JOHN F. DEANE was born on Achill Island, County Mayo, in 1943, and now lives in Dublin. He is the founder of Poetry Ireland, the national poetry society, and of The Dedalus Press. His novels and short stories – *In the Name of the Wolf*, *The Coffin Master and Other Stories*, *Undertow* and *The Heather Fields and Other Stories* – are published by Blackstaff Press. He won the O'Shaughnessy Award for Irish Poetry in 1998 and the Marten Toonder Award for Literature in 2001, and his poetry has been shortlisted for the T.S. Eliot Prize and the *Irish Times* Poetry Now award. His latest collection, *A Little Book of Hours*, was published by Carcanet in 2008. He is a member of Aosdána and in 2007 the French government honoured him as a *Chevalier de l'Ordre des Arts et des Lettres*. In February 2010 he won the inaugural Gregory O'Donoghue International Poetry Prize. Columba Press will publish a book of his essays, *The Works of Love*, in December 2010 and his next poetry collection, *Eye of the Hare*, will be published by Carcanet in June 2011.

Where No Storms Come

John F. Deane

BLACKSTAFF
PRESS

BELFAST

First published in 2010 by
Blackstaff Press
4c Heron Wharf, Sydenham Business Park
Belfast BT3 9LE
with the assistance of
The Arts Council of Northern Ireland

John F. Deane has asserted his right under the Copyright, Designs
and Patents Act 1988 to be identified as the author of this work.

Typeset by CJWT Solutions, St Helens, Merseyside

Printed in Great Britain by the MPG Books Group

A CIP catalogue record for this book is available
from the British Library

ISBN 978-0-85640-858-8

www.blackstaffpress.com
www.johnfdeane.com

Heaven-Haven

I have desired to go
   Where springs not fail,
To fields where flies no sharp nor sided hail
   And a few lilies blow.

And I have asked to be
   Where no storms come,
Where the green swell is in the havens dumb,
   And out of the swing of the sea.

GERARD MANLEY HOPKINS

TIME AND THE CHILD

Aunt Lily Graham stepped off the green midday bus from Westport and entered the household at the crossroads like a summer storm. Aunt Lily was big – very big. She was big in bosom, in head and in voice. She was big in stature, in gesture and in passage. And she placed herself quickly in front of Dolly, offering her a gift that she hoped would ensure the child's affection for ever. This gift was big. It was a panda bear, almost as large as Dolly herself, hauled about under the big arm of Aunt Lily Graham and dumped onto the small body of the girl who keeled backwards under the weight of the cuddly gift and fell on her back on the tiled floor of the hallway. Dolly almost cried with the sudden fright of it, and almost cried again with the shock of falling on her back. But Aunt Lily was installed for the length of one summer and Panda was installed upon the affections of a startled Dolly.

'Oh what a little fairy you are to be sure, to be sure,' Lily would shout at her. Dolly simply sulked at that but Lily did not seem to notice. Until one day, about three days after Lily's irruption into the household, Dolly came downstairs and into the kitchen, a big question bothering her. Lily was sitting on one side of the kitchen table, a cup of tea in her right hand, held up high because her elbow was on the table, a bad-mannered thing to do, Dolly had always been told. And Dolly's father was on the other side of the table but he was reaching his hand across the flower-patterned and scuffed oilcloth and was laying it over Lily's other hand, rubbing it gently. When Dolly came in the door her father withdrew that hand.

'What will we be when we grow up, little fairy?' Lily said to her. 'Will we be a nurse or a teacher or just a big fairy?'

Dolly ignored the stupidity of that. She turned to her father. 'We're going to Salthill soon, aren't we, Daddy?' she asked him.

'Soon, soon, pet, but not for a while yet.'

'But we always go to Salthill in the summer, and it's time to go now.'

Lily laughed, irritatingly. 'The child's a fairy!' she said again. 'The child is quite a fairy.'

'It's not time yet, Dolly,' her father said, a trifle nettled. 'Your aunt Lily is here for a holiday for herself and then, after that, it'll be time for us to go to Salthill.'

Dolly looked up at Lily. She spoke quietly to the big woman: 'Will you be going back to Westport tomorrow, Aunt Lily?'

'Oh yes, tomorrow and tomorrow and tomorrow, dear child, then I'll be gone. Soon it won't be long, I promise you. Then I'll pack up my po and my toothpaste and go home to my lonely little house with nobody to love me and live all alone and lonesome again.'

'How many tomorrows is that, Aunt Lily? Three?'

'Well, it might be a little bit more than three, dear fairy. Just a tad more. But then a day will come and you'll be able to say, my lovely aunt Lily is going home tomorrow, and it'll be true, and then you'll be sad and sorry to see me go. Won't you, child?'

Dolly hesitated. 'I don't know what I'll be when I grow up, I'm too young yet.'

'Maybe you and me should go up and join the nuns up in St Ruth's, Dolly,' Aunt Lily said. 'We'd not be lonely up there, now would we?'

'No, Aunt Lily, we'd not be lonely. But I don't think I'll go. You can go, if you like.' Dolly paused again. 'Yes, I expect I'll be sorry to think of you all alone and lonesome, Aunt Lily,' she said, and she turned sharply and went back out the door of the kitchen.

It seemed to have happened overnight but that could not have been the case. Dolly always slept without closing the curtains on her bedroom window; she liked to watch the moon, or the stars, or even the complete blackness and she had not been wakened during that night by lights, or by noise, or by hammering. But in the morning there it was, the biggest tent she had ever seen, erected in Henry Locke's bottom field. There was a small blue flag swinging from one of the high poles and it sent her spirit into a quiver of expectation. And for the space of a blessed time, the presence of big Aunt Lily in the house was forgotten.

At first she thought it was the circus, back again after its slow circling of the villages of Ireland. But one look at the tent, rectangular and off-white, made her wonder; this was not the circus high tent with all the stripes, like wild pyjamas. This was different. This was … pictures! A picture show! Moving pictures! She had heard of them, but this was to be the first of her life. Imagine! And imagine how they found enough space in Henry Locke's field that was dry enough to support such magic. The circus tent had always found space down on the sandy banks, a safe distance from the village.

That day went by too slowly. The whole schoolroom was in a state of tense excitement and Dolly's mother got irritated several times, trying to curb the nervous anticipation, the distraction among the girls in her class. She even threatened to give them so much homework that none of them could possibly make it to the tent. But she was not that hard on them, she could not be. And it was clear that she, too, was excited.

The entire world went along that evening, all of the children wildly chattering, all the adults pretending that they were not really bothered, one way or another. After all, they had seen so much in their lives already. And movies! Just some newfangled way of wasting valuable time. But soon everybody was happy, settling noisily onto the most uncomfortable forms and hard chairs that mankind could ever invent but all agog, prepared to fork over their thruppences without demur. If there were flies in that tent they would be in trouble; they would all be swallowed whole by mouths sagging open, and all the in-breathing excitement that was in the air.

Dolly knew that she would never forget that night. The

movie was *The Wolf Man* and Lon Chaney Junior played the unfortunate Laurence Talbot bitten by Bela Lugosi who gave him the disease, if that's what it was. He suffered the curse of the wolf man. The village folks all screamed; they called out warnings to the screen; they put their heads between their hands and watched from between their fingers. Some of the smaller children cried at times, in fright, and their parents had to reassure them; there was a general rustling of sweet wrappers, of silver foil being hurriedly taken off bars of chocolate. Some of the children, and some of the old grannies too, buried their heads in their hands completely and would not watch, especially at those times when the chilling music told them that something unmentionable was going to happen. Oh it was wonderful! Dolly kept her eyes firmly fixed on the flickering images though there were moments when even she had to hold on tight to her mother's elbow. And when the full moon came out they knew what would happen next and watched with utter fascination how the hair grew on Chaney's hands and face and how those big eyes widened and, oh my and oh dear, how he set about his gruesome night activity! Then his great shadow grew along the walls of the city, his awful hands clung to railings as he lifted his gruesome body towards the innocent maiden in her fine black dress, her face growing white as snow, the black cape of the wolf man blotting out all the light as he came towards her. It was heady. It was beautiful. It was deadly. They loved it. They hated it. They kept explaining to each other how it was done, how all of this was not real, it was all done, the adults said, in a tank, it was moving pictures, it was cinema. Fantasy. Fantastic.

Several times the machine whirring somewhere behind them broke down in the darkness, failing with a slowly throttled sound. Everybody groaned, though many of the older grannies complained with a certain sense of momentary relief. A small naked white bulb came on then, because now that blackness about them had become terrifying. The bulb threw an even more eerie and sickly light on the village folks, turning their faces a deathly white. And then it started up again, cigarette smoke lifting in slow grey-blue clouds through the beams that travelled so closely across the darkness above them, like shifting clouds of dust, and the man with the wolf inside him, or the wolf with the man outside him, got on with the awful business of his living. Once it rained, heavily, and Dolly pressed more closely against her mother as the sound of the raindrops on the taut roof of the tent played its own somewhat comforting music. She relished the gentle, kindly hand of her mother brushing reassuringly against her hair. She felt peaceful, even though the world portrayed on the screen was frightening, exciting and, eventually, secure. It was all black and white; it was all simple, unbelievable and utterly credible. And Dolly relished every body-checking moment of it.

As they came out from the tent onto the damp grass of Henry Locke's field, the young girl felt as if she were stepping out of another world that was in some ways more real than that of her own village, though she held tightly to her mother's hand and made sure her strong father was never far away. Almost at once she felt her shoes sinking into the soft clay of the field and she was saddened that her new white knee-socks might be ruined. And yet, what was all of that against the suffering of the poor wolf man who was two people, or two beings, whose death came as a relief to himself and to all of the people who had screamed and clutched and warned throughout that night.

Mother paused to talk to someone as eager and excited as Dolly was and for a moment the young girl turned and looked away, over the nearby ditch, down across the fields, to the sea. There was only a quarter moon idling on its back, not very bright, and clouds came and moved quickly across it. Dolly was surprised that it caused her no fear. The distant light from Clare Island, from that great lighthouse up on the headland, was shining wonderfully across the bay, lighting up a quickly shifting track over the ocean, sweeping around from left to right then disappearing before appearing once again on the left. It was fascinating to watch, and even tiny glimpses of the shore and the harbour down below them could be seen. That light gave her a sense of security and wholeness that countered at once the notion that there might be a wolf man in the neighbourhood, and that, indeed, it could be Dolly herself, or her father, or one of the village lads if some day one of them was bitten by a local Bela Lugosi. How wonderful it is betimes to shudder at vicarious horrors; how exquisite to see your father standing by, big and unfazed and prepared.

Dolly had never wanted a panda. What she really wanted was a watch, a big fob watch like her grandfather had, held by a chain from the high buttonhole in his waistcoat to a small pocket over his heart. He would put two fingers of his right hand into that pocket, delicately, withdraw the watch, keeping his left hand on the chain; it was like a bird's beak, Dolly thought, dipping into a beaker. Then he would hold the big watch in his left hand, his thumb pressing on a catch on top of the watch, the silver-chased cover would spring open on a perfect hinge and the great white face would peer up at him, offering him its wisdom. Even more wonderful than all of that was the way the figures and the big hand and little hand of that watch were painted a gentle light green and when grandfather looked at his watch in the dark, the figures and hands would glow and he could tell the time right at midnight, or even in the darkness of the cupboard under the stairs.

Grandfather always wrinkled his nose a little and sniffed when he had found out the time and then he snapped the watch shut again, taking not much care this time, and dropped it back into the little nest of his pocket. Some of the boys in the boys' school had waistcoats, too, and they had watches like that, but not as fine, not as big. 'Turnips' they called their watches, and they were very proud of them, taking them out so very often that Dolly sometimes mocked them but still, she was envious. Even though they were lesser watches, with lesser chains, and even though they broke easily, she was still jealous. In any case, and Dolly tossed her curls when she noticed this, some of the boys did not know the first thing about telling the time.

In her bedroom Dolly had her own clock. Her grandfather gave it to her when he saw how intrigued she was with clocks, with watches, with time. 'What is time?' she asked him, as if he should know, he the old one, he who had skipped about in the nineteenth century, so very long ago. 'Time is something we don't have enough of,' he would reply, grinning at her, stooped as he was now, and stiff all over. Sometimes he would smoke his pipe, knock the bowl of it against the fireplace and then spit into the fire; there would be a hissing sound that always terrified Dolly, something dark and ugly about it, something unwholesome. 'What time is it now?' she would ask him, over and over until he got so tired of it he gave her the small gilt carriage clock he had been presented with when he left the Royal Irish Constabulary, years ago. 'You must wind it up every night, like this,' he told her. He clicked open the glass back to the clock where you could see all the strange mechanisms, so clean and golden and perfect, all of them moving, some so slowly you could scarcely notice, cogs and springs and wheels. There was a double-ended key hanging on the glass at the back, one end to wind up the clock in the evenings, one end to shift the big hand if it was not keeping time accurately enough; 'It's like feeding the pigs, Dolly, they need to be fed, you know how they come grunting and shoving when you go out with the slops?' and he put one end of the key onto a little golden stick and turned it, slowly. It made a loud, hard ticking sound that Dolly loved. 'But you must turn it only twelve times, no more, else it's overwound and might break. The other end of the key goes here, but that's to move the hands, in case the clock goes slow or fast, too fast.' Grandfather paused, and gazed at the young girl. 'Too fast, too fast,' he said again and again.

Dolly kept the clock on the mantelpiece in her bedroom. It was a big room and its great window opened out onto a meadow. She would remember that meadow as being a great green space surrounded by a high and fragrant hedgerow of escallonia bushes, a place of miracle and pleasure, of wonder and excitement, where she watched her father, stripped to the waist, the white-grey hairs of his chest like the feathers on a cygnet, as he started to swing his scythe from somewhere in the centre of the meadow, swinging with the rhythm of a pendulum – slow, careful, perfect. From her window she could even hear the released sigh, soft and lazy, of the grass as it lay back before him. He circled, the circle widening all the time, until the whole meadow lay like a wonderful racing track and you could run round and round and round until you reached the centre, the safe house, home. And every now and then he would stop, dip the whetting stone in a bucket of water and whet the blade of his scythe, *crrraaaaaaasp, crrraaaaaaasp* down the right side of the blade and *psaaaaaaarrc, psaaaaaaarrc* back up the left side, quickly, the noise of it grating at Dolly's ears, but grating with a pleasing irritation. She would sit against the gable wall, underneath her own window, sit there where a climbing rose bush covered the lower half of the wall with scented blossoms that were filled with the humming of bees. For moments, then, life was perfect, and all things were well and more than well with the world.

Not long after Dolly had seen her first movie, a local entrepreneur, electrician, general handyman and grocer-cum-butcher-cum-coffin-maker, opened the Night of Dreams Ballroom in Baile Mór. It was at once denounced by Father Tiernan who devoted a sermon to it the following Sunday and for several Sundays after that. Dancing! Among Catholic young people! *And* in a shed with a galvanized roof, right on the bog-edge of the town! In a place where none of the elders of the community, the leaders of the people, could know with ease what kind of things were going on within! Sin, sin, and more sin. Whist drives, now, if the Church had some hand in them, that would be fine. But imagine the occasions of sin where lights were low, where young men and women danced close together without supervision, where the music was performed by some foreign band from somewhere up the country, bringing with them the black hooliganism and pagan practices of Dublin or London or Las Vegas! Oh dear, this was Satanism rampant in Baile Mór. Dances, properly organised by the members of the gun club, where strict dress codes were followed, or Irish dancing sessions with the parish priest as Master of Ceremonies, or the headmaster of the technical school in charge of the music, now that would be for the good of the people. But oh my God! What has Ireland come to at all, at all, at all?

Under such pressure, and after a third night where no more than five or six couples braved the wrath of Father Tiernan,

Barney Cooligan bought a cinema projector and the Night of Dreams Ballroom became the Night of Dreams Emporium. Dolly went along to see Lon Chaney Junior once again, this time in *House of Dracula*. Because this hall had been intended for dancing, the seating was a row of forms along the side walls and some hard chairs that could be brought out into the centre of the floor for those prepared to pay a few pennies more. Dolly was sitting on a form against the wall. She had to lean out and turn her head towards the left to see the screen, and keep it turned. And sometimes she had to move out onto the floor and kneel there so she could see past the bigger boys and girls who were able to lean out further to see the movie.

She was again enthralled; she saw the heavy coffin rising up through the waters of the mere, dark flowers growing round it, the mists moving, and the beautiful woman in the long, white chiffon dress who came, innocent as a ghost, across the moors towards that coffin. And oh, that handsome man, the black suit, the cape, and those teeth, those beautiful, dreadful teeth! In a moment of truly sweet and heightened tension Dolly cried out to the screen, 'Please, please don't open the locks on the polished coffin …' She was more than ever thrilled when the locks were open … and utterly delighted when Dracula's son was joined by the wolf man, both of them pretending to the doctor that they needed cures for vampirism and lycanthropy, when all they were after was the blood and the flesh of the lovely heroine. Oh dear, what a pleasurable thrill ran up and down Dolly's spine and tickled the hairs on the back of her neck! She was glad that the Emporium was showing movies, and not holding those ridiculous and noisy and too-late-at-night dances.

When she sat back on the form against the hard wall, when the naked bulbs in the hall again gave a small and sickly light to the field of excitement while a reel was changed somewhere, a boy leaned over to Dolly and spoke to her.

'You're very stupid, shouting at the screen. Don't you know the people on the screen aren't real?'

'They are, too, real!' Dolly insisted.

The boy was small and a little too fat, his face was red, his eyes were red too, perhaps from watching up at the screen, but Dolly was annoyed that he should think her stupid.

'And I'm not stupid, I know the name of the actor, it's Lon Chaney, so there!'

'It's not Lon Chaney!' the boy answered, triumphantly. 'It's Lon Chaney Junior, so there to you!'

But Dolly wasn't interested in carrying on the conversation. The boy was wearing a new waistcoat over his white shirt, and there, yes right there on this rude, fat boy, was a watch chain, leading from one side of the waistcoat, across that podgy belly, into a small pocket on the other side. Oh dear, Dolly was silenced, she knew that she, being only a girl, could never wear a waistcoat and could never have a watch like that. The boy turned away, certain of his victory in argument, certain of his superiority. After all he was a boy, she was only a girl, a silly, stupid girl.

Her parents feared that Dolly might be scared to be alone in her bedroom in the dark nights, after seeing such movies, after the wolf man, the bloodsucker, the vampire, after the blood-curdling howling, after the music that tore your insides to shreds. But Dolly was not scared, not at all. She left the curtains of her window wide open and sat, sometimes, in her nightdress, gazing out on the wonders of the darkness across the meadow and further off, the gleams of the light from stars or moon over the fields and ditches, and further still, out over the sea. It was all so beautiful, she thought, and if a shadow of some dark creature were to pass across that dim light, so much the better. Then the sluggard life of the village might be quickened for a time and the dullards of the boys' school might shut up their mouths about her stupidity and the slowness of the girls.

And then, in the warmer summer nights, came the time-keeping of the corncrake. The land rail. That secretive, endangered creature that set up a ratchet through many of the night hours, haunting the darkness with its strange, harsh and enticing call. Dolly sat entranced, that tick-tock-tick-tock hoarse-throated time-keeping of the bird was close to her own heart. As she sat in the embrasure of the window peering onto the night, sometimes she thought she glimpsed this shyest of birds move warily over the meadow. She saw bats, too, flitting by at great speed; she saw small dust storms when the meadow was down and the grass lay waiting to be dried and gathered up. And she saw the moonwalks across the waters of the sea, and dreamed her own dreams. Some nights she fell asleep on the chair and half-woke when her body slumped against the window, crawling then into the luxurious arms of her bed. But never did she fear any of the shadows or humped darknesses she saw out there in the night, rather her sense of compassion rose up, for the creatures that are threatened by the world, the corncrakes hiding before the awful blade of the scythe, sheltering their young, the small furred creatures that lurked at the edges of the meadow and that were pounced on by the long-eared owl and carried off into some awful nest to be torn apart, to be shredded into pieces for the young of another species.

She shuddered in sympathy with the man who knew that within himself was a beast, lurking and awful, waiting to be released so he could wreak havoc about him and destroy what he himself was most in love with. And the vampires, too, she longed for them to find some peace to that awful restlessness they knew, that need for blood, for its sustenance, that could only be found amongst the vulnerable living, that turned them, too, into creatures of the night that would live in anguish for centuries. Of course Dolly knew that this was all invention, but she knew too that there was truth in the darkness, a truth she only vaguely discerned, a truth that made her heart swell with compassion, and no fear.

Dolly was sick with a kind of fever one day. She missed school and had to stay in bed. Her strong father came in to her, sat on the edge of the bed and laid his cool, firm hand on her brow. Then he put his strong fingers gently through her hair and murmured some sympathetic words. Dolly smiled up at him, deeply happy. Soon her mother came in, much more business-like, dressed already for her day's work in school. She had the thermometer in her hand; Dolly hated that thing, she hated how it felt stuffed in under her tongue so that she could not swallow.

Her mother shook it briskly. 'Open up, young lady,' she said. She was clearly suspicious.

'You know, Dolly,' she half-scolded, 'Archbishop William John Murphy will be coming soon to the school for the confirmation class! A lot of the girls will be confirmed this year, but only if they know their catechism. I will need you in the classroom to help the girls with their answers. You'll be confirmed, please God, in a year's time, but you know the catechism, you will be an example to the others. I need you …' Her mother being the teacher, Dolly always had to be on extra good behaviour because her mother would have no favourites; indeed, she went to the other extreme and was much harder on Dolly. It would be no harm to miss … Her mother took out the thermometer, held it against the light, screwed up her eyes and then shook it briskly once again.

'Well, it's up to a hundred and two. You're sick, poor Dolly, you must have a flu. I'll get Aunt Lily to send for Doctor King later on. I'll tell her to bring you up a cup of tea now and some toast. You'll be able for that? And then you must stay in bed. Stay warm. You'll be well in a day or two. Tuck in there now, there's a good girl. The silly girls will have to learn for themselves, for a day or two, anyway.'

Her mother lifted her head gently from the pillow, plumped up the linen and, finding the top side a little damp, she turned it over, plumped it up again and laid Dolly's head back down. Then she drew up the blankets, tucked the sheet in under her chin, patted her softly on the brow, and went out.

Dolly felt really pleased, though hot and a little bothered. She lay, listening to the usual morning sounds from downstairs and from outside. The clanging of iron on iron was her father taking the ashes out of the old range. There was the back door opening and shutting; he was bringing the ash-bucket up to the ash pit behind the house. Silence a while. Then the back door again and a sound of the vigorous poking of the smouldering fire in the range. A small clattering of cups and saucers and things. She dozed off. She woke soon again to hear the Ford starting up outside, father bringing it out across the yard, round the corner of the house as far as the back gate; a pause, that engine sounding rough and wheedling; she could hear the gate opening, the car moving, the gate closing. Then, with a small sense of loss, she listened as the sound of the car diminished into the distance. Silence. She dozed.

When she woke again, sunlight was brimming in her room. There was a tray of toast, with butter and marmalade, lying on a chair beside her bed. It was cold and hard. She glanced at the clock on the mantelpiece. It was after midday. Had the doctor been? Who was in the house? There was a luscious silence. She could hear a robin singing outside her window. In the distance she heard a cock crowing, crowing again, and being answered from somewhere further down the village. A dog barked, lazily, somewhere. She almost laughed at the pleasure of it. The girls would all be in catechism class now, learning those strange and difficult words by heart, repeating them aloud together, not understanding them. 'The seven deadly sins ...' 'The commandments of God ...' 'The commandments of the Church ...' Was there seven of everything. Or was it ten deadly sins and seven commandments? What was sloth? And 'the pride of life'? The girls would be upright in their desks; tense, expectant of difficult questions. They even had large lobs of old testament stories off by heart; the Red Sea; Abraham and the pillars that fell down; or was that Samson and Jacob? And the coat of several colours, Joseph, wasn't it? And the seven cows and the seven lean years. Seven again. A holy number? Or was that ten cows and ten lean years? And what did it all mean anyway? Dolly grinned; she did not have to worry today; her mother would not call her out and show her off in front of the other girls. She snuggled down under the bedclothes and floated away into her dreams.

But they turned dark, those dreams, dark and filled with flowing streams of blood. She lay, she did not know how long, neither asleep nor yet awake, she tossed under the weight of the sheets, she squirmed under the too-loud ticking of the carriage clock, she grew so hot she thought she had become a trickling stream of sweat, she grew cold and shivered and when her eyes shut tight she could see the strangest and most distressing figures of nightmare advance towards her. Not vampires, nor wolf men; the figures of her terrors were real men, big and ugly and violent, with ash plant knobbly thick sticks in their hands with which they rained down blows on the backs of donkeys and cows, and black and hairy fists big as saucepans that held her own small hand in a grip of death.

She shook herself into wakefulness and sat up in bed. The clock's ticking became less insistent. Somewhere outside she could hear the pitched calling of a chaffinch. Otherwise the silence was refreshing, even a little comforting. Until she heard voices, a quiet murmur of voices that seemed to come from the living room downstairs. But, she thought, her father was away in Baile Mór, at work; her mother was down in the school, teaching the village girls; there were two weeks left before the holidays were to start; only Aunt Lily was in the house. Was she talking to herself? Or had her father come home, for some reason? Dolly got out of bed, slowly; her nightdress was clinging to her overheated body. She twinked it looser about herself, then put on her purple dressing gown with the white cord that she tied tightly about her. She rubbed her forehead against the edge of the sheet and moved out quietly onto the landing.

She felt dizzy and had to hold on to the banisters for a moment. But she was correct; voices came, still indistinctly, from downstairs. When she recovered her equilibrium, she passed across the landing window that faced out over Locke's field; there was no tent there now, only a few sheep mooching about amongst the thistles and wet grasses. Then she moved slowly down the steps of the stairs. The door to the living room was closed. She could hear a woman's voice, and a man's. They were talking earnestly, but she could not quite make out the words. She opened the door, softly, and stood there, gazing in.

Her aunt Lily was sitting at the table, her big elbows resting on the oilcloth, holding a cup between her two hands, as if warming herself. And on the other side of the table, facing Aunt Lily, was a priest. He was sitting back in his chair, his right hand lazily holding a cup on its saucer where it rested on the table. His face turned towards the door. He sat, simply watching as Dolly stood there, watching, too. There was a silence as he looked at her. Aunt Lily looked at Father Scott for a moment, then followed his gaze and when she saw Dolly, she called out, a soft call, not one of those high piercing and terrified screams, but one of simple surprise, mixed perhaps with a little fright.

'Dolly!' Aunt Lily said. 'Dolly, are you all right?'

Dolly nodded and felt suddenly a little weak. She moved cautiously over to the table and came up to her aunt. She stood beside her then, gazing up pleadingly at the big woman.

'Oh the poor little fairy, she's unwell, you know, Father Scott, she's quite unwell, the little fairy.'

Aunt Lily put down her cup, shoved her chair back a little from the table and reached for Dolly. The young girl hesitated, then quickly climbed onto Lily's knees and laid her head down against the great bosom.

'Oh, the little creature, oh the darling little girl!' Lily cooed, holding the fevered head against her bosom and beginning to rock ever so slightly. Dolly turned her hot face towards Father Scott. The priest was good-looking, with a fine mane of shining black hair and a small, neat moustache. His black suit seemed impeccable and his black stock shone like silk. His white collar was as pure and unstained as fresh snow and his face, at this moment, was relaxed and smiling slightly.

'Well,' he said to Dolly. 'So we're sick today, are we? No school today, then? Too sick to go to school today, are we? With Archbishop Murphy coming, too, coming soon. Maybe the little fairy is scared of the big Archbishop?'

Dolly felt at peace leaning back against her aunt, feeling the strong arms around her, the great body rocking gently with her. She smiled at the priest, but there was a small triumph in the smile and Father Scott noticed it. Dolly had her right hand in her hair and was slowly twirling her fingers through her curls.

'I'll go, Lily,' the priest said, rising slowly and languorously from his chair. 'I'll go. And we'll talk again, soon, I hope, very soon.' He looked again at the young girl and hesitated. 'Maybe after Benediction this evening, if it's fine, maybe you can come to the sacristy, come around to the back of the chapel, wait for me.'

Lily was nodding. 'That's fine, Jim, that's fine. I'll come round after the Benediction.'

'Jim', Dolly thought. It was the first time she had ever heard a priest's name. She thought it was always Father Scott, or Father Tiernan, or Father Quinn. She did not know priests had names like Jim. Jim. It felt very strange. She gazed again at the priest. Father Scott was tall and slim and his movements were alert with restrained energy. She noticed that the back of his hands had a good deal of black hair. She thought, suddenly, of the wolf man, and she snuggled more deeply into the soft bosom of her aunt.

'Get well quickly, little fairy,' Father Scott said. 'Get well, go to school, where all little girls should be. You're a slug in the cabbage of bliss, you are, a little fairy maybe, but none the less a slug in the cabbage of bliss.' He laughed lightly, came and rubbed his fingers through Dolly's hair in a kindly and gentle manner.

Dolly cuddled more snugly into her aunt's body, one hand still twirling through her hair, the thumb of her left hand moving instinctively into her mouth.

'Ah, the little fairy and her great big aunt are the best of friends now, aren't we, the very best of friends,' Aunt Lily cooed, pride and contentment in her voice.

It was only a few days later when Dolly, remembering, felt that she had betrayed herself. How could she possibly have climbed onto Aunt Lily's lap? How could she have given herself away like that, to this big woman who bowled over everything in her path? How could she give this loud and parrot-coloured woman a hold like that over her? And Aunt Lily made the most of it, telling father and mother, over and over again, how the little fairy had appeared at the doorway, a vision from another world, tears in her eyes, her face pale as a ghost's, and how she had run, yes positively run, to the lap of her favourite aunt and climbed up for comfort, for love, for care. How she had stuck her finger in her mouth like a small baby, how she had dozed in safety on Aunt Lily's bosom. Dolly, feeling strong and healthy again, longing to get away from such sugar and cotton wool measliness, cringed and tried to hide.

It was one of Dolly's special pleasures to be taken to Sunday Mass with grandmother, with Nanna. Nanna and Ted still lived in the big house just down the road from Dolly's house and sometimes Nanna would stop on the way to Mass and wait for Dolly to come out and walk with her to the chapel. It was about half a mile and Dolly always felt singled out and special to be alongside Nanna; the old woman was almost eighty now, Dolly knew, but still strode out with vigour, her head held high, and a smile on her face for everybody. The people greeted her, and greeted Dolly who walked along delightedly, holding her Nanna's hand. Then together they walked up the centre of the village chapel, found a bench not far from the altar rails, genuflected and knelt in along the bench.

All the women and girls of the village took the benches on the right-hand side of the chapel. The men and boys took the left-hand side. It was not appropriate for a girl to be on the left, or for a boy to be on the right. Dolly had never found this strange; in fact, she had never even thought about it. What mattered to her was her Nanna kneeling beside her, a big prayer book open before her, and a large and noisy rosary rattling against the bench. Nanna prayed a lot, you could hear the sibilance of her whispers as she prayed, her mouth moving, her eyes closed. Dolly loved the gentle talcum smell that came from her; she loved the big presence, she loved the softness of the old body when she leaned against her, she loved the kindliness and the affection that shone in Nanna's eyes.

In a niche at the top of the women's side was a statue of the Virgin Mary; it was a crude affair, a simpering woman, vaguely gazing downwards, her hands held at her side but her palms open to the women before her. Dolly was always taken by the right hand of the Virgin, how it had broken off, and a wire frame that served as bones for the fingers protruded uglily. Around the head of the statue was a wreathe of twelve stars that were supposed to light up during Masses and other devotions. But two of the stars were broken and did not light up, and another flickered weakly, as if exhausted. One of the eyes of the Virgin was badly painted and this made Dolly think that the Virgin had a squint, and that the one good eye seemed to be vaguely watching out towards the people. The girl loved that thought; she found the Virgin, in her country simplicity, her blue and white gown that looked vaguely like a priest's and vaguely like nightclothes, homely and agreeable, simple and approachable. Like her own Nanna was. Her mother had sometimes whispered to Dolly that, just perhaps, she might be blessed enough to find a vocation in the service of the Mother of God. And Dolly found she could say her prayers easily before the statue.

Her mother rarely came to pray in the woman's side of the chapel. She took the girls from the school who could sing up into the gallery every Sunday where they chanted hymns, sometimes in English, sometimes in Latin which nobody could understand, and sometimes in Irish, which Dolly could scarcely follow either. Her mother played the harmonium; Dolly could hear the wheezing and catching of the old instrument as her mother worked the pedals; then the music came and Dolly didn't like it; it was nothing like the piano at home, nor was the music as pleasing as the songs her mother would sometimes play when there were visitors down in the parlour. The hymns, Dolly found, always seemed to her to be square things, not rounded and lingering, but squat and boxy, and some of them were repeated so often that they had lost any meaning for her. Dolly could not sing; she could squeak, she could follow a song and try to sing it but her mother always stopped her, saying she was off key, she was out of tune, she could not keep the rhythm. Dolly didn't mind; she preferred to be down in the chapel with Nanna, rather than up there with her mother and the other girls.

Dolly loved to examine the scarves that the women wore. Every woman, every girl, had to come to chapel with her hair covered. Some of the strange women from the hillside wore old caps like berets; some of them had dull hats that were square and boxy, like the hymns. But the younger mothers and the girls had scarves that were colourful and picturesque and Dolly loved to enter the world of the scarves. A woman nearby had a light yellow scarf with the head and neck of a most beautiful horse looking out from it; as she moved her head a little the horse seemed to come to life, its eyes were big and real and Dolly could imagine it racing about a field in a summer breeze, tossing its mane, flicking its tail at the flies. There was a scarf in the bench just two rows ahead that had several racing cars on it, a shamrock green scarf with cars that were bright red and blue and silver, and under the cars Dolly could read words, when the woman was still, and they said 'Monte Carlo Grand Prix'. Dolly could close her eyes then and hear the engines revving up, she could hear the screech of tyres round some dangerous bend, she could see the chequered flag raised and waving frantically at the winner.

Sometimes Nanna nudged her to answer the prayers, to kneel down or sit up, or join her hands. But she always did it gently, she never seemed to get cross. Dolly tried to pick up and answer, she could use phrases like 'et cum spiritu through – oh', or 'glory day Patrick', or 'Deo grassy ass'. But she did not like them though she had a notion of what they all meant. And then one day the girls in the choir were signing a hymn that Dolly really loved, it was 'Hail, Queen of Heaven, the Ocean Star', and Dolly, watching up at the Virgin in her niche, wanted so much to join in. She tried to join in the refrain but the sounds came out sideways and a bit wrong from her mouth and her Nanna looked at her, grinned and shook her head slightly. Dolly knew that the second verse began 'Oh gentle, chaste and spotless Maid'; she thought she would try to sing the words quietly to herself, the way Nanna said her prayers. She shaped her lips into an O, she took a deep breath, she began and found herself, to her complete astonishment and delight, whistling! Yes, whistling! She had been trying to do that for ages; all the boys could do it easily and many of the girls could manage it. Her mother didn't allow the girls to do it as she said it wasn't ladylike, girls didn't whistle, that was a thing that rough boys did. But the girls were particularly proud when they could whistle and Dolly really wanted to be able to do it. Now, suddenly, there on the women's side, she had done it. She was so startled and pleased with herself that she simply could not stop. Even though the woman with the horse on her scarf looked around at her sharply and her Nanna gave her a big nudge in the elbow. Dolly whistled the first line of the hymn and it sounded to her as if she were in tune. Then she stopped. Horse-scarf turned away. Dolly tried again, just to make sure she hadn't lost the skill already. She hadn't! She whistled the third line of the hymn. Then she stopped. She looked over at the men's side of the chapel, quite by accident, but also with a certain pride in her heart, and she caught the eye of that boy, that Packie Brennan; he was watching her, and grinning; he had heard her, too, even there, right across in the other side of the chapel. She half smiled at him, pleased with herself, and he raised his thumb to her in recognition. She was pleased. She looked up at the statue of the Virgin Mary and winked at her.

Dolly's great worry, when her father was out cutting the grass in the meadow, was the corncrake. What if that secretive bird was caught in the path of the dreadful scythe? What of the nest, with its tiny and innocent young, hidden somewhere in the deep meadow grass? Would the long curved blade not slice right through them? Her father told her he would keep an eye out, that never yet had he killed a corncrake, that he expected the young were fledged already and able to fly and make a safe place for themselves. But once Dolly had seen them, she had seen the mother rail half-fly half-run while calling out of the grass at the edge of the meadow, not far from her father's swingeing scythe, and the bird was calling desperately, and then she had seen two small birds, young land rail, dark and head-high and awkward, run clumsily through the grasses and disappear into the sedge in the drain. She had only worried the more.

That had been earlier in the summer, when the weather was up, the sun shining, but all the older men were forecasting rain and storms and her father said there was a trap door opening in the world before him and he would have to pass through, take the chance and save the hay. Dolly thought she understood but she worried all that day and long into the night. The night was extra still and she sat in her nightdress at the window, the curtains not drawn closed, and gazed out into the meadow. The grass lay in symmetrical rows where it had fallen, like a perfectly drawn spiral with pathways through between the grasses, from the centre out to the very edge, and she imagined that the silence was stronger than before, if such a thing could be. But then she heard them again, she heard that welcome scraping sound of the corncrake, and an answering call from further away, from somewhere beyond the meadow, and she felt that there was a new, safe family out there, mother and chicks secure and well and sound.

The next day was sunny, too, and Dolly moved out into the meadow with her mother and her father. They each had a long rake, a lovely-to-handle wooden rake with wooden teeth at the end, gently curved, and she loved the way the still green grasses yielded to the pull of the rake and gathered themselves into little piles about the meadow. She noticed, too, the places where the grass had lain overnight were slightly more yellow than the places where the grass had been cut down. She found nests, one glorious nest that her father said was a nest of the humblebee; there were tiny honeycombs and the honey within tasted sweeter than any she had ever tasted before. There were wild flowers, too, among the grasses, beautiful orchids, buttercups, clovers and they lay streeled and miserable among the piles. Perhaps the cows would find the hay the sweeter because of the flowers. Dolly hoped it would be so.

The day after that was Sunday. Dolly went with her parents to early Mass; she sat, with her Nanna, on the women's side. She shuffled in her place and Nanna glanced down at her a little crossly. She fiddled with the tiny silken tassels of her prayer book and Nanna, for the first time ever, pinched her on the wrist, hard, so that Dolly let out a small cry. She tried her best to hold herself, on her knees, without stirring, but her knees so quickly began to ache, and her elbows hurt against the hard wood of the pew. She distracted herself by watching the altar boys and how they moved, ungainly and awkward, about the altar, muttering their strange Latin phrases, shifting book and bell from place to place, the priest in his colourful robes turning and twisting and announcing, too, strange Latin phrases. Then came the sermon when they all sat back up on their benches and Dolly tried to remain calm, to listen, to remain still. But she could understand little of the words the priest spoke; it was Father Scott again, but he looked and sounded so very different from the Jim that had been in her living room that she thought it couldn't really be the same person. She could see the altar boys, too, who were sitting on the altar steps, leaning on one elbow, watching out towards the people and she recognised one of them, it was Packie, though looking so different now. He looked so steady and serious. He was listening to the priest though his eyes were roving over the faces of the congregation. He looked good, in his white surplice and his black soutane, and she could see his homewool thick socks underneath the soutane and just over the black slippers he was wearing on the altar; and on the top of his socks she could see the white flesh of his legs, just below his knee. She was fascinated. She whispered to her Nanna:

'Nanna, look at the legs of the altar boy!'

But Nanna tut-tutted at her, put her finger to her lips, and did not answer. And then suddenly, the sermon must have ended, everybody stood up and Father Scott was announcing some big prayer, again in Latin. It all sounded lovely, but distant, unreal, and very holy. The two boys were standing, too, their backs to the people again. Dolly put her finger into her hair and began to twirl her curls slowly.

Dolly waited in the sunshine until her mother came down from the gallery, blessed herself at the stoop, nodded to some of the girls who had been in the choir. Then father came out quickly after them and he was talking to another man. Dolly could hear something about the weather, the need for hurry, the rain was coming, the hay would be spoiled. It was Sunday but Father Scott had said it would be all right, it was necessary work and it would not be a sin to work on that Sunday, they could start by eleven o'clock. The man was nodding; it was Mister Brennan, Packie's father, and they lived down in the lower part of the village, about half a mile from Dolly's house. There was excitement, a rush about things, and then Dolly and her parents were hurrying home.

This was the part of the Sunday that Dolly loved so much. After Mass she was able to take off her special dress and cardigan, take off her shiny black shoes, put on the old shirt and grey-blue dungarees she loved and felt relaxed and easy in. Then they had the special Sunday breakfast of fried eggs, toast and bacon, the scent of the bacon filling the house and making her mouth water. And today they had to hurry; the Brennans were coming to help with the saving of the hay; the weather would break too soon; they dared not risk losing the harvest.

It was fun out in the meadow. Dolly already felt prepared, in her dungarees. She tied a new white handkerchief about her hair to keep it from falling down in front of her face, and to keep the sun from bringing out too many freckles on her cheeks. It was warm out in the meadow and she felt closest then to her father and mother, especially when they began to make the big cocks of hay and she was hoisted up on top to help make them firm and tight. They all raked and gathered and the drying grass felt good and fragrant in her arms as she gathered up the stray wisps and leavings and carried them to where they would build the cock. The Brennans came, Mr Brennan and Mrs Brennan and young Packie Brennan and soon the meadow was as busy as ever it could be. Packie and Dolly scarcely spoke to one another; he was in short pants, his braces heaved up over his naked chest; he wore heavy boots and Dolly thought he would be burned and his feet would sweat. Packie worked well, without talking, without whistling. Dolly was quiet for a while but then she could not resist whistling a tune and calling out to her parents, especially when she was on top of the growing mound of hay, trampling it down, gathering the wisps together, firming everything, the saved hay rising, and she rising with it, into the warm afternoon. The greatest thrill was when her father decided the cock was high enough; then he threw a rope up to Dolly, she caught it and threw it down the other side of the cock to Mr Brennan; the two men tied the cock tightly to heavy stones on either side and then they threw more up to her, and a small canvas sack, opened and flattened out; this formed a kind of cap against rain. At last the moment came when Dolly had to sit down on the cock and let herself slide gloriously down to the ground, her father waiting to catch her lest she fall too heavily. That was great. It was exhilarating. She crowed.

They had lunch out in the meadow. Her mother left them

for a while and went in to prepare sandwiches and a great flask of tea. When she was ready they all gathered by one of the cocks, sat down, leaning back against the saved hay, and relished the thickly cut bread, the hard-boiled eggs, the lettuce and tomato sandwiches. The adults drank tea in great mugs from the flask; and there was lemonade for Dolly and for Packie. And that was the only time the children really came together, Dolly pouring the mineral for them both into two glasses.

'Thanks,' Packie said. She sat down beside him; he had a tiny blob of yellow egg on his face, at the side of his mouth. She giggled.

'Where's your fob watch?' she asked him.

He looked at her. 'It's in my waistcoat, at home. Can't bring it out in the meadow. Might lose it.'

'Does it keep the right time?'

'Of course it does. It's brilliant. I have to wind it up every morning and every evening. Sometimes it loses maybe a minute in the day, but it's easy, all you have to do is turn the thing at the top a bit and it's perfect again.'

'You're lucky!'

He looked at her. 'You're lucky. Look at the big house you have. And your father has a car. And you have a bike. We have nothing.'

She looked at him. She noticed now that his trousers were a little soiled, that there were small rips just under the pockets; she noticed, too, that one side of his braces was tied up by a piece of string. They were poor, the Brennans, she knew that. She drank her lemonade. Nothing would spoil this day. Nothing.

'Would you like another sandwich? There's one with tomato ... ?'

'Yes, please!'

'I saw you serving Mass today. You were giggling.'

'I was not giggling! The Latin is hard, you know, and me and Tommy, we were saying funny things to each other and Father Scott wasn't really listening to us, so we could say them.'

'Like what?'

'Well, there's a bit where we have to say "*mea culpa, mea*

culpa, mea maxima culpa" and me and Tommy said instead "me a cowboy, me a cowboy, me a Mexican cowboy".'

Dolly wondered. 'That might be a sin, mightn't it?'

'It's not a sin, how could it be a sin? And sometimes we just say, over and over, fast like, "cabbage and bacon, cabbage and bacon, cabbage and bacon," and it sounds, if you say it fast, like Latin.'

Dolly hesitated. 'He's called Jim, you know?'

'Who?'

'Father Scott. His name is Jim. Jim Scott.'

Now it was his turn to look at her, astonished. 'How could it be? He's a priest. He's Father Scott. You call him Father. That's all.' Dolly didn't like to tell him any more. He was poor, but he had that wonderful watch.

Next morning the rain was heavy and falling steadily. She could see the haycocks from her bedroom window; they stood finished, proud and capped: they would do. Aunt Lily's room was the one across the landing from Dolly's; the door was shut when Dolly came out to go downstairs. The girl tiptoed to Lily's door and opened it, softly, softly. It was dark within, the curtains drawn tightly across, but Dolly could see the big shape under the bedclothes, she could hear the heavy breathing that was almost a snoring. She wondered. She closed the door, softly, and tiptoed downstairs. Her father had already gone to the office when she came into the kitchen and her mother was wrapping some sugar sandwiches in greaseproof paper for Dolly's lunch. Sugar sandwiches; Dolly loved them, especially with a mug of cocoa when she could sit like a normal girl amongst all the normal girls at lunchtime in the yard.

'Mam, where was Aunt Lily yesterday?'

Her mother looked at her. 'Father Scott took her to visit her cousin in the hospital in Castlebar,' she said, quietly. 'You know Lily's cousin, Peggy Leslie, has been ill for a long time. They left after Mass. Father Scott is very, very kind.'

Dolly said nothing. She took her breakfast of porridge with sugar and milk, then a slice of toast. Her mother kept urging her along, hurry up, we'll be late, I can't be late, I have to open the school … Every morning the same. Every morning. But now there were only a few days left before the summer holidays, before freedom!

Monday, and it was raining hard. Many of the girls arrived wet and cold; they shook out their poor coats in the little porch and hung them up on hooks under the window. They gave off a strange and unwholesome smell all day and some of the girls had wet hair. Mrs Lohan brought those girls up to stand a while in front of the fire where she made them bend low over the blaze to try and get their hair dry. She scolded them for their stupidity, she spoke about umbrellas, about hats, about having an extra coat and pulling that over their heads but Dolly knew that a lot of the girls were lucky to have even one coat, a lot of them could not afford to buy an umbrella – what was her mother thinking of? And the more Mrs Lohan scolded the more Dolly would likely suffer for it during lunchtime. She quailed in her seat and tried to read over the poem they were supposed to know by heart for today, something about going out to a hazel wood and fishing for fishes with berries on a thread; such a silly poem, Dolly thought, who would ever go fishing with a berry and a thread?

But the day went well; there was a fine sense of ease in the classroom when everything settled down and the roll had been called. Dolly knew that most of the families would have got the hay saved over the last few days, and some of them would have brought the turf home from the bog and raised clamps up against the wall of the house. Mrs Lohan, after the period for sums, asked several of the girls to recite the poem and as they stumbled and staggered along the stony road of it, Dolly followed them mentally and knew that if she was asked she would be able to say it off pat. She relaxed. The warmth of the fire and the gentle hum that came from the rote learning in the other room lulled her into a sense of comfort and peace. And if it kept raining the girls would be allowed to stay in the classroom during lunch break and she wouldn't have to try and find a corner of the yard to be alone in, or see if maybe Joan or Margaret Mary might allow her join them in a game.

And then the door flew open and Father Scott came swinging in! He always came in like that, unannounced, suddenly, bursting in you might say, wishing to startle everybody awake. All the girls stood up together, noisily, to sing out 'Good morning Father Scott!' Several books fell off several desks, a few pens and pencils clattered onto the wooden floor; one awkward girl hit the edge of her desk as she rose and the desk-lid banged down again, hard. Father Scott waved them all a great, benign wave and they sat down, gathering their things back together. Father Scott moved over to Dolly's mother and they began to talk together quietly, half turned away from the girls. There was silence. Dolly could not make out one word of the whispering but for some reason she thought it must be about Aunt Lily. She idled through her reader; there was a lovely picture, in black and white, of ducks on a small pond and there was an easy poem going with it, 'Four ducks on a pond, a grass bank beyond ...' That was nice, Dolly liked it. And there was a story about four boys who went out fishing together on a boat they stole from some harbour; they got into trouble with the waves and the wind and a lifeboat had to come out to fetch them safely back. Dolly knew where that story was heading.

Suddenly Father Scott had finished speaking with Mrs Lohan and was eyeing the class of girls. He liked to question them, but carefully, making sure he never asked questions they might not be able to answer, in case he might embarrass Mrs Lohan.

'What's the name of the thing you cut the meadow with?' Father Scott asked the class, in a general way.

Every hand shot up. 'Yes, I bet you know that one,' Father Scott went on. 'But do you know how they keep the scythe sharpened? Hah? Do you know that one?'

Several hands shot up. Father Scott was moving jerkily across and back at the top of the desks, restless as ever, his words jittery and jumpy, as if he was the nervous one. Mrs Lohan stood behind him, near the blackboard, a smile of condescension and sureness on her face. She knew her girls would not let her down.

'Well, Gráinne,' Father Scott asked, pointing to a tall girl in the front desks.

'A wet stone, Father,' she said.

'Good-good-good, good girl Gráinne, but it's a whetstone, not a wet one, whet, whet, to whet something means to sharpen it. There's a h in it; whet. Whetstone.'

Dolly's hand shot up into the air.

Father Scott looked at her. 'Well, Dolly, what have you to say for yourself?'

Dolly answered at once. 'I was at Mass, Father.'

Father Scott hesitated. 'Yes, Dolly, good girl, so you were. I saw you there. Now, girls, how many are the laws of the Church?'

There was a pause. This was a quick switch, a difficult question. Mrs Lohan's smile was not as broad. Dolly's hand was up again.

'Yes, Dolly, have you the answer?'

Dolly said again, 'I was at Mass, Father.'

'Yes, yes, Dolly, we know that, you told us that but what I want to know now is this, how many are the laws of the Church.'

'I was at Mass, Father. I was at Mass.'

Dolly spoke quietly. She was insistent. Father Scott was taken aback. He looked at her, then he looked about at Mrs Lohan.

Mrs Lohan said crossly, 'Now Dolly, that's enough. That's not what Father wants to know. Let one of the girls answer.'

Breda MacNulty had her hand up. 'Yes, Breda,' and there was relief in Father Scott's voice.

'There are seven laws of the Church, Father.'

'Good girl, Breda, good girl. Seven. Yes. But now, you know what I'm going to ask you next.'

Dolly's hand was up again. 'I was at Mass, Father.'

Father Scott was exasperated. 'If you say that again I'll put a bee buzzing in your lug, Dolly, now that's enough. We've heard you. We know you were at Mass. Now, can anyone name for me the seven laws of the Church.'

'I was at Mass, Father, I was at Mass.'

Father Scott simply stamped his foot against the hard wooden floor of the schoolroom, turned and walked quickly out of the school, banging the door shut after him. There was a long silence. Mrs Lohan came down and took Dolly by the ear and led her to the furthest corner at the back of the class. There she had to stand, in utter disgrace, until it was three o'clock and time to go home. Dolly was not repentant; she felt she had done nothing wrong; but she knew, too, it was not right. When the other girls asked her later on why she had kept on saying that, Dolly was never able to answer them. She simply did not know. She must have had a reason, but she did not know the reason. And she could not explain it to her angry mother, either then or later on, at home. When her father heard about it he was silent; he was not cross; he simply took hold of Dolly, gently, rubbed her hair and said that the girl was simply confused, that was all, she was confused.

When she went home Aunt Lily was sitting at the kitchen table, a big mug of tea in her big hands. Mrs Lohan told her the story of Dolly's misbehaviour at once and Aunt Lily looked at the girl, angrily, and hissed at her: 'Such a silly thing, such a silly creature. How dare you, Dolly, how simply dare you!' Dolly said nothing and left the kitchen. She went straight upstairs to her room, took out the black and white panda bear from the wardrobe into which she had stuffed it, and began to shake and pummel it with her fists. Then she went downstairs, quietly, and out the front door, around the side of the house, across the meadow to the far ditch and flung the sad creature into the depths of the hedgerow that ran along between the meadow and their neighbours' fields. Then Dolly went back into her room, flung herself onto her bed, and wept.

One of her favourite places to go, when she was alone, was in the pine grove at the side of the house, a grove planted in her grandfather's early days to give the house shelter from the Atlantic winds. They were very high now, Scots pine, dense with their branches and pine needles; several of them higher than the house. And she loved to climb them, one of them in particular where the lower branches were strong and low enough for her to clamber up easily.

She climbed, and the rough bark felt welcoming to her

hands, the little sweatings of resin daubed her fingers with wonderful incense. Now and then a robin came and watched her curiously from a branch or a small breeze moved surreptitiously through the trees and cooled her. She knew each branch, each reach and hold and soon she was sitting in a fork of the tree high above the world and could watch out over the island, the whole way down to the sea and the whole way back to the bogland slopes of the mountain. Of course they knew she was up there, the adults, but they would pretend they did not know and would call her name aloud to thrill her, to make a greater treasure of her secret place. At times, on wilder days, she would not climb to the top fork of the tree but stay a little lower down and then the trees would all lean and sway under the rough winds and she would thrill, holding on and leaning, swaying with them, and she was on a ship that sailed the seven oceans and took great seas on board, surfacing again, indomitable, making its way to port.

And then one day she climbed, high, high, only to find her secret hideout violated. There he was, Packie Brennan, sitting and grinning down at her, astride her special fork, there at the top of her special tree. She could see the scratches on his bare knees, she could see the broken laces on his old boots, that he wore no socks, and that his shirt, an old one from his father or even his grandfather, without a collar, torn and missing a few buttons, still had a large breast pocket from which the chain of his fob watch protruded, goading her.

He laughed when he saw the surprise on her face.

'Packie Brennan! What are you doing up here? This is my place. Come down.'

'Your daddy told me I could come and climb the trees if I wanted,' he said to her. 'And this is not your tree. You didn't plant it, did you? You weren't even born when it was planted, were you?'

'That's not the point. It's the tree I have chosen to be my special tree, and that's the place where I always like to sit. It's mean of you to be here.'

'Well, it's a free world, you know, and I like it up here.'

She looked up at him for a moment; she could think of no

response; she could not think how she might get rid of him. She gave up. She began to climb down again. That nettled him into some action.

'I bet you can't hang from a branch and let yourself drop,' he challenged her. Now, Dolly always did drop from one of the last branches; it was fun to hang for a while over the ground, and then let go and drop through the air for a second. Over the weeks and days she had raked together a heap of dead pine needles to form a fine cushion down below. She was good at this. She was an expert.

'If I do that will you go away and leave my tree alone?'

He considered. 'Well, only if you can drop from a place higher than me.' He was beginning to clamber down after her. She moved out along a thick branch, still holding to one above her. She had done this before; there was no problem. She was at about the height of a man, her father, say, from the ground. 'Watch this,' she said. She slithered herself along the branch until she was laying across it on her stomach, then, carefully, she eased herself over the branch until she was hanging from it with her two hands. She looked up at him. She let go. She landed on her feet and did not fall over.

'Sure the cat could do that,' he said and followed her agilely until he too had hung from the same branch and dropped easily onto the ground.

'What about that one up there?' he said, pointing to one that reached out from the tree much higher than this one. It was at least twice, maybe more, the height of her father. Her stomach heaved a little at the thought. 'I bet I'll do it!' he said and began to climb up the tree again. She followed him, a little nervous at the prospect. Soon he was standing on the higher branch, moving out carefully, gripping branches above him and to the side. He glanced down. Dolly was sure that he hesitated. She looked down from where she was, holding onto the bole of the tree. It was high, very high, but her heap of pine needles was below and she could drop onto that.

'Ladies first,' he said, moving further out onto the branch. He was grinning. 'I bet you're scared, girls are sissies, they're always scared of things.'

'I'm a bit scared,' she admitted to him. 'It's high. And it's only good to be scared, then you don't just do all stupid things. And it's always good to tell the truth, too. So I'm scared, and I bet you're scared, too.'

'I'm not scared!' he said. 'Come on, you go first then get out of the way cos I'll be down fast after you.'

As Dolly moved out along the branch their combined weight began to make it bend a little. She felt for a moment she would lose her balance and she gripped more tightly onto the smaller branches above her. Then she was out over the pine needles. Slowly, and with her whole stomach in a knot, she slithered down onto the branch and lay over it on her stomach, still holding on tightly. She glanced down again. It was a long way down. She hesitated. 'Cowardy cowardy mustard!' he began chanting at her. 'Cowardy cowardy mustard!' She looked up at him. 'You're a bit stupid,' she said, 'it's not mustard, it's custard. Custard. Cowardy ...' but he had moved over on the branch above her and began to jolt it up and down, jumping on it so that she lost her hold suddenly and fell. She screamed. But it was over at once; she fell, safely, onto the pile of leaves, she fell face down and lay there, a little winded, but delighted that she had made it. Nothing broken. No damage done.

Then she heard Packie call out above her and oh boy but he was scared now! What had he done? 'Are you OK?' he shouted down and there was panic in his voice. 'Oh my God, are you all right?' She ignored him. She simply lay there, not moving, but laughing to herself. She heard him muttering 'Oh God, oh God, oh God' as he clambered back down the tree. He did not drop from a branch, he simply climbed down, carefully. Then he was standing just over her, and asking 'Please, Dolly, are you OK?' She did not stir. 'I'm sorry,' he said, 'Really I'm sorry. I didn't mean ...' She moaned, just a little bit and suddenly he ran, he simply turned from where she was and ran. He's going to get somebody, she thought, but when she lifted her head, cautiously, she saw him run out the back gate and head away, down towards his own house. He was leaving her, simply leaving her. 'And I could be dead,' she said to herself, 'My back could be broken!' 'Now who's the coward?' she thought, and

she was delighted. Now he would not come back to invade her
space again.

Dolly picked herself up and looked back at the high branch
with pride; my God, she had dropped down from up there!
That was a special drop, she was chuffed. She would tell her
mother, not about Packie, but about the drop, how high it was,
how she had loved it, and how it was safe because of the pine
needles piled beneath.

She came out the small gate of the grove into the yard. There
was a red Ford Anglia car parked in the yard. She was surprised.
It was Father Scott's car, red and busy, like Father Scott himself,
and everybody knew that he always drove too fast in it,
sometimes even, they said, reaching thirty-five miles an hour.
But that was, people said, when he was rushing to somebody
who might be dying, somebody who might need extreme
unction. Dolly opened the back door of the house and walked
into the kitchen.

Father Scott was standing with his back to the fire; he was
lifting himself up and down on the balls of his feet, restless as
usual. He grinned when Dolly walked in.

'Look what the dog dragged in!' he said. 'Dorothy. Who goes
to Mass! Now she's all covered in pine needles.'

'I dropped from a high branch,' she answered.

Dolly's mother was seated at the kitchen table, wrapping
something up in a paper parcel. 'Look at you, you're all covered
in dirt and things.'

'Been crawling about on your tummy, have you Dorothy?'
Father Scott laughed.

She began to tell them. 'No, but I was up in the tree …'

'How often have I told you not to be climbing trees!' her
mother scolded again. 'It's not a thing that girls should be doing.
I've told you that.'

Dolly noticed that her mother was not really cross; there was
something else bothering her. She was only giving half her
attention to Dolly.

'A wasp in the honey jar of joy!' Father Scott smiled at her.

'But Packie Brennan …' Dolly began. The door from the
kitchen into the hallway opened suddenly. It was Aunt Lily and

she was dressed in her big coat with some furry animal about her neck. Dolly could see how red her eyes were. She had been crying. Lily glanced at Dolly and said, but without conviction, 'Look at the fairy, all covered in dirt.'

Dolly wanted to leave the kitchen, to clean herself of pine needles, but as she was opening the door into the hallway Aunt Lily spoke gently to her.

'Goodbye, Dolly.'

Dolly was surprised, at the word, and at the sadness in the voice. She hesitated and looked back. Everybody was watching her. Aunt Lily was fiddling with the black and white gloves she wore; she was really dressed up, Dolly could see that. But was she really going away? That would be nice. For a moment Dolly felt very bad for that thought, after all, Aunt Lily seemed very sorry indeed. Dolly left the door open, came back and tried to hug Aunt Lily, but her face simply buried itself in the dark coat.

'There's a fine fairy, a fine fairy,' Aunt Lily murmured, rubbing Dolly's hair.

'Goodbye, Aunt Lily,' Dolly said, then turned and went out into the hallway.

It was Friday night, and father, mother and Dolly, and even grandfather, were going to go and watch a movie in the Night of Dreams Emporium. It was already summer holidays and everything seemed warm and good to Dolly. This was a movie she wanted to see, it would be funny and it would be frightening: *Abbott and Costello meet Frankenstein.* She had seen a trailer for it some weeks before and, anyway, she loved Abbott and Costello. And it was rare enough that grandfather would come with them; he wanted a good laugh, he said, and he wanted to see what all this was about.

Nanna had made potato cakes and Dolly simply loved them, with parsley, butter and a fried egg. Grandfather was full of talk during the meal but Nanna was strangely silent. When they were finished Nanna went out into the hall and beckoned to Dolly to join her. Nanna closed the door quietly and left the others to clear up.

'Dolly, I want you to do something very special for me, please, there's a good girl.'

'What is it, Nanna?'

'I want you to stay at home with me this evening and not go to that old film.'

'Oh but Nanna, this is a special film, and I've really been looking forward ...'

'I know, Dolly, I know, but you see grandfather is going and I'll be all alone in the house. And I'll be scared, very scared. I'll be frightened.'

'Scared of what, silly?'

'Of ghosts, Dolly, ghosts. Devils. All of those terrible things that can happen to old women on their own. Even someone breaking into the house.'

'But there's no such thing as ghosts, Nanna, and we'll be back soon and nobody will break in.'

Nanna reached into the little purse she carried in her apron and drew out half a crown.

'Of course I'll pay you to stay with me, and please Dolly, please don't tell anybody I asked you. Just say you wanted to stay and play cards with me, or listen to the play on the radio. Please, my own sweet Dolly.'

'Oh Nanna, don't ask me to do that. I really want to see this film.'

Nanna considered, then she drew out a yellow ten-shilling note and offered it to Dolly.

'Now, that will show you how scared I am. I'll be terrified here, all on my own, and grandfather doesn't know that either, I can't ask him, he so rarely goes out.'

'Why don't you come with us, Nanna?'

'I hate those old movies, and anyway I'd only be scared even more. Werewolves and all of that. I have enough of my own dead who might be wandering about the world tonight and might come in and terrify me. I ask you again, my own Dolly, please, just for tonight. And look at all the money you'll have when you go to Salthill; you can go to ten movies there. And we'll have fun together, the radio, a game of cards, and look, I have bars of chocolate.'

She reached back into that deep apron pocket and produced two bars of dark chocolate. Dolly looked into her face a moment. She was old, she had too much talcum powder on her cheeks so that there was a heap of it piled into the lines that crossed her forehead, too much of it on her chin and the netting that held her hair in place did not properly cover the coming baldness that she would suffer from. And Dolly could see that she was pale and anxious, but … this was a special night, she couldn't miss it, she simply couldn't.

'Sorry, Nanna, not tonight. You'll be perfectly all right, you'll see, and I'll make sure we come straight back immediately after the film is over. And I promise I won't tell anybody that you asked me.'

Dolly was already moving away and had her hand on the knob of the kitchen door. Nanna sighed heavily. She handed the two bars of chocolate to Dolly then turned and went out into the front garden for a while, to stand and watch down over the fields towards the sea.

Dolly greatly enjoyed her night at the cinema. It was only after the shorts and the newsreels and the trailers were over and when the lights came up again for a short while, that she remembered the bars of chocolate. She took them out. But then she put them back into her pocket and sat back silently in her seat. The people chattered eagerly around her; grandfather nudged her and winked.

'This will be great!' he said to her. She simply nodded.

When they got home, quite late in the night, Dolly was already sleepy. She could see that every light in the house was switched on. Nanna was sitting in the kitchen; she had the radio on, quite loud. But she was asleep in the easy chair near the dead fire. Grandfather jollied her awake. Only Dolly could see the traces of tears down the old woman's cheeks, tears that had left soft, pink lines through the talcum powder. She felt guilty, so guilty. And after all, it wouldn't have been too hard to stay with her grandmother. Didn't the preparation for confirmation say how important love was in life, to be a Christian, a good Christian. And somewhere, deep down within her, Dolly had responded already to the notion of being a nun that her mother had hinted to her. Nanna smiled at her and she went up, quietly, and slipped the two bars of chocolate back into the deep pocket of the old apron.

The film that moved her most deeply was called *On Moonlight Bay*. It starred Doris Day, and there was Gordon MacRae, a handsome man, strong and formidable, a little like she imagined her own grandfather to have been, when he was younger. She had one scene in particular always before her eyes, a scene with Gordon rowing a small boat in a lovely place, trees around, the moon warm and watchful, and Doris sitting in the stern of the little boat; and there was love between them, and music, and the song that said 'you have stolen my heart, now don't go 'way', and Doris scarcely knew what was meant by it all. Yet there were tears in the young girl's eyes, in that smelly old cinema, with the seats already torn and the reels sometimes breaking down and the voices going all froggy and slowing into foolishness, 'you have stolen my heart', and oh the soft music of it, the big eyes of Doris Day wide with the wonder of love and the dread of the war that hung over the scene, 'as we sang love's old sweet song on Moonlight Bay'. And when, in the end, Gordon MacRae marched off to that dreadful war and Doris stood, holding back the heartbreak, promising to wait, to wait for him for ever, Dolly was so sad and so happy at the same time that she could scarcely breathe.

When she came out from the cinema it was a warm, still night; the moon was shining, away over the ocean and the light from the lighthouse on Clare Island swept with a silent reassurance across the bay. She could see the high cliffs and the distant mountains stand out clearly in their humped shapes, reassuring, too. Her father paused to light a cigarette and gaze out over the bay and Dolly was glad of the darkness and the pause before they would have to head off home and he would discuss the film with her. She hated that, especially with this one, she wanted to hold it close inside her, hold Doris's love and promise, her joy and sadness, deep in her own being and not have to spoil it by talking about it. She moved away a little from her father; these were stirrings that disturbed her and gave her immense joy at the same time; she was growing up, she would become a woman. Soon she would have finished primary school and the world would be opening up before her. It was exciting, challenging, and a little disconcerting.

Just then Packie Brennan came around the corner of the cinema; she knew him, in spite of the dimness of the night, she knew that somewhat stumped figure, that swaggering walk, the hands stuffed down into his trouser pockets. She saw that he was wearing long trousers, she saw too that he was slouching away from his parents and that he wanted to light up a cigarette … Imagine the foolishness of that, Packie Brennan wanting to smoke a cigarette! He saw her at once.

'It's you,' he said, familiarly, and a little angrily. 'Wasn't that such a load of old rope, that film! God, such a silly story, like chocolate cake that had gone sour and someone had dropped it on the floor and someone else had jumped on it. Jeez! A real load of rubbish.'

'I thought it was brilliant! And I thought Doris Day was lovely. And the music, too. I thought it was brilliant.'

He looked at her, scarcely seeing her, as he watched about furtively for his parents; he was cupping his cigarette in the cave of his hand and occasionally pulling quickly on it.

'I really liked Doris Day,' she repeated. 'And the story was lovely. It was about love.'

Packie hesitated. 'I thought it was a bit silly, and soppy,' he said. 'And you're not Doris Day, Dolly Lohan, I can tell you that. It's all so unreal, and I sure as hell am not George MacRae, that's for sure.'

Dolly looked at him. 'Gordon MacRae,' she corrected him. 'Gordon, his name is Gordon, not George. And by the way, my name is Dorothy, please know my name is Dorothy, not Dolly.'

He was taken aback. 'Sorry, sorry!' he said. 'It's been Dolly as long as I've known you, that's for sure. Why is it changed all of a sudden?'

'It's not changed. My name has always been Dorothy. Dolly is just a kind of a nickname, and I don't like it any more. And I agree with you, Packie, you're no Gordon MacRae, that's certain. You'll always be Packie Brennan, and you'll kill yourself with the smoking, it's stupid, that's what it is, and it'll make you sick and you'll die before I do because I don't smoke, and you'll be dead and see if I care!'

She turned from him at once and went to take her father by the hand. She did not look back at the boy. But she found that she was crying again, crying softly to herself, and there was such a sadness in her soul that she had to take in deep breaths to keep herself from calling out in fright. Then she heard Packie coming quickly up behind her and his voice calling, very quietly, 'Dorothy! Dorothy!'

She turned. 'What?'

He hesitated. He found it difficult. 'Dorothy, I'm sorry about knocking you off the tree that time. You know, when you fell? And I'm grateful you didn't tell anybody. I got scared, that's all. I'm sorry.'

'That's all right, Packie Brennan. That's all right.' Dolly smiled to herself across the darkness as she came up to where her father stood, watching out over the bay.

WHAT NEEDS TO BE UNDONE

Packie Brennan lived with his father and mother in a tumbledown house just beyond a small bridge, down from the road that led to the pier. The river that flowed by his house came all the way down from the hills, gathering peaty water as it descended, widening and deepening and, just by his house, meeting the incoming tidal waters. Twice a day there was a very big pool of water just beyond Packie's home, almost a small lake, and it was here that Packie played. Here he was able to imagine himself the captain of a great ship that sailed over and back across the ocean. For several hours, before high tide when the water filled the basin with a rich gurgling sound that slowly fell into quiet, then during that long period of high tide when the world appeared to stand still, and for some time after the tide began to flow out and the runnelling and chunnelling of the water began again, Packie took his home-built craft and moved around on his own ocean.

The boat was hammered together from old planks and two by fours; the whole covered over with canvas that he had painted several times with thick hot pitch and left to dry. It served, and it served well. Packie preferred the quiet evenings where he would drift up to the bridge with the incoming tide, then row his way back down again; sometimes drifting, sometimes rowing. The water beneath him changed colour, from bog-peat brown to salt-sea emerald, sometimes frothing gold and white. In the shallows he could watch the mullet roll their bodies just under the surface of the water; he would have caught them, save that his father said they were ugly fish, feeding on dirt and slops and their flesh was impure. Sometimes, a salmon or a sea trout might leap from the deepest part of the pool, trying to rid itself of the vermin its body had picked up out at sea and that splash, that arced and shimmering leap, would stir Packie's soul to its depths. If he was lucky, and that wasn't too often, he might sometimes catch a brown trout, small but very tasty. The old pared branch he used for a rod, with a length of twine and some green-coloured gut he had found in an abandoned trawler, was not great for serious fishing. But it served, and at times it served well.

At high tide, the waters intermingling seemed to hold a whisperful conversation with the pitched boards of his little craft. The water brimmed in the great pool, Packie sat without moving, simply allowing his body to drift with the drifting of the boat that moved itself with the movement, or lack of it, of the world's tidal power. His mind would fall empty; he would be absent a while from all the niggardliness and demands of the world, his eyes half-glazed with the simple pleasure of bodily being, until the boat would butt its prow against the bank, and he would have to take the home-made oars and row himself back up towards the bridge. Packie, without knowing what it was, had a strange but glorying sense that he would be part of all of this, part of the movement of the water, part of the great power of the ocean that shifted and deepened and widened just beyond the bend of the river, part of the mountain above that sent this stream of water out of its very core, down through the boglands of the island, to meet the upwelling of the sea. He could not put words to that feeling, he scarcely ever tried to think of what it meant to him, but when, at last, the midges that gathered in the dusk began to drive him shorewards, or when the darkness began to fall too early in the latter part of the year, or when his grandfather called to him to come in to say the rosary, it was with reluctance that Packie dragged his craft up on the shore, up onto the grasslands beside the house, turned it over and placed two cement blocks on its upturned belly, in case the island or the sea winds should cast it about, and move grudgingly back into the world of the adults, willing himself to move indoors, knowing a feeling of defiance and of self-defence.

Grandfather led the rosary, announcing the mysteries, saying the first decade. The second decade was taken up by Packie's father, and his mother took the third. Packie led them on the fourth decade; then the fifth, with all the extra prayers, the trimmings, were said by Grandfather once again. Old Ned Brennan had been a fisherman, had spent days and nights out on the seas in a medium-sized half-decker, trawling. It had been an impossible life but Ned had relished it, every toss and turn of the sea being known to him, as every toss and turn of his wife had been known, before she had been roughly torn from him, many years ago, by tuberculosis. For years now the old man's bones were creaking and sore, they were dried out he used to say, and he spent large parts of every day simply sitting in a cosy chair near the open door of the house, watching out over the river where Packie played, or simply listening to the histories the sea and its tides were reminding him of. He did not complain. He had his pipe. He could spit out across the small yard towards the few ducks and hens that bothered the poor soil before the house. He had his pension which he handed over in its entirety to his son, Edward, and to Edward's wife, Nora. He caused no trouble in his own home; he never entered into dispute with his son or daughter-in-law; they would have the house soon enough, he might live in a modicum of peace until then. Nora was good enough to him and only complained at times, in the loud darkness of stormy nights when she thought the old man could not hear her over the grumbling of the winds and the seas. And Edward knew that her complaints were not really against the old man, but took another source, the poverty in which they lived.

Grandfather's one remaining joy was in his grandson Packie; the old man's great ambition was that one day he might see that boy heading away to a seminary to become a priest, to escape the poverty trap of the seashore house, and bring glory at last on the name of Brennan. But he never spoke that dream aloud, in case it be shattered, utterly, before it had even been spoken.

That was why old Ned Brennan had offered the whole of his savings when Packie told his parents about the day Father Scott came into the boy's school and spoke to the class about the need for acolytes in the church.

The boys were scared of Father Scott. He seemed to prance in front of them, asking questions and always expecting them either to give the wrong answers or not to have an idea of what he was talking about. And Brother Juniper simply smirked and rubbed his hands in a kind of glee when Father Scott moved down between the rows, asking questions.

'Now you clods and sods of damp turf you,' Father Scott began. 'Here's a chance for you to be something special. I want acolytes. Acolytes. Yes, Michael Bergin, and what are acolytes?'

Michael was one of the Bergins from the mountain and everybody knew that they were not too bright up there. Michael turned round.

'Em, Father, I think it's a kind of … a kind of timber, Father.'

Brother Juniper laughed aloud. Father Scott came up to Bergin and stood, looking down at him, trying himself not to laugh. 'A kind of timber, is it? Well, well, well, like the stuff in your skull, Bergin? Eh?'

All the other boys had their heads down over their desks. 'Nobody knows then, oh Brother Juniper how do you survive with all these jackasses about you?'

Brother Juniper only giggled.

'All right then,' Father Scott went on. 'I'll have to give a hint. Acolyte. A helper of some kind. Of a very special kind. A good boy. A holy boy. Oh dear, sure there isn't a chance of finding one of those here now, is there?' He gazed around the class. Packie Brennan happened to look up at that moment and caught the priest's eye.

Father Scott dived! 'Ha, Packie Brennan! Maybe you're a holy boy now, eh Packie? Do you know what an acolyte might be?'

'An altar server Father,' Packie answered. The words had come to him out of some kind spirit in the air. Father Scott was stunned. 'Correct, saint Packie Brennan, an altar server is correct, and you, Packie, you will be the very first to come to the altar to serve. Your father will be proud of you, Packie Brennan, well done!'

Packie, even more astonished at his success than Father Scott or Brother Juniper, sat in his desk, his mouth hanging open. Father Scott went on to ask for five other boys who would volunteer to be acolytes, to serve the morning Mass in the monastery or the Sunday Mass and evening rosary and Benediction in the parish church. Then he told them to go to Sweeney's stores and buy a surplice, a black soutane and altar slippers and be ready for practice the following Saturday at the sacristy.

That afternoon Packie was given a clip on the ear by his father. 'And where do you think we're going to get the money for all that expensive stuff, tell me that! An acolyte indeed, next thing you'll want to be off to become a priest or something, or a monk like Brother Juniper.' And again all Packie could do was stand, his mouth fallen open, dreading what Father Scott might say if he failed to turn up on Saturday. That was when grandfather Ned produced a five-pound note from the depths of his waistcoat and handed it proudly over to Packie's father.

'You ought to be proud of the boy, Edward, you ought to be very proud. A son of the Brennans up on the altar serving Mass! That's a great honour indeed, close to the priest and close to the Holy Sacrament. Get the boy what he needs, get him a pair of stockings, too and I'll tell you what, get him a new fob watch with the change! He deserves it, and all the boys have one. An acolyte, Packie Brennan an acolyte. Sure we'll be as good as any family in the parish, lad, well done, well done!'

And on the following Sunday, at first Mass, Packie Brennan was on the altar in his starched surplice and his long black soutane and he knew the movements, the duties, and most of the answers to the strange Latin prayers. And his grandfather knelt in the front pew of the church, on the men's side, and beamed. And scarcely noticed the one grey sock and the one green that showed over the altar slippers and underneath the hem of the black soutane.

Packie was no angel, even if the white of the surplice made him look a little more like a cherub than his father could wish. For

Edward Brennan was angry with life, a life that had given him a father who had made little of the poor land down by the shore and had placed on his shoulders the added burden of having to care for an old man as well as his own wife and son. And so he tended to punish Packie for the sorrows of his own life. He had his special technique, too; if Packie came home wet from the pool, having fallen in the water, or simply damaged a shirt, a trousers, or taken a real fishing rod without permission, then Edward Brennan would stand the boy in front of him, make him hold out both hands, the back of the hands upwards, and he would slap him, hard, with a piece of two by four timber. Sometimes Packie's knuckles bled. Sometimes he cried aloud. Sometimes he held back the tears, but always, after such punishment, he was placed for at least an hour in the dark and cluttered closet under the stairs. There was a sickly smell in there, of must and dust and old polishes, there were battered ancient suitcases, sweeping brushes and the two good fishing rods his father kept. There was no light in there, save for the chink that showed under the door. The one ease Packie found was that he could cry quietly in the darkness so that his father might not have the pleasure of seeing his tears. And he could hold his hands in under his armpits to ease the pain.

Sometimes, while he stood in the cupboard, for there was nowhere to sit down, he would hear Grandfather shuffle his way to the door outside and try to comfort him. Ned did not dare go counter to his own son's wishes; after all, he was relying now, till the end of his days, on his son's patience and tolerance. But he felt so for Packie that he would come and whisper outside, promising a bag of aniseed balls or a bar of chocolate when Packie would be let out. 'Just come down to my room, when all is quiet, and I'll hand it out to you. There's a good boy. Your father's having a tough time. That's all. You're a good boy. You'll just have to take more care. That's all. That's all.'

Packie would press his face against the door of the closet and reassure his grandfather. 'It's all right, Granddad, thanks, I know it was wrong to fall into the water, and I won't do it again. I'll be careful. Don't worry, please don't worry. I'm all right now.'

Ned had a room down at the end of the house, because he

was not able to climb the stairs any more. Every evening, after rosary, he would shuffle his way down to his room, and nobody would see him again until late the next morning, when Edward would have gone out into the yard and Packie's mother had his own porridge prepared for him. But sometimes Packie would sneak down to the old man, before going up to his own small room and boy and grandfather would whisper secrets to each other by the light of a candle or, in the darkest nights of the winter, by the yellow light of a small oil lamp. And those were special moments, for both of them.

The bed in Grandfather's room was huge. He kept a bolster on the inner side of the bed, where Granny had slept – to remind him that he was never alone, Ned said to Packie, that Granny was always with him. And he kept all her clothes still in the old wardrobe, her shoes under the bed, and her mirror and hair brush on the small uncluttered dressing table. And once he showed Packie a long white and woollen shirt, with a big picture of a crucifix sewn onto the chest; he told him they were to dress him in that when he died, for it was made by Maggie's own hands, made for him to help him over the winters, made warm and strong for him, because, Ned said proudly, she had loved him, Maggie Connors had loved him, and that made him know that he had lived and had known what living was about. And when she died he had sewn the bit of linen that had the crucifix on it, onto the shirt and had put it away, to wear only once more, when he would be laid to rest in the same grave as Maggie so that she would know how he never forgot her, how he still loved her, and how happy he would be to be with her once again.

Packie listened to his grandfather and kept all those secrets to himself. But there were times when he hesitated at Grandfather's bedroom door, convinced that the old man was weeping inside, weeping at the loneliness of his life and the emptiness of it, there on the scrambled poor acres at the edge of the shore, acres that forced his son into a state of almost perpetual crossness and that made Edward's own wife too ragged and thin. It was that quietly rasping sound of the old man's weeping or sighing that would be the sound to haunt Packie Brennan's living for ever.

'Do you cry in here sometimes, Grandpa?'

Ned looked at the boy and drew him closer to him. The old man was sitting in the wicker chair that always stood near the head of the big bed.

'Yes, Packie, I do, sometimes. For lonesomeness. And there's no shame in it, boy, there's no shame in a man knowing sorrow. Nay, nay, it's good for a man to know sorrow for this life is a vale of tears, it's in the prayers, the Hail Holy Queen we say every night, mourning and weeping in this valley of tears, because it's our need to purge ourselves of this world, so that we may become as pure as possible to enter before the sight of God. How can we enter the purity of heaven, Packie, if we're all black with sin and pride? Hey? How can we? So we must purge ourselves, and it's only suffering that can do that, fretting us away till we become spirit and lose the shame of this mortal flesh that drags us down into the dirt. That's what it's about, lad, it's about cleansing, and sacrifice, and suffering, till we're ready to be saints and stand in the radiant glory that is in the court of God. So don't be worried about me, Packie, I'm ready for it, I'm getting ready for it and it won't be long now, I can feel it, you know the way you can feel it when the tide is at the full, you can feel it in the air about you, you can feel it in your bones, in your hair, it's a kind of distant tingling sensation, a quietness and you know that the tide will turn any moment now, and begin its way back out to sea. Well, I feel it, Packie, I feel it often now and it lifts my heart to my own Maggie, and if I cry, lad, it may well be tears of relief, that my sufferings here may soon be over and I'll be happy for ever with my own dear wife Maggie.'

'I'll miss you, though Grandpa, I'll really miss you.'

'You're a good boy, Packie Brennan, a really good boy, and I'll be with you always, and my own Maggie will be with you, too, so one day you'll join us all in heaven, and we'll all be together again, without this suffering, this pain, this loneliness. Now, let's read a little bit more this evening and then you'll have to slip away to bed. Quick as a flash. Where were we? *The Old Curiosity Shop*, wasn't it? And little Nell …'

★

Sometimes Packie wandered away from the shore, especially those late afternoons when the tide was out and the pool before the house was too shallow to be any use, and he always liked to play, alone and peaceful, either in the pine grove beside Lohan's house, up the village, or in the hedgerow that ran around that large holding, dividing the meadows and the gardens, the orchard and the peat acre. If he slipped around behind the pine grove there was a kitchen garden with carrots, parsnips, potatoes, with the staked-up rows of beans and peas; between grove and garden was a small opening in the ditch where the wire fencing had been broken and here Packie would slip onto the alien property, make his way across the end of the garden and into the high and long hedgerow that was hollow enough within to hold his body secret from the world. He could creep and crawl along in there, and watch out through the fragrant leaves and flowers, sometimes held back a little by the rhododendron bushes that grew here and there along the hedge. But it was a tunnel; it was his; he was unobserved. From places here he could see the fine holding of the Lohans, he could envy the richness and depth of their soil, the dryness of their turf, the fine cocks of hay in the meadows.

The earth in the hedgerow was hard, it was dry with leaf mould and blossom-droppings; here and there tiny roots or stones in the ground stippled his palms and knees; but his journeying around the holding was a fine adventure for him, he was a pirate on dry land, at the edge of an island where his ship had anchored down by the shore. Thrush and robin watched him warily; now and again a blackbird would scoot out of the branches with a high alarm call, startling him. And there were insects, strange and beetly, that sometimes frightened him with their ugliness, the awful throbbing of their wildly-coloured and lacquered bodies, their pebble eyes that swivelled and seemed to remain forever open. And there were small spaces within the hedgerow where he could pause and sit up in a certain comfort, where he could fall still and remain silent, fixed in place like the branches, part of the earth, conscious of its slow pulse beat, its steady rhythms. He could absent himself, unconscious of what was happening to him, and receive some breath of being that moved into him from far beyond the normal dullness of his life down by the shore. At those times a strange and unfocused longing rose in him, accompanied by a sadness he could not name. It was not envy of the wellbeing of the family whose acres he haunted, it was not fear, it was a sense that there must be a great deal more to living than he could ever see himself a part of. And so he sat, still as an egg, allowing sadness its spaces within him.

Until the day he was sitting, utterly still, his mind vacant, his body motionless, and watching out through branch and leaf towards the gable end of the Lohan house. Here there was a small fruit garden and Packie knew there were redcurrant bushes, blackcurrant bushes and gooseberries and, he suspected, even strawberries growing in neatly ordered rows. The lower part of the gable wall was covered with a climbing rose bush and the blossoms were plentiful, Packie imagining he could get the scent of the flowers from where he sat. The sun was shining brightly on wall and climbing rose and the window above was mirroring the brightness of the day. Packie saw the upper half of the window slowly lowered and a young girl appeared, leaning out, watching down into the garden.

Something shifted in Packie's chest, something that hurt him sorely as he saw the perfectly white dress the girl was wearing, and how she seemed to be singing quietly to herself. She was wearing some kind of a wreathe of flowers in her hair, roses perhaps and, as Packie watched, she began to take the blossoms out and pluck the petals, letting them float down over the garden as she hummed, or sang. There fell a slow and gentle stream of pink petals that floated easily away on a small breeze. Gradually the richly dark hair of the girl was loosened and began to fall about her face and shoulders and Packie knew that he was gazing at something that was beautiful, and something that closed him out from a wealth and glory that he might be allowed to glimpse during his life, but never share. Dolly Lohan, he knew, was beyond him.

He watched a long time, minutes and seconds being meaningless. Then the girl disappeared and the window was closed after her. All he could see was the glass once again mirroring the world outside, of which he was still a part. He sat on another while. Now anger grew in him, and he broke off several of the escallonia branches about him, determining to build in there a small shelter where he could often come, and sit, and watch. Later that evening, after his own supper, he took a thick slice of white bread, sprinkled sugar on it and went out to sit on the ditch outside the door and watch the heron move ever cautiously in the shallows beyond. He had his own world, his own riches, here, at the edge of the pool, amongst sea-things and tidal rhythms and the great sky.

On his way home from school, Packie would linger by the roadside, kicking stones into the ditch, taking his time, sometimes able to pass a half hour or so with the other boys. They talked of many things. They talked of the cinema that had been built back in the next village, of the films that were to be shown every Friday night. Among these boys was Tommy James Molloy, a big boy, red-faced, iron-fisted, ignorant and a bully. Packie was hugely scared of him. When they had left the school far behind and had turned onto the road that led through a low tunnel of fuchsia hedges, Tommy Jimmy Molloy produced a packet of cigarettes. It was here, many afternoons, that Packie learned how to smoke and though at first it made him feel quite sick, he soon got used to it and felt himself grown up and important. Anyway, his father smoked, and his mother took an occasional cigarette. Packie often found half-smoked cigarettes around the house; he had easy access to them and, in Tommy Jimmy's company, he felt proud to be able to produce a collection of almost perfect smokes and share them out. He would have Tommy Jimmy Molloy on his side, if ever battles in the school should occur.

Then, at the crossroads, Packie was left to carry on home alone. He had at least another mile and a half to walk. Sometimes he loved that passage down the slope of the hill towards the river, the bridge, the estuary, and his house. Sometimes, when the sun was shining, he could watch the montbretia in the ditches, their lovely orange flowers, or the fuchsia with the clusters of blood-red strange-shaped flowers hanging down. He could name the birds in the small fields, the stonechat, the wheatear, the finches, and he could anticipate the animals, cows or sheep or donkeys, that would be in each small holding that he passed. It was a pleasure to him to be alone again, to live in his own half-thinking mind, absorbing the world, relishing it.

Sometimes he hated that last walk, and tried his best to linger, and arrive home as late as he could. Because sometimes Edward would be back from the village, and he might have too much drink taken and be angry again, angry at the cheating world. And then Packie's mother would simply disappear, into the sheds at the back of the house, or down along the road towards the pier, because Edward could be rough in his angers, and prepared to strike anyone that came within the flooding estuary of his contempt for himself and the life that was given to him. Packie knew the signs from the morning agitation his father might display, from the promise that he might head for the fair out in the town, perhaps try to buy and sell a cow, or a few sheep. And from a distance, even from the way the smoke from their chimney rose or did not rise into the late afternoon sky, Packie could tell the news of the sad little house beside the pool.

Grandfather would take to his own room on those occasions of wrath and lock his door. He would not appear then until his son came to knock fretfully on the door, to call out his apologies, to plead again with his own father for forgiveness, to plead with his God for strength. One day, when Edward had begun that dismal afternoon by striking Packie across the back of his legs with the strap from around Edward's own trousers, and sent him out into the shed to spend the evening there without supper, when Packie's mother had disappeared, away up to a neighbour's house, when Edward had finally taken to his own room and fallen on the bed to snore, fully clothed, for a few hours, when Packie had crept quietly back into the house to wash his face and prepare some kind of a supper against the return of the poor normality he knew: Edward staggered back out of his room, his face red with the sorrow and misery of his own failures, shook his head sadly at his son, and turned to knock on Grandfather's door.

'Ned,' he called, from outside the locked door. 'Ned, I am going up tomorrow to Father Scott, I will take the pledge, I promise you. I have made up my mind. I will take the pledge. I won't go into Hogan's pub again, never, never. Ned, please forgive me. Ned, I'm sorry.'

He waited. There was no response. He knocked again, a little more loudly. 'Ned, tell me you forgive me. Please help me, talk to me. I promise …'

There was no reply from the room. Edward turned and looked anxiously at Packie. Grandfather was always quick to respond to Edward's sorrow. But this time there was no sound, no noise from the stirring of the bed springs, no coughing from the old man. Nothing. Edward knocked again, very loudly this time, a little frantically. He called. There was no response. Edward put his strong shoulder to the door and heaved; the door sprang inwards and Edward stumbled into the room after it. Packie came to watch. He could see Grandfather lying back on the bed, his face as white as chalk, his body twitching slightly. His eyes were half open, he was gazing up at the ceiling. Packie was scared.

'Quick, Packie,' his father shouted. 'Quick as you can, boy, run up to Murphy's store and ask them to call for Doctor King. Something's wrong with Grandfather. Something's seriously wrong. Get the doctor to come, immediately, it's urgent boy, run, run, run!'

Packie was clambering quietly through the Lohans' rhododendron hedgerow on an afternoon of great stillness. His whole mind was numb from the sorrow of his grandfather's illness. Packie felt now that he had no real friend left in the world, nobody to shelter him, nobody to advise him. He stopped at his favourite spot from which he could see the Lohan house, Dolly's window, and the finely cut meadow just before him. He crouched down carefully in the bushes, on his hardened patch of dry ground. He took out a cigarette and lit it, carefully blowing out the match and dropping it deep into the shrubbery around him. He inhaled. He sighed deeply. This was good. This was escape. This was living.

He heard what sounded like a cough and he quickly hid the cigarette in the heel of his hand and tried to wave away the smoke around him. Then he heard a gentle rustling just outside the hedge and, carefully, he craned his neck and looked out onto the meadow. Just beneath the hedgerow was a drain, overgrown with iris and grasses and ferns, and almost dry. There was a fox, a large and beautiful fox, moving carelessly by outside. It was so close to him that Packie could almost make out each russet hair sun-burnished. He was greatly taken by the long and breathfilled brush that ended in white hairs and that seemed to him like a king's train, an old guardianship, as if this magnificent creature stalked the earth with authority. Packie could see that eye, rounded and, he thought, sorrowing and he was disturbed to see a moon-sliver shape of white in the eye. The fox's long tongue lolled from between its sharp, yellow-white teeth and Packie could fancy that the creature was smiling to itself, grimly, as if it had vanquished some of the pathetic machinations of mankind to destroy it.

For a long moment Packie held himself enthralled. He was as still as some of the thick roots of the escallonia and rhododendron bushes that lumped themselves out of the earth around him. He knew that this beautiful creature was hunted and hated and even feared, that it was an outcast, a loner, and a killer. It was probably on its way to some henhouse right now, or to some patch of yard where hens were rooting foolishly. A tiny shiver of fellowship ran up and down Packie's spine and at the same moment a kind of guilt moved through his blood; for he knew himself part of a predatory species, part of a rough and cruel kind that killed and destroyed what was often so utterly beautiful, ransacking the lives of creatures whose only intent was survival, and perhaps the rearing of its own young. And he thought at once of his own father and his violent rages, his obscene drunkenness, and the miserable attempt made at home to shape a good and worthy life. Packie ground his teeth and, without thinking, crushed the cigarette he was smoking so hard in his fist that it quenched and he knew no pain at its burning.

The moment passed, as suddenly as it had come, and Packie lost sight of the fox. A magpie let out an ugly ack-ack-acking sound somewhere near by and flapped its body loudly among the foliage above him. Something had entered into Packie Brennan, an awareness that human beings are not quite animal enough to know how cruel and thoughtless they are; how men go scattering blood over the earth as they might scatter water off their fingers. Packie remembered his grandfather, Ned, who had carefully gathered off the earth a greenfinch, oh long ago, that had flown foolishly at its own reflection in a window and had plumped down onto the ground, stunned. Ned had cradled it gently in his fists, had stroked that head, had shown Packie the half-closed eyes, the loveliness of the olive-green of its feathers, and how the slit along its beak was tinged with a golden streak. And after a short time the bird had stirred in the old man's hand, and he had laid it gently down on top of the ditch. When Packie looked again it was gone and he never knew whether it had lived or been taken by some predator lucky enough to come across it. Now Packie crawled hurriedly out of his hiding place, made his way back along the hedgerow to the road and ran the whole way back down to the old house where his grandfather lay, sick and almost abandoned.

It was Sunday evening. Packie Brennan and Thady Roche were the two acolytes during the devotions that began at seven o'clock with a long and tedious rosary. The acolytes had to kneel on the hard marble altar steps for all of those prayers, and then the Benediction of the Blessed Sacrament began. Up in the small choir loft the girls from the school began to sing out their 'O Salutaris Hostia'. Packie loved this part of the evening; there was the incense and he was in charge of that, the thurible, the charcoal smoking and waiting, and the delicious rattling and running of the golden chains. He could wield that strange thurible with expertise, holding it open while Father Scott sprinkled on the grains, then shutting it and handing it to the priest; how they all loved that glorious scent that rose and spread throughout the little chapel while the girls up in the loft sang the 'Tantum Ergo Sacramentum'. But it was after the blessing that Packie stood quite simply enthralled at the music of the 'Panis

Angelicus', the most beautiful music he had ever heard, even though he understood nothing of the words except the first one, bread. Priest and acolytes stood while the choir sang that piece, then they genuflected together and went back into the sacristy.

This evening, however, Packie could see his mother down on the women's side of the chapel. He could see no sign of his father. This could only mean one thing: Edward Brennan had found his way back into the pub and would come home later on tonight in a rage, and shake the house to its foundations and his little family to their bones. That old familiar strain in Packie's stomach started up and grew in intensity as he helped Father Scott take off the heavy robes and fold them away into the drawers in the sacristy. Then Packie took the long quencher and went out onto the altar to put out the flames in the six high candles behind the altar. The people had almost all left by then and he was able to lurk in behind the altar, the smoke from the candles tapering slowly away up into the rafters. There was a stool there and he sat for a long time, not thinking, scarcely aware of anything save the lingering scent of the incense and the memory of that glorious tune. He sat, forgetting time, until suddenly the lights on the altar were turned off and he heard Father Scott shut and lock the sacristy door. Packie was startled.

That was when the notion came to him that he would not go home at all that evening; he would stay in the chapel and creep home in the morning when his father would have snored off all his rage, his mortification, his despair and when a modicum of benevolence would have found its way back into his life. The idea gave some sense of relief to the boy. He sat on a while longer; he heard the main door of the chapel opened; he knew it was Father Scott coming in to see that everything was in order and that the chapel was empty. He heard the priest shuffling about; he heard a vague, half-hearted whistling. Then the door was shut again and the key was turned in the heavy lock. Packie Brennan was alone and locked into the little chapel.

For a while, delighted, he sat quietly where he was. The locking of the heavy door had sent echoes, hollow and raw, through the chapel. When he was certain that there was full silence about him, Packie went back into the sacristy, took off and hung up his soutane and surplice, changed out of his altar slippers and put on his shoes. As he tied one of the shoes the lace broke and he cursed aloud; he noticed again how shabby those shoes were, how there was a split under the toe where water could get in. He tied a small tight knot that he felt he could not open again but what did it matter? This was the start of something new in his life, and oh how wonderful it would be, to be independent, not to live in dread of his own father, or of school. He tried the sacristy door; it was locked from outside. He went back out into the sanctuary.

The light in the chapel now was dim, evening fading quickly and sending only a grey dull light through the high windows. Packie stepped out of the sanctuary and walked down the centre aisle. His shoes made a loud noise as he walked and he delighted in the sound; he coughed, loudly and laughed as his cough echoed through the high rafters. He tried the door at the back of the chapel; it, too, was locked from outside. He could not get out now, he knew, until Father Scott came to open the chapel for early morning Mass. Then he could simply hide in the confessional box and slip out when the priest went into the sacristy. Tonight he could sleep soundly, perhaps up in the choir loft, or even in one of the great cupboards in the sacristy.

He climbed the stairs to the choir loft. The spiral steps creaked under his feet. He had never been up here before and he was surprised at the way the gallery opened out over the chapel and all the benches below. He stood a while and gazed down; he noticed how quickly the light was fading. For a moment he felt a little scared. Then he shook himself; that was foolish, very foolish. He opened the lid on the harmonium and touched some of the yellowing keys. There was no sound. He sat on the stool and pretended to play. His hands moved rapidly over the keys and he swayed his body to the imaginary tune. Then he reached for the sheet music that was laid out on top of the piano. He found the music and words of 'Panis Angelicus'. He grinned.

He took the music sheet and went down to the edge of the gallery. He lifted the words and music before his face and, in the scarce light there was, he began to sing out the words. Packie knew well that he could sing. Sometimes, in school, Brother Juniper got him to sing the notes for the other boys at their music lesson. He had a sweet boy soprano voice, the timbre rich, the notes sure. Now he sang aloud that lovely hymn, stumbling only a little over the Latin words. He was delighted at the way his voice appeared to fill the entire chapel. He opened his lungs and sang as loudly as he could. If there were angels still lurking sleepily in the rafters they would have sat up and listened, and admired. Packie sang the hymn through once, then again. He enjoyed it. He felt a certain power sweep through him; he had never enjoyed singing, the other boys had teased him, he had a girl's voice, he should join the girls' choir, he was a sissy, a baby … But here, alone and in command, Packie Brennan sang, and he knew the music was good and his pleasure in it was very great.

By the time he came back down into the body of the chapel it was getting quite dark. He had to pick his way carefully round the last few steps. When he stepped onto the stone flags of the floor again and his shoes made a loud, clacking sound, a sudden fear gripped him in the stomach. Quickly he sat in to the very edge of one of the pews and fell quiet. The chapel now seemed to him to have a lot of noises in it. The benches creaked now and again, for no reason, unless the dead were there, praying out of their purgatories, for Packie believed that no evil spirit could come into the sacred Presence in the chapel. Then he heard what sounded like a voice hissing in a high register! It came from somewhere not far away and he felt shivers of fear on his spine. He tried to crouch even lower in the bench. He was already sorry he had tried this trick. Perhaps there was a way out … Then something zipped past him, very quickly, and he felt the slight breeze of it in his hair. He cried out in fright and his cry echoed and re-echoed in the chapel. Soon all was still again, apart from the occasional moan from the old timbers of the benches.

Packie scolded himself for his foolishness. It was a bat! It had to be a bat and now that the chapel was dark and quiet they were flying out of the high rafters, or in through the slightly open upper parts of the top, unreachable windows. He strained to see them. He could not, but he did hear the occasional soft whoosh of their flights and he reassured himself. Bats, yes, that's all, and there were bats in the old hayshed down by the shore, and they were harmless. It was all right. He was fine.

But still ... he decided to try and find a way out of the chapel, just in case. He worked his way around the aisles, under the windows. They were all shut and even though there were thin ropes that could be pulled, they only opened a small slit high in the windows; he could not reach that high and even if he could he knew he couldn't get out through the slits. He went back into the sacristy. It was very dark in there and he switched on a light. He expected nobody would notice, from outside, the chapel being all by itself over on the edge of the hill. He tried the door again. It was locked. The windows in the sacristy, too, were the same as in the main body of the chapel; there was no way he could get through them. He would have to spend the night.

He opened some of the cupboards that held the vestments the priests used. He could see there would not be much of a chance of sleeping in any of them. There were a lot of vestments; perhaps he could wrap himself ... but the thought worried him; these were sacred items, and the Devil was very real. There was a red silk cushion that was used sometimes when the bishop came for confirmations; that might make a good pillow and the Bishop only used it to kneel on. He went back out onto the sanctuary and decided that a good place to sleep would be in the narrow space behind the altar. He began to gather up the kneelers, small rubber mats that the acolytes used, and he laid these down on the hard flags of the floor between the back of the altar and the back wall of the chapel. It wasn't great, but it might serve.

It was now getting almost fully dark and Packie found himself quite nervous. Now and then a swishing sound went through the chapel and each time he decided it had to be a bat. He did not dare turn on any of the lights; it would not do to be caught in the chapel; what would he say? How could he excuse himself? Then he remembered the two statues in their niches at the foot of the sanctuary; a statue of the Blessed Virgin and one of Jesus and the Sacred Heart. There were large candleholders in front of the statues; he could light some candles; that would be a comfort to him, until he felt sleepy, and they would go out by themselves when he had fallen asleep. He stood in front of the statue of the Blessed Virgin. He saw the iron of the circle of stars about her head, how rusty it was; he saw that her right hand had fallen off, there were merely iron protrusions that had once held the clay; it was sad. Packie searched; there were a lot of thin candles, about three or four inches high. There was a box of matches. He was in luck. He took out several candles, fixed them into the holders, lit one of them, then lit the others with that one. There was a modest warmth from them, an even more modest light. They at once began to drip their grease. He sat back on a bench, to rest, to watch, and to think.

He sat for a while. Once only he looked back into the body of the chapel and was at once frightened by the intensity of the darkness back there. There mustn't even have been a moon or stars out, there was no glimmer at all through the windows. He turned back quickly to the candles and was dismayed to see how quickly they were burning out. He went up and lit three more. Some of the warm grease from the first candles fell onto the brass base of the holder and he scooped it up and began to mould it. It felt lovely between his hands, though a little greasy. He gazed up at the sorrowful, downward-gazing face of the Virgin; he decided he would give her some fingers. He began to shape the grease, carefully, and soon he had three fingers, reasonably recognisable, reasonably shaped. He clambered up on the altar rail and fixed the fingers to the wire bones; they didn't look half bad. He sat down on the bench again to admire his work.

He sat, growing aware of the depth of the silence around and behind him. Everything was dim, even close to where the candles burned, but behind him the darkness was intense. He did not dare look back. There was a gentle blood-red flame in the sanctuary lamp and this gave him a tiny comfort; it meant that the Real Presence was here, and he began to feel sorry that he had never paid much attention to what that meant, but he hoped that it meant that God was here, and God was good, and would take care of him. But then, wasn't he committing grave sins, wasting away the candles intended for the prayers of the faithful and for the upkeep of the chapel? Wasn't he deliberately placing himself in the awful position of taking over the chapel for his own selfish ends? Wasn't he hurting his mother? He suspected his father would, as yet, know nothing of his disappearance, and he knew his grandfather was too ill to know, or to be worried about him. But his mother ... wasn't it a sin, against the third, or fourth? commandment, he tried to say them to himself, but couldn't really get past the first of them. And the candles burned on, and the Virgin stood above him, her three fingers already falling out of shape.

Packie was dismayed. He didn't think it would be as hard as this. Suddenly there was a loud bang from somewhere in the darkness behind him and he screamed, leaping up and rushing to the base of the statue to hold on. The echoes went rapidly around the chapel. What was it? Who was it? He tried to look back but all was darkness, and silence settled back quickly. He could think of nothing other than the word Devil: just the word was enough to throw him into a dreadful panic. Quickly he took out all the candles that would fit into the brass holders and he lit them all, using several matches, dropping the spent matches on the floor. And even then there was little light. He heard another swishing sound somewhere behind him, a bat, no doubt, but then hadn't he seen movies about Dracula, about Werewolves, about vampires ... and surely anything at all could be back there. He stood, then, out before the statue of the Blessed Virgin and tried to pray, but nothing came to him. He tried out loud: 'Hail Mary full of grace ...' but the sound of his own voice frightened him and he could go no further. And then he decided he would sing: he rose up onto the bench, he held his hands out wide towards the Virgin, he closed his eyes and sang, to the very best of his ability, '*Panis Angelicus*' ... He sang, on and on, making up the words where he didn't know them, humming when he had to, and his voice filled the little chapel and if there were saints or angels about they would have settled to relish that singing. The Virgin would be pleased; perhaps he might go, soon, and try to sleep, there behind the altar, before the candles had all burned out.

He began to climb down off the bench when he had to scream again: all the lights in the chapel had suddenly gone on. Packie fell down on his knees, crying out 'Oh God! Oh God! Oh God!' He buried his face in his hands. He was crying convulsively. Then he felt a hand gently on his shoulder and a voice calling him, 'Packie, it's Father Scott. It's all right, it's all right.' Packie looked up. It was not the devil. It was not Satan nor Dracula, it was not the Werewolf. It was indeed Father Scott. Packie blessed himself hurriedly and got to his feet. 'I'm sorry, Father, I'm sorry ...'

But Father Scott was beaming at him. 'It's all right Packie, you're all right now. I was called down to the shore, your grandfather isn't too well, and I gave him the Extreme Unction. And he asked after you, Packie, he asked after you, and we hadn't missed you till then. But suddenly I remembered you had been out quenching the candles and I remembered closing the doors and maybe, I thought, just maybe, I locked you in. And I was right, you see!'

Packie was, indeed relieved. 'Grandfather?' he asked. 'Is he ...'

'He's all right, Packie, for the moment. But he's not well, you know. He's not well. But he'll be glad to see you. Come on, now, I'll drive you home.'

Packie was pleased to be sitting in the front seat of Father Scott's red Ford Anglia. There was a strong smell of leather and Father Scott drove erratically, but Packie was happy that he was going home, and that Father Scott didn't scold him.

'I tried to open the door as quietly as possible,' Father Scott told him. 'I saw the strange light in the chapel and I wondered. But the wind took the door from my hands and it banged. I think you were frightened.'

In the darkness of the car Packie only grinned.

'But before that, for a little while,' Father Scott went on, 'you got up and began to sing. Do you know, Packie, you have a wonderful voice. Truly wonderful. I will ask you to sing that hymn, '*Panis Angelicus*' wasn't it? I will ask you to sing that some day, maybe at Benediction.'

'Oh God Father, don't ask me to do that. They're all girls ...'

Father Scott laughed. 'OK Packie, for the moment I'll leave it. But really, you should do some more singing. You'd make a great priest, do you know that? A great priest.'

The journey from the chapel down to the shore did not take long. Just as they drew up outside the house and Packie opened the door to get out, Father Scott laughed again. 'And by the way, Packie, you must owe the Blessed Virgin about thirty shillings for all the candles.'

Packie stood in the gentle light that shone out through the windows of his home. He was stunned again. Thirty shillings. Where would he get thirty shillings?

Old Ned Brennan held on, suffering mildly, for several weeks. Every afternoon Packie came hurrying home from school and into the room at the lower end of the house. He found it, now, the saddest place; there was a smell of age and decay in the dark room so that even the sounds of the birds from outside increased the sense of sadness there. Ned spent all of the day half propped-up on pillows. The top of his faded pyjamas was open, there was no button, and small wisps of grey hair, like tufts of soiled down, were visible. The neck was rough and ugly and spittle occasionally dribbled from his mouth.

'*Psah*,' Ned used to say at any dirt found about the house when he was stronger; '*psah, psah*, I can't stand dirt.'

Now, lying on what he knew was to be his deathbed, the old man seemed to gather about himself a kind of surety. He spoke of it to Packie though the boy scarcely knew what he was talking about. 'I am fading out, Packie, child. And it is a wonderful thing. I am become small, dependent only on the goodness of God. I am waiting, and she is waiting, too, your grandmother is waiting for me and the only way I can get to her and out of this dark, sad world, is to disappear from this place, to become nothing, Packie, nothing. To become invisible so that it's only God can see me, and so I can see God. To become nothing, Packie, nothing. That's what this life is about. Not to become rich and famous and fabulous, but to become nothing. And that's what's happening to me, and it's a wonderful thing, boy, a wonderful thing.'

He could not put words on it but Packie, too, knew a diminution of his own spirit before the sight of the old man whom he loved, he knew the first unsheddable shiverings of grief. The old man smiled when Packie entered the room; the boy came and touched his lips to the cold forehead and the man's hand, thin and hard, tried to grip his arm and shake it. There was a small, difficult smile on the white lips. Soon Ned could not speak aloud but he whispered to Packie.

'Father Scott's been,' he whispered. 'He tells me you are a mighty singer. A mighty singer.'

Even these few attempts seemed to weary the old man.

'Don't speak, granddad, I'm only OK as a singer, only OK. But I like it.'

'He tells me, he tells me you do the '*Panis Angelicus*'.'

'That's right, I think I know it fairly well by now. It's a nice tune.'

'You will sing it for me, won't you? Packie, I love that old tune. I just love it.'

Packie stood back at once and opened his mouth to sing. But Ned Brennan lifted his stringy arm and shook it, no, no. Then he whispered: 'No, I want you to sing it for me on my big day. My big day, Packie.'

The boy was puzzled.

Ned beckoned to him to come closer; there was a strong smell of sickness from the old man and Packie tried to hold himself back a little.

'When I'm in my coffin, Packie, and lyin' in state up at the top of the chapel and all the people are thinkin' of me and prayin' for me and all to that, then I want you to stand up and sing, just for me, '*Panis Angelicus*'. That's my last request, Packie. Will you promise me, like a good lad?' The old man fell back into his pillows, exhausted with the effort. He closed his eyes and for a moment Packie thought he was dead. But the eyes flickered open again and fixed themselves on the boy.

Packie nodded. 'I promise, Granddad, I promise.'

A slow smile spread across the old man's face. He tried to raise his hand but he was not able. He sighed heavily. Packie stepped back from the bed and waited. A stray light was coming in through the small window. The old man's clothes were folded neatly over a chair near the bed. The large wardrobe stood like a great sentinel, like a monument to the old woman who had died a long time before. There was a picture of the Sacred Heart on the wall, though it was dim and faded now. Packie looked up at it and tried to pray. For some reason the only words that came into Packie's mind were from a nursery rhyme, 'all the king's horses and all the king's men couldn't put Humpty together again'. The words went round in his head, and round again. He tried, 'Our Father, who art in Heaven …' but it was no good. Only the same foolish rhyme returned to him. There were a few tall yellow irises in a vase near the window; they were wild, from down by the river, and they were drooping miserably already. Packie crept away out of the room, feeling utterly incapable.

The day that old Ned Brennan died, Father Scott called to the school to collect Packie and bring him home. The priest glided quickly into the classroom; all the boys stood, noisily, and Father Scott waved vaguely to them to be seated. Then he whispered for a while at the top of the class with Brother Juniper. Once he turned and glanced at Packie and the boy knew, at once, what this visit was about. Scarcely aware of it Packie stood up in the room and shouted out 'No!' and Brother Juniper came down quickly to him, took him gently by the shoulder. 'It's all right, Packie, dear boy. It's all right. He's in heaven now, and he's happy, and we still have to wait and suffer until we are like him.' But Packie simply stood and looked, unseeingly, towards the priest.

The house by the shore was very strange when Packie came in. There were women there whom he scarcely knew, sitting in the kitchen, talking quietly. He did not see his father or mother but one of the women was going round among the others with a plate of sandwiches. Against another wall men were sitting with bottles of stout in their hands. There was a difficult silence for a moment at Packie's entrance and then, as Father Scott came in, everybody stood to acknowledge the presence of the priest. Father Scott took Packie by the shoulders and led him down to the lower room.

His father was standing in the room, dressed in his best suit. His mother was near the head of the bed, straightening out the pillow and the top of the white sheet. She looked very pale. She glanced up and said, simply, 'Father,' then came quickly round the bed and held Packie's hands in hers. She kissed him gently on the forehead, then faced him towards the bed.

'He's gone, Packie, gone, he's with Granny now, and with God. We must be happy for him.'

The old man lay high on the pillow. Somebody had placed big brown penny coins on his eyelids and Packie could see a bandage tied under his chin and up around his head. They had folded his hands and wrapped a rosary beads through his fingers. The tiny humps his body made under the sheets told how little of the man was left. Packie's mother pushed him slowly towards the bed. 'Give your Granddad a farewell kiss, now, Packie. He was very fond of you, you know.'

Packie felt deep within himself that this was not his granddad; there was not the remotest resemblance to the man he had known and loved. Unwillingly, and for his mother's sake, he bent forward and touched his lips to the brow. It was cold, very cold and hard, and Packie drew back quickly.

Outside, Father Scott beckoned to him, leading him out the front door onto the hard-packed earth. 'Packie, child,' Father Scott began, 'your granddad wanted you to sing for him, at the Requiem Mass, day after tomorrow. You'll do that, like a good lad? I already spoke with Mrs Lohan and she's happy for you to go up to the choir loft and sing from up there. At the Communion of the Mass, Packie. You'll do wonderfully.'

Packie climbed over the rocks, further up the coast where there were low cliffs and he could clamber down to the sea's edge, over barnacled boulders, crevices and danger-places. The ocean rose and fell beautifully here, especially on those days of storm when the spray lifted in over the rocks and moved, in the wind, up over the salt and unproductive fields. Back at the shore house they had taken his grandfather and placed him in his coffin. Ned Brennan lay, as he had lain the day before, but without the pennies and the bandage. He seemed more peaceful though Packie knew that the real man was simply not there. They had dressed him in that shift he had set aside for himself. His hands were clasped around the big brown rosary. He looked comfortable enough. Packie had simply nodded. He left the house. People were coming and going all the time, murmuring in low and mournful tones that made Packie feel wretched and scared. He needed to get away.

He sat on the rim of a cove. Here, after storms at sea, there was a gathering of the world's detritus, caught in the crevices, washed up between the rocks. Packie often found bits of wooden fishing crates and frayed rope-ends. There were small, dunted buoys wedged firmly between the rocks so that you'd need a hammer to prise them out. Now he found a piece of polished wood, about a yard long, flung by the sea onto a ledge below him. He lay on his stomach and reached down, fetching it up. It was beautiful, some kind of dark wood polished until it gleamed, mahogany, or polished oak, and on it was stencilled in gilt letters the word 'Panama'. Packie held it up; there were two holes on either end, where the wood had been screwed onto something. 'Panama': Packie thought it might be the name of a ship, or even a person, or – and he thought he had come across the name in school somewhere – perhaps it was a country, way out there somewhere, far beyond the horizon. He set it on the rocks behind him; it would be a treasure.

And then he saw, floating on the surface and almost invisible in the foam and froth from the breaking waves in the cove, a string of coloured feathers, many of them frayed and scuffed down to the naked quill, all of them linked together by a thin, but strong, piece of twine or fishing-gut. He took the wood with 'Panama' written on it and fished out the chaplet of feathers. He imagined it could be the headgear of some great Indian chieftain, like those he had seen in the cowboy movies back in the cinema at Baile Mór. Some Indian, murdered perhaps by invading white men, flung into the sea far, far away from home. But he saw a small hook still adhering to one of the feathers and he knew then that it was merely some fisherman's line, one that had perhaps been dropped over the gunwale of a boat into a shoal of mackerel and that had been snipped away, maybe even by a shark, or some enormous and exciting fish. He set the piece of wood and the feathers behind him on the rocks. Then he glanced around him; there was nobody in sight. The sea was breaking softly this afternoon, making a low and lulling sound, and only the easy breeze could be heard at times, coming from the land behind him. He stood up on the rocks. He sang.

As the notes came out Packie felt, at first, wholly self-conscious. He knew he would feel worse than that tomorrow, in the chapel, up there with all the girls giggling and looking at him. If he could get the words off by heart, and be sure of them, then he could close his eyes and not see the girls at all. He had the words written out for him by Father Scott and now he sang them, carefully, the training he had got in Latin from serving all those Masses came in quite useful now. And because Father Scott had explained the meaning of the words to him, it began to come more easily as he sang.

Soon he felt he knew the whole thing pretty well; it wasn't that long, after all. Twice he sang it right through, without a mistake, and he even enjoyed it, feeling the vigour in his lungs and the pleasure that the singing gave him. He began to feel he might just do fairly well, tomorrow, for his grandfather.

When he turned back from the sea he was startled to find someone sitting on the rocks not far away behind him. It was Dolly Lohan. She was watching him. And for a little while he felt embarrassed. He sat down again on the rocks, facing the sea, his back to the girl. There was silence for a while. He heard her moving down over the rocks towards him. She came and sat beside him, drew her legs up to her chin and said nothing, simply sat there. Packie felt that this was all right; indeed he felt a little pleased. Then she spoke.

'I'm very sorry about your grandfather, Packie, I'm sorry for your trouble.'

Packie had heard this said by the adults. He knew what it meant all right, but it sounded strange. He nodded. He did not know what to say in response.

'You sing beautifully, you know,' she continued.

'How long were you there?'

'Oh, a while. I heard you singing the song a few times. I liked it very much. Are you going to sing it at the Mass?'

'Yes, Granddad wanted me to do it. But I think I might make a mess of it, so I came down here to practise.'

'It'll be very lovely, I bet,' she said. And then she reached out her right hand and touched him on the left shoulder, gently. He was surprised that she should do that; he glanced up at her; she was watching him and her eyes were big and blue, her face filled with sympathy and kindness. To his great shame he felt tears beginning to come from his own eyes and he turned away, quickly, and rubbed them off. He chucked a few small stones in the water for a while. They disappeared in the waves, almost without a splash. He sniffled, loudly, and stood up.

'Look what I found,' he said, and he showed her the timber and the feathers. 'It says, Panama, on the wood. I think it might come from a shipwreck or something.'

'Panama,' she said, 'is a country, in South America, I think. It's very, very far away.' She held up the piece of timber. 'The writing is very beautiful, isn't it?'

'And look what else I found!' he said, triumphantly. He picked up, from just underneath the rock where he had been sitting, a large, dusty panda, black and white, torn and broken, the straw stuffing sticking out from it here and there. Now he was laughing as he saw her astonishment.

'Where did you get that?' she asked him. 'That was mine, but I threw it away.'

'I found it, in your hedge. I sometimes climb in there, to be alone, and I found it.'

She took it from him, carefully. 'It's a panda,' she said. For a moment she held it to her chest but it was soiled and little bits of leaf and twig adhered to it here and there. 'I'm glad to have it back!' she said, and laughed, slightly embarrassed now, too.

'You can have the wood with Panama written on it. If you like,' he said. 'You can keep it up in your favourite tree. I know you keep stuff up there. I keep stuff, too, up in a nook I have made in the big hayshed at home. I have things there.'

She looked at him. 'Do you want to keep the panda?' she asked him.

He looked at it. 'Not really, I think. It's yours.'

She laughed in response.

'But I'd like the feathers better,' Dolly said then. 'Some of them are very beautiful. They'd go well up in my little tree house.'

'OK then,' Packie said. 'I'll keep the Panama thing, but if you'd like it …'

For a short while they watched the waves bobbing gently against the cove walls below them. They were silent. Then the girl said, 'I'd better be going home. They'll be wondering. Thanks, Packie, for the feathers. And for rescuing my panda. You can come and visit the tree house, if you like.'

Packie grinned at her. He watched as she clambered carefully over the rocks towards the fields and the laneway that led up towards the village. Then he turned back towards the sea and watched a large black-backed gull come swooping low over the waves. As it passed along just beyond the rocks and gliding wonderfully between the low waves, Packie felt a peace and even a touch of joy that seemed to wash through his whole being. He looked up at the sky, the clouds thick and grey but without darkness in them. 'Thank you, Granddad,' he said. 'Thank you. For everything.'

Packie sat in the back of the church loft. All the girls in the choir were in front of him, in their rows. None of them had giggled at him; some of them had even nodded and smiled at him. One of them, a bigger girl, Patricia McCarthy her name was, had shaken his hand and said 'I'm sorry for your troubles, Packie.' Again he had felt a tiny surge of tears, but he held them back and simply nodded his head. Mrs Lohan spoke kindly to him, too. She told him he'd do fine, that everybody would be proud of him, especially his granddad, listening from Heaven.

The Mass dragged on below. The priests, who sat on chairs and faced each other across the sanctuary, drew their slow voices, like great fret-saws, over and back across the mourning hymns; their black vestments, the smoke rising from the candles high-standing about the coffin, the dull responses of the people, all threw a sour savour over the morning. At last, as Packie's stomach churned with anxiety within him, the people began to step out of their pews, in order, to head up to the altar rails for Communion. Mrs Lohan got up from where she was kneeling beside the girls, nodded to Packie and headed over to the harmonium. She sat on the seat, took down the music, began to turn it over in front of her. Nervously Packie had taken out the sheet of paper on which he had written the words. He stood up and moved forward to the edge of the steps that led down to the front of the choir loft. But just then Mrs Lohan began to play and yes, it was the music of the 'Panis Angelicus'. She played a little, then paused and turned to Packie, nodding vigorously. Packie began to sing but he was confused, he had not expected the music, he felt his voice was too quiet to be heard over the sounds of the wheezy harmonium, he faltered, he stopped. Mrs Lohan kept on playing the notes of the hymn. Packie was deeply embarrassed; some of the girls glanced around, they were nervous, too. Packie glanced down and all he could see, there before the gilded small gate that led into the sanctuary, was his grandfather's coffin. He felt the old man was waiting for him, that he would not be released until Packie had fulfilled his promise.

He turned then towards Mrs Lohan, found the courage somewhere and said: 'Please stop playing!'

Mrs Lohan turned round to look at him. She could see the intensity in his face, the determination in his stance. She stopped playing. Packie turned away, drew a deep breath, and began again.

He was able to pitch the hymn to his own voice. For the first few phrases he sang accurately and sweetly, but it was, perhaps, too quiet. He noticed several faces turning round down below in the body of the chapel, to gaze up in curiosity. He took another deep breath; he closed his eyes, trusting to whatever powers, whatever God there might be, to bring him through. He sang. And as the beauty of the melody and the soft and lovely sounds of the Latin words flowed out into the rafters of the little chapel, he felt a great surge of power in his voice. With his eyes closed he could almost see the words hang like a rainbow, there in the dimness above him. He could feel his breathing grow stronger; he could sense how the ceiling of the choir loft seemed to throw his voice out over the people down below, he knew that his grandfather heard and was pleased. He sang, and all his heart and soul and mind, as well as his chest and all his breathing, were in the song. When he finished he could hear the echoes of the last notes he had sung move away like angels reluctant to leave the chapel, and he sat down on the bench, buried his head in his hands and sobbed, quietly, to himself.

Packie was in the grove up at Lohan's house. It was afternoon and now that his grandfather was no longer around, Packie was reluctant to head home. In the grove the light was dim; there was a fragrance from the pine trees and from the early summer blossoms of the rhododendron. He climbed into the lower fork of one of the trees and sat, waiting. Perhaps Dolly might come in, and together they might climb up to the little tree house she had put together high in her favourite tree. He waited. He was peaceful. He drew out half a cigarette from his jacket pocket; he had a small box of matches. He lit the cigarette, inhaled deeply, and eased his back against the bole of the tree.

He sat there for a while, listening to the breeze move gently through the pines. He heard his name called out from down below: 'Packie, it's me, I'm coming up.'

Dolly was standing at the foot of the tree, just below him. 'Sure, come on. It's easy.' He stood up in the fork of the tree and moved onto the end of one of the branches. Dolly climbed and sat in the fork of the tree, facing him.

'You shouldn't smoke, Packie, don't you know? It's really disgusting. And it's not good for you.'

He grinned at her. 'You're not my mother, you know, nor my father, either. And I'll do just what I like, if you don't mind.' He drew heavily on the cigarette and coughed a little.

She grinned at him. 'There, you've a cough already. And oh,

by the way, I think you were wonderful at the funeral the other day. You sang beautifully. Everybody loved it.'

'Thanks,' he said, a little embarrassed. He flicked the rest of the cigarette into the air and it soared off towards the far hedgerow. They sat quietly for a short time. Packie drew out his watch from its pocket and gazed at it. 'I'll have to go soon. Thanks for letting me onto the trees. It's peaceful.'

Dolly said nothing for a while. 'You're lucky, you know, that watch, I'd just love to have a watch like that. I'd love it.'

'I'll swap you it, if you like. Have you anything …?'

She thought a while. Then her face lit up with excitement. 'I've a bike,' she said. 'They gave me a bicycle last Christmas, and I don't ever use it. I don't like cycling. I'll swap you the bike for the watch!'

He was astonished. 'But, a bike? My God, that's too much … your parents?'

'Oh they won't care, they know I never use it anyway. Come on, I'll show you.'

An hour later Packie Brennan cycled into the front yard of the house at the shore. The bicycle was small, neat and coloured blue. It was a girl's bicycle, without a crossbar, but Packie was delighted with it. He could bring it to school; it would save him about an hour's walking every day, half an hour there, half an hour home. And it had only cost him a watch! He could scarcely believe his luck. He called his mother out to see it, and she seemed pleased, though a bit bemused.

'Them Lohans, they're well off, I suppose. And you can always use a bike, Packie.'

But his father, when he came in from the shed, was angry.

'We're not so poor as we have to get charity from the Lohans or from anybody else. We have our pride. You'll take that bloody bike straight back up there and get back that watch. Who does she think she is, that little bitch, to think she can win you over with something like that? If we want a bike we'll buy our own bike. Take it back, right now, or I'll give you such a belting you'll never be able to sit on a saddle again.'

As he cycled slowly back up the hill towards the Lohan house, Packie knew, or he thought he knew, that his father was right. Who did she think she was, this girl, getting rid of a bike, a girl's bike, for his lovely watch? Of course his father was right. Of course they'd buy their own bike when they wanted a bike. Of course they would, and it'd be a proper bike, a man's bike, with a proper crossbar, and big grips, and a dynamo and a light. Soon. They'd buy one soon.

He knocked on the back door of the Lohan house and Dolly came out to him. He was a little shamefaced as he told her what her father had said. She looked sad, and hurt. For a moment he hesitated.

'But you can keep the watch,' he blurted out. 'Really, I've had it a long time. Why don't you keep it, I know you've always wanted a watch.'

She looked at him. 'No, thanks, Packie. No, I can't do that. Fair is fair. But I will go right now and ask my father to get me a watch. And you're very good to think of it. You remember what I said to you after that movie?'

'What movie?'

'We were standing outside the cinema back in Baile Mór, we saw *On Moonlight Bay*, and I said you didn't look a bit like Gordon MacRae and all of that, do you remember?'

'Gee, I thought that was a real soppy old film. With Doris Day in it, and all that stupid singing. I remember. And you told me your name wasn't Dolly, it was Dorothy.'

'Well, I'm sorry I was cross with you. Not that you're like Gordon, you're not, you are, you know, a bit … well, pudgy.'

He laughed. 'That's all right. You're still not like Doris Day. But you …' and he blushed suddenly, 'you are nice. Dorothy.'

He swiped the watch out of her hand and turned and ran out of the yard, through the gate, heading for the shore and his own house.

Father Scott was closeted in the house on the shore for quite some time. Packie, home from school, had seen the priest's car, that cranky old red Ford Anglia, parked outside in the yard. He did not want to go in while the priest was there. He left his schoolbag under the thorn bush that was as old, he thought, as his grandfather had been and was now as crooked, twisted and bare as the old man had been before he died. But it was a landmark; it served. He loved it.

He shoved out the boat onto the brimming tide. The midges would be swarming about the water later on so now was a good time to drift and dream. The tide was almost at the full and the water in the pool was deep and dark and swirling dangerously. He had homework to do but, in any case, if Father Scott was there, he wouldn't get a chance to do it. And he had the whole weekend ... A sea trout jumped at the lower end of the pool where the fresh water met the salt, and it arced itself beautifully for a moment before plopping back into the water, the drops falling from it as it hung that ecstatic second in the air. Packie let out a long sigh of admiration. And if he could catch a fish like that, how wonderful it would be.

He felt the boat swing on the swinging of the tide; again he knew himself to be part of the great forces of the world, intimate with tide and flow and deep, only the thin boards of the small craft between him and the currents. He heard the door of his house slam shut. He saw Father Scott get into the car, heard its engine start, rev up and he watched as the priest drove out through the dirty yard and turned onto the small road that led up towards the village. He listened as the engine groaned its way up the hill, listened as it faded slowly into the afternoon. He did not like the way the door had slammed. There was something not right at home. Perhaps his father had been drinking again. Perhaps he had insulted the priest. Packie's stomach churned a little at the thought of having to face back into that house, and suffer whatever mood his father might be in.

He took out his makeshift oars and began to row upstream towards the bridge. The water from the hills came brown and fecund, having made its way through field and bogland, and came rushing to meet the high-tide water at the lower end of the bridge. Here the meeting frothed white and gold and the tide-waters churned against the fresh-water falls. Packie was not paying sufficient attention. His small craft was caught in the swirl of the water and flung swiftly towards the rocks at the further side of the pool. The wood crashed against a rock as

Packie tried to push with an oar against it. He pushed too hard, the oar slipped suddenly off the wet side of the rock and Packie found that the boat's gunwale was dipped deep into the water and held. With a strange and frightening slowness, Packie was flung out of the boat and into the water at the edge of the pool. It was not deep. He fell on his hands and knees and scrabbled himself quickly upright in the water. He was not hurt, but he was wet, and the boat was drifting away from him, the one oar floating near him in the pool. He grabbed the oar and reached to hold the boat. Slowly he drew it back towards him; there was a lot of water in it but Packie had an old can that had held beans and he began to empty the water out of the poor stricken boat. Tears began to blind him as he worked. Why did it always have to be such a difficulty? Why did he now have to face his father who might be angry with him, or with the world in general, while he was drenched with sea-water and had made an utter fool of himself? Why did it have to be so difficult?

Packie rowed slowly back across the pool and drew the craft up onto the grass. It was slightly damaged, but nothing too serious. He heard the door of the house open; he ducked down behind the grassy bank that divided the shore from the yard of his house. He peered over the top and watched his father move towards the sheds at the side of the house. He was stomping along angrily, but he seemed sober. Packie heard the ugly squealing of the stable door as his father opened it; he heard the even more ugly noise of it being shut. Then there was silence. Packie quickly collected his schoolbag and went across to the house. Perhaps he could sneak past his mother and change his clothes? but as he opened the front door as quietly as he could he heard his mother's voice.

'Ah Packie, it's you. Come in here, love, quickly. I've a bit of news for you.'

His mother was in the kitchen. Packie stood before her, crestfallen and dismayed. She scarcely glanced at his wet clothes but took him gently by the right shoulder and looked into his eyes.

'You're wet, a grá, go quickly and change. Put on your best. You're to go up to the priest's house at once. Father Scott has something to tell you. And I hope you think it over carefully.

It's a great chance for you, a great chance. Run now, there's a good lad, quickly now, before your father comes in. He's none too pleased. But I think it's a great chance, a great chance.'

In less than an hour Packie Brennan stood at the door of the presbytery and knocked. The house was a bungalow; there were flowers on each side of the path leading to the door. There were fine curtains on the bay windows on either side of the small porch. Packie could see the red car parked over at the side of the house. The garden had shrubs of all kinds growing in it and the lawn was neat and well trimmed. Packie wore his best suit, the one he wore on Sundays, the one he had worn for all the big events of the last three years. The trousers were long; the knees of the trousers and the elbows of the jacket had been patched by his mother with small leather patches. He had a good tie on, too, and his mother had made sure that the knot was right. Ellie Quinn opened the door to him.

'It's yerself, is it?' she said, curtly. 'Father's expectin' you. But you'll have to go round by the back of the house. This door's only for the quality. Father's in the study. Go round the back an' I'll open for you.'

Packie walked carefully round on the concrete path that led past the bay window on the right, around the side and into the back yard. This, too, was all concrete; there was a small puddle of oil where Father Scott must park his car; there was a crack in the concrete before the yawing door of a garage and there was some small plant growing through the crack. But the yard was not wet and muddy, like the yard at the shore house, and the walls were white-washed and looked clean. The back door was coloured cabbage-green but there was a small window in it and Packie saw Ellie Quinn's face watching out for him. She brought him in through the scullery. Packie was astonished at the size of the kitchen; there was a big cooker and there were several pots on it, the heat coming from it into the kitchen would have been enough to dry his wet clothes at once. There was a smell, too, of mutton, he thought, and of something gorgeous, like an apple tart. His stomach lurched a little as she opened the door into the hallway. She beckoned to Packie as she stood in front of a door just next to the kitchen. She looked at him, straightened his tie a little, smoothed his hair gently, smiled at him and winked. Then she knocked on the door.

Father Scott was sitting at a big writing desk in an alcove of the room, just inside the window. His back was to the boy. The room was furnished with a deep leather armchair, a large shining table with four chairs, a cabinet filled with glasses of all shapes and sizes, and a sideboard with silver tureens and cut-glass bottles. There was a sense of opulence that made Packie feel deeply uncomfortable.

'Here's the boy, Father,' Ellie Quinn murmured. Then she left the room, closing the door softly after her. Father Scott wrote for a few moments more, then swivelled his chair rapidly round to face Packie.

'Packie Brennan, the very man!' the priest said. He stood up and moved over to the sideboard, opened the lower cabinet and took out a bottle. 'A little drop of sherry is called for, I think, don't you, Packie?'

The boy wished he had a cap or something in his hands, to squeeze and fiddle with. 'I don't know, Father.'

'Of course you don't, but I do.' He poured himself a modest glass of the dark golden liquid, then returned the bottle to the cabinet. 'Sit, Packie,' and he gestured vaguely to the room. Packie sat, stiff and uncertain, at one end of the table.

'I've just written a letter to Father Mills, at St Canice's, you know,' Father Scott said. 'You do know about Canice's don't you, Packie?'

'No, Father.'

'Oh dear, oh dear. Your father … Never mind. St Canice's is a college, a secondary college and a scholasticate, over in Grangewilliam. I've been watching you, Packie, this while, you know, both at home, in the chapel, and in the school.' Father Scott lowered himself carefully into the big leather armchair. 'And I've talked with Brother Juniper. And this is the thing. I think you might have a vocation, I just think you might.'

Packie looked blank.

'For the priesthood, boy, the priesthood. Canice's is a secondary school. You'd need to get your Leaving Certificate. Six years or so. And at the same time there's the scholasticate.

You'd get preliminary education there, in the priesthood, make it all easier for you, and faster, too, when you'd go on to Grange Seminary. You're a bright young lad, so Juniper tells me, so your mother says, though your father ... And you know the Latin, and you're good about the altar, and you were magnificent in the chapel at your poor grandfather's funeral. There now, I think that's the whole of it.'

The door opened cautiously. Ellie Quinn came in; she had a white cloth in her hands. The boy and the priest were quiet as she laid the cloth over the table. She smoothed it out. She glanced at Packie and stood, waiting.

'You'll have supper with me, Packie, won't you?' Father Scott asked.

'Oh no, thank you Father, I'll have to be getting home. We'll have supper at home. Mother has ... and Father ... No thanks, Father, I can't. Really.'

'But you'll at least have a good slice of apple tart before you go? To celebrate, I mean.'

'Celebrate, Father?'

The priest waved Ellie Quinn away.

'You see, Packie. The diocese has three scholarships to St Canice's, every year, for boys we think will study well and might just go on to the priesthood. That means all your expenses will be paid for you, your clothes, your travel, your lodging, your teaching. All of it. For the whole time, until you graduate. And then, if you think it's right, and if the diocese think it's right, you'll go straight on, to Grange Seminary, to be a priest, lad. There now, that's something to celebrate, isn't it? I've been on the phone to Father Mills; he's agreeable. I'm sending him on a letter, and Brother Juniper has written one, too. It's a gone conclusion, Packie Brennan. We'll make a good priest of you before you know it. Here's your health!' and the priest drained his glass of sherry.

Ellie Quinn came in again. This time she had a big blue bowl and a large slice of apple tart in it. It was steaming hot and a great glob of cream was melting over it. She set it down with a great grin on the table before Packie and plonked down a large spoon beside it.

'Ladle that into yourself, Packie Brennan, there's a good lad now,' she said.

Father Scott grinned. 'Let's see, Ellie. How about … Father Packie Brennan. Hmmm. Don't like it. Packie. The name's not really Packie, is it, Packie?'

'No, Father. It's Patrick. Patrick Joseph Brennan.'

'A good solid name for a good solid lad. OK, then, now let's see. How about … Father Patrick Brennan, sounds good, Ellie Quinn, doesn't that sound good to you?'

'Wonderful, Father. We might have a saint in the parish yet. But he'll have to get that fine apple tart inside him, for a start.'

Packie lowered his head and grinned. He picked up the spoon.

His father and mother were at table when he got home. There were thick slices of bread on a large dish; there were pats of white butter. There was a jar of home-made jam. It would be good and wholesome. There would be tea.

His mother stood up to greet him. She was flushed and eager.

'Well, Packie, what do you think?'

He sat down quietly at his place. 'I'm going to St Canice's, on a scholarship,' he said, proudly.

'You're not then,' his father said, equally quietly. 'You're needed here, on the farm, in the house. Like your father before you, and his father before him, and his father, back and back. You're finished school in a week or two. And that's all the schoolin' you'll need. You'll stay here and keep this place goin'. I'll be needin' your help. The place needs you.'

'Now, Edward …' his mother began. But his father suddenly banged his fist on the table and stood up, knocking over his mug of tea.

'That's it, now,' he shouted. 'I'm the boss here. And I'll have no son of mine, me only son, goin' off for fancy learnin' in a college, miles and miles from here. Boardin', no less, the priest says. Won't be around for turf, nor hay, nor the cattle, nor nothin'. I'm not havin' it, an' that's final.'

He sat down again. His mother began to mop up the tea from

the table. The old yellow cloth was stained. She picked up the cup. She stood near her husband.

'But a vocation to the priesthood, Edward, that's something very special. We just can't …'

Edward raised his fist threateningly.

'Woman, don't cross me now, or you'll feel the weight of this, I promise you, and I'm stone cold sober, as you well can see.'

Packie stood up, too. Very quietly he went round the table, drew his mother a little back and stood between her and his father.

'If you ever strike my mother again, I promise, I'll kill you.' Packie spoke with vehemence, but he spoke quietly.

His father laughed, uncertainly. 'You, you fat little squirt you. You and whose army?'

'I might be a fat little squirt to you, but Father Scott thinks I'll be a priest some day. And I'll get education, and all free. And I'm going to St Canice's. And maybe I've no army now but I'll grow up and I'll keep my promise. And that's the end of that. In September I'm away to St Canice's. I'll help out here when I'm back, but you will not stop me. You will not stop me.'

For a moment his father's fist remained raised. He stood up, slowly, from the table. He drew back his fist as if to strike his son. Packie's mother moved forward and caught his arm.

'Our son is going to college, Edward, and that's the end of it. I'll not see him destroyed on this shore, I swear it, he'll go and make something of himself. Even if it kills me, I'll see him ordained one day, I'll see him ordained.'

There was a long moment of silence. All at once, the big man murmured, 'Let me go, woman. It's all right. Let me go. I'll not stand in his way, so. If he's determined. And you, too, determined, like. I'll not stand in his way.'

Edward sat down again. And so did Packie and his mother. They ate the bread quietly for a while.

'And my name's not Packie, by the way, my name is Patrick. I'm Patrick Edward Brennan, and I'm proud of it. And I'm going to college, and I've a vocation, that's what the priest says, and the college will have me, and Brother Juniper thinks so, too.'

His father looked at him. Edward Brennan seemed to have grown smaller in himself. But he looked more relaxed. He smiled, wryly, at his son.

They ate on in silence. After the meal, Edward proposed the rosary. 'I'm wore out, all of this is too much for me. We'll say the prayers and I'll hit for bed. And we'll pray, mother, we'll pray for three things. First, for Packie, that if God wants him God might have him. And not let us die for the want of a son. Second, for me, that I might get over this curse of the drink that has me, has us, ruined. And thirdly, thirdly … ah, I don't know, for everythin' an' anythin' else, the third thing.'

Later that evening, Packie lay on his bed in his own room. He was still in his best suit. He was still trembling. His stomach was filled with moths and butterflies all aswarm, his head filled with words and thoughts and pictures he could not get hold of. He heard his father's heavy stride as he headed for his own room. The steps hesitated outside Packie's door. There was a quiet knock.

'What is it?' Packie called out, sitting up quickly on the bed.

'Only me,' Edward spoke through the door. 'Only me. Goodnight … Patrick Edward.' Packie heard him giggle beyond the door. 'Father, ah sure why stop there? Bishop Patrick Edward Brennan, of the Shore. Oh Jesus Christ the Woodman! Packie, say your prayers and sleep well.'

The boy grinned.

'I will, Dad. Goodnight.'

THE GARDEN OF EARTHLY DESIRES

Sister Francesca came striding into the classroom, her black habit swishing about her. She strode up to the front of the class as if she were driven by anger and contempt. One of the girls got up and quietly closed the door after the nun. Sister Francesca was tall and gaunt, her face high and thin, her brow disappearing into the white stuff of her wimple. She let her armful of books drop down on the table with a bang. The girls cowered; the signs were ominous. They had all stood together as the nun had entered; Dorothy was in the row nearest the window, about fourth desk back and fairly out of the way of the nun's gaze that froze the girls into immobility.

'In the name of the Father …'

After the prayers the girls sat down, none of them daring to glance at any of the others. The grounds outside the convent school were bathed in sunshine and Dorothy could see the tops of the poplar trees, how they were already turning gold before the full onset of autumn. They scarcely moved in the soft breeze.

'I have been suffering you girls now for four years!' Sister Francesca began. 'And as yet, with your examination coming up at the end of this year, I believe that scarcely one of you has any idea what poetry is about. It is not, I repeat, not, intended for your amusement. You are to learn the words by heart, you are to be able to repeat the words perfectly when required so that you can quote whole passages when you answer your examination questions, and you are to learn, to accompany the poems, the notes I have given you. It is that simple. And yet, and yet ...'

She picked up one of the copies she had brought into the classroom with her. Homework. Each girl shuddered and whispered a prayer that she was not the one about to be made an example of.

'Maureen Hanly!' the nun called out.

A plump girl, her cheeks red as beetroot already, stood up quickly and her hands nervously brushed her skirt into shape. She was on the row nearest the door. She coughed, awkwardly.

'So, Maureen, out of Ballyshannon, isn't it? God help us all, Maureen. And you in a town where one of our great poets lived and worked. To whom am I referring, Maureen?'

The girl sniffled loudly and looked down at her desk. Nobody stirred. Nobody even thought of whispering.

'Yeats, Sister?'

'Yeats! Dear God, dear God! But never mind, girls, if I have to suffer my purgatory here on earth then I will not have to suffer it again when I am mercifully released into the arms of God. And I have to thank you, Maureen Hanly, for offering me this opportunity to suffer. Yeats, indeed. Every girl in this class knows to what county William Butler Yeats was attached. You, for instance, Jennie?'

A small girl who sat perfectly still right in front of the Sister's desk stood up slowly in her place. She was pale and already trembling with a kind of dread.

'Please Sister, I think that Yeats was from ... em, Dublin?'

Sister Francesca put down the copy she held in her hands. She turned away with a long loud sigh and moved to the high window. She leaned her elbows on the sill, her forehead against the glass, and gazed out onto the lovely gardens of the convent.

'"I will arise and go now, and go to" ... Terenure? Is that it, Jennie, Jinnie, Jinnie the donkey, are those the words of that lovely poem?'

'No, Sister.'

'No, Sister. No, indeed. But do you know the words Jinnie the donkey?'

The nun spoke with a rapier quietness that chilled all the girls.
Jennie began:

' "I will arise and go now and go to Innisfree" Sister.'

'To Innisfree Sister, indeed. And *Innis* we all know, because
we are Gaelic scholars one and all, means island and everybody
knows that Dublin is an island, isn't that so Jinnie the donkey?'

'No, Sister. Em, I think it was Donegal, Sister.'

The nun laid her head down on the windowsill in weariness.
There was silence in the classroom for a long while. Jennie and
Maureen remained standing, not daring to look at one another,
not daring to glance at any of the other girls. Eventually the nun
turned back to the classroom. 'Sit down, Jennie, sit down.
Donegal indeed. How stupid can you get? Dear God how thick
and stupid can you get? Is there anybody in the whole class who
might tell me what county our beloved Yeats comes from? Our
great national poet, surely somebody must know. Anybody at all?'

She gazed slowly over the heads of the girls. Now it was only
Maureen who remained standing. There was not a sound in the
room. At last a hand rose, slowly, into the air.

'Hah!' Sister Francesca pounded. 'It is our genius Norah, out
of Ballinasloe in the County of Galway. Tell us Norah, tell us,
please do.'

'Sister, Yeats was born in a tower in a place called Ballylee,
in Galway, Sister.'

The nun again sighed deeply. She waved her hand vaguely
towards Norah and Maureen, indicating that they should sit
down. Then she sat herself behind the big teacher's desk.

'I suppose you gave it a try, Norah out of Galway. But you
are wrong, stupid and ignorant and wrong. But what's the use,
what's the use? What you will all do for me is open the college
notes you have before you, turn at once to page fifty-three
where you will find a neat summary of the places and dates of
the life of William Butler Yeats. You will proceed, now, to
learn that page by heart, quietly mind you, I don't want to hear
any murmurs and mutterings from any of you. And in ten
minutes I shall pick out five girls and they will recite for me the
whole of that page. And when that is done, if I can find five girls
bright enough to do it, we shall proceed to page eighteen where

we will find the same information, only this time relating to the
Ballyshannon bard, our own dear William Allingham. I shall
then find five more girls, including you, Maureen, who will
give me those details by heart. After which I shall once more ask
five more girls, perhaps the same ones, perhaps others, to recite
for me the fifteen lines you were supposed to have for me
today, from the poem 'Il Penseroso', by John Milton. From what
country, Dorothy Lohan?'

The nun had switched quickly and had noticed Dorothy's
attention drawn by a wasp that seemed to be knocking against
the window. Dorothy was startled, but she stood up quickly
and said:

'John Milton was from England, Sister.'

'Good girl, good girl! The first answer that comes even near
knowing something about something. From England indeed,
that Godforsaken country of Protestants and colonists. Indeed,
indeed. And where was I? Yes, Milton and 'Il Penseroso', the
thinking man. And while you are learning all of this by heart –
sit Dorothy, sit, sit, sit, do you expect a reward or something? –
I shall give you back the trash you handed up to me last evening
by way of homework. Trash, trash, trash ...'

All the heads in the classroom bowed low over the books.
There was a soft murmur of voices as they worked to make sure
they had the texts and the poem by heart. Sister Francesca sat
behind her desk. For a while she watched the bowed backs, the
lowered heads. There was a momentary smirk of satisfaction on
her face. She turned to gaze out the window to her right; from
where she sat she could see the fields beyond the poplar trees;
she knew the blackberries were almost fallen into rot; the fields
were emptied of haycock and cornstook; she shuddered at the
thought of late autumn, its bleakness, its gathering cold, its
yellow-gold and wet thickness across the roadways and the
garden paths. She would miss the quiet and warm afternoons
when she could move gently through the convent grounds,
saying her office, praising the God of last things, the God of the
world to come.

Sister Francesca sighed; she turned back to the classroom.
Her face clouded over. She began to pick up the copies, one

by one, opening each one of them, saying the girl's name. Then she simply flung the copy through the air in the general direction of the raised hand. The copies flopped and flipped their pages open as they flew and fell and slithered across the wooden floor or thumped on a desk. The girls worked on. Heads bowed.

At length Sister Francesca called out: 'Right, my fine idiots. Let's see how well we know our Milton. Myra Ryland, please, tell me all about '*Il Penseroso*'. Delight me. Sing it out to me.'

A small, intense-looking girl stood up, near the back of the class. She coughed. She had black hair wound tightly into a bun at the back of her head. The white school shirt was open at the neck, the navy blue jumper was frayed at the collar and at the sleeves. She began in a weak and unsteady voice:

> Hence, vain deluding joys,
> The bread of folly without father bread,
> How little you bedstead …

'Oh dear, oh dear, oh dear, Myra Ryland, prime idiot, "the bread of folly without father bread", and "how little you bedstead", indeed, indeed. What stupidity, poor Milton, if he was still alive he'd die on the spot. How you destroy him. It's "The brood of folly", and "How little you bested, bested", bested. Go on, well, no, you've already killed the poor man. Let's hear from you, Grace McHugh.'

With a soft sigh Myra sat down in her desk. Another girl, two rows ahead of her, stood up. Grace was tall and thin in build like Sister Francesca, but her narrow face and thin carroty hair made her look desperately anxious.

> Hence, vain, em, deluding joys,
> The brood of folly without father bred,
> How little you you, em, you bested
> Or fill the fixed mind with all your, em, em, toys, Sister.

'"Toys, Sister", "toys Sister"? Is that what Milton says? Grace McHugh, when are you ever going to get sense. Sit, sit, sit.

Myra Ryland, Grace McHugh, you will both stay in the classroom this evening after classes, four o'clock, and you will write out the entire poem, neatly and carefully, five times each, and I will ask you the first ten lines again after that.'

And so the hour progressed. Not one girl was able to recite the poem with any fluency. At last Sister Francesca, greatly irritated, called out: 'Enough! Enough! I will die, you will kill me, as well as killing the poor dead poet. Let me hear it properly. Dorothy Lohan, I am sure you know the ten lines by heart. Let me hear them, please, let me hear them. Take me out of this my misery.'

Dorothy stood up at her desk. In front of her she saw the bowed backs, the cowed girls. She knew the silence in the classroom was a silence of misery and hopelessness. She glanced to her right. Ursula Horan was sitting there, a big girl, pleasantly plump, her round face pale now though it was usually quite healthy and red. Her hands fidgeted with the brown paper covering on her textbook. She looked up at Dorothy and there was a small sneer of hatred in her eyes. Ursula Horan had got about three lines of the poem out before she came to a shuddering stop. Dorothy decided.

'Sister, may I ask you something first?'

'You may, child, you may.'

'Sister, I don't understand the second line. And so I find it very hard to learn it by heart. And there are some strange words, "fancies fond", "gay motes", and the last line, Sister, it's very difficult.'

The good nun looked at Dorothy. 'Difficult, is it? What's difficult, may I ask, about learning words by heart? All you have to do is go over it, then repeat it. And in your examination that is all you will have to do. Rattle it off, child, rattle it off.'

Dorothy took a deep breath. She began: '"Hens vain deluding joy …"'

'"Hens", Dorothy, "hens"? Is this a poem about eggs and chickens? Milton the great poet writes a poem about hens and chickens. Can you believe it? The word is hence, hence, meaning away, away.'

Dorothy began again.

> Hence vain deluding joys
> The brood of folly without father bred,
> How little ... how little ...

Dorothy stopped. She glanced down at Ursula Horan who was gazing at her, open-mouthed. Then she looked back at Sister Francesca. 'I'm afraid I find myself unable to get it off by heart, Sister.'

There was a long silence. A chill breeze blew across the classroom. Sister Francesca was gathering up her books. 'You will all remain in the classroom at four o'clock this afternoon. Then you will get down to your work and you will not leave this classroom until everybody knows this poem perfectly by heart.' She swept out of the room. There was a clattering of desks as the girls stood. Sister Francesca banged the door shut after her. There was a great sigh of relief as the girls sat back down again.

They began to chatter excitedly. Ursula Horan looked over to Dorothy. 'You didn't know the poem?' she asked. 'That's the first time Sister's pet has missed it.' That sneer was still on the plump and somewhat ungainly face.

'It's just not fair, Ursula,' Dorothy said. 'I love the poem, and I do know it by heart. But I only understand bits and pieces of it. And you can't know something if you don't understand it. She is making me hate poetry, the way she's killing it for us.'

'So, you really know it by heart, then?'

Dorothy rattled off the first six or seven lines to Ursula, and grinned.

The red-faced girl grinned back. 'Well, I have to admit, the fact that Sister's pet made a mess is good for all of us. Even though we have to stay back. Though I think Sister'll now be madder at you than at anyone. I hate poetry. I hate it. It's rubbish!'

Every Saturday afternoon Dorothy was allowed home for the weekend. Classes were let off at noon. The girls who lived too far away to go home had to play games, or do some manual work in the grounds of the convent and the school. It was always a great joy for Dorothy as she ran down the long cinder track to the bicycle shed at the far end of the convent grounds. It was early autumn; already the trees, the poplars and the oaks that bordered the grounds, were turning a beautiful ochre and yellow colour. This afternoon the sky was clear, although a frail full moon was just visible low on the horizon. Dorothy's heart lifted. She would cycle the ten miles home and at the end of the ride she would sit down to a plate of hot potato cakes with butter melting on top and parsley liberally sprinkled. She had homework to do; she strapped her schoolbag on the carrier of her bike. She wheeled the bike out towards the big gate that led onto the road. She wheeled it slowly; she would relish every moment of the ride.

She mounted the bike and freewheeled easily down the hill of the small town. People were shopping and some of them waved to the girl, clearly identifiable as one of the convent girls, as she cycled easily by them.

Always, on this slow journey home, Dorothy remembered the words of a poem that she truly liked: it was by Gerard Manley Hopkins, and it began 'The world is charged with the grandeur of God.' Today she knew what that meant; as she turned from the main road out of town onto the narrow lane that led towards her own home, she revelled in the thick hedgerows that were now turning all kinds of shades of yellow, amber and gold. There was a long line of grasses mingled with daisies, dandelions, vetch, tiny cresses and trampled-down plantain, a line that stretched away down the middle of the lane where the cart wheels, the cars, the animals, did not usually pass. Trees reached out over her head and thrushes and blackbirds called from their hidden tasks and lurking-places. Times she was able to let the bike roll freely down a hill, round a bend and into another lane from which the distant hills could be seen, today all clear and green with, here and there, small dots of white that were grazing sheep. Her heart was warm and, in spite of her mother, in spite of Sister Francesca and the whole grim barrenness of the convent, she felt perhaps there was a God up there, and that the wonder of the world hid Him most of the time, but at moments like this He shone forth, like the sun coming out from black clouds.

There were cows grazing at the side of the lane as she came to about a mile from her home. She cycled carefully along the hedge that bordered the farm of Peter Joseph, PJ, Hannafin's messy farm. PJ was the son of a farmer who was the son of a farmer, and the line, like that on the centre of the lane, went on and on into the far distant past. But the meadows and fields had deteriorated under PJ's handling, through his drinking habits and his general indifference to the ways of the world. He had, Dorothy knew, taken the grandeur from the fields. How could he allow his cattle out onto the road like this, to mess it up with their dung and their churning of it, to push their big and heavy bodies against the holly saplings and the blackberry bushes that still held onto a few hard, green berries? As she pushed her bike carefully around and through cattle that were totally indifferent to her passing, she saw PJ himself idly smashing a stick against the hedgerow near his gate. He turned to watch her coming. Instinctively, as she mounted the bike again, Dorothy straightened her skirt down over her knees and cycled with great caution. He grinned at her.

'Hey there, young Dorothy Lohan? And how is the scholar this fine day?'

PJ was a big man; he wore Wellingtons that were soiled with dried-on clay; his trousers were baggy, grey too, and he wore braces over a white collarless shirt that had pink stripes running vertically along it; the neck was open and tufts of grey hair showed through. His shirt sleeves were rolled up over thick, strong arms and the hand that held the stick was big and powerful. PJ's face was kindly, though his eyes were bloodshot and his nose a little too large and too red. He smiled and showed a set of teeth, distinctly off-white and yellowing. His hair was black and unkempt. Dorothy slowed down and he came and reached for the handlebars of her bike. She stopped.

'Hello, Mr Hannafin. How are you today?'

'Mr Hannafin, is it? Aren't we the formal colleen now? Convent educated an' all. Well, well, well, I hope we're not gettin' too high and mighty now, to say PJ to our own neighbour. What?'

Dorothy stood on the ground, unwilling to dismount fully, straddling the frame of the bicycle, wishing to move on through the afternoon as quickly as she could. There was a strong smell from the big man, a smell of farming, an unwashed smell, an animal smell.

'No, indeed, PJ, but they teach us to be mannerly and respectful. That's all. Lovely day, isn't it?'

'I've something I want to show you, now, Dolly Lohan, an' I think you'll like to see it, too. Just leave the old bike there by the gate an' come on along with me.'

Dorothy flinched at the old name.

'I think I'll just keep on going, PJ, if you don't mind. They're expecting me home about now.'

'Come on girl, only take a minute. You young girls like to see beautiful things, now don't you? What?'

He was pulling the bike away towards the gate and Dorothy had to hop off or she would have fallen. PJ simply let the bike fall on its side against the grass verge to one side of his gate. He waited. Dorothy followed him, stepping carefully through the muddy entrance way. A rough clay path led from the lane up towards the farmhouse; to the left, before the house, were sheds that looked dilapidated and dirty. PJ began to walk ahead of her.

'What'll we be when we grow up, Miss Lohan, then? A doctor? Lawyer? A farmer's wife?'

'I'm not sure, PJ, though my mother thinks I should become a nun.'

'Join that convent, is it? What a waste of a fine strappin' young lady like yourself. What?'

'How's Mrs Hannafin, PJ? Is she well?' Dorothy was keen to turn the subject.

'The old hairpin, you mean? She's within in the kitchen, where she ought to be, doin' what she ought to be doin', washin' an' shinin' an' polishin', but she's in good shape, Dolly, in good shape.'

He turned into the first of the sheds; it was a small space, the floor covered with straw, with bales making a fence around the centre. There was not a lot of light coming into the place, save that from the open door and from a small window high up in the wall. PJ stepped inside, then stood back inside the door and beckoned Dorothy in. There was a strong animal smell that made Dorothy hesitate at first, but there was something appealing, too, about the smell. She could hear a small but persistent cacophony of yelps and barks. Then she moved forward, delightedly.

'Oh,' she called out at once. 'Puppies. Oh they're lovely!'

There were six tiny white puppies creeping and crawling over one another, and nuzzling into a large and beautiful bitch that lay peacefully back against one of the bales of straw. They were white, but with a hint of a light orange-brown shading that whiteness; their ears were a gentle brown and the same brown shaded their faces down to the black tip of the nose.

'Butterscotch!' Dorothy called out at once. PJ was smiling broadly at her.

'They're Labrador,' he said proudly. 'Labrador retrievers. That's the mammy there, I call her Princess. And I will be looking for homes for these little fellas. Butterscotch, now there's a grand name for one of them should anybody want him.'

'Can I pick one up?' the girl asked.

'Sure, take one up, here, I'll help you.'

PJ moved forward and bent in over the bales; he gathered up one of the puppies and handed it to Dorothy. Then he stepped back a little behind her.

Dorothy cuddled the little creature against her cheek; the wide dark eyes seemed to gaze at her with a familiarity that touched her. It did not make any struggle. She was thrilled.

Then she felt the two big hands of PJ Hannafin reach round from behind her and cup her breasts. Dorothy was still small in that way but his strong touch and his quick caressing of her breasts hurt her. She stood stock still. She was terrified. She exhaled loudly, 'Ohhhhhh …'

'It's all right, girl, don't worry,' PJ murmured from behind her, his mouth close to her left ear. 'Sure you're a fine an' a growin' woman now an' you need a strong hand to make you know it. You'll make someone a fine wife one day, no surer thing. Don't waste your livin' on them nuns.'

While he spoke he moved his hands roughly over her breasts and she felt his fingers feel for the button of her blouse. She flung the pup back onto the straw and began to struggle away from the hands. But they were strong, very strong and firm and he tightened his grip to hold her.

'Don't worry, now, it's all right, it's all right,' he kept saying. 'I won't hurt you, it's all right. I'll let you have your pick of that crop of puppies, all for free, for yourself, just stand quiet a moment, there's a good girl.' He was breathing heavily and his face was leaning down now over her left shoulder. She struggled, silently. She backed against him, forcing him to move backwards, too, and for a moment his hold slackened on her and she quickly darted away from him. He was blocking the door. She felt trapped. She moved away to the far side of the bales, keeping the pups and the bitch between them. She put her hands behind her and felt the coldness of the rough stone of the wall. He stood quite still, watching her. She could not see his face now, the light from outside throwing him into shadow.

Dorothy felt her whole body sag; it was a kind of weariness that, taken with the suddenness and the fright of what had happened, sapped her strength. She was glad to remain there, against the cold and slightly damp stones of the wall behind her. She watched the man. She could still see the six pups grope around on the straw and her heart melted again for the creatures, and for herself. They were so beautiful, so much a part of what could be wonderful about the world and why, oh why, had she not been allowed to touch and hold them as she so much wanted to? The man moved and the blackness of his form against the light terrified her; he seemed to loom there, black and utterly dangerous. She screamed. At once the bitch leaped up in fright and started to bark, loudly, and to move protectively towards her pups, towards the looming figure of the man.

'Shut up, you dirty bitch you!' JP shouted at the dog. Then he jumped in to the frame that the bales made and aimed a kick at the bitch. He missed and his impetus flung him onto the straw. Before she knew it Dorothy was out of the shed and running as fast as she could, over the dung-covered, muddy path down to the laneway. She did not look back. She could still hear the barking; she heard a loud screech of hurt. She picked up her bike from where it lay and she mounted it, her schoolbag hanging from the carrier and an end of it dragging against the ground. As she pedalled furiously she grew aware of the tears that were pouring out of her eyes. The whole day had darkened; the trees and shrubs along the sides of the lane had blurred and misted; the small stones and loose debris of the laneway impeded her; she cycled on, her form bent forward over the handlebars.

'I kind of half fell off the bike onto the side of the road, along Hawthorn Lane,' she told her mother who stood in the kitchen, waiting for her.

'What were you doing on Hawthorn Lane? That's a long way round. I have your meal ready for you this half hour. It's going to dry up, there in the oven.'

Dorothy looked at her. She felt the tears coming to her eyes. She opened her mouth but no words came. How could she tell? What would her mother think, what would she say? Sex, sex, sex; it was a bad word in this house, a word not to be used, not to be discussed and now, if she should blurt out the truth of what had happened, she felt her mother would blame her, blame Dorothy, and she would be disgraced in this house, this family. 'I'm sorry, mother,' she said. 'It must have been all the fallen leaves along the lane. I skidded. I like Hawthorn Lane, the trees, the bushes, the birds.'

'Don't cry, Dorothy. A grown girl like you must not cry. Are you hurt?'

Dorothy held out her right hand, palm upwards. There was dirt on her palm, perhaps from handling the puppy, perhaps from reaching back against the shed wall behind her. There was no scrape, no blood, no scratch. Her mother took her hand and looked at it. 'Can't see anything wrong with that,' her mother said. 'Just wash your hands and I'll give you up your potato cakes.'

'I don't want any potato cakes!' Dorothy shouted, in spite of herself. She brought her hands to her face and covered her eyes and cheeks and rubbed furiously at her forehead. 'I'm sorry, mother, I think I just need to have a bath. Thanks for the cakes. I'll be back down. They'll be grand …'

She moved quickly out through the kitchen and up the stairs to the bathroom. She heard the kitchen door bang shut behind her. She locked the bathroom door and leaned back against it. She closed her eyes and sighed deeply. A sense of her own filthiness came upon her, like a weakness, and she began to tear her school clothes off and fling them onto the ground at her feet. She ran the bath quickly; the water was scarcely warm but a small steaming rose from it and at once she began to feel better. She stepped into the water as soon as she could and sat down in the bath. She let the water keep running. She took the red Lifeguard hard soap and began to soap her body all over. She shuddered. She had never felt so dirty. She scrubbed and rinsed and soaped herself again. She gazed down at her breasts and for a moment she hated them. She brought her hands up hard and thumped her breasts, hurting herself. They were small yet, but pert and white and perfect. She covered them with the soapy water and rinsed them, over and over and over. She dunked her head in the water and held it there until she found her breathing difficult. Then she sat up straight again and turned off the tap. She lay back in the bath, her two hands holding the sides. She closed her eyes and tried to let her troubles fall away from her.

'Guilty!' was the word that kept coming to her. As much as she tried she could not get rid of the word from her mind. How was she guilty? Had she done something to provoke PJ Hannafin's attempt? Had she ever said something, or moved in some way that had roused him? And her own mother, how could she ever tell her mother anything about all of that? It was a word her mother would surely come out with at once, 'guilty', 'guilty', 'guilty'. And there was all that prompting from her mother, that she should grace her family and become a nun, a great and holy vocation, her mother said. Dorothy shook her head and opened her eyes. The bathroom window was open at the top and she could see thin clouds of steam make their way out into the fresh air of the day. She wished her guilt could go with it. She wished her body could feel clean again. Clean and whole and wholesome.

The walls of the bathroom were of a dull brown colour that Dorothy found, for the first time, a little nauseating. The ceiling was white, but it was a white tinged with a yellow stain from years of rising steam. And she thought at once of the Labrador she had picked up, the one she would love to own, that she would call 'Butterscotch', the colour, Dorothy thought, of early autumn, of a sweet and lingering gentleness. But now she could never have a dog like that! She did not deserve to have a dog like that. How could she? She was dirty, she was guilty, she was lost.

It was almost an hour later that her mother came and knocked on the bathroom door. 'Are you all right, Dorothy, are you in there, are you all right?'

The girl came back into the world from a lethargic and dreary half-forgetfulness. She sat up in the water that showed a slight scum of dirt around the edge. She was cold. She shivered. Her flesh was white and covered in goose pimples. Her breasts were whiter than ever. She put her hands over her breasts to cover them. 'Yes, mother, I'm fine,' she called out. 'I'll be down in a minute.' She reached forward in the bath and pulled the stopper from the plug. The water began to swirl out, making an ugly, sucking sound. Dorothy had rarely felt so cold in all her life.

After Christmas the weather grew menacing. Dorothy sat and watched as the sky seemed to grow into the very colour of her own feelings: it was dark by mid-morning; the sky seemed to be heavy and to hang just over the fields. There was a bleakly soft-green dimness everywhere. Dorothy sat at her window and found herself crying, quietly. She still felt soiled and empty; she found nothing to rouse her or to please her. She would be content to sit there forever and let the earth take her to itself. Now the quiet and secret life of the convent held a small attraction for her.

The first flakes of snow began to fall. They were scarcely perceptible at first, coming down out of that heaviness so slowly they could have been individual small moths seeking shelter.

Quickly the snow began to thicken; it was falling straight down, no breeze there to move it slantwise or to blow it into swirls. When Dorothy looked up at the sky she could see only great spots of snow as they fell, and it was the silence accompanying that gave some strange beauty to the fall. Dorothy sat on. The window was open at the top and now and then a large flake floated in, landing on the windowsill inside, or sometimes touching so softly on her hair that she scarcely noticed. She gave herself to the day.

By afternoon the snow had blotted out the light. A small breeze had risen and the flakes began to blow about in different directions. It was, Dorothy thought, like a great swarm of white butterflies in chaos about the world. The evening darkness fell early; lights were on in the house from early afternoon but even her mother was reluctant to pull the curtains over against the whiteness. By nightfall the snow had stopped and the wind had fallen again. Dorothy stood outside and saw that the sky was beginning to clear; there were stars everywhere and a great coldness took the earth and made her shiver. The light from her house glimmered beautifully on the front lawn; everywhere was white where the snow had covered hedge and field and road and had piled up high against the walls and hedgerows, blanketing everything in a soft orange glow under the gleaming lights from the house. Dorothy stood for as long as she could bear the cold. She was grateful, then, to go indoors and snuggle in with the family around the noisy fire.

The whole world, next day, seemed to play a symphony in the key of white. There was not a breath of wind though the day was as bright as summer and the sky was a clear and lovely blue. The snow sparkled on lawn and road, on field and bush and meadow, melding everything into one delightful and beautiful white music. Dorothy tried to walk from the front door down to the gate; her feet sank in the snow which had a brittle frozen surface, making walking difficult; after the gentle breaking of the frosted surface her feet made a crunching sound as the softer snow compacted under her boots. Her breath nested before her face in gentle visible puffs and she laughed, she laughed gaily for the first time in months.

In the afternoon her father came back from shovelling the snow away off the backyard pathway.

'They're all going back to the lake!' he called, and there was excitement in his voice. 'The water's frozen solid. We're going to skate!'

Even Dorothy's mother came, dressing herself carefully. The lake was a bogland mere, formed where a quarry had been abandoned many years before, a lake now reputed to have such a soft-peat and muddied bottom that you could sink forever through its blackness. Usually it was unlovely, a matrix lake, a fern-world at one side, a dangerously inviting garden of tall reeds on the other. Near the bank on the farther side Dorothy had once discovered a large hole dug out of the soft peat; on the grass bank before the hole she had found hen-feathers and some small bones. She knew at once that she had found a fox-den and the darkness within had made her shiver. But she had not told; she felt at one with the secrecy and innocence of the creature whose existence she knew, but which she had never seen. Now the reeds rose rigid out of the ice; even though the sun shone brightly from a clear sky, the air remained chilled and the ice simply thickened.

The lake and its black water had become a silver-white playground. The boglands about, the ferns and heathers and peat-banks, all lay in shades of white and off-white that glistered and shone with exceptional beauty. There were many children gathering at the end of the lake nearest the road, where the lake-edge was shingled and safe. There were adults, too, many of them doubtful about the lake and its safety. One of the men picked up a rock from the edge of the lake and flung it as far as he could out onto the surface. There was a high saxophone note from the fall and the rock stayed, the ice-skin around it stiffening a little, but not cracking. The lovely note rang for a moment about the hills and heather spaces, gathering further mystery from the soft greys and near-whites of the snow on all the land and water round about. Gingerly the children, and some of the adults, moved out onto the ice.

Within minutes the excitement was great; adult and child skittering and sliding and skidding, most of the children falling almost at once, some of the smaller ones crying in frustration but being chivvied along, rising again, beginning to pick up their balance, running a little and then sliding on great hobnailed boots along the surface of the lake. There was no grace to it, the boots, more used to striking sparks off the stone roads, now scutting small smoke-showers of ice into the air. But there was happiness to it, bodies moving through the slight gloom, the adults more slowly, the children skimming, that slow take-off into a nervous run and that slide, half-sideways, hands clutching at air for balance, small splicks of ice lifting behind them and settling again on the surface, like white dust; scarves blew in the air, the darkness of coat and jumper was strong against the white, but there was noise, laughter and cries, challenges and calls, it was a small world transformed for a while into the exotic, the dangerous and the beautiful.

Dorothy was nervous. At first she moved only a little out onto the ice, testing every inch before her, standing stiff and uncertain only when she was sure the ice was very thick beneath her. One of the girls came past her, moving quickly, so quickly that she rammed straight into Dorothy and they both fell onto the ice, Dorothy's sorry, 'Oh, oh, oh' filled with instant wretchedness. But the girl picked herself up at once, laughing, and caught Dorothy's hand and hoisted her up, too, then pulled her, still laughing, along with her. Dorothy found herself moving easily. 'Let go! Let go!' she shouted, and she was sliding, slowly but certainly, with a certain grace. Soon she had found her feet and was beginning to move at speed about the ice, the tough soles of her shoes giving her sliding power, the coldness on her body beginning to transform into pleasurable warmth. She began to whoop with delight, body after body, small and large, moving randomly about on the surface of the lake.

Dorothy was astonished then to see her mother move out aggressively on the ice. Mam. She was dressed in a long red coat and a black scarf was wound tightly about her throat. Dorothy watched as the woman quickly picked up on the game and was moving fast, her arms flailing, her face red with joy, the woollen cap that Dorothy's father used for fishing trips packed down tightly on her head. Soon she seemed expert, the child within the tightly controlled woman breaking out, seeking naughtiness as she turned and skated, reaching and gaggling like the best of them and suddenly the bog-hole lake had become a ballroom and they could do eight-hand reels to their hearts' battering, trouser legs of the men tucked into socks, the music of their laughter and basso profundo of the ice lifting gleefully into the clean-blue sky.

Dorothy heard an excited barking at the end of the lake where the road passed. Then she saw it, that beautiful Labrador retriever she had seen keeping an eye on the pups in PJ Hannafin's shed. The bitch was barking excitedly and racing about, too, on the ice, slithering helplessly, turning in an utterly undignified scrabbling for hold, her barking almost as articulate as the cries of the humans. 'Butterscotch!' Dorothy cried out with joy and she began to slide towards the dog. Her mother came sliding after her, laughing, pretending to bark, the child in her more a child at that moment than Dorothy was. The dog came slowly up to Dorothy, wagging her tail and the girl was at once hunkering down to pet her when she remembered that PJ Hannafin himself would most likely be somewhere on the lake, too. A great cut of sorrow hit her and she stood back from the retriever. Mrs Lohan came and caught the dog and began to pet her, urging the animal, too, into excitement, her heavy-wheeling self balancing then more fancifully than Dorothy's or than the dog's till they both went belly-heavy and scattering out over the ice, leaving Dorothy laced to the surface of the lake, nailed to sadness and to an overwhelming emptiness.

It was at that moment that a body came sliding loudly into hers, almost knocking her over once again, though she turned quickly and held on, sliding a little way with the new arrival. There was laughing and a small riotous noise of joy from the person who now held her as they both came to a halt, a little unsteadily, not far from one of the shores of the lake. For a moment, her head buried in the black wool of his great coat, Dorothy thought that this must be PJ himself, his hands gripping her tightly, their bodies pressed too close together. She screamed, weakly. Then she looked up, all the while struggling to get free.

'It's OK, Dolly,' a voice said. 'It's me. It's only me.'

She was backing away awkwardly from him; it took her a short time, but at last she knew him, though he was taller and slimmer than she had ever known him. His hair was a rich and gleaming black and his blue eyes were as clear and sparkling as that day's sky.

'Are you OK?' he asked her. 'I'm sorry; I saw you, and came sliding over. Then I couldn't stop or turn, and I went straight into you.'

She laughed, more with relief than pleasure. 'Packie Brennan,' she said. 'I'm so glad it's only you.'

He giggled. 'How do you mean, only me?'

She took him by the sleeve of his huge coat and tugged him cautiously aside. Together they glided in a somewhat ungainly way, to the shore of the lake. She stepped out onto the frozen grass.

'You must call me Dorothy, now, don't forget,' she said, seriously. 'I'm a woman now, you know.'

He laughed. 'I forgot, for the minute. And you must call me Patrick, you know, no more Packie for me. Sure I'll be finished at the scholasticate soon.'

She looked up at him again and was surprised at how good-looking she found him. She glanced around; the retriever was still skidding and barking and jerking her body around on the ice but there was no sign of her owner. 'Patrick,' she said. 'It's just, I had a bit of a fright recently, that's all, and you gave me a fright, too, bumping into me like that.'

'Sorry,' he said again. Then, for a long moment, they stood together, out of the press and swing, the jollity and noise of the people. They were silent.

'So,' he began. 'How is it going at St Jude's? Do you like it?'

'I hate it! I hate the nuns, and I hate everything to do with them!' Her voice was vicious, her face flamed with anger. 'And you know what? I hate their God, and their lessons, and their false piousness and their hypocrisy, and I don't know how on earth you can even think of becoming a priest. It's all stupid and lies and false, that's what it is! And you know what? I'm not even going to Mass any more.'

He was taken aback. 'Well, your mother won't be …'

'It's nothing to do with my mother. I'm old enough now to do what I want to do myself. And if you don't like it, Packie Brennan, don't think that I care!'

She turned from him then and began to walk away from the lake, over the grass, back towards the laneway that led down to her house. Patrick stretched out his hand after her and held it there, but no words came to him. He let his hand drop back, heavily, by his side.

Dorothy drew further and further away from her mother and from her home. She was glad, now, to be away for most of every week, in school. She had a new friend, too, a girl called Evelyn Harris, a bright and very pretty girl and they sat together as they both entered on their final years in secondary school. There were rumours that Sister Francesca was unwell. The nun opened the classroom door; the girls rose. The nun walked slowly up to her rostrum; she seemed stooped, the habit hung more loosely about her, her face was pale and all the animation was drawn out of her. She laid her books down on the big desk, said the prayers lethargically, and sat down. The girls, too, sat, making a great deal of scraping noises with their chairs and desks. Sister Francesca simply looked down at her books and waited.

Evelyn Harris had piled her books up in front of her and opened the English poetry book behind them. She grinned across at Dorothy.

'Right, girls,' Sister Francesca began. 'Please look over the Gerard Hopkins poem you have for today. I expect you will have it by heart. I will give you ten minutes to go over it. To make sure.'

There was a loud and irritating shuffling of books, of feet under desks, of coughing and sneezing. The girls glanced around at one another and smiled. Sister Francesca scarcely looked up at them.

Dorothy raised her hand and waited. Sister Francesca ignored her.

'Sister!' she called out. The nun looked up, took off her spectacles slowly and gazed at Dorothy.

'What is it, child?'

'Sister, I don't understand those lines in the second part of the poem …'

'In the sestet, Dorothy, the sestet.'

'In the sestet, Sister. I don't understand them.'

'What do you not understand, Dorothy?'

'It says, "O the mind, mind has mountains; cliffs of fall, frightful, sheer, no-man-fathomed. Hold them cheap may who ne'er hung there." What does that mean, Sister?' Dorothy looked over at Evelyn and winked.

The nun put her spectacles back on, carefully. She sighed and glanced out the window.

'It means, child, simply this, that people suffer from great darknesses in their lives, sometimes, sadness, hurt, misery, and that this is a terrible suffering, depression, and that we can fall from a high place of happiness and peace into the lowest abysses of pain and loss. That's what the mountains in the mind are, and the falls, too. The falls. The misery. The trouble.'

Sister Francesca lowered her head over her own books once again. Dorothy was quiet. There was an echo of that in her own mind.

Evelyn Harris had raised her right hand and was clicking her fingers.

'Yes, Evelyn, have you a problem?'

'It says, "no-man-fathomed", Sister. What does that mean?'

'It means, child, that there is no person on this earth who has gone down so deeply into sorrow that he, or indeed she, knows all that there is to know about human pain. No man, no person, has ever understood fully what pain is. Except, perhaps, Our Lord Jesus Christ, on his cross.'

Another hand was raised, and another pair of fingers clicked. It was the plumper-than-ever Ursula Horan, sitting hunched over her books at the back of the classroom.

'What does it mean, Sister, when he says "no worst, there is none". What does that mean?'

Sister Francesca took off her spectacles again and looked over the whole classroom. The girls fell silent. A late autumn sun fell across the room at an acute angle, half-blinding the nun. An edge of blackboard gleamed a moment and darkened as a cloud passed outside. 'Must I spend my whole life trying to explain things to you, girls? We did this poem last year. Now we are revising. Do I have to start at the beginning all over again?'

Dorothy's hand was up again.

'Sister, you never explained this poem to us before. We simply don't understand it. For instance, "pitched past pitch of grief". I know what grief is, but pitch? I know they put pitch on the bottoms of boats, but what is pitch of grief?'

Evelyn Harris added: 'And "schooled at fore-pangs", Sister, and fore is spelt wrong, it should be f-o-u-r, but it's not.'

Another girl spoke up: 'It says, "here wretch creep", who's the wretch, Sister? and why is there a whirlwind in the poem suddenly?'

Somebody laughed. Then several girls began to speak together. Sister Francesca rapped loudly on the top of her desk.

'Enough!' she said. There was silence.

At that moment a stray wasp wandered in through the open top of the window and buzzed its way down over the classroom. One of the girls waved her hands wildly about her hair. 'Oh! Oh! Oh!' she called out, and knocked several books off her desk. A girl at the very back of the class leaped out of her desk, waving her arms about too, as if the wasp had got stuck in her hair. The girls laughed. Sister Francesca watched them, without expression. Dorothy watched the nun. Evelyn Harris was giggling loudly and making a pattering noise on the wooden floor with her feet. Several other girls began to wave their arms. Somebody banged down a book on the top of her desk and called out 'Missed!' Dorothy saw Sister Francesca rise slowly from her desk. She gathered up her books, very carefully, and took them under her arm. Then she stood a long while, simply gazing out of the window, ignoring the girls and the classroom. Gradually the girls grew silent. The wasp had flown high up onto one of the windows and was crawling about, out of harm's way. The girls settled in their places. Evelyn glanced over at Dorothy who had grown pale and very still.

Sister Francesca sighed loudly, turned from the window and walked very slowly out of the classroom. She left the door open after her. The girls were stunned. They did not know what to do. There were some nervous titters, somebody clapped for a moment, then fell silent again. The absence seemed to swell the classroom with heat and tension. Dorothy got up quickly and ran from her place, out the open door, down the short corridor and out into the air. She leaned over at the base of a tree in the college grounds, expecting that she would throw up. She was hot and sweating. She sat down on the damp grass, closed her eyes and laid her head back against the bole of the tree.

After the common evening study in the great hall, all the girls trooped out and headed for the chapel, to attend Benediction and the saying of the rosary. They moved in single file, and in silence. Ursula Horan manoeuvred herself to get beside Evelyn Harris and Dorothy Lohan; the three of them made signals to one another, they nodded, winked and lined up one behind the other. As they passed out of the study hall Ursula moved quickly away down the dark passage to the right of the long hallway; Evelyn slipped after her and Dorothy, with a quick glance around, followed. They stood quietly for a time in the darkness of the passageway, waiting. The shuffling of the other girls gradually fell away to silence. They heard the study door being shut, and the clacketing footsteps of Mother Mary as she followed the girls along the corridor towards the chapel. Then there was silence. 'Right, let's go!' Ursula whispered. They ran, pushing against one another, until Ursula opened the door that led out into the grounds of the college. The evening was mild; the horizon was already dark grey, the trees rising, still as posts, into the dimness. The whole earth seemed at peace, though lying heavy under the coming night. There would be no stars; the clouds lowered over all. The high nets of the netball court hung limp and torn; the cinder pathway of the convent walks looked black. The walls of the toilets loomed ugly and forbidding. The three girls slipped in quickly.

'Now, girls, I have news!' Ursula whispered with great excitement.

'Hold on a wee minute, first things first,' answered Evelyn. The toilets were open off either side of a small, cobbled yard; the wooden doors hung green and ugly, opening into blackness. The girls moved quickly down to the furthest cabin and Evelyn stepped inside. The other two stood outside, listening and watching. 'It's OK, I'm sure,' Dorothy said. 'We're safe as houses. Nobody noticed.'

Evelyn took out a packet of cigarettes and offered one to Ursula. Dorothy shook her head.

'Smoke away, girls, I simply don't like it, though I love the smell of cigarettes.'

The other two lit up their cigarettes, holding the flame in their fists, blowing the smoke into the darkness of the cabin. They could not be seen from the college chapel but then you never knew if one of the nuns might be walking about.

'Did you hear?' Ursula whispered urgently. 'About old Francesca?'

'No, what about the auld bag?' Evelyn asked.

'She was seen, in civvies! Ya, in civvies, a green wool skirt, a cardigan and a green scarf about her shoulder. She was seen, several of the girls spotted her out of the classroom window. Just about at the end of the afternoon. In civvies. Like a real woman. And she had a small battered suitcase in her hand!'

'She's left?' Dorothy whispered anxiously.

'Got the hell out of the nuns, that's what she's done, and good riddance to her, too!' said Evelyn.

'I heard she was suffering, she was ill, depressed or something, for a long time,' Ursula whispered, still excited. 'And when she walked out of our class, that was the end of it.'

'Jesus, that's awful!' Dorothy said. The other two looked at her.

'It's great, Dorothy, we've got rid of her, the auld hairpin!'

Dorothy was silent. They could hear, faintly across the dusk, the sound of the organ in the chapel; it was playing out the music of 'O Salutaris Hostia'.

'Oh no but it's awful,' Dorothy said. 'Imagine what she must have gone through! God help her.'

'She was a bully!' Evelyn said. 'And she couldn't teach for

peanuts. She made me hate poetry. And she made me hate religion, too. All that self-righteous stuff she went on with, all that so-called holiness, that purity, that Latin blather, those stupid hymns and prayers and everything. She put me right off the Catholic Church, and that's the truth of it.' She blew a great gasp of smoke into the darkness behind her.

'Somebody drove up in a broken-down old car,' Ursula went on excitedly. 'Francesca was waiting, under one of the big trees near the front door. All alone. The suitcase at her feet. And I'll tell you something else, too!'

'What?' whispered Evelyn.

'She was smoking a fag, that's what!'

'My God,' Dorothy said. 'Smoking, too. I wonder who came to collect her? Do you think she has parents or something?'

'Well, I suppose she must be a human being, after all,' Evelyn laughed. 'Maybe she has a mother somewhere. Oh but it's good riddance, I'm so happy she's gone. I hope she is, really gone, I mean; the place will be better without her!'

Dorothy was silent. The girls smoked happily. Now they could hear the sounds of the 'Tantum Ergo' coming from the distance. Darkness was already settling in over the trees and there was silence in the yard, apart from the slow drip, drip, drip of water somewhere nearby. The girls blew the smoke carefully down into the basins of the toilets. Dorothy found there were tears in her eyes. She sniffled.

'What the hell's the matter with you, Dorothy?' Ursula asked.

'I don't know,' Dorothy said. 'Somehow I feel so sorry for the nun. For Francesca. Or whatever her name is. She might be Mary Murphy for all we know. And we did give her a hard time. Maybe it's our fault she's lost. Maybe it's a sin …'

'Lost? A sin?' Evelyn sneered. 'She's not lost. She's a tough bird. She gave us a miserable time and made me lose my faith. Maybe I'm the one that's lost. And sin? I thought we didn't believe in sin any more, do we?'

Ursula laughed. 'Don't they even say it's a sin to smoke? And there she was, your saint Francesca, smoking away, waiting. I'll bet she'll find some poor old man who'll take her in and marry her, God help the poor old fool.'

The three girls paused a moment at that vision. Then they laughed and the tension passed, the way light eases softly from the base of a tree.

'There's one problem, though, one worry,' Evelyn went on. 'Who is going to take her place? Maybe we'll get some other old battleaxe, Sister Mary Francis of the Weeping Armpits, somebody like that.'

They laughed again.

Sister Bernadette was a small nun, curls of chestnut-brown hair peeping from under a somewhat carelessly worn wimple. She was pretty, her eyes a deep green, her skin fair and complexion smooth and unblemished. She smiled easily and moved softly about the classroom, filled with a quiet enthusiasm.

'Hopkins,' she was saying, 'Oh what a wonderful man. But sad, girls, oh so sad. You know he died in Dublin? Yes, in our own capital city. Didn't like the place either. Came down with a kind of depression, you know, far from home, from family, and he had to teach in the university and correct exams, and his eyesight was failing. Oh so miserable. And in spite of the fact that he was a priest, and a Jesuit, too, there were times when he thought that even God had abandoned him. Haven't we all had moments like that? All of us. And we need someone we can talk to, someone who'll listen and help. And he had nobody, because God, at times, doesn't seem to be there. Amn't I right?'

Evelyn's hand was up. She looked quickly towards Dorothy and winked.

'I don't believe in God at all, Sister Bernadette!'

'Oh yes, dear girl, Evelyn, isn't it? Yes, I understand. Oh yes indeed, there are dark times in all our lives. Very dark times. Times when we want to get away from it all, just hide, really, and let the whole miserable world pass us by. Thank you, Evelyn, for that. But doesn't it all help to explain that difficult poem of Hopkins? "O the mind, mind has mountains; cliffs of fall … " and haven't we all hung on those cliffs, sometimes at least, dreading to fall, knowing we might fall into despair? Oh yes, poor man, poor, poor Hopkins.'

The nun fell silent. She was gazing down at the floor in a kind of absence. Dorothy watched her. The nun was pretty, very pretty, Dorothy knew, and now she was sad. Sad because of some old poem that some old priest had written, years and years ago. But Dorothy agreed, yes, yes, there were moments like that, 'hold them cheap may who ne'er hung there'. And Dorothy looked at Evelyn Harris, she was a girl who did not ever seem to hang on such cliffs, she was always merry, always cheerful. Dorothy read the lines of the poem to herself again. Sister Bernadette sighed and moved back up to the front of the classroom.

'But Hopkins finds a small comfort, there at the end of the poem, a comfort in the knowledge that no matter how bad a day is, it will end in sleep, and no matter how miserable a life is, it will end with death. And then there will be a kind of peace. Now, Evelyn, I find no faith in God in that poem, do you? And this is a priest, mind, a good priest, a good man, an honest man and a lovely poet. And he doesn't appear to have faith in God, at least not when this poem was written, does he?'

Evelyn was taken aback.

'How can that be, Sister, that a priest does not have faith?'

'Oh he came out of that misery, after some time. He wrote many other sonnets, many of them bleak and black, indeed many of them asking God where are you? Where is your comforting? And he really found no answer. Faith in God is a matter of will, not feeling, you see, and in another poem, not in your books, I'm afraid, he simply said "Enough! the Resurrection". He was willing himself back into some belief in the Resurrection. Just like now, look, girls, look out at the boughs of the trees. Look, look at the blessed white on the hawthorns! Come on, let's all stand a moment at the windows, quietly girls, we don't want Mother Veronica to hear a clatter in here, she might come in, we don't want that, now do we?' and the little nun giggled to herself.

The girls rose, quietly, and moved over to gaze out the windows. They were watching out over the private gardens of the convent; these were laid out geometrically, with low box hedges dividing pathway and lawn, flowerbed and rose garden.

There were daffodils in profusion in the beds, with a row of dark-blue hyacinths running around the edges of the rose beds, crocuses, yellow-gold and purple-white and white, were already hanging their heads in shame at their imminent dying. The trees, chestnut and lime and sycamore, offered a baby-green that was soft and promising, their leaves as yet tightly held in bud or opening out gently to the new year. A whole row of apple-trees was bright with white blossoms and in the easy breeze a few petals blew about like small, dreamy moths.

'See!' urged Sister Bernadette; 'there's Sister Mary Alacoque, sitting on the bench under the pear-trees, there, at the far end of the garden. See how peaceful she is. She is reading her Offices, Terce, Sext and None, no doubt, whispering prayers of praise and love to her Master. But do you think her life, that long life dedicated to this convent, to the children of this area, to learning and to prayer, do you think her life has been without stress, depression and even, at times, despair? No, indeed, there is nobody on this earth who will escape some suffering, but the important thing is to see it in perspective, to see it as God's long and reaching finger, coming to probe and touch and seek for love, for patience, for the will to continue in God's love even though everything is darkness and pain? And that is what Hopkins did, that is how Hopkins came through – with patience and by understanding the place of pain in life. That is what makes the honesty of Hopkins's dark poems so wonderfully true. Because he, too, understood that all that is left for us in life is desire, longing, hope for that wondrous country where every tear will be wiped away and every sadness overcome, when we shall all be forever in a garden of peace and loveliness with our God. Oh girls, how blessed are we all, and how blessed, too, to be able to see and love what there is in the world about us.'

The girls stood, dumb and stirred, watching the world beyond as if it were wholly new, listening to the words of the small Sister as if they were opening up new territories, new glories.

'Now, girls, back to your places, please, and as quietly as possible.'

The girls moved back, carefully, and sat at their desks.

Dorothy gazed up at Sister Bernadette and there was moisture in her eyes, she was deeply moved by the Sister's words, and she was stirred by the emotion and commitment she had heard in the nun's voice. For a while there was a rich silence in the classroom. Then Sister Bernadette moved quietly to the window again and looked out for a moment: '"Nothing is so beautiful as spring,"' she quoted, '"When weeds, in wheels, shoot long and lovely and lush." Hopkins again,' she continued, turning back with a great smile to the girls. 'Think of it, how the rest of us see weeds and feel that we must instantly chuck them out of the earth. But what does the poet see? He sees their beauty, how they shoot long and lovely and lush. And listen now, listen to this, does this not stir your hearts and minds?' The nun moved back to the centre of the classroom and smiled down at the enraptured girls. She half-closed her eyes and recited, by heart:

> I have desired to go
> Where springs not fail,
> To fields where flies no sharp nor sided hail
> And a few lilies blow.
>
> And I have asked to be
> Where no storms come,
> Where the green swell is in the havens dumb,
> And out of the swing of the sea.

She paused, closed her eyes fully and swayed gently. The music of the words, their urgent sense of longing and desire, all sank deeply into Dorothy's soul so that she felt herself lifted to a new level of awareness. Sister Bernadette sighed deeply.

'Hopkins again, of course, girls, that great and holy poet, Gerard Manley Hopkins. That poem is called "Heaven-Haven" and it has another title, too, "A Nun Takes The Veil". That is what we seek for, not only we who are blessed to be called nuns, but priests, brothers, everybody, "thou hast made us for thyself, O God, and our hearts are restless until they rest in thee". Only in God's love, girls, only in accepting pain and suffering of every kind with a quiet equanimity, because we know we are destined for things most wonderful, for a world beautiful and for a joy filled beyond our wildest dreams, only then are we able to accept the deepest suffering and only then, only with that faith and deep desire is a poet like Hopkins, a priest like Hopkins, able to cope with the despair and depression that came upon him. Let us return to this week's poem again, dear girls, dear children, dear friends of Jesus, and let us see how meaningful it may have become to us, to the readers, almost one hundred years after the poet wrote the words.'

Again Dorothy watched, her whole body feverish with awareness and excitement, as Sister Bernadette half-closed her eyes and recited the poem by heart.

'"No worst, there is none. Pitched past pitch of grief ..."'

All Dorothy's being urged her to reject the ugliness and heartlessness of what she saw as the world's beliefs, their hardness and rigidity, their insistence on rule and law and regulation. While all about her the earth offered itself anew to the young woman's eyes: the springtime in the convent grounds swelling towards the promise of summer everywhere she looked. These weekends she always cycled home by a circuitous route, to avoid having to pass down Hawthorn Lane and perhaps meet PJ Hannafin again, a route that took her by the old canal where an almost wholly overgrown path brought her through flowering blackthorn bushes, hawthorn hedgerows and brambles, where even the untouched growth in the damp ditches offered glories of half-hidden beauty, wild orchids, primroses, vetch. And there was that disturbance in her whole being which she attributed now to Sister Bernadette, not only to the way she opened up Dorothy's soul to poetry and words, but the way her very presence sent small flutters of anxiety and excitement through her, body and soul.

When she went up to the front of the class to collect an essay she had written on the poet William Butler Yeats and his poem 'He Wishes for the Cloths of Heaven', Sister Bernadette took her by the hand and turned her to face the class: 'Here, girls, is an essay on Yeats which I find as good as any essay I have ever read.' Dorothy could feel her face burning. 'Dorothy takes the words, "But I, being poor, have only my dreams", and she lets her pen fly along with the words, the words that touch all of us in our deepest hearts, for what is left to most of us but our dreams, and this bright girl shows how important the lines are to those who find that their dreams have been trodden on, and how that will move to destroy our souls. And she is right, girls, she is right, and she has shown how important poetry can be in touching the deepest reaches of our most secret souls. Well done, Dorothy, I have given you full marks.'

Sister Bernadette was still holding Dorothy's hand and the girl felt a strange and guilty tingle in the touch. She glanced at the nun who was smiling at her and her heart – she felt it truly – gave a small lurch within her.

'I think you are in love with Sister Bernadette!' Evelyn teased her after class.

'I am not! I will never be in love with anybody!'

And Dorothy moved quickly away from her companions, holding her copybook close against her breast. That evening she did not skip away with her friends to go out into the grounds; she followed the rest of the girls into the chapel and knelt, enraptured, while the incense rose against stained-glass windows through which the evening sunlight shone beautifully, she listened carefully for the first time to the words of the prayers, Mystic Rose, Tower of Ivory, House of Gold … and all of them touched her so that she felt tears come to her eyes and she bowed her head with a new gladness. Again she thought of that poem the nun had recited, 'And I have asked to be where no storms come …' Was it possible to escape the storms, the Hannafins of the world, and live at peace in the convent?

As she knelt on after the other girls had left the chapel Dorothy felt a hand touch her gently on the shoulder. She looked up. It was Sister Bernadette, smiling down at her. 'Can I have a quick word outside the chapel with you, Dorothy?' the nun whispered.

'I was a little anxious about your essay, Dorothy,' Sister Bernadette began when they stood out in the dark gallery that led from the chapel to the refectory. 'Certain things about how your dreams had been trampled on, your essay became so rich and personal that I knew it was written from your heart. If there is anything you would like to chat over, anything at all, perhaps something you might like to get off your mind, things bothering you, there is someone who will listen, someone who promises two things, firstly, that nobody will ever know what you have told her, and secondly, that she will understand, whatever it may be. If you would care to come to my office, perhaps tomorrow, after class … ?'

Dorothy nodded, dumbly, her hands held tightly together against her mouth, the tears, almost always there now, ready to come rolling down her cheeks again. Once more she felt her whole body grow hot and tremble and she almost reached out to the nun when the good Sister touched her gently on the cheek and smiled. 'All right so, Dorothy, tomorrow, say at 4.15.'

There was a fascinating light system outside the door when Dorothy arrived; it reminded her of traffic lights. Beside the bell-button there were three lights, green, orange, red; they were not lit when Dorothy pressed the bell but almost at once the small orange light came on. Dorothy smiled, and waited. Then, after a few moments, the green light lit up and Dorothy pushed open the door.

Sister Bernadette's room was spacious; large windows opened directly onto the convent garden and there was a warm and bright light shining in on a large desk covered with books and papers; copy books were neatly piled on one side of the desk. Behind the desk was a large swivelling chair. The room had cupboards and against one wall a small sink with a kettle and crockery on a shelf above it. There were two large, brown leather armchairs that stood on a darkly polished wooden floor; small, slightly frayed carpets were crumpled and crinkled here and there and against one end of the room was a curtain pulled right across. Dorothy believed there was a bed in there and she imagined a crucifix on the wall, prayer books on a shelf, a wardrobe.

Sister Bernadette stood against the window, watching Dorothy. It took the girl some moments to become used to the light; then she saw that the nun was smiling warmly at her. 'Do sit down, there, in that armchair, Dorothy,' she said, pointing to the armchair nearest the door. Dorothy sat, rather stiffly. But she felt excited to be in the room; she grew aware of a gentle fragrance, talcs perhaps, mingled with the scent that papers give off, and, perhaps the lingering scent of coffee.

'I bet you'd like a cup of tea!' the nun said, moving swiftly to the kettle.

'No, no thanks, I really wouldn't, thanks Sister.'

'Very well, but I do have some very nice biscuits here, springy ones, with some sort of coconut topping, and raspberry jam. I'm going to have some of these and I hope you will, too.' She proffered a plate and Dorothy took one of the biscuits, holding it gingerly over her lap while the nun sat in the armchair next to her and bit into one of the biscuits.

'I wonder if you'd like to tell me about the anxieties you have, dear Dorothy. You have anxieties, I feel? Now I have promised you, and I will keep my promise, that not one word of what you tell me will ever be passed on to anyone else. And I want you to promise me that you will not breathe a word of what I say to you. So that we have complete trust between us. Is that fair? Do you agree?'

Dorothy nodded violently. In a kind of automatic way she began to tell the nun about her encounter with PJ Hannafin. Sister Bernadette listened intently, nodding her head often and murmuring sympathetically.

'And then there's your mother, I don't think you can tell your mother about such things. Am I right?'

Dorothy hesitated. 'I don't want to blame Mother, it's not her fault, I think it's mine. I'm just a bit scared, I don't know the words ...'

By now the biscuit in her hands had been broken into fragments that were spilling down onto her lap. Sister Bernadette came and knelt before her; holding a plate in her left hand she gently swept the crumbs off Dorothy's skirt with her right hand, then she smiled up at her, still kneeling before her. 'Our job, as Sisters, our calling indeed, rather than our job, is one of service. I'm here to help you in any way I can, dear

Dorothy, and indeed I have been sensing that you have many things that you want to say to me. Am I right?' She rested her right hand a moment on Dorothy's knee and the girl trembled.

'I think I want to be a nun, Sister, like you …' Dorothy blurted out.

'Hah! I thought so, indeed, I prayed so. That's wonderful, Dorothy, truly wonderful. We must thank God for this, we must truly thank God. You have seen what the world is. You are strong, and yet you are very weak. Like all of us. You know what family life is, a wonderful thing indeed, perhaps the most wonderful thing of all, but you have seen the difficulties there, too. Here, in the convent, we have a hard life, a dedicated life, but it is given to our Lord, not to man, it is given in love, and love will be our reward.'

The Sister rose and stood before Dorothy.

'I am going to tell you a little bit about my father, Dorothy. Yes, my father, not my Father in Heaven, not God,' and she laughed gently. 'My real father. Tony Doran his name is. A man I love very much, but a man who exemplifies what goes on in the world, and where real sorrow lies. And then I am going to go back to that little poem of Hopkins that I spoke, you remember? "I have desired to go where springs not fail, to fields where flies no sharp nor sided hail and a few lilies blow"? That longing to leave the worries and troubles of the world and to find peace in the service of the Lord.'

Dorothy nodded. She watched as Sister Bernadette moved slowly over and back across the room in front of her. The nun lowered her head a moment onto her folded hands, as if in deep thought. Then she looked at Dorothy, smiled again, nodding slowly.

'Yes, my father. Tony. Daddy. I can still see him sitting at the kitchen table of an evening, oh any evening, almost every evening – a big man, his hair white, stooping a little; his hands are big and strong, but very, very gentle. See him? There, scattered over the kitchen table are magazines, many of them are seed catalogues because there is a large garden behind the house.'

Sister Bernadette paused again. She moved over to the

window and looked out. 'Here, Dorothy, we have a fine garden, neat and ordered and well-kept. Flowers. A great variety of flowers. And behind the convent we have a kitchen garden, vegetables, fruit. But we have a full-time gardener who lives in the little house down at the convent gates, you know him, all the girls know poor old Johnny Traynor. He has been with us for years, forever, it seems. You know him?' She turned back to Dorothy.

'Yes, Sister, I see him often. He moves a little shakily, always with something in his hands, a rake, a wheelbarrow, weeds ...'

'Yes, yes, that's him, dear old Johnny. A fine gardener, and he gives his whole life to it. And he's not very imaginative, you know, straight lines in the gardens, no frills, useful vegetables, flowers for every season that he can gather for us to lay on the altar. Carrots, potatoes, celery, then roses, lilies, oh I don't know what. You will not find a weed nor a chick in Johnny's garden. It is predictable, Dorothy, but truly lovely.'

Dorothy nodded. She was not quite sure where this was leading. Sister Bernadette began to move back and forth slowly again, across Dorothy's line of vision.

'Unlike my father, Dorothy, very unlike. For my father had imagination, and ideas. Indeed my mother called them notions, not ideas. Your father has notions, she used to say to me, notions and God help us they will forever remain in the realm of the notional. It took me a long time to figure out what that meant, Dorothy, but I worked it out. There was nothing straight-lined about my father. He used to say that a straight line was a boring thing. He wanted curves, twisting flowerbeds, up-and-down vegetable plots. And he was not satisfied with carrots and potatoes and celery, no indeed. That's where the magazines on the kitchen table come in. You see he used to write away to somewhere in England for catalogues, and these coloured gardening magazines arrived every so often in the house. Father would sit at the table and pour over them, almost drinking them in, admiring the perfect tomatoes, the whiter-than-white button mushrooms, the fantastic flowers, exotic and rare, oh all of that. And he would be excited, God bless him, sitting in our drab kitchen, dreaming of great and productive gardens.'

The sister paused again. Dorothy did not stir. She was taken by the intensity of the nun's remembering.

'Did you ever hear of mangetout, Dorothy?'

'No, sister. It's French, isn't it. Eat everything?'

'Exactly, exactly Dorothy. Eat everything. It's a pea, that's what it is, a variety of the humble pea. But you can eat the pod and all, the peas, the pod, everything. Delicious. And have you heard of the cherry tomato? Of the aubergine? Of mung beans, lima beans, adzuki beans? Well, not only did I hear of them all but I sampled them all. Father ordered his seeds from these catalogues, and we tried the weirdest and most foreign foods he could find. But nobody in the house, nobody in the neighbourhood, bothered with them, they preferred, we all preferred, our cabbage and potato, our leeks and turnips and bitter apples. He was the first man in our county to grow mushrooms, beautiful, white button things, delicious when roasted with salt and butter on the top of the stove, night-sweating creatures, he grew them in the outhouse, spending hours, hours on end, preparing the straw, the manure, oh I don't know what, and we had mushrooms until they were coming out our ears! Poor Father. Everybody mocked him, everybody went back to tea and toast, and many people were scared stiff of his mushrooms, they expected to be poisoned. Poisoned! But this was his way of learning the world, Dorothy, what he was doing was disciplining his dreams, earthing his longings, it was his attempt to set the ground in order, to bring the great world in which he dreamed and longed and wondered into his own back yard. Poor Father, poor, dear Father.'

Sister Bernadette moved back to the window and stood watching out so that Dorothy could not see her face. 'I don't know,' the nun continued, 'which came first in his life, the alcohol, or the dreams. So many evenings then he would not come home from work anywhere near the time he was expected; he would turn away, turn into the nearby public house, drink away his failures, drink to stop the loud and accusing noises in his own head. I think he was frustrated with the everyday boredom, with the day-after-day sameness, the round, the getting nowhere that is in most people's lives.' She turned back again to Dorothy. 'I think it was a way of drowning out his feelings of guilt, too, guilt that he had not achieved any of the dreams he had when he was younger, any of the hopes, that he was getting nowhere, not even his garden was appreciated by anyone other than himself, and even he found that the stuff he was hoping to grow and develop simply would not grow well in the dampness of our climate. The world frustrated him, Dorothy, and he hid that frustration in the dark night of alcohol.'

There was a long silence as the nun seemed to lose herself in her memories. She sighed then, and looked at Dorothy, a grim smile on her lips. 'He died, oh a couple of years ago, I still think of him as alive, as you see, but long before he died his catalogue dreams had fallen into nightmares, the garden fell neglected, mouse-eared chickweed grew in the cracks of the walls, and lovely mosses and lichens flourished in the crevices. The apple tree grew scraggy and knuckled and produced few, and those mealy, apples. What can you do, dear Dorothy, except kneel down and implore the Lord in silence, implore him for the soul that seems, for how do we truly know, to have lost its way in the terrible grip of the world? I remember, a few short years ago, about a year after Daddy's death, I was in his old garden; it was April and the blossoms from the old plum tree were blowing about, everywhere; there were small snow-flurries of them and the grass lay like a memory of winter. I saw something sticking out of the ash-pit, an ugly old pit that seemed lovely for the moment because the plum blossoms covered it. It was the corner of some old full-colour photograph of perfect flowers, bright red with yellow stamens, impossible creatures, too exotic by far for our old country farm. Mother must have thrown them out, but she must have torn them apart, too, those old catalogues, in frustration or anger or a simple sense of loss, as if she had been tearing apart the illusions that had made his life so sorry, her own life so filled with sadness.'

She paused again, then sat down in the armchair beside the young girl.

'Forgive me, Dorothy, for going on like this. Why am I telling you all of it? Because, I think, I see something special in you, something in your eyes and demeanour that leads me to think that you are not of this world, that the world of peace and prayer and service may be where you will find fulfilment in your life. Remember the poem by Hopkins that I quoted: "I have desired to go where springs not fail ... And I have asked to be where no storms come"? Well, there will be storms, of course, but I promise you that there will not be disappointment. Give your life to the love of Jesus and there is no disappointment, no disillusions, only love, real love, and perpetual contentment. We carry about in us the living of the man Jesus and the eternity of the Lord Jesus, we know the tasks, the every-moment tasks that will help us to that love, we will not be overcome by the heaviness of the matter of our lives. We will not be like those, shoals and shoals of them, who drift through life with every violent current, turning and twisting while we are going nowhere. We will be "Where the green swell is in the havens dumb, and out of the swing of the sea".'

The sister's voice, in the slowly darkening room, had grown soft but thrilling in its intensity. Dorothy watched the pretty face with absolute awe; she longed, now, to be taken into the arms of this small nun, to know her fingers moving soothingly over her face, through her hair, along her body, those fingers that were fine and long and cared-for, unlike the rough and dirt-laden fingers and broken nails of PJ Hannafin. There was silence for a while. Dorothy stood up, slowly.

'Thank you, Sister Bernadette, thank you. Everything you have said is wonderful, and true. I know it. I think I have always known it, but you have made me certain. I want to be a nun. I want to be a Sister and to give my life for Jesus. I really want it.'

BODY OF THE BEAUTIFUL

It was May. Trees were standing astonished once again by their own maiden loveliness, the cherry tree, the chestnut, the oak. Patrick Brennan was happy. Today he had been to Sweeney's Stores to buy clothes for the scholasticate. It was Father Scott himself who had received a sum of money from the headmaster at St Canice's and had gone with Patrick to the stores. Now, packed away in a new suitcase, were two dark-coloured suits with long trousers, white shirts, black ties, and an assortment of socks and underwear. He would not stand out among the other scholars for his poverty and shabbiness. Soon he would finish in the 'small school', easy exams, and then a summer of preparation and excitement.

He stood in a small grove of fuchsia trees; he felt, for the first time in his life, complicit in the beauty and wonder of the world about him, he felt now, too, complicit in its rebirthing, its youthful greens, its budding. A blackbird came close to where he stood, calling with a harsh staccato anger, hesitant before its nest. The boy felt engaged with the world, with his grandfather, rest him, and with God. Freshness was the word that resonated in his mind. He came out to the edge of the grove; down across fields was the sea; he would miss it, of course, but he would be delving deeply into the knowledge that the world of men and women had accumulated down all the centuries; he would know everything, he would be a part of the changing and miraculous universe. For a while he watched a pair of goldfinch sifting for seeds amongst the dandelions and wild grasses, so beautiful they were, coloured with a generous and smiling brush, and he felt, somehow, complicit in that generosity, too. He knew that what would be asked of him would be a simple contemplation of this generosity, that he would make no demands of the world of the beautiful but accept the promises it made, the appeasement, eventually, of the hungers in his being, hungers he felt now that he was beginning to understand.

St Canice's was a grey, huge building. It stood far back from the road, behind a long row of sycamores. On either side of the road were fields, great meadows and trampled pasturelands. Behind the building Patrick could see playing fields, the high white poles of goalposts, the hanging nets of tennis courts. He was overwhelmed by the corridors, the staircases, the dorm-itories, the classrooms; he was small, he knew suddenly, very small and lost. His stomach churned and he felt no relief to see other boys as nervous and shaken as he was. They were all given supper in a huge refectory, the ordinary boarders to one side, the scholastics separated from them by a low, wooden partition. Patrick heard the boarders talk and shout to each other, a certain joy and familiarity in their voices. Many of the scholastics, already dressed in more sober, dark suits, were restrained and tense. Patrick was relieved when night prayers were said in the enormous chapel, prayers that ended with the singing of the 'Salve Regina' to the great thundering music of the organ, and at last he was shown through a long dormitory with separate cells divided by wooden partitions, into a smaller room where there were a dozen beds, without partitions.

'This is the new boys' dorm,' an older boy explained to them. 'After a few months some of you will be moved into the scholastics' dorm, with partitions and your own space, because some of the older men will be moving on to the seminary at Grange. But for the moment, find a bed for yourselves, put your stuff into the locker, your suitcase under the bed. Go to sleep, lights out in ten minutes, and the bell will waken you tomorrow at ten to seven.' He was grinning; he had been here a few years already; he was happy not to be in this dormitory any more, without privacy, among boys who were utter strangers. Patrick's heart was heavy. He moved carefully and found a bed not far from the archway that led back into the larger dormitory. He climbed into bed and lay awake for a long, long time.

The windows were high and large and without curtains. Uncertain September light kept the dormitory bathed in a faint glow, from moon, or stars, Patrick did not know. He heard shuffling and stirring from the others around him; he thought he heard sighs, and someone sobbing. Gradually the night darkened, gradually he began to doze. He slept, but the sleep was restless and he dreamt he was climbing through tunnels of trees and into sea-caves where everything was dark, where threatening figures loomed out of the branches and reached down from the dripping roofs. He tried to cry out, for help, but his throat would not sound. And then something enormous, black and white, like a bear, came crashing loudly through the fuchsia and rhododendron tunnels and a great black paw, the claws sharp and extended, began to reach for him. He woke, suddenly. He was sweating.

Patrick was cruelly at a loss when he woke. He was sitting on a hard, wooden floor, somewhere. He was in his pyjamas but he had a thin eiderdown wrapped about his body. He was leaning back against a wall and a pale light glimmered in on him from a high, uncurtained window. He found, too, that he was crying, softly, to himself. For a while he believed he was still in some strange dream; he had no idea where he was, nor even who he was. Only gradually did his awareness return; he was frightened and astonished to find himself in the large dormitory, with the separate cubicles, all of them with their curtains drawn across the entrances. He was at the other end of the college from his own small dormitory and he had no idea, except that he had walked in his sleep, how he had come there. For a moment, after he stood up, he felt like shouting for help. He stopped himself, in time. He gathered the eiderdown around his shivering body and tried to gauge the direction back to his own bed. Judging by the light of the quarter moon that was low on the sky, he began to move, very slowly, holding his body against the wall. When the darkness fell completely as a cloud came across the moon, he groped along with one hand in front of him, his body gliding against the wall. Eventually he reached a wall that came out at right angles; he turned along with the new wall and continued to move. He came to an opening. He paused. He had no idea if he was right or not. He waited. Soon the moon came out again, shedding the smallest light but sufficient to show him he was back at the archway into the small dormitory. With enormous relief he moved, quickly now, back into his own bed and lay down.

He was very cold, and very frightened. He felt, right now, that he might not be able to last long in this place. It was a world too different to the world he knew – everything was alien to him. He had never felt so alone in his life. Around him he could hear some of the others, restless too in their sleep. One of the boys was whimpering, softly, like a kitten lost under floor-boards. It was, strangely, a comfort to Patrick; at least he was not the only one disturbed by the night, the difference, the un-known. He sat up for a moment and reached to the small locker beside his bed; he had left his fob watch in such a way that he might be able to read the time from his bed, but it was too dark. He took the watch and tried to read it under the faintest of light still coming through the window but it was no good. For a moment he thought of Dorothy and the image of the girl, his friend, soothed him. He listened for a short while to the gentle ticking of the watch, then he left it back on the locker. Soon, he slept again, a deep, blank sleep, scarcely moving until the sudden shrill scream of the electric bell ripped him out of the bed into a dark morning. His new life had begun.

In the classroom, first year, Elements, Patrick found himself among some thirty other boys, several ordinary boarders, some three scholastics like himself, and a small handful of day pupils, local boys who went home in the afternoons. Each of them carried a bundle of books balanced on a thick slate. They placed the books on the desks before them. They waited.

Patrick was sitting towards the back, at the wall. Beside him was a plump boy still dressed in short trousers. Patrick was glad of his scholastic suit now, and proud of his shirt, his jacket and his black tie. He felt already advanced in the world. He just nodded at the plump boy and then glanced around at the rest of the class. They were all nervous and timid, touching their books, opening them desultorily, waiting.

Father MacShane was a big man. He came sweeping into the classroom, his long black gown like a trail of angry wind behind him.

'Stand up, all of you, when I come into the classroom!' he shouted.

The boys stood, terrified.

Father MacShane said a few quick prayers and the boys murmured 'Amen'. The priest slammed down a few books on his desk and turned back to the class. 'Sit!' he ordered, and they sat. Patrick felt at once that this was going to be difficult; he tried to cower even more into his seat, to hide. In front of him was one of the boys who had spent the night in the same dormitory as himself; he was a big boy, and Patrick could see that the sleeves of his new suit did not quite reach over the cuffs of his shirt. The back of his head was shaven; his hair had been cut by someone using a bowl and the black hair was tufted now into the shape of that bowl, giving the boy a sadly comic appearance. Patrick could see sweat already on the back of the boy's neck.

Father MacShane moved menacingly back and forth at the head of the class. He had fair hair, neatly arranged over a big, intent face, great bushy eyebrows shading sparkling grey eyes, freckles on the round face and a nose that was too large and suffering from tiny perforations. 'Latin!' he bellowed. 'We are going to begin Latin. You will love it. It is easy. This class is called Elements, Elements so it is, and we are only beginning. If you follow willingly and intelligently you will come with me into a great world of classical wonder and linguistic magic that will open up the whole of Europe to you. Europe, its history, its languages, French, Spanish, Italian, and on even into the bad English that you speak. It is the language of the Church, is Latin, so it is, and therefore it is a holy language and therefore this class is a sacred place and you are going to live in the blessed comfort of the Church. Are you with me, boys, are you with me?'

There was silence. Yet something had already stirred in Patrick's soul, some excitement he could scarcely comprehend. He could see the small and muddied pool before his house down at the shore, he could hear the angered muttering of his father and see the dark and unwholesome entranceway into the small house, he could hear the cries of hungry sheep in the small fields and the howling of the winds in off the Atlantic through the scrawny and arthritic limbs of the thorn bushes. He remembered how the mysteries of the Latin he had learned for responses to the Mass had intrigued him with their music and difference. And already this priest, this frightening, large man, had opened up archways that he said would lead them into worlds of magic and wonder.

'Right!' said Father MacShane sarcastically. 'I see we have a bunch of linguists here, linguists who do not know how to speak! But on we go, on we go, we'll see, boys, we'll see. Open up your book, your Latin grammar book and let us make a start. Page one, chapter one, the verb, to be. *Sum: es, est, sumus, estis, sunt …*'

The day passed in a haze of wonder for Patrick and one new subject shifted into another, one new teacher left and another came, the boys opened new and strange books, French, algebra, English, Irish, history, geography …

At supper all the scholastics were assigned specific tables and places and they were to retain these all through the year. Patrick found himself sitting beside the great big boy whose suit was just a little too small for him. William John Mills was his name and he shook hands awkwardly with Patrick. His eyes were glittering with tears already, his hand was a little sweaty, his black tie was askew and the top button of his shirt was open. But there was gentleness in his face and Patrick thought he had never seen eyes so dark, perhaps only in the eyes of exotic women he had seen in films.

There were ten of them, all first years, all dressed in their black suits, their black ties, their white shirts, all of them still feeling awkward and lost around the big table. The Brothers served them great plates of white bread, big dunted tin pots of tea, small pats of butter with the crest of the college on them, and then a dish with some streaky bacon and almost-burned mushrooms. William John Mills groaned when his plate was put in front of him.

'I'm ravenyous,' he said to Patrick. 'An' I hate muchrooms. I hate 'em.'

Smiling, Patrick lifted his bacon from his own plate onto Mills's, then scraped the burned mushrooms back onto his own plate. Mills's eyes brightened.

'Thanks, you're a butty,' he said.

After their supper they were all ushered out into a large quadrangle, bounded by the four high walls of the college, the buildings housing the boarders on three sides, the fourth that of the scholastics. They had a half hour to kill here and were expected to walk sedately around the gravel path of the quadrangle. William John and Patrick stayed close together.

'It's goin' to be not possible,' Mills said.

'What is?'

'This Latin, this French, all this stuff. It's awful hard, so it is.'

'Oh it's not, really,' Patrick answered enthusiastically. 'You see it's all linked up, I can already notice that. Like take *est* in Latin, for he is, and take *il est* in French, also for he is. I mean the *est* is the same except in French it's a different pronunciation, but the word is the same. And *sumus* in Latin means we are and in French it's *nous sommes*. *Sommes*, *sumus*, almost the same. You can hop from one to the other and see how they link. I think it's exciting.'

Mills looked at him; he was taller than Patrick and much bigger.

'Maybe you're a lot brighter nor me,' he said. 'I never noticed any of that.'

'I'll help you, I'll be delighted to help you. Maybe we can do some study together. And you can help me with the algebra, I saw that you were good at that.'

'Yes, I was, wasn't I? It's just that name, algebra, I know the stuff, I think it's simple, but it's the name.'

'So!' Patrick stopped in his walking. 'Have we a treaty, man? Me Buffalo Bill, you Big Chief Muchum Eatum, let's have a treaty, let's help each other, you big algebra man, me big Latin man. OK?'

William John Mills stopped too; he looked at Patrick and
grinned. His face was lit up now with some pleasure. They
shook hands, laughing. A bell rang for prayers in the big chapel.
After that there would be an hour in the study and Patrick was
already eager to go back over the wonders he had been
introduced to during the day. Then there would be night
prayers and they would file up quietly to the dormitories. He
believed he would sleep well tonight.

'Now, I want the present tense of the verb to be. Rattle it out
for me. You boy …' and Father MacShane pointed to some boy
towards the front of the class. Patrick's head was held high; he
longed to be asked; he longed to display how excited he was by
this new learning, how the universe was suddenly a miracle in
his eyes, how he was diving into its mysteries with great hope.
The tall boy in front stood up and rattled off the tense and was
duly praised. Father MacShane did not ask Patrick to recite
anything, not yet. They began a reader and again Patrick's heart
leaped with excitement as he was able, almost at once, to
decipher what was going on. The priest read out loud:
  '*Julia puella parva est* …' He stopped and looked out over the
class. He spotted Patrick's eager face. 'Well, you boy, with the
big open eyes, what do you think that means?'
  'Julia is a small girl, Father.'
  'Excellent, excellent. Now, that leads me to explain
something to you. Adjectives. Small is an adjective. *Parva* is an
adjective. An adjective, so it is. But because it's beside a
feminine noun, girl, *puella*, *parva* too must be made feminine. In
Latin, that is, of course.'
  It was clear to Patrick. He glanced over at the puzzled face of
William John Mills. He was shaking his big head from side to
side, slowly. The priest noticed him.
  'You boy, big boy, you seem puzzled. What's the worry,
boy?'
  William John looked over first at Patrick, then stood up.
  'Sorry, Father, I don't know what an adjective is.'
  There was a rustling sound about the class, like a small

breeze touching across a poplar copse. William John blushed beetroot-red.

'What's your name, boy?'

'William John Mills, Father.'

'William John Mills. Hello, William John Mills. Willy Milly.' There was a sniggering among the boys. 'And can you recite for me the present tense of the verb to be, Willy Milly? Or, let us say, Willy Nilly, shall we? The verb to be, you can say it for me, can't you?'

'Yes, Father,' and William John did so. Correctly. For a moment Father MacShane appeared disappointed but he proceeded to explain what an adjective was.

Patrick was slightly hurt that the priest had fixed a silly name on his friend. He was hurt, too, that the other boys had laughed. He knew the name would stick. He knew his friend would be saddened and humiliated by it. He put his head down over the book.

The next day, Father MacShane picked on William John once more. He asked him to recite by heart the first three lines of the text, beginning '*Julia* ...' William John struggled through the lines, mispronouncing many of the words, but he got to the end of it. Father MacShane then asked him to translate what he had learned by heart. William John began: 'Julia is a small girl, Father.'

'A small girl Father?' Father MacShane laughed. 'What, may I ask, Willy Nilly, is a small girl Father?'

'I meant a small girl, and then I just said Father, Father.'

'Are you teasing me, Willy Nilly?'

'No, Father.'

'Go on.'

'Julia is a small girl. She is a ... she ... Sorry, Father, I couldn't understand the rest of it.'

Father MacShane seemed pleased.

'My dear Willy Nilly,' he began in a reasoning, gentle tone of voice. 'You must keep up with the rest of us, you know, we cannot lose you, you cannot be left behind. You, dear boy, are a scholastic. You will go on to be a priest, God help us, just like me, God help me. So, you must know your Latin through and through. Now, I am going to show you how I make sure that scholastics keep up with everybody else. And watch!' he shouted suddenly and gazed around at all the other boys. 'Watch what I do to make sure. Willy Nilly, come up here, please.'

William John left his desk, his face wearing a stunned look. Father MacShane turned to the blackboard and picked up the duster that lay on the ledge. He stood the big boy in front of him, took the boy's left hand and turned it over, bunching up the hand so the knuckles offered a small, pale area. Then he wrapped down hard on the knuckles with the wooden back of the duster. There was a horrible sound of wood against bone. William John looked up at the priest in astonishment.

'Now, boy, there you go. That's to remind you that you are going to be a priest, so you are, and that your Latin is a very special gift you must gather up into that fine head of yours. Back you go now, and down you sit.'

William John gazed down for a moment at his knuckles, then up again at the priest's face. He looked for a moment at the boys who sat stunned and silent before him. Then he went back quietly to his place.

Patrick held his head down over his book. '*Julia puella parva est* ...' he read, over and over again.

In the yard that evening, there was a game of football with goalposts chalked up against the gable wall. There was screeching and yelling from the older boys. Patrick and William John and several of the first-year boys, still awed and hesitant in this strange new world that was yet grey and louring over them, stood apart, hands in their pockets, shoes idly kicking at loose stones, their conversation desultory, their eyes still furtive and scared.

'Did it hurt?' Patrick asked.

William John laughed.

'No, not a wee bit. But it was the shock of it, and the sound of it, that crack. And when I looked down at my knuckles they were red. No, it didn't hurt. It was weird. But I've been learning that stuff about bloody Julia, I'll tell you that.'

Just then they saw Father MacShane making his way towards them. He looked big, here too, in their yard, his black soutane floating against the wind, his shock of straw-coloured hair blowing wildly. He settled the small cape about his shoulders and came straight in amongst the new boys.

'Now lads,' he began, his voice gruff and filled with bonhomie. 'This is something I do every week, only for the first-year boys. That's all. To help you along. You know.'

They looked at him suspiciously. His face seemed much gentler now, even kind. He reached into some pocket deep inside his soutane and took out a small, red, leather-covered notebook.

'Now, I will take orders. You'll pay me when I come back, tomorrow evening. Here, same time. Anything you want me to buy for you, in town, I mean. The boarders will have their town leave on holidays, but you scholastics, you won't get into town, except when there's a match on. So this is your chance to buy. Whatever you want. Tell me now. I'll write it here, your name, your wishes. I'm like the good genie out of the lamp, so I am. Just try me.'

He held a small pencil poised over the page. Nobody spoke.

'Nobody wants anything, then? Well, here we go. I always suggest some Tiger Balm. Who'd like some Tiger Balm?'

They looked blank. Nobody spoke.

'Tiger Balm? Is that what you asked me? What is Tiger Balm?' He was laughing heartily.

'Well,' he went on. 'Tiger Balm comes in a small tin, and it's a balm. A salve. An ointment. It smells great. There's camphor in it, menthol, olive oil. You rub it on and it soothes your aches and pains. It's true. And it warms you up, so it does. And it smells so good. For instance, where's William John? Ah, there you are. For instance, you get a wallop from the duster and then you rub in Tiger Balm and you feel better all at once. And let me tell you boys, once and for all, come, lean in …' He leaned in towards the group of boys conspiratorially, glanced around to see who was listening, and smiled. The boys began to come closer around him. 'There's Father Michael Erraught now. He's the Dean of Studies, you see. And in class, I don't know if it's happened yet, when you misbehave or don't know your lessons, you get a docket. Right?'

One of the boys, a small, wiry boy with his tie wholly askew, was nodding furiously.

'Yes, yes, I got a docket already. From Father Beaver. And there was a big two written on it. I had to bring it to Rat … I mean to Father Erraught. And he gave me two slaps. With a leather. And it hurt. My God, it hurt.'

'Right, that's it. Good lad. That's the way. That's his job, he's like the executioner, he has this pandy, and he hands out the punishment we teachers think you deserve. And it hurts. It stings, so it does. The pandy is a rough lad, he's sharp, he's mean, he cuts. And this is where Tiger Balm comes in. It soothes. Have it in your pocket, boys, rub it on, no, rub it in, well before you visit Father Erraught, rub it in so he won't see it, and then rub it on after, and I promise you, you'll feel better, quick.'

The boys looked at him in astonishment. They looked at one another. Father MacShane grinned at them. 'Well?' he said.

William John Mills suddenly asked him: 'Could you get me a Crispin, Father?'

'A Crispin, Willy Nilly. Now what would that be?'

'It's a biscuit, Father,' the boy answered excitedly. 'A biscuit, with chocolate. I can't get them, and I love them.'

'I've the order written down, Willy Nilly, and I'll find them for you, you can be sure.'

William John grinned happily, even proudly.

Someone else began shouting, 'For me, liquorice allsorts, Father, and bulls' eyes.'

'I'd like to order a box of nougat, Father, them ones with the paper on them, that you can eat.'

'You can eat the paper, too, yes, yes, I know those …'

He wrote down the orders, the wish list, and the names of the boys that went with each. Patrick said he would like to get the Tiger Balm.

Father MacShane looked at him. 'You're a good student, Patrick, you will not need it, I hope.' And the priest laughed. In Patrick's mind the crack of the duster on William John's knuckles still sounded, and the sound hurt him. He pushed for his order. And he had also seen the big, proud-looking and aristocratic Father Erraught. He had a dread of that pandy, he feared physical suffering. He would be prepared. Father MacShane left them and headed back into the bowels of the college. The boys were excited and for the first time they felt that perhaps, just perhaps, they had somebody big and important on their side. 'He's a bear,' one of them said. 'He's a big panda bear,' Patrick added, 'a big soft panda bear, coloured black and white.'

Every Saturday morning the scholastics had to sit an examination in one of their subjects. The examination lasted an hour and a half, from eleven o'clock until 12.30. The papers were taken up and results were read out in class on Monday or Tuesday. During the class for the subject just examined, the door would open unceremoniously and Father Erraught would enter, nod to the teacher and turn to the class. The Dean of Studies was a tall, erect man, middle-aged, heavy with the importance of his position, inclined to suspect the pupils of wrongdoing and keen to maintain the strictest discipline that would enable him to stand tall, remote and feared. He was strongly built; his grey hair was softly curled, parted in the middle and he wore slightly tinted spectacles that did not allow the boys to know exactly where he was looking. He kept his left hand always inside his soutane, up at the height of his chest, where the pandybat was kept waiting. He held the results sheet in his right hand. He paused, sensing the dread that lurked in the small bodies before him.

'I have here the results of your examination in Latin, and Father MacShane expresses himself quite satisfied with your work. But that is not how I see it, gentlemen, that is not how I see it. There are four failures here, four boys with marks under forty percent. That will not do, gentlemen, that will not do at all. And those four boys will follow me out of this classroom when I leave.'

There was a dreadful silence. Father MacShane stood at the

blackboard, his eyes on the floor. Father Erraught paused dramatically, then lifted the scroll and glanced at it.

'First place, with one hundred marks, Patrick Joseph Brennan. Well done, sir. Come up and collect your card.'

Patrick's whole body relaxed; he had sat stiff and terrified although he knew he had answered the questions well. He got up and approached the priest. Father Erraught nodded haughtily towards him and handed him a card. The priest nodded again and Patrick returned to his seat. It was a finely printed card, gilt-edged, coloured red and on it was the college crest, his name, the subject, the date, and the mark, with a big First Place printed on it, and red Celtic patterns inscribed in each corner.

'You will keep these cards safe,' the Dean of Studies said. 'You will either send them home, or keep them to show your parents during holidays. They are a record of your achievement. They are a reward for work well done. Second place, with a mark of eighty-three, goes to James Rotherham. Mr Rotherham, well done, but I shall expect a little higher next time ...' James collected his card; it was blue, for second place. The third place card was green, and the mark allotted was seventy-two. Patrick was aware how quickly the marks were falling towards the failure mark.

The four boys who failed had to stand and listen to a tirade from the Dean. Amongst them was William John Mills whose total had come to thirty-five marks. Patrick glanced at Father MacShane; surely he could have given the boy a few extra marks, to save him. William John stood, his hands gripping the edge of the desk, his head hanging low. The Dean told them that it was a disgrace that they, and in particular those privileged to be scholastics and hoping one day to be priests in the service of the Church, could not even pass their easy Latin examination. Did they think they were on holidays here? What? What? What? Did they think that Father MacShane was simply passing the time of day with them? Did they? Did they? What were they thinking of? Gentlemen! Gentlemen! Were they reading the *Beano* during study hours? 'What were you doing, Mr Mills, during your hours of study? Were you chewing gum, sir? Were you dreaming?'

There was no answer. The boy kept his head low. His face was pale. Patrick could see the knuckles against the desk were very white.

The priest quickly turned on his heels and went out of the classroom, leaving the door open after him. There was silence and hesitation. Father MacShane beckoned to the four boys who had failed to go out after the Dean. They went out, some of them trying to warm their hands under their jackets, some rubbing their hands hard together, to warm them. As they passed by him, Father MacShane whispered, 'Don't forget the Tiger Balm, boys. Hurry back.' William John, the last out of the door, turned and grimaced towards the boys who were left behind. He closed the door softly after him. There was silence.

The boys remaining in the class listened intently, while Father MacShane began to talk about the accusative case. But he spoke softly; he was watching, and listening, too. Then they heard them: two loud slaps, leather hitting flesh not far away, outside the classroom door. Four times they heard the slaps, and they winced each time, several of them rubbing their palms together, unconsciously. The door opened and the four boys filed back in, quietened, without looking about them. They went straight back to their desks and sat down. Father MacShane said nothing; the four boys bent forward over their desks, but it was clear that they were hugging their hands against their bodies, trying to ease away the sting. Patrick looked over at William John; there were a few tears on his cheeks, his teeth were clenched together. Patrick glanced up at Father MacShane, who nodded at him, and Patrick drew out the little tin of Tiger Balm and handed it across. Soon the tin had been passed among the boys, Father MacShane kindly turning his back to write something on the blackboard. A rich scent of camphor, menthol, of healing, soon pervaded the room. When William John handed back the tin he grinned at Patrick and nodded. It helped, it definitely helped.

Over the next five weeks Patrick came first in every subject and never fell below ninety-five percent on any paper. He worked hard to help William John Mills whose marks improved a little, sufficiently for him to avoid further contact with the pandy. On the first Monday in November, the days darkening and the world falling drawky under its dampness, the lights had to be put on in the classroom. Father Erraught, 'The Rat', walked into the classroom in his usual domineering and challenging way. The subject had been French, and Patrick and William John had spent several hours together, going over the work, preparing the verbs, the vocabulary, the tenses. William John was confident.

'First place,' the big priest began, 'well, I am getting fed up of this.' He grinned, but his grin was still cold and threatening. 'First place, Patrick Joseph Brennan. One hundred percent. Mr Brennan, your card, but I have something else I want to say to you. Come with me, please, after I leave the classroom.' Patrick collected his card and returned to his seat, his whole being filling up suddenly with dread. What could it be? Had he done something he was not aware of? Had somebody reported him for something? There were three boys who had failed this time, two of them having failed several other examinations before.

'You three boys will also follow me out of the classroom,' The Rat said, his face severe. 'And you, Mr Ryan, and you, Mr Sheehan, both of you have now failed far too often. It appears to me that you are not putting your heart into it. I will have to give you a stronger hint, I'm afraid. Don't you think so, Father O'Regan?' and he turned to the teacher of French.

'Ah, Father Erraught, some of these boys think they can pick up French simply by eating chocolate in class. I found two of them chewing chocolate biscuits. Not these two, mind you, two others. But these two, ach! They do not appear to be bothering at all.'

'And who, Father, has been eating chocolate biscuits in class?' Father Erraught asked.

'Well now, interesting, isn't it? One of them is William John Mills, Willy Nilly, I believe he's called. But I have to say he has been improving, his homework has steadily got better, neater, more accurate. And the other boy, ach! I hesitate to say it, the other boy is Patrick Brennan. And I feel that perhaps this time, seeing as how the two boys have worked so well this week, we might forget the facts, Father Erraught, don't you think so?'

Patrick glanced over at William John who had blanched, his hands already moving down on his knees, beginning to rub himself warm. Patrick's stomach began to churn, so, this was it, eating Crispins in class. Yes, he was guilty. And yes, it was William John who had given them to him, in his gratitude, in friendship. Father Erraught hesitated. He glanced at the two boys.

'I'm surprised, Father, very surprised. Don't we feed these boys well enough? Eh? Eh? Well, Mr Brennan, are you hungry in class? Tell me, sir, don't you eat your breakfast?'

Patrick stood up in his desk. The Dean was still smiling. 'I'm sorry Father, yes, I eat breakfast ...'

'All right, sir, all right,' the Dean said impatiently. He turned to leave the class. The three boys who had failed stood up to follow him. Patrick stepped out from his desk. The Dean turned back a moment.

'Oh Mr Mills, you must come with me, please.'

William John looked distraught, but he stood up, too. They trooped out after the priest.

In the corridor outside the classroom Father Erraught paused. The boys gathered together in a line against the wall of the classroom. The Dean put the exam results sheet in a pocket inside his soutane and in the same easy movement drew out the pandy. Patrick shuddered.

The Dean beckoned to the first boy who came forward, his right hand stretched out. The Dean slapped each hand, twice, with the leather. Four slaps. The boy winced at each blow. So did Patrick. 'Next!' the Dean said. The second boy came forward and was given two slaps on each hand, and the third boy suffered the same. Patrick was shivering with fear and he hated himself for doing so. He must overcome this dread. The three boys went back into the classroom, their hands held fiercely against their chests.

'Now Mr Mills,' the Dean said, grinning at the big boy. 'Eating in class. Just about scraping through your examination. What kind of place do you think we have here, eh? Butlin's holiday camp? What?'

William John did not reply. He held out his right hand. The Dean raised the pandy and brought it down, twice, viciously on the boy's hand. 'Left!' said the Dean and William John held out his left hand and was given two more slaps. Patrick was utterly dismayed. The sound of the pandy against the flesh echoed loudly in the corridor. The Dean held himself erect, haughty, cool. William John brought his two hands to his mouth and began to blow onto them. He turned, glancing quickly towards Patrick, then went back to class. The Dean turned with a small smile towards Patrick, then moved down the corridor towards the office that was at the end of the long hall. Patrick followed, terrified.

The Dean's office was small; it was crammed with books but there was a large desk against one of the walls, an armchair against the far side of the desk, and a small wooden chair this side. The Dean went round behind his desk and left the exam results paper in a drawer in the desk. He nodded to Patrick to close the door. The office was small and very intimate with the door closed. The Dean sat in his armchair behind his desk. 'Sit, Mr Brennan, sit!' he said.

Patrick sat on the very edge of the hard wooden chair. The Dean grinned at him. Patrick noticed how the priest's hair was grey with streaks of the original black here and there, how it was neatly ordered in small curls across his head, distinguished looking; he saw, too, how the Dean's face was red from the pandy exertions. The Dean picked up a paper from his desk.

'I have here your exam results since you came to St Canice's, Mr Patrick Joseph Brennan,' he began, his voice gentle. 'And I have spoken to all your teachers. We are agreed. You are wasting your time in Elements. I intend to move you, at once, up to the second classes, we call them Rudiments. You will begin on Monday next, is that clear?'

Patrick gazed at him in wonder. 'Yes, Father,' he said, but he was far from sure.

'You will move into Father Beamish's English class first thing on Monday morning next. I will be coming in with the results of this weekend's English examination for that class. You will not, of course, take that examination, you will continue to take this final examination in your old class, in Elements. But after that you will be expected to continue your hard work in the new class. Is that clear?' Patrick nodded. 'It will be difficult, for a while, you will have to catch up. But you will catch up, we have no doubt of it. Well done, boy, well done. You have saved yourself, and your father, and,' he glanced a moment at the paper in front of him, 'you have done Father Scott, in your home parish, proud. It was he who urged us to take you on as a scholar. He was right, Mr Brennan, he was right.'

The Dean stood up. Patrick leaped to attention. The big priest came round the desk, stretched out his hand and Patrick shook it. It was hot and firm, but Patrick smiled with satisfaction. A whole year saved. A new class already. It was wonderful. A challenge. But a triumph, too. He thought at once of Dolly, the satisfaction he would have in telling her how he had got on, when he went home for Christmas. He gave a small skip of satisfaction as he went back up the corridor towards his old class. As he came near the door he glanced back down the corridor; the Dean of Studies was standing outside his office, watching him, his hands behind his back. He stood tall and sphinx-like, there, in the near darkness of the corridor's end, a frightening figure, Patrick thought, and he shivered with a small exultation that he had escaped. And then a hard thought struck the boy; he had been found eating in class, along with William John Mills; the bigger boy had been punished and Patrick had not. It was not just. Perhaps the Dean of Studies had simply forgotten. Patrick turned and walked slowly back towards the Dean's office, his head low. He stood a moment before the priest, then looked up at him and said, his voice trembling:

'I think, Father, you have forgotten that I, too, was eating in class. Along with William John Mills. I, too, ought to be punished.' And he held out his right hand.

The priest laughed aloud. 'Well, well, well, I think this is the first time a student has volunteered for punishment. You are a fool, sir, a fool. You have been singled out for your application to your studies; we reward application, we do not punish application. I, and Father O'Regan too, decided you were merely helping out the thick boy. We shall overlook the misdemeanour, this time, sir, this time. Now clear off out of my sight and do not be found wanting a second time!' The priest turned away sharply, went back into his office and shut the door.

'The body parts,' the Rudiments science teacher was saying, 'I will name them, and you will learn what they are. We will picture them, we will put them together. Like taking a bicycle apart, the wheels, the saddle, the ball bearings, the nuts, the oil, and we will spread them out before us. And we will name each part and find where it goes and what its function is in the whole. Are you with me, Mr Brennan?' he asked suddenly.

Patrick was sitting at the very back of the new classroom. He had a whole new set of books. He was, as yet, confused.

'Yes, sir,' he answered, cautiously. Mr Jack O'Shea was a lay teacher, small and vole-like, his nose long and sharp, hairs peering out of that nose, long loose strands of hair drawn across a bald skull. Patrick had taken a dislike to the man, though he did not yet know him. 'Jacko,' he was called, and he held his class taut in expectation of punishment and sarcasm.

'Good, Mr Brennan, good,' Jacko went on. 'Nice to know that you will catch up to the rest of us, who are so stupid it took us more than a full year to get here. But you came leaping in, didn't you? Oh yes, some boys can get away with murder. Our own Dean of Studies must have taken to you, what? A boy from the island, of course, the seaweed in his ears, what?'

The other boys in the classroom snickered. Patrick flinched.

'I will name the bones, I will point out the skull, the skull, that dry and ugly bone left over when the flesh falls off and the brains fall out, and I will show you the jugular notch, the costal cartilage, oh yes this is English, boys, and I challenge you all to know the language. The language of the bones, and all the linked and linking parts, the femur, pelvis, fibula, the metatarsal bones. And then there are the muscles, the blood cells, and the brain itself … Where is your brain, Mr White?' and Jacko made a sudden lunge towards a boy who was gazing abstractedly towards a window.

'Eh, my brain, sir?'

Jacko took the boy by the ear and half dragged him out of his desk. 'Your brain, boy, yes, your brain. You are called Mr White, are you not? Have you a white brain, boy? Is it white? Or were you looking at something special out there, outside our window? Tell us, tell the class what you were smirking at.'

'Nothing, sir, I was thinking, sir, that's all, about what you were saying.'

'You were thinking, were you, Mr White? Too much effort for you, I'd say. What were you thinking about, if I may ask? Tell me what I was talking about, do.' He kept hold of the boy's ear which had turned very red under the pressure.

'Em, you were talking about the bones, sir.'

'Good. Good. What bones? Name some.'

There was a pause. 'The elbow, sir, the finger-bones.'

'Hah!' shouted Jacko with some satisfaction. 'I thought so. Not listening. Thinking about some girl out in the city, eh?'

'No sir, no sir.'

Jack released the boy, went back to the teacher's desk, took up the punishment notebook and began writing out a docket for the Dean of Studies. He handed it to White. Every afternoon, after classes were over, all the boys with such dockets had to report to the Dean of Studies to receive the number of slaps written on the docket. The next day, the docket, stamped, would have to be handed back to the teacher.

'Proof, boys,' Jacko went on in his acid voice. 'Proof that even if you have all the bones and the flesh and the blood in the one place at the one time, you will not necessarily have a person. Like Mr White, he's there, but he's not *there*. Ha, ha, ha!'

There was no answering snicker from the class.

'If you put all the bicycle parts down on the table in front of you, spread them out, you have not got a bicycle. Right. So, it is not bones and flesh and blood cells that make a person. Let's take music. Let's take Mozart. You can take each individual note he wrote down in one of his symphonies. I don't know, let's say three hundred thousand different notes. You can say how far one note is from the next; you can count all the marks he made on the paper, you can see his individual scrawl. But you cannot hear the music until it is all played and put together. The orchestra, the conductor, together they will draw the music out, by rehearsing it, over and over until they capture what the notes say. The music. And that is our world, boys, that is the world of science. We must know the individual parts of our world, but we will not be any the wiser until we fit it all together. Until you learn, you troop of idlers you, until you learn!'

Patrick was moved by Jacko's words, but he was scared of the man. That evening he studied hard, science was a new subject for him, and he loved it, even before he dipped his toe into it. And afterwards, in the yard, he spoke with excitement to William John Mills. The latter walked slowly along beside Patrick, hands in his pockets, head down. 'It's an exciting and a beautiful world, William John. It really is. And I am going to figure it out. I am going to learn everything about it. It is God's creation, don't you see? And when you know the creation then you will know God. It's clear. It's wonderful.'

William John held up his two hands before his face. That day he had been given four more slaps of the pandy and his hands were still red and sore-looking.

'I'm no good at learning, Patrick,' he said. 'I'm just not bright. And I can't keep things in my head. So I get biffed all the time. The world is not wonderful for me. Not the world in this place, at least.'

'But you do want to go on and be a priest, don't you?'

'I used to. But when I see people like Ratty, like Hairy Harry and Smelly Sammy, and they're supposed to be priests, then I'm not sure I want to be like them.'

'No, but you can be like yourself, William John. And you're kind and gentle and good to other people. And I'll keep helping you as much as I can.'

'You've already gone far ahead of me, I can't keep up. And I've used up all your Tiger Balm already, and Father MacShane is going to get me more, instead of Crispins, I have to keep buying the Tiger Balm.'

The big boy's face looked so glum that Patrick had to laugh.

William John laughed, too, and for a moment a brighter light seemed to shine in the grey, walled-in yard.

At the end of term two leaders from each class were brought on an outing. Even though he was scarcely six weeks in his new class, Patrick was chosen as one of the leaders in Rudiments. The twelve boys, from Elements right through to the sixth year, Rhetoric, were taken first into the priests' quarters for a 'feed'. They were brought into the parlour with its polished floor, its high windows, great leather armchairs around the walls, fine high-backed chairs set around a gleaming mahogany table; there were sideboards, great bulked ones and they were covered with food, cakes, jellies, fruit, even chocolate bars. Quietly, when none of the priests were in the room with them, Patrick pocketed four Crispin bars to bring to William John.

After the meal they were taken into town by three of the priests, Father Cusack, a small, baldy-headed man with a kind face, Father Holohan, also small and thin, with a cruel-looking face and tiny, thin lips; and Father McAdoo, an elderly man, the music teacher, whose soutane was deeply soiled by years of chalk-dust and unthinking dribbling of food. They were brought to a concert hall and had to listen to a real orchestra playing real music. Several of the boys grumbled at this 'reward' but Patrick was overwhelmed by the size of the hall, its comfort, and by the people of the town, so many of them dressed in suits and fine frocks and all talking animatedly together. All the members of the orchestra were gleaming in black suits or dresses, the men with white shirts and dickey bows, the women with elegant flowing sleeves. More panda bears, the boy thought to himself, and giggled. Patrick was stunned by the shifting and noise of preparation until somebody played a note and all the instruments began to search through the air to find that same note. Then the orchestra held the note for a long time, the people settling expectantly. There was silence. A door opened at the side of the stage and the conductor appeared, a small white baton in his hands that he held as if it were one of his fingers. There was great applause. The music began and

Patrick was again carried away into a world of wonder and beauty that he had never even dreamed of.

It was Beethoven's violin concerto. Father McAdoo was sitting in front of Patrick and he could see the old man shake with pleasure. There was dandruff down the back of his soutane and Patrick could see the rough hairs on the back of his neck but he knew that the priest, too, was thrilled to be there. Patrick felt exalted as the violin burst into sound. The soloist was a small, stocky man, with a moustache hanging down either side of his mouth. His hair was unkempt and blew about his head in the excitement of the playing. He stood waiting while the orchestra built up the music at the start of the concerto. The lights had dimmed in the hall but were bright on the orchestra and the soloist. His eyes closed, he played, swaying to the music as if he were on the deck of a ship on the rough seas, his face moving with concentration, his lips stirring as if he were mouthing words to his violin, sweat appearing on his brow, moving down his cheeks, but the music! the music seemed to rise out of the floor of the hall, to pour in from the walls and to drop from the ceiling and it hauled Patrick up out of his everyday living into somewhere else he had never been before. The rock face of the violinist, his unprepossessing figure and stance, the stumpy fingers that seemed to move like flames over the strings of the violin, all of that together with a sadness on the soloist's face made Patrick sit uncertain before what was expected of him, unsure how to respond to the surge of emotion within him, but soon he simply gave himself to the evening, to the awesome power of the music, to a sense that the whole of life was in harmony behind the individual with the violin, there was intelligence there, and it was there, Patrick felt, as the music seemed to send a cold shiver up and down his spine, it was there that God resided and it was there where he and all the audience, even the orchestra players and the conductor, had no right to be, they were interlopers on a world that was almost too beautiful to bear, on a world that was demanding, lovely beyond belief, striking until it was almost unbearable.

At the end of the playing the soloist stood, as if exhausted, as if he had been swimming against a fierce current and had at last reached shore. The audience burst into wild applause and many of them stood up, to clap the louder, to cheer, to call ... Patrick, too, stood up and applauded but he felt wholly weary, incapable of speaking, tired past anything he had known before and yet exalted, taken out of himself into a world far too great for his keeping, far too wonderful for his small shoulders to carry. He grew ever more determined, deep down inside himself, to bear witness to the greatness and the wonder of that world.

It was Christmas. Patrick was happy to be home again. His mother greeted him with tears, holding him back from her and gazing at him with pride, the suit, the shirt and tie, how he had grown, was he happy? How was he doing? Were the boys nice? Oh and she wanted all the answers at once, and she wanted all the answers to be positive. She would have a son a priest, and what was there greater in the life of a household than to have a son a priest. She ushered him into the kitchen; she sat him down at the table; she served him at once a meal of boxty bread where the butter oozed and spread under a sprinkling of parsley; she served him rashers of bacon and home-made blood puddings, she served him her own brown soda bread and a great mug of tea. Patrick's father sat quietly, though he had welcomed home his son, shaking his hand as if he were a stranger, shy of him, and uncertain. Patrick told them of his friends, of the priests, of how soon he had moved from the first class into the second, how that would mean he would be finished in the scholasticate a year sooner than expected and that Father Scott would be proud of him. He would move on, then, to the seminary, and start the courses that would lead to his ordination.

'Only,' his mother breathed with tense enthusiasm and expectation, 'only to live that long, that's all, only to live to see my own boy say Mass, above there in our own chapel, and all the neighbours crowding in to see and hear him, my own boy, my Patrick. Please God spare me. And your father, too, your father, too.'

'Aye, aye,' his father answered from the fireside chair, 'that would be a day, rightly.'

Patrick was happy to be back in his own familiar room that evening. He had drawn back the curtains and set a lighted candle carefully on the windowsill where it would stay lit until it went out by itself, it would welcome the coming of the Child on this sacred night. Patrick stood in the dim light of the candle and gazed out the window, watching the stars shining over the sea, stars that appeared close but sharp and very, very cold. He thought, too, of William John Mills, how he was missing him from the classroom, how he looked forward to spending the evenings with him in the yard, and then, quite suddenly, he thought of Dolly Lohan and his heart lurched strangely within him. He undressed slowly and climbed into the bed. His mother had placed a hot water bottle between the sheets and Patrick, as he prayed silently before sleep, offered up a very special prayer for her. He looked forward to meeting Dolly at Mass the next day, Christmas Day, he looked forward to telling her of St Canice's, he looked forward to telling her how he had already skipped a year, he saw himself standing outside the old chapel, looking fine in his suit and shirt and tie, talking to her, talking to Dolly.

Christmas morning dawned with a strange brightness. He got out of bed quickly and fell to his knees on the cold, cement floor. The Christmas Mass would be early; he hurried to dress, brushing any dust from his suit, straightening the tie and ensuring that the shirt was properly buttoned, the collar neat about the tie. There would be no breakfast until they came back from Mass. His mother was already waiting for him, her heavy long black coat buttoned to her throat, a woollen scarf, dark red with yellow flowers, on her head. She was smiling, her face was red with delight and a scarcely contained excitement; her breath formed tiny clouds in the chilled air. There had been snow; it would be a white Christmas. Together Patrick and his mother headed out into the yard; his father would not go to Christmas Mass, too much fuss, he would complain, too much fuss; he would stay at home and prepare the goose for the day's feasting.

There was snow crowded against the fences and blown in under the stems of the hedgerows. The fields were scattered with snow that had caught in clumps of scutch grass and rushes. It was very cold, but it was a clean coldness, the sky a lovely blue with seagulls almost transparent circling high up against the brightness. He stood awhile beside his mother as they inhaled the sharpness of the morning into their lungs. A small breeze stirred along the hedge tops. The snow had made the angular bleakness of the yard appear lovely for the moment but Patrick was unaware that the sharp frost had made the path dangerous. He moved ahead quickly, his boots scattering sparks off the stones of the roadway. His mother moved cautiously in her heavy coat and scarf. She turned for a moment to look out over the sea and slipped on a patch of ice over one of the water-holes on the road, and she fell with a small cry, as of a tiny furred body caught in the teeth of pain. It was the sound her body made against the ground, that thump against the hard earth along with the cry that entered into Patrick's soul and made him shiver with a kind of world-sadness he would never after be able to shake off.

He hurried back to her; she lay, as if she would lie forever, as if suddenly she knew herself worn out by her living, and hurt beyond healing. Her face was white, her eyes watched up at him, and she appeared vulnerable and bleak in the awareness of flesh and of the fleshly consequences of human ageing. He was too young yet to comfort her and by the time he would be old enough to have true words of comfort, he could find no words with which to soothe his own spirit. He helped her off the earth; she was more heavy than he could have believed. She limped, slowly, leaning on him, and they went back into the house. His father was still in bed, so he sat her down by the fireplace and worked to get the fire into a blaze. She sat, in coat and hat, in her blackness and her silence and her hurt, and already a strange doubt and anger had forced its way into Patrick's life.

It was Saturday morning. The final term of Patrick's third year in the college was already drawing to a close. The scholastics were in the study, taking their weekly examination, this week it was English. Their papers were handed out. Father O'Brien was supervising; he was a wide priest, squat and heavy, his hair was the colour of straw and he was continually drawing out a handkerchief to blow his nose, which he did quite loudly. When he supervised their examinations he spent most of the time walking up and down between the rows of desks, glancing down at the work, sometimes twirling about suddenly and turning back, hoping to catch somebody copying. But because of the small squeaking of his shoes under his weight, and because of his habit of blowing his nose, the boys generally knew where he was.

In another three weeks the public examinations would come; the boys were already getting nervous, it was essential to pass these so that you could move forward into the final two years. Patrick had his head down over his paper. He was writing furiously. Suddenly he heard a bang and he looked up. Father O'Brien was standing by the desk of William John Mills. He had just banged his open hand down on the answer paper before him and had lifted, with his other hand, a small slip of paper. He held it up before everybody.

'Mr Mills has been copying out a poem, I am sorry to say,' the priest spoke out loud, addressing the hall. The boys knew he was not sorry at all. 'This is cheating. We cannot have cheating, especially amongst scholastics. I will have to send for the Dean of Studies.' He beckoned to another younger boy and whispered something to him; this boy left his desk and went down the hall and out through the door at the back. Father O'Brien stood triumphant, his hand still down on top of William John's desk, a wide grin across his face. The boys waited. William John was already rubbing his hands together in anticipation of further punishment.

The door at the back opened again, loudly. Nobody looked around. They heard the soft-shoe approach of the Dean of Studies. Father Erraught came up and pretended he knew nothing of what had been happening.

'Well, Father O'Brien, what is this all about?' He spoke aloud, so that the whole hall could hear.

'I'm afraid I have to report that this boy ...'

Father Erraught interrupted. 'William John Mills, this boy, Father?'

'Mr Mills, to be sure. Here I have in my hand a piece of paper on which the poem by John Milton, "On His Blindness", is written out in small letters. And here, on the examination paper, is the question: What does the poet Milton intend us to know about his coping with blindness? Quote from the poem in answering the question.'

'I see, Father. A clear case of copying, I should think. Cheating, I call it. And from a scholastic, too. William John Mills, what have you to say?'

Both priests were enjoying their little charade before the students. William John kept his head down and murmured something.

'Nothing to say, nothing, indeed. Of course, nothing, because there can be nothing to say. Guilty, is the word I expected to hear. What is the word, Mr Mills, what is the word?'

There was another murmur from the boy.

'Louder, please, the students cannot hear you.'

'Guilty, Father,' William John said aloud.

Father Erraught had kept his hand inside his soutane. Now he took out the pandy and swished it loudly against the black cloth.

'I shall have to make an example of you, boy,' he said. 'Before everybody. There are public examinations coming up and if any boy is caught copying, cheating in any way, he will be expelled and his whole future will be thrown into jeopardy. So, punishment now will avert more serious punishment later on. Stand out, boy!'

Father O'Brien had moved away. William John stood up and stepped out of his desk. Father Erraught swished the pandy once more against his soutane. He stepped back.

'This time it will have to be six,' he said to the hall in general. 'I shall have to administer six slaps to this boy. Six. On each hand. Learn from this, all of you, learn that you must not cheat.'

Patrick could see William John's shoulders hunch in anticipation of the pain. He saw him stretch out his right hand. He saw Father Erraught raise the pandy. And then, before he knew what he was doing, Patrick had leaped up and shouted, 'Stop!'

Everybody looked at Patrick. There was a small murmuring of surprise. Father Erraught stopped, astonished. William John looked around at Patrick and shook his head, slightly.

But Patrick had left his desk and had come up along the aisle towards William John. Patrick was trembling, with fright at what he was doing, but with anger also.

'William John was copying because he was scared, that's all,' Patrick said aloud to Father Erraught. 'He was scared because he knows that if he fails you will beat him again. You have beaten him too often. He should not be slapped because he is not as intelligent as some of the other boys. It's not fair. It's not fair. And, it's too much.'

The Dean looked at Patrick with amazement.

'How dare you, Mr Brennan, how dare you!' he ground through his teeth. 'Go back at once and sit down. Sit down, boy, before you get into the same trouble as your friend here.'

'Are you going to give him six slaps, Father?' Patrick answered. His voice was not trembling now. He had gone too far. He would go the whole way.

'None of your business, boy. Get back at once into your seat.'

'I will not let you slap him again, Father. You hurt him because you are mean and because you love hurting people. And it's wrong. It's very wrong. And if any of us leave the scholasticate it's because of priests like you. You're supposed to be helping us, you're supposed to teach us Christian love and kindness, but you love punishing people, especially poor boys like William John. It's a very beautiful world we live in but you have made it ugly, with your pandybat and your punishment. You are destroying what is beautiful, and you are destroying William John's hopes and happiness.'

He stopped. He was breathless. There was silence. William John was gazing at Patrick. Father Erraught's face had grown white. He had lowered the pandybat. Patrick bowed his head. Then somebody clapped, quietly, towards the back of the hall. Somebody else joined in. And somebody else. Quickly the applause grew to a loud roar all over the hall. Several boys cheered. Many of them banged their feet against the wooden floor. The noise was tremendous. The hall became a theatre and the boys were the audience, Patrick and William John the heroes, and Father Erraught the wicked spirit. The Dean stood, amazed and uncertain, while Father O'Brien waved his hands in a hopeless effort to quieten the boys. Patrick stood, unabashed now, more certain. William John stood, too, head bowed, a new fear clouding his eyes.

At last Father Erraught brought his head close to Patrick and shouted above the din of the hall: 'Well, Mr Brennan, so, this is what you are really like. Well, you have not heard the last of this, I promise you. You have not heard the last.' Then he lifted his voice as loud as he could, he banged the pandy down hard on the surface of the desk, 'You shall all hear more of this, I promise you, I promise you!' Then he stalked quickly down between the desks while all the boys turned and cheered, applauding still. The Dean passed out the door, banging it loudly after him. Silence returned, slowly. Patrick sat down and tried to continue with his examination. William John turned and walked, quietly, down between the aisles after the Dean.

'Mr Mills,' Father O'Brien called out after him, uncertainly. 'May I ask you … ?'

But William John simply continued his walk, head bowed, between the desks. He opened the door of the hall and closed it, quietly, after him. Papers rustled in the examination hall. Father O'Brien's footsteps began to be heard again, softly, up and down between the desks.

By lunchtime the excitement among the boys had grown into a fever. They all entered the great refectory and stood at their tables, chattering amongst themselves, waiting. Eventually Father MacAdoo entered and went up to the high desk and said the grace before meals. At the quick 'Amen!' the boys sat down, noisily, and the chattering began again. William John Mills's place was empty at the table. Patrick Brennan sat, quietly, the other boys watching him. They ate and drank, without paying much attention to what they were doing. And at last the Rector, Father Gabriel MacAllister himself, walked into the refectory, went up to the high desk, nodded to Father McAdoo and took his place. He rang the hand bell on the desk and there was almost instant silence among the tables.

Father MacAllister was a tall man, his body spare, his hair white and carefully groomed. He was clean-shaven and stood and spoke with undoubted authority.

'A very grave incident has occurred today, among the scholastics. I am deeply saddened and distressed over this incident. The details I am certain you all already know. I will not rehearse them here.'

He paused and gazed out over the silent grove of faces. He coughed, delicately, bringing his hand to his mouth.

'Mr Mills will be leaving the scholasticate from tomorrow morning. I have decided to send him home. Without a reference.'

He paused again. Patrick, at his place, laid his elbows on the edge of the table and rested his head on his hands. He sighed deeply.

'It gives me, however, even greater pain to have to send one of our best students home, too. I am afraid that it was Mr Brennan who initiated the – I can only call it a riot – in the examination hall this morning. This simply cannot be tolerated. From tomorrow morning, Mr Brennan, too, will be sent home. Without a reference.'

Several of the boys murmured softly amongst themselves. The sound moved like the rustle of a slight breeze across the hall. Patrick did not move.

'I have asked the parents of both Mr Mills and Mr Brennan to attend tomorrow, here in the college, after morning Mass, to collect their sons, and to receive explanations. And I have to tell the rest of you, scholastics, boarders too, that misbehaviour of this kind, should it occur again, will have the most dire consequences for all.'

He paused again, his stern face moving slowly over all the raised faces.

'I shall be in my office from three o'clock this afternoon, and I expect both boys to come and see me then, so that we can have further discussions. And,' he paused again, 'if any boy wishes to come and apologise through me to Father Erraught, or if, indeed, any boy wishes to add anything in explanation to this morning's behaviour, I shall be glad to see him. That is all.'

He blessed himself, said the grace after meals out loud, the boys answering a quiet 'Amen', then he came down slowly from the desk and left the refectory hall. Patrick got up from his place and moved quickly out of the refectory. As he passed the tables several of the scholastics patted him on the back, some of them said something to him, but he did not hear. There were tears of utter desperation forming behind his eyes. He moved quickly outside, down a corridor and out into the grey yard of the scholasticate.

At three o'clock there were many boys queuing up outside the Rector's office. Patrick was surprised when he came to the great black door with the old-fashioned bell-pull outside. Over the door were two small lights; one would flash red if the Rector did not want to see you; the other would show green if you were to enter. There was no sign of William John Mills.

Patrick approached the door. The boys nodded and smiled at him, several of them greeted him, still as a hero. One of the bigger boys was prefect of the scholastics; he was tall and heavily freckled, with rust-red hair. He was always immaculately dressed and was known for his punctuality in all things, for his love of detail and the niceties of the rule. He greeted Patrick, too.

'We're waiting, Patrick,' he said. 'Father Cusack is actually inside at the moment. He's been in a long while. I expect he's pleading on your behalf. I expect so. And that's what we're all here for, too. We're going to go in one by one, before you, to tell him what we all think about Father Erraught, and how we all support you in what you said. So you just wait until we're all through, then you can go in, and we'll see how it goes.'

Just then the Rector's door opened and Father Cusack came out. He held the door for the prefect who knocked gently on it. The voice of Father MacAllister was heard calling 'Come!' and the prefect closed the door softly behind him. Father Cusack at once spotted Patrick, beckoned to him, and moved away from the boys down the corridor. He was a very small priest, very slight in build, so that he always seemed to be looking slightly upwards; he was almost completely bald although his face, round and cleanly shaven, was soft and gentle. He was a kindly man and was the Dean of Scholastics, in charge of the general welfare, spiritual and physical, of the boys.

'I have just been inside with Father MacAllister, Patrick,' he said, in a low voice. He was holding Patrick's elbow gently. 'I have been telling him how our em, Dean of Studies was, or rather is, a little, shall we say, over-enthusiastic in his punishing of the boys. I was saying to him, and I have the voice of many of the other Fathers, that I think your friendship for poor William John was, is rather, such a fine thing, shows such a good side to your character, I mean on top of your studies, of course, and that a second chance at the very least, ought to be extended to you. And, of course, we all take your point, announced rather bluntly in the examinations hall, so I am led to believe,' and the priest laughed a little dryly, 'that William John was probably frightened into his pathetic attempt to cheat. Now I may say to you, and you must not say this to anybody, you see, you must not pass this on, OK?' and Patrick nodded, 'I promise, Father', and the little priest, raising his head even further, said 'Good, good, our good Father Erraught may in fact leave the position he holds in this college and move on to better things. In Dublin perhaps, in the mother house. So that might be one thing to make you boys quite happy, I say, quite happy, and I hope that you will be given another chance. Good boy, good boy.' He gave Patrick's elbow a squeeze and moved swiftly and silently away down the corridor.

Patrick's heart rose a little and he turned back towards the Rector's door. The prefect had come out and was chattering excitedly with some of the bigger boys waiting to go in. He turned and smiled at Patrick. 'We're telling him,' he said, 'we're all telling him. I mean, how unfair Father Erraught has been, and he's listening. He's not saying much, but he's listening.'

At that very moment the Rector's door opened again. This time it was the Rector himself, and he stood, gazing at the boys queuing up before him. He smiled, ruefully.

'I see I'm going to have a long afternoon. I shall shorten it.

Any boy who has come here to complain about Father
Erraught, you may simply pass before me now, and I will
understand, without you having to say it, what you mean. Any
boy with anything else to say, you will remain. Mr Brennan,
you will wait until these boys have seen me. Then you may
come in. All right now, let's see who we have here.'

The first boy stood forward, the Rector nodded at him,
murmured his name, and the boy turned and went back down
the corridor. The second boy followed. Patrick counted; there
were about fifty-five of them, and some were not scholastics but
boarders, and they all filed slowly past the Rector, who said the
name, nodded and remained grim and serious.

Once they had all passed in front of him and had gone away,
Father MacAllister turned to Patrick.

'Mr Brennan, Patrick, I have heard from Father Cusack and
now I have heard from many of your colleagues. I must think it
all over. I shall, in fact, talk on the telephone with your Father
Scott. Tomorrow morning, after Mass, you will please come
back to me here. Say ten o'clock. Then we shall see what is to
be done. Good day to you, child.'

Patrick said 'Thank you, Father,' and turned, too, to leave.
He was gratified by the word 'child'. But he wondered about
William John, where was he? What was he doing?

Patrick woke up sometime in the very early hours of the next
morning. He found himself sitting, wrapped up in one of his
blankets, leaning back against a wall. He did not know where
he was. He was terrified. This had not happened to him since
the very first night he had been in St Canice's. He sat, steeling
himself to remain calm. He felt cold, very cold. There was a
moon but it was already low in the sky, though a vague and
sickly light came in from a window facing the wall against
which he found himself. He tried to find out where he was.

Slowly, in that faint light, he realised he was out on one of
the corridors. On the wall opposite him were windows, far
apart, and behind him were the rooms of the priests. He was in
the Priests' Corridor, a place where, in fact, the scholastics were

never allowed to go. He stood up, quickly. He was wearing his pyjamas, but the blanket was well wrapped about him, as if he had set out deliberately to go somewhere and had prepared himself that way. At the further end of the corridor he could see the banisters of the stairwell. He was on the top floor. His dormitory was on the first floor. He had climbed, in his sleep, up those stairs and down along this corridor. It was not where the Rector's room was. He had never been in this place before.

He held himself for a while against the wall. He told himself to remain calm. He closed his eyes. There was a small squeaking sound that suddenly chilled him, coming from somewhere behind him, in the deeper darkness. He turned quickly, but he could see nothing. Then he remembered this was the infamous corridor where all the scholastics said there was a ghost, the ghost of some priest who committed suicide by throwing himself out of one of those very windows. He walked, they said, this corridor almost every night, seeking peace, searching for forgiveness, a soul lost and without hope. For a long moment Patrick's body froze in horror. He closed his eyes again. There was silence.

At last he began to move, very slowly, trying to make no sound at all, down along the corridor, keeping close to the wall, passing the doors of the priests' rooms. Every now and then he glanced back, expecting to see some terrifying figure emerge in the moonlight from that furthest darkness. And slowly, too slowly, the top of the stairwell came closer. Then he paused, at the top of the steps. The stairs went down into blackness. He would have to go down the two flights to find the way into his own dormitory. But first he would have to leave the half-shelter of the wall and make it to the steps. He hesitated. He looked back again at the darkness behind him. Only the faintest gleam of light came through the windows, falling onto the wooden floor of the corridor. He felt colder than he had ever felt before. If only he could make it back to his own dormitory …

Then he rushed for the stairwell. The blanket seemed to fall free of him but he gripped it more tightly around his body. For a moment it hampered his legs and he felt that any second now he would scream in complete abandonment to the terror that flooded through him. Without looking back at the corridor he moved, his left hand holding the banister railing, his right gripping the blanket tightly to him. His bare feet grew colder yet against the granite steps of the stairs. He rushed down, and it felt as if a great wind were rushing against him. He reached the floor below and continued as fast as he could down the next flight of steps. When he reached his own floor he could see at once the entrance to his own dormitory; the door was closed. He rushed against it and burst it open. Then he closed it behind him and lay back against it. The blanket dropped away around his feet. But he held his shivering body close to the door and tried to breathe, slowly, back into quietness. He knew now where he was; around the partition to his left, fourth curtain along on that side was his own cubicle. Patrick bent and gathered up the blanket from the floor, then he rushed around the corner and slipped as quickly as he could inside the curtain of his own space. He knelt on the floor beside his bed. He leaned his head down on the covers and he thanked God, from the bottom of his heart. As he climbed back into his bed, half afraid now of falling asleep, there were tears streaming down his cheeks.

After Mass, Patrick presented himself at the Rector's door. He was still in a sort of stupor from the happenings of the day and the night before. He drew himself together as best he could, took several deep, deep breaths, and tugged on the bell-pull outside Father MacAllister's door. There was no answering light from above. He waited. And then the door opened for him and Father Scott stood in the doorway, holding it open, and smiling.

'Ah, my own good student, my best lad,' Father Scott said at once. 'Come on in, come on in. And don't worry. It's sorted out. Everything is OK. Come on in and let's talk with Father MacAllister.'

As he held Patrick about the shoulder and gently drew him into the big room, Father Scott continued his reassurance.

'I know you're a great student, Patrick, and Father MacAllister knows it, too. Indeed, Albert and I studied in the seminary together for a few years. We know each other well. He rang me yesterday. I told him I would tell your parents but I didn't, Patrick, I came on down myself last night, and stayed in the presbytery just down the road. I've had a long, heartfelt chat with my good old friend. And everything is worked out. Your parents need know nothing. Nothing.'

About half an hour later, Patrick came out the front door of the college onto the driveway. Father Scott was with him. The complaints about Father Erraught, from so many of the students, from Father Cusack himself and from some other priests, were enough to persuade the Rector to have the Dean transferred to the mother house for a while, to see where there might be a better position for him. Father Scott and Father MacAllister agreed that, though what Patrick had done was a little forward of him, it showed, in fact, that the boy had the wellbeing of others at heart, rather than his own. And he was forgiven. For this time.

There were two cars on the driveway in front of the great oak door. One was the old-age red and battered Ford Anglia of Father Scott, its one windscreen wiper hanging like a dead eel from its place, the front bumper askew, dunts and scrapes along its sides and a delicate though large spider-web-shaped crack in the back window. The other was a sleek and beautiful new car, the top half in soft yellow, the lower bodywork a coffee brown. It was long and low, the windows slightly tinted, the hubcaps gleaming silver. For a moment both Patrick and the priest stood to admire it.

The left-side door opened suddenly and William John Mills got out. He was dressed in light blue shirt, dark-blue pullover and cream trousers and looked well and happy. From the other side a large man dressed in a camel-hair cream coat belted carefully around his portly shape, stood out and lit up a cigar. He was smiling towards William John. The latter came up to Patrick, shook the hand of the priest and grinned at his young friend.

'Patrick, I wonder if I can introduce my father to you,' he said, indicating the man by the gleaming car. 'Excuse us Father, please.'

'Where were you, William John?' Patrick said. 'What's going on?'

William John's father shook Patrick's hand warmly up and down, 'Good fellow, good fellow,' he said. 'Have a few words with my boy, then we'll head off, he and I.'

William John told Patrick that he had simply walked out of the college the day before, when he heard he was being expelled. He took a bus into the town and booked himself into a hotel. He went to a movie that evening, after phoning home to his parents.

'I went and saw a great film, Patrick. I really laughed and laughed and laughed. You must see it. It has Danny Kaye in it and it's called *The Secret Life of Walter Mitty*. I don't think I ever laughed as much in my life. And do you know what? Yesterday, when I walked away from here, I suddenly knew how miserable I have been in this place, and how much I need to get away from here. My father picked me up this morning at the hotel. I'm simply going home. Get into the family business. Give up this idea of the priesthood. It was stupid of me ever to think of joining up. It's not for me.'

He told Patrick that his father was delighted and that he had never wanted him to be a priest. He needed someone to take over the business, a smoked salmon exporting business run from one of the port towns in the south. And the car?

'Oh that. She's a beauty, isn't she? She's a Borgward Isabella, a German lady, brand-new. A Hansa 1500, whispers across the roads like a saint, I'm going to drive her home, away to hell out of here. But listen, Patrick, I want to leave something with you. You were so good to me, the only one, and here is a little gift, something to remember me by.' He produced a packet from his pocket and handed it to Patrick. There were six tins of Tiger Balm inside, 'to replace all I used of yours, and just in case you ever get pandied yourself!', and a dozen Crispin bars. 'But most of all I want you to have this,' William John said, holding out a fine silver fob-watch chain, 'I know you keep your watch on the locker, the chain is broken, so this will help, it won't break. And look! I have attached my own silver sodality medal, my name is on it, it's yours, just as a remembrancer, that's all.'

'But it's a special medal, that, you won it, and it proves you're a member of the sodality of the Blessed Virgin, I can't accept that, William John, it's too much.'

'Please, please, take it. And all this stuff about medals and the Blessed Virgin and God and all of that, it's all rubbish, Patrick, that's how I feel. How can anyone possibly believe in anything with that cart-load of priests in there? I don't want to upset you, but for a long time I've been losing any faith I ever had in religion. My father agrees with me, though he never said it before! And so, I'm off into the big world, with cars, and movies, no Latin, no algebra, no French, nothing but salmon, and money, and women, Patrick, women!'

He shook hands quickly with his friend, then turned back towards the beautiful car. His father ducked quickly into the passenger side and William John, with a final wave of his hand, climbed into the driver's seat. The car started with a low growl that settled into a gentle purr. Patrick watched as it glided with immaculate grace down the avenue, under the trees, out the big gate on the main road. William John Mills had gone. Patrick felt bereft, exalted at the loss of Father Erraught, but deeply saddened and lonely after his friend.

Over the next few years, Patrick worked steadily in the scholasticate. He found life easy now, he did well in all his subjects, he was popular, almost a hero and he succeeded in his examinations. But in his heart his faith was beginning to grow cold. He found himself mentally arguing with all that he and the other scholastics were being taught about their beliefs. But he remained silent; he wanted to finish his time in the college, get his final examination, and head out into the world, the way William John had done. Patrick knew he would need his examination results as he had no immediate prospect of anything more than the miserable acres down at the shore where his parents still struggled by.

The Christmas before his final examinations, the weather grew unusually cold. At home, Patrick found the time dull on his hands; there was little to do about the place. Christmas passed with a vagueness and imponderability that he found disconcerting. He remained ill at ease. He was bored. Then came the days after Christmas and the weather grew grey and menacing. Patrick sat at the kitchen window looking out at the grey-green darkness of the day; he loved the snow falling in total silence, the large flakes beginning, by afternoon, to blow slantwise in a growing breeze. How beautiful the world is, he thought, and he remembered the music, he remembered the days he would float innocently on the pool below the bridge, dreaming, not fully aware of how grand was creation. Now, though, the thought that there was a personal God hidden behind such beauty had been set to one side, Patrick's consciousness of an accompanying sorrow and miserliness in the earth itself, driving the image of God into some misty background.

The whole world, next day, seemed to play a symphony in the key of white. There was not a breath of wind though the day was as bright as summer and the sky was a clear and lovely blue. The snow sparkled on lawn and road, on field and bush and meadow, melding everything into one delightful and beautiful white music, and Patrick's spirits soared like a white gull into the clarity of the blue sky. He went out and found the ground in the front yard as hard as a rock, the water in the little mud-pools and slither-holes frozen stiff. Even the edges around the sea-pool were frozen. It was bitterly cold, but exciting, and Patrick guessed at once that with a frost as strong as this, people might be out on the lake behind Lohan's house, sliding, skating and having fun.

He dressed at once in warm coat and scarf; he put on his thick boots with their steel studs and he cycled cautiously up the hill and back the road to the lake. Well before he got there he could hear the screams and chattering, the excited laughter of young and old voices, and the barking of dogs. He left the bicycle by the roadside and ventured out on the ice. He was greeted by many of the people he had known in school, and soon he was sliding, cautiously, over the ice. He knew he was not much good at this but if he managed to run a little he could then skid, his boots raising tiny showers of ice-specks before him, for a good distance. And then, suddenly, he spotted Dorothy and found himself sliding directly towards her. He called out but it was too late, he bumped into her but without knocking her over. If there was a God, he thought suddenly, then this is the kind of accident he should be managing.

For a moment, standing a little aside, they chatted easily, Dolly again, and Packie, but too soon Dorothy's anger over something to do with her school became a small storm, incomprehensible to Patrick and she hurried away from him. He stood, stunned and astonished. What had he said? And why had she attacked him, was it over his aiming to be a priest? 'I'm not going to be a …' he called out after her, but she was too far away already, and was stomping away along the frozen grasses to her home. 'I'm not going to be a priest,' he whispered aloud, but so that nobody could hear, 'I'm going to marry you, you beautiful, lovely girl!' And he began to flail his arms about wildly again, and impel himself forward on the ice.

Before Easter, that final year of Patrick Brennan's scholasticate, all the boys were taken, one by one, by Father Cusack for a 'serious conversation'. The boys joked about it, about his seriousness, his innocence, but Patrick knew that behind their mockery he had touched them. He felt, as his turn approached, that he must be careful, not to admit that he would not go on to the seminary, not to admit to his serious doubts about God, nor to his thoughts, indecent and shameful, of Dorothy Lohan. He would set up a wall of silent obtuseness, this small priest would not get behind it.

'Sit down, Patrick Brennan, sit down,' Father Cusack said, ushering him to an uncomfortable chair in front of an enormous desk. Patrick sat, stiff and watchful. The priest fiddled around a little on his desk for a while, selected some papers, smiled at Patrick, then sat down in his own swivel chair on the other side of the large desk. 'Ah!' he said suddenly, smiled again, then opened a drawer in the desk. He rooted around in there, then took out an already opened box of liquorice allsorts, and a brown paper bag with some other kind of sweets. 'Allsorts, or mint, Patrick?'

'No thanks, Father,' Patrick said, wishing to remain unembarrassed and unselfconscious.

'Love these myself, if you'll excuse me,' Father Cusack said, dipping into the paper bag and taking out a few sweets wrapped in crinkly paper. He smiled again, left the sweets on the desk and closed the drawer.

'I suppose I don't have to tell you the facts of life, Patrick?' he began, without embarrassment, though looking sharply at the boy.

'No, Father, my own father …'

'Ah yes, of course, of course. Then I'll just stick to the question of the seminary, OK?'

'Yes, Father.'

Father Cusack glanced through the notes he had in front of him, looked up once or twice and smiled. Then pushed the papers to one side. 'All most satisfactory there, Patrick, most satisfactory indeed. A model student, including, if I may refer to it, the episode with Father Erraught, some time back. Splendid! Splendid! Spoke volumes, really, volumes. And then your help with that boy, I forget his name, Mills, wasn't it? Excellent! And your results, all exemplary, everything steady. Ideal! Splendid!'

The priest sat back in some satisfaction and swivelled himself a little on the chair. He joined his hands then and brought the two of them to his chin.

'And now, Patrick, the priesthood. The seminary, all of that. How do you feel, are you looking forward to your studies there?'

There was an innocence and openness about Father Cusack that Patrick could not resist.

'I'm not sure, Father,' he began, in spite of all his watchfulness. He felt, now, it might not be fair to pretend. 'Ever since William John Mills went away I've been troubled. I've had doubts. And I know that I am very happy when I'm at home, when I'm in the world, like. There's so much …'

'Ah yes, I see, I see, the world, the flesh … yes, yes, all of that, all of that. I understand, of course.'

'It's all so beautiful out there, Father, I mean, there's the world of nature itself, the trees, the sea, the mountains, all that freedom, and there's things like music and travel and all of that, things a priest could not do, and there's, em, there's …'

'There are women, Patrick, and family, and love. All of that, yes, yes of course. All of that. It comes down to what we want out of life, Patrick, I mean, in the end it comes down to what we have done, what we have achieved. Cars and houses and journeys are all wonderful, don't get me wrong, and family, love and all of that, quite perfect and holy and wonderful. It's a question, Patrick, of desire. Will we ever find satisfaction for our desires, that's the question. It comes down to that, what we long for in our lives, what we see as our heart's desire. Let me tell you a little story, if I may.'

Father Cusack leaned forward and laid his elbows on the desk before him, his hands still joined, as if in prayer, on the desk. He looked at Patrick for a moment.

'I am going to tell you about my father, Patrick, my own father. You will be kind enough, I know it, I know it, not to pass along any of this to your friends, it's private, between you and me, OK?'

'Of course, Father, of course.'

'My father was a fisherman, Patrick, I don't mean professional, I mean he fished for pleasure. In the river Blackwater that flowed not far from our home. His great urge was to fish, his longing to spend as much time as he could on the banks of the river, or sometimes wading out into the flow, fly-fishing. I don't know if you've ever done that, Patrick, but it is a fascinating and a specialist pleasure. I used to watch him, when he came home from work of an evening, on those calm evenings, and I could see at once that he was almost overcome with longing, to be out there, fishing. And I would watch the prelude to his great plans, the laying-out on the kitchen table of the artificial flies he kept in a leather-wallet pouch. It was folded over and over and he would stretch it out, exposing all the range of flies that he had. He would look out at the evening, the light, whether the alders were bending with the wind or just whispering to themselves, and then he would bend down over that pouch with complete attention, choosing the perfect lure for that evening. I remember the names of some of them, great names like attractor nymphs, the blue-winged olive, the cinnamon sedge, the thunder bug. Can you imagine it, Patrick, a small artificial fly called thunder bug?' The priest laughed quietly, and Patrick smiled in response. The boy felt surprised, his hands were sweating a little, he rubbed them secretly against his trousers.

'And some of them, their colours, the hairs or feathers or whatever they were, some of them were really beautiful, Patrick, beautiful as anything in the world could be. There was turquoise, fawn-gold, emerald, bright orange, and all sorts of stripes and streaks and tails, like miniature peacocks. But what always hurt me, Patrick, always, were the hooks, small and cruel, copper-coloured usually, and their desperate barbs were hidden and camouflaged in the beauty. You see what I'm getting at Patrick, you surely see. He would choose, put aside the three or four for that evening. Then he would get dressed up, a special old jacket in which he stuck the flies, his rod that came in pieces that he would have to put together, carefully, oh all the preparation, the anticipation, that was the greatest part, the desire, Patrick, the desire. And the waders, pulled up over an old pair of trousers, right up as far as his waist. And I would see him move up and down the bank of the river, watching, gauging, even listening, yes I believe he was listening for the chattering of trout, and sometimes he would wade out into the water, bracing himself against the flow, he would test his wrist, flicking beautifully the almost impossible thinness of the rod and I'd admire how the light green line would curve out over his head, over the water and the fly would land, oh just so, just so. Wonderful, Patrick, wonderful. And yet, do you know, he was always uncertain, my father, something would always hurt that longing within him, some sense that this was a waste of time, that he would catch nothing, nothing, that he ought to be elsewhere, at his duties, oh something Patrick was not quite right, not like the Fisher of Men that we know and love, not like the Christ, Patrick, not like the Christ. And so often I would see him, that big body of his would droop in a kind of disappointment, a failure, even if he had caught two or three reasonably sized trout, I would see how his eagerness would die into weariness, I would watch him restore the flies to the pouch, he was packing his longing away, for the moment, for now. And so often, as night came down, I would see him walk the floor, Patrick, at a loss in himself, he was like a fox, taut and watching, and I imagined and I think I sometimes heard, his whispering lisping words as he prayed, Patrick, as he prayed for something more, something neither he nor I nor indeed my mother, ever could put a name to. And it was that pacing to and fro on the kitchen floor that convinced me, Patrick, convinced me utterly that I had to be certain about my own life, certain about what was important for me, certain of where I would lay my desires, so that when night comes I will not be pacing hopelessly, and wondering, Patrick, wondering …'

Father Cusack's talk entered Patrick's soul where it lodged, disturbing in the weight of its quiet presence. Over the Easter break the boy spent a long time idling on the waters of the pool below the bridge, trying to clarify the world to himself. His father muttered about idle hands, wasteful hours, but Patrick ignored him. He never spoke to his parents of Dorothy, but her image as she floated like a beautiful vision across the ice before him, her image troubled and disturbed every vision of himself that he tried to place as priest, serving others, serving a God of which he was in doubt.

On the last Saturday before final term began in St Canice's, Patrick helped his father plant a few rows of potatoes behind the big shed that stood ends on to the shore. He grew weary, stooping and rising, choosing and planting, covering over the cold seed potatoes with the poor earth of the holding. He knew then that he would have to leave this place, this house, these fields, even this shoreline, and a great sadness held him. After a meagre supper taken in almost complete silence, Patrick rose and went back out to push the old boat onto the pool one last time. He rowed slowly up as far as the bridge, the dark brown water purling gently about the boat, then he let it drift with whatever current would take it, slowly down from the bridge towards the sea. He trailed one hand in the water, feeling the cold freshness against his fingers.

He heard his mother call to him, gently, from the shore and he rowed in towards her; she was standing on the bank, her coat still on, and her scarf loosely about her head. She waved at him, and smiled.

'Patrick, I've been up to Confession, for tomorrow, you know, Easter Sunday. Mass tomorrow, by the way, is at nine o'clock. And do you know who I met just outside the chapel?'

'Who, mother?'

'Dorothy. Dorothy Lohan. She stopped me, and me only in my dull rags, you know, she's a lovely girl, Patrick, really lovely. She was eager to chat, I could see. You know I'm not one for chatting, but she began by asking after you. I told her how well you were getting on in St Canice's. She said she hadn't seen you since the day on the ice, up on the lake.'

'That's right, I haven't seen her ...'

'I told her you were starting your last term in the scholasticate and that come September, please God, you'll be moving on to the seminary. She was glad to hear it, Patrick, very glad. And do you know what?'

Patrick was shocked and hurt by this news but his mother did not notice how he shrank into himself, how his face blanched a moment, how he gripped more tightly the gunwale of the old boat.

'What, mother?' he managed to ask.

'She told me she'll be entering the convent herself, immediately after the examination, in June, she'll be going on to become a nun. There now. There's the two of ye, isn't God good, two of ye as used to be great pals, I remember the films and all that, two of ye from the one small parish, a priest and a nun. Dorothy said she's joining up, with others, friends of hers, it seems, from the college. It's great, Patrick. I'm so proud, so happy.'

She turned away, her slight figure buoyed up so that she walked tall and straight to the door of the dilapidated house. For a moment Patrick held the boat against the bank. Then he pushed hard with the makeshift oar and the little skiff moved back out into the flow where the river began to broaden into the flats before the sea. He breathed deeply and let the boat take its course. It moved slowly, drifting gently out into the small current that took it towards the great sweep of the bend before the pier came into view, the few small fishing boats, and the sea. The sky was grey now, clouds heavy and threatening. On the bank nearest him he saw the yellow iris already beginning to swell, there would be a fine show along that bank before summer. A pair of mallard floated leisurely near him and he admired again the show that the drake made, that emerald-green head with its sheen, even in the grey of evening, the golden-yellow bill tipped with black, its white collar and above all the intense dark blue of its wing-feathers edged with white, and the black-tipped tail twitching proudly. Just then three swans came low over the estuary waters, their great bodies heavy on the air so that the sound of their wings came like laboured breathing; they flew towards the small craft then veered away when they saw the human.

But Patrick's spirit could not lift. For a moment he closed his eyes. The small boat drifted on, beginning to turn slowly in the gathering strength of the current where it met the incoming tide. He drifted on further until a loud sluppering sound against the boards brought him back to himself. Should he drift much further he would be caught in the sea-current and it would be very difficult to labour the boat back towards his home with the poor oars he had. But he had made his decision. Without her knowing it, Dorothy Lohan had decided for him. With a strong pull on the oars he turned the boat and began to row for home.

THE USES OF ADVERSITY

Dorothy had a dream of Jesus. There was, of course, sunshine; there were wide spaces of greenery with rivers sparkling through; there were trees, shade, and love. She saw a castle in which there were quiet chambers and great archways through which a rich landscape could be glimpsed; there was a Lord, distant and serene, there were tables with good things to eat and there was wine, though never in her life had wine passed her lips. Her Jesus was chaste; she saw Him dressed in flowing robes, His hair and beard were black, not a sheened black, rather a gentle warm-night black; His eyes were blue, a deep and penetrating blue, and His hands were soft, the long fingers raised in greeting. *You are fair, my loved one, your eyes are as doves, and where we rest is leafy and caressed by warm breezes.*

She stood awhile before the convent door. She held her small brown suitcase in both hands before her. She gazed up at the two-panelled door, its brass knocker, the large and gleaming doorknob. She had never been this side of the college before, the convent itself being strictly out of bounds for the students. St Monica's. On either side of the door were three storeys, small windows on the first and second floor, large windows with white lace curtains on the ground floor. High over the door, on the apex of the roof, rose a stone cross. There was silence, apart from the birds in the high poplars and the oak trees; roses bloomed in the tended flowerbeds on the gravel driveway. She hesitated. She was not sure. But were not several of her friends joining with her? She drew herself up; she took hold of the brass knocker. She knocked.

There were nine girls joining the convent that June. They were welcomed by Mother Mary Justina, a large and grave woman dressed in the dark brown habit of the Sisters of St Francis of Sepolito, with the heavy brown veil and the grey pelerine. The nine postulants were led together into a small dormitory where they were given cubicles. Dorothy's cubicle faced the end wall and she was lucky to have a small window looking out over the fields and down towards the river. In the cubicle there was an iron bed and a locker with a delft jug and basin for water; a dark blue curtain could be closed over to give her some privacy. There was nowhere to put the few items of clothing she had brought with her so all the girls were given a small cupboard in a common area at the end of the dormitory, near the door. They had been given the clothes they would wear all through the summer months, black wool stockings, clumpy black shoes with laces, a long black skirt, also woollen, a white blouse and a black cape that covered their shoulders, coming down in front to be joined by a small chain across their breasts. They wore a white lace veil bound across their heads by a brown clasp. At once Dorothy felt encumbered and hot, she moved awkwardly, she was anxious.

'You need wilderness in your lives,' Sister Mary Clare, mistress of postulants, told them as they sat together, cowed, in the dark room at the rear of the convent. There were only two windows here, high in the wall, and the little light that came in kept the room dim and cool. 'I want you to imagine a wilderness, a desert even, with only a few stumps of dead trees, the rest sand, stretching away to far distant horizons. Here you place yourselves, young women now, who have already found the world a bleak place in which to live. But you have found Jesus, our hope and strength, our fortress against the blandishments of the world and a saviour from the predations of mankind. Here, in this desert, you will start afresh. You will imagine a world beyond that is brimming over with the wrath of God; you will see yourself flung from the highest, most gilded pinnacle of that world, flung out on the air and falling. But you are held, dear daughters, you are held above the surface, because it is the angels that will bear you up while all about you the others fall to their destruction. So you will spend these few preparatory months on your knees, in prayer. Thanking God for your deliverance. Kneel with me now, here on the hard floor, kneel, and while you are on your knees know that this is the most appropriate position for a human being to be in, kneeling, eyes closed, pleading with the great and terrible, but the loving and kindly God, pleading for your soul and for the souls of others. And while you kneel, here in the safety of our sacred House, you will yet know that there can be no rest nor peace for the soul seeking the love of Jesus …'

Late that night, Dorothy lay on her hard bed, a faint light coming through the small window in her cubicle, and all about her was silence, otherness, and barrenness. She felt a great sob welling up within her but she held it back; I am a lily among thorns, she sounded in her soul, an apple-tree standing amongst the trees of the wood, and my beloved gazes at me with his eyes of a dove. The only sound that came in through the window was the sound of a summer breeze stirring the high branches of the oak trees, and once a small shriek, as of a night-creature pierced suddenly by the talons of an owl. It was almost dawn before she slept.

Dorothy's task was to keep waxed and perfect the polished wooden floors of the convent's ground floor. In her heavy clothes, the veil sometimes slipping down over her face, she knelt on a small piece of rubber, took the can of wax polish and, moving backwards over the floor, rubbed it in hard until a matt sheen was left across the surface. She rose, stood a while, easing her back. She took a heavy brush topped with a large felt cloth and began to sheen the floor until she could see the windows reflected in it, until not but an inch of floor was gleaming. It was difficult, but she relished the silence of the parlour, of the hallway, the others being at their own tasks, most of the nuns away on retreat or preparing the college for the coming year.

Sister Mary Clare, one day, came through the parlour, her hands hidden in the folds of her sleeves. She had been in the convent grounds, the day was damp, the lawns recently cut.

Sister Mary Clare moved, slowly and deliberately, across Dorothy's waxed floor and left a trail of footprints with tiny streaks of mud and small grass clippings behind her. Dorothy gasped aloud, kneeling on the floor over against a wall.

'Child,' Sister Mary Clare announced, 'between God, the source and sustenance of our being, and us, poor and sinful creatures, the obstacle is suffering. We carry about in our bodies the dying of the manGod, the Godman, the Jesus who loved us and died for our sakes. Our flesh is destined for destruction, we live under a clouded sky. We move, dear child, in a world of sin and darkness, we can only reach rebirth and light through labour, suffering, pain, all of it offered up to that sinless person who is our Lord and Master. God be with you, child.'

Dorothy stood, the polishing cloth in her hand. For a moment her fist clenched about the cloth, then relaxed. She bowed her head before the nun and then went to the cupboard and got out more cloths, a hard-straw brush, a mop, and began work again at the parlour door.

That afternoon the postulants were allowed to leave the convent for a walk carefully mapped out for them, down by the river. They walked in threes, and Sister Mary Clare walked with them. Down by the river the hydrangea bushes were loud in the purple of their blossoming; the river-water moved with an eagerness that sparkled under a gentle sun and the small waves breaking over rocks and stones nearer the banks were almost transparent in their racing. Dorothy's spirit rose in praise. Beyond the bridge there were children playing; they were barefoot, raucous, ragged, but raced and leaped with as much gaiety as the river itself. They were kicking a ball against the gable-wall of a public house; they had painted-on white goalposts and the yard where they ran was dirty with nettle-flowers and the tiny pimpernel. As they rushed about, dust-puffs rose around their feet and a wind-swollen small brown paper bag that had held sweets skipped about at their feet like a tiny, silent pup. They stopped and watched, in silence, as the young women walked quietly by on the river path, hot in their black skirts and capes, in the strange and covering veils, in their black shoes and black-wool stockings. The postulants passed, silently, in under the arch of the bridge. The children began their shrieking and arguments once more.

They left the edge of the town and moved into the woods that rose along the hillside. It was cooler under the trees and Dorothy relaxed a little. Beside her was Nuala Coyne, and with them walked Maura Raftery, two girls who had been in college with Dorothy. They had never been close in those days but now circumstances forced them to spend time together. Sister Mary Clare walked ahead with two other postulants; behind them came the next group of three, then Dorothy's group. Nuala was a heavy girl and moved more slowly so they fell behind a while; Sister Mary Clare and the other girls moved on at a steady pace.

When they were out of earshot Nuala giggled. 'Hey, girls,' she said to Dorothy and Maura. 'Do you miss them? Tell the truth, now. Do you miss them at all?'

'What? Who?' Dorothy asked.

'You know, fellas, lads, boys. I mean, we're all girls together, takes getting used to, you know, after all the lads we mixed with down the years. So, do you miss them?'

Dorothy glanced across at Maura. Maura was pretty, a well-formed young woman whose raven-dark hair was now cooped away under the veil. She shook her head, doubtfully.

'I know we're not supposed to think of anything but Jesus, God, the Holy Spirit, that kind of thing, and Mary, we're supposed to think about the value of virginity, of being a virgin martyr, even. And no, I don't think I miss the boys. I mean, I never went to dances or anything like that.'

'What about the films, Maura?' Nuala pursued her. 'In the back row, did you ever, you know, kiss a boy? Did you ever, oh dear, fondle a boy?'

'I did not!' came emphatically from the pretty postulant.

'Well, I did,' Nuala pronounced. 'I remember at a film, I forget the name of it, but that actor with the strange face that should have been ugly but wasn't, you know, the man with the crooked nose? What's his name?'

'Are you talking about Jack Palance?' Dorothy prompted.

'Now you're talking, Dorothy, Jack Palance it was. He was

an Indian in the film. But I missed most of it. I was sitting in the back row with Mick Dwyer, you know, the good-looking fella from up at the top end of the town. Oh boy, he was frisky, I'll tell you. We had a time, a good time of it, and I enjoyed every second of it. I don't mean we did anything wrong, like, no way, I wasn't that foolish. But I know I was really happy, I was excited, it was special. I miss that, you know, I think I'm going to miss that a great deal.'

The three girls moved along in silence for a while. There was a great exhalation from the hillside pines, a fresh and health-giving scent on the air. Their heavy shoes tramped on rough, dry earth, but it was covered with yellow and brown pine needles from earlier years. While they walked, Dorothy began to think of Patrick, and how he had bumped into her on the lake that day, she remembered the sudden rush of pleasure his presence and his touch, though accidental, had given her. She sighed deeply and shrugged her shoulders.

'I don't think I'm going to miss any of that, you know,' she said. 'I was groped once, and that was enough for me.'

'Groped?' Nuala asked eagerly. 'Tell us about it. Was he good-looking? Was he young?'

At that moment Sister Mary Clare stopped up ahead and looked back. The three girls fell silent and when they reached the nun, Sister Mary Clare decided they would all turn back, they had walked enough, they would be tired. Then she changed the order of the girls and she, Dorothy and Maura, walked together. Nuala was moved along with the pair that had already walked with the nun. She grinned conspiratorially at Dorothy, winked, and they began their return walk.

Towards the end of those strange, unreal summer months, the postulants were in the study-room, reading from the works of the founder, Blessed Mary Evangeline Morrow who had had several schools and convents built around the country, including this one, with its postulancy and novitiate. All the nuns were praying fervently that one day soon Mary Evangeline Morrow would be made a saint and then the glory of the sisters would

be on an even stronger footing. Dorothy sat enthralled; late
morning, the summer warmth finding its way into the room,
dust-motes shifting slowly, the silence exalted by the soft
turning of pages, the quiet noises of absorption. She felt wholly
contented, here, knowing she had been called by the True
Lover, *arise my loved one, my beauty, and come away, into the fields
where flowers grow and no tempests come* ...

There was a sudden disturbance behind her, she heard a harsh
gurgling sound, the rattling of a desk and when she turned she
saw Nuala Coyne tumble out of her seat onto the floor. Some
of the girls screamed with fright. Nuala was lying on her back
now, her whole body trembling and in spasm, her hands
gripping wildly at the air, her face pale as a whitewashed wall,
her eyes had disappeared and her mouth was foaming, her
tongue gagging out and in. The postulants watched, frozen in
terror. Nuala rolled onto her side, rolled back, her hands now
clutching at her throat. The brown veil came from her head and
the noises in her throat were like the interrupted fall of water
from a spring. One of the girls rushed to the door, opened it and
shouted out for Sister Mary Clare. She returned, leaving the
door open, standing helplessly over the writhing girl.

In a moment Sister Mary Clare was in the room, bending low
over Nuala.

'Give her air, girls, she's going to be all right. Don't worry.
But give her air.'

She loosened the blouse at Nuala's throat, then glanced
around quickly at the postulants' desks, snatching a wooden
ruler from one of them. This she placed, as gently as she could,
in Nuala's mouth, over her tongue. She shushed her, held her
firmly against her own body, spoke soothing words to her and
gradually the girl quietened, and fell still.

'Dorothy, one of you, run quickly to the phone in the
hallway. Dial four. You'll get the post office. Tell Mrs Maguire
we need Doctor Weir up here as quickly as possible. Emer-
gency, tell her, don't let her dawdle. Don't answer questions.
Go, go, go!'

Dorothy ran as quickly as she could from the room. Within
about half an hour Nuala had been taken from the convent by

ambulance, the postulants huddling together as they waited for news, for explanations. 'Poor Nuala is an epileptic, girls,' Sister Mary Clare told them. 'She has had a seizure, that's all. It's known as *le petit mal*. Not the terribly serious form of the illness. She will recover perfectly, and probably won't remember a moment of this. She is particularly blessed. As you know our own Blessed Mary Evangeline Morrow was an epileptic and offered up her sufferings for the salvation of the world. It is a great grace Nuala has been offered. She must use it well. We must pray for her, pray for her, and for ourselves, and for all human kind.'

Sister Mary Clare sent them to the little oratory reserved for the postulants and they knelt, praying, their heads down in their hands. Dorothy was distressed. Yet she knew within herself that this terrible moment must teach her something. Now she would be even more determined to find her peace and security here, within these walls. Nuala had brought in with her things that were not wanted, not in here, in this world safe behind thickened walls and silvered glass. She thought, too, of PJ Hannafin, and Hawthorn Lane, his crude and dirty fingers groping her. And how had she deserved? and how had Nuala deserved? The fathers' sins, she had heard, are visited upon the children; perhaps there is not enough love in the world to go round. The quizzical face of Patrick rose for a moment before her mind and a short cry of pain rose to her lips; she suppressed it.

Early in September the great day dawned for Dorothy. Today she was to take the habit. Mother Mary Thérèse came from the Motherhouse in Paris and there was fuss around the convent all morning. The postulants were finishing their retreat. Dorothy walked in the private part of the convent grounds. In the distance she could hear the girls from the school out on their mid-morning break; the postulants were living almost on an island of their own, where the world, even the world of the professed nuns, the teaching sisters, would not touch them.

At the far end of the convent garden, where limited chaos still had hold, nettles and thistles grew in rigorous abandon. Dorothy sat on an old, half-rotting, garden bench, her heart lifted in her joy. She sat so still, her hands held inside her sleeves, that the life of the world carried on about her, indifferent to her presence. She watched a pair of goldfinch on the thistles, relishing the seeds; she sang praise for the wonder of their colouring, their russets and gold, their yellows, that tawny effect, and the jerky, self-satisfied glory of their small yet plump bodies. There was a hazel tree over against the wall, and on it she saw three small birds whose names she did not know; they were light green, like a finch with a black crown and black bib, and small yellow patches on its wings. They were busy, twittering rapidly amongst themselves as if in a great and important haste about something. And further down the clogged footpath that once led from here to the river, were hawthorn trees, their limbs twisted with age. Dorothy had learned many things in the few months of her postulancy, she had learned how the distorted body may house a mind electric and in shoal, and how the distorted body, too, may house a mind slow-burning, disfigured, and at loose. And each of them, and all of them, were beloved of her own great Lover, Christ, to whom she was making her first, beautiful vows.

Scarcely an hour later she was lying face down on the altar steps of the great chapel, the other postulants lying on either hand. The nuns, in choir, were singing a Latin motet, there was incense on the air, there were high candles everywhere; there was solemnity, ritual, and a great and sudden pressure on Dorothy's heart. Behind her, she knew, holding their own emotions, were her father and mother; somewhere back there, too, was Aunt Lily, older now, more plump and blatherful than ever, but, Dorothy quickly thought, beloved, too, of her Christ.

When her name was called out, solemnly, by Mother Superior, and when she gathered herself up carefully to her feet, Dorothy felt suddenly scared, incapable and distressed. She stepped forward, onto the lower step of the altar, and held her two hands forward, close together. She scarcely heard Mother Mary Thérèse's monotonous voice intone the words, in Latin, that she had so longed to hear; *arise, my love, my fair one, and come away … daylight and candlelight and the black-blood flickering flame in the elaborate sanctuary lamp.* Mother Mary Thérèse laid across her wrists a silken chord and wound it gently round; 'Do you,

Dorothy ...' and the young girl answered, 'Yes Mother, yes, yes, I do ...' And then she heard it announced, for the first time, her new name, the name by which she would be known for ever more, Sister Mary Evangeline. One of the assistant nuns laid across her outstretched hands the black habit of the order, the white pelerine, the girdle with the large and heavy wooden rosary. She bowed, and stood aside. And soon, with the others, she was led into the sacristy to be robed in the habit. She was helped, this first time, and with a thrill of joy and pain she noticed that her sponsoring nun was Sister Bernadette, her curls of chestnut-brown hair, her gentle hands, smiling, sure, deft. Sister Mary Evangeline bowed her head, grateful, smitten again, solemn-eyed.

She was stripped, first, to her underwear and stood, abashed, before Sister Bernadette. She brought her arms over her breasts to cover them and waited. There was a shift, an off-white linen underdress that Sister Bernadette helped her draw over her head. Then the black habit; it was heavy, the pleats of the skirt coming down almost to her ankles, the top half buttoned to the neck. Sister Bernadette buttoned it for her, slowly, smiling at her, remaining silent. Sister Mary Evangeline shrugged herself into some sort of comfort inside it. Then the pelerine; it was of linen, too, white and beautiful, ironed to a pleasing stiffness; it was down over her breasts, almost to her waist, then tied by long linen tapes behind her back and behind her neck. She found it difficult to tie it at her neck and her fingers fumbled against the fingers of Sister Bernadette before it was done. She was handed the rope girdle, white and hard, and shown how to draw it round her waist, slip the tasselled ends through the loop, draw it back and tighten it so that the ends hung down almost to her ankles on the right-hand side. Into the girdle she looped the heavy rosary beads, each bead of rounded wood, small brass chains holding it all together and at the end of it a wooden cross without its Christ.

Finally, Sister Bernadette came and stood in front of her, holding a brass crucifix with the figure of Christ Crucified, also in brass, the cross linked to a leather thong that was tied in a loop; Sister Bernadette kissed the crucifix, leaned forward and gently kissed Dorothy's cheek, then slipped the loop over

Dorothy's neck; the crucifix hung down over the pelerine and Dorothy held it up and gazed at it, wondering. She put the black veil on again, wearing still the white band that showed that she was not yet fully professed. Then she stood and waited.

When the other postulants were ready, the assistant nuns moved away, all except Sister Mary Clare. She lined them up near the door and waited, listening. They heard the pealing of the great organ in the chapel; Sister Mary Clare opened the door. 'One behind the other, Sisters,' she whispered, 'and follow me. Heads down. Hands joined in prayer.' The choir intoned the solemn '*Te Deum*'; Sister Mary Clare walked out slowly onto the sanctuary, the new sisters following. To the great majesty of the music, Mother Mary Thérèse would welcome them by name, and individually place around their shoulders the black cape of the order, joining it under their chins by a small brass clasp. They were professed.

Almost in a dream Dorothy, now Sister Mary Evangeline, welcomed her father and mother, blushed and bowed before Aunt Lily, and walked slowly with them around the convent grounds. Sister Mary Evangeline knew a fine intoxication in the love of Christ; she spoke modestly, her head lowered, her hands hidden in her sleeves, but her heart was singing, the '*Te Deum*' rang still in her soul, and the words of the Song of Solomon echoed through her brain …

For once, Lily was almost wordless. She had grown old, Sister Mary Evangeline could see, quite old. Her large body seemed to have shrunk, her eyes were dulled, a dark green beret sitting on top of her head did not disguise her near baldness. There was too much talcum powder on her face and her lips were too red with lipstick. She was, today, a discordant note but Sister Mary Evangeline accepted her, as she did her parents, flesh of her flesh, bone of her bone. From now on, and forever, Sister Mary Evangeline thought to herself, my spirit will never leave Christ's side; I will assent to suffering, to isolation, to labour.

Sister Mary Evangeline studied hard and enthusiastically, the rules and constitutions, the lives of the saints, the spiritual exercises of The Foundress. She joined the professed nuns in the main chapel, rising at two o'clock every morning to sing Matins with them, though she found it always difficult to remain awake, difficult to concentrate on the words, difficult to make her way back to her small room in the body of the convent, and to undress again, to get into her nightshift, and to sleep. When the convent bell would waken her again at six o'clock, she would have to wash in cold water in the delft jug on her locker, robe herself again in the difficult habit and pelerine, the girdle and beads, the veil and cape, and go back down to the chapel for Lauds. She lived in a lovely stupor, in spite of her tiredness; the word 'love' was everywhere, in her prayers, her singing of the Office, in the Mass, the meditations. She was happy. She knew it. She was at peace.

The days, the weeks, the months, flowed gently by for Sister Mary Evangeline, they flowed like a dream-river, and she lived in the dream and loved the dream. *How beautiful you are, my love, how beautiful, and your eyes are doves behind your veil.* The novices studied, morning, afternoon and evening, and all their study was love, the love of Jesus. *Before the dawn-wind blows, before the shadows drop away, I will make my way to the mountain of myrrh, I will travel to the hill of frankincense.* Though each day began in tiredness, though the habit was a weight on her developing body, though the routine of silence, of meals taken while listening to a nun reading from the lives of the saints, was deadening, though she occasionally had to take a class in the school or supervise a dormitory at night when one of the older Sisters was unwell, Sister Mary Evangeline's life was rich and contented, fervent and allayed. *She is a garden within high walls, my beloved, she is a garden enclosed, she is a fountain sealed.*

During the first summer of her noviceship, Dorothy and the other novices were given days of relaxation and recreation. She had not seen her parents since the day of her taking the habit; she would not see them again until the day of her first profession, after two years of the novitiate. She did not mind. The world and its blandishments were kept strictly at bay. But that month of July the days were very warm and the heat penetrated even the coolest hidden corners of the convent. The novices were brought, in the two convent cars, several miles to a secluded cove where they might picnic and swim. The cove was small, hidden by high cliff walls; the ground was rough and stony but the sea here was gentle, there were boulders to shelter them from the ocean winds; and from any prying eyes that might touch the spot.

They laid their towels out on the surface of some flat boulders. They moved carefully in behind high rocks. They had already donned swimsuits before they left the convent so they were able to leave their heavy habits, their cloying shifts, with ease. They swam and gambolled noisily, washing away the hours of silence and tension in a small riot of confused pleasure. This, too, their novice mistress told them, this is the grace of Jesus, this is the Jesus body, these erratics and these sloped sea-shores, these washed-up lives from the mysterious depths of the mid-Atlantic, sand-veins in the flesh of the mountains, stumped seams of granite across bared cliff-walls. And on the grassy slopes nearby, the swift umbel-shapes of dandelion, the wild iris blossoms that were soft as tissue-paper and strong as the force of the ongoing revolutions of the planets, all of these, too, were the Jesus-fingers, the love-song of the Creator for the world. *How beautiful are your feet in sandals, O daughters of the King; how the white curve of your thighs is like the curve of a necklace of finest pearls, the work of the Master's hands. And oh, how your burgeoning breasts, my lovely one, are like two fawns, like the twins of a gazelle. How beautiful you are, my love, how charming, you are my delight and the King himself is captured in your fairness.*

She swam out, then, Sister Mary Evangeline, away from the others, away from their easy chattering and excitement, out beyond the mouth of the small bay. She swam, relishing the power of her body, the supple strength of her limbs, the life and energy of her whole being. She swam slowly, powerfully. Then paused, turned on her back, and allowed herself to float under the clear and cornflower blue of the sky. The waves bore her up; the swell was gentle, a soft ululation of the water, an easy lift and fall of the tide. She stretched her arms out wide and floated freely. Her body felt complete, at peace, and her whole spirit was buoyed up.

Then, out of some association in her mind, the old song came back to her and the words and melody sounded in her brain: 'We were sailing along, down Moonlight Bay. We could hear the voices ringing, they seemed to say: "You have stolen my heart, now don't go 'way"...' She closed her eyes in recollection; she thought, at once, she heard a voice call her name, his voice, Patrick's, calling her, distant but distinct, 'Dorothy! Dorothy!' and her whole body jerked upright. For a moment she sank under the surface with the suddenness of her movement but there was no sense of panic, only that wonderful silence that the underwater holds, and that pounding sound of her own heart in her ears. When she surfaced again she saw that she was very far from shore. She felt her body being taken, slowly but ineluctably, by an invisible current that must sweep in and around the mouth of the bay. She began to swim as strongly as she was able, back towards shore.

She breathed hard. She urged her body to its greatest strength. She looked up again, towards shore. She was still very far out though she could see a figure away on the cliff-top, as if gazing out towards where she was and, foolishly, she imagined it must be Patrick, and that he was calling to her. She swam more urgently. When she looked up again the figure had disappeared and, for some reason, a memory of the day she had sat on the sea's edge with Packie Brennan came to her mind; that carefree day, a day of some strange intensity, a movement of thrilling sensation in her young flesh, and then that old black and white teddy bear that her aunt had given her ... and suddenly Dorothy felt a great surge of panic. She did not seem to be making any progress; she was as far out as ever, from the shore. She lifted her body in the water and tried to call out, but all that sounded was a faint cry, 'Help!', that would not have carried more than a few yards. She found herself under water again for a moment and when she surfaced she raised her body once more and waved her hands in the air, frantically. And sank again.

She had seen figures on the shore, the novices, her companions, but they were not watching out to sea; they were seated, eating sandwiches, drinking from their flasks of tea, and several of them were sitting on the stones in behind the rocks.

They could not hear her. They might not even have missed her yet. And as she surfaced once more she found herself saying his name, quietly, intensely, over and over, Patrick, Patrick, Patrick … She discovered a small calmness in saying his name aloud. She forced herself over onto her back where she could rest and float a while. She urged herself to be calm, to remain collected, to focus. She breathed deeply. Then she turned and began to swim again, as powerfully as she could, with a controlled movement and energy. She put her face into the water, breathed out, lifted her face, breathed in, and she was swimming more powerfully than she had ever done before. She grew aware that perhaps the tide had been turning, too, and whatever current had been there may have slackened. She was making progress. She would make it. She would be safe. She was glad, then, that none of the novices, and particularly Sister Mary Clare, had noticed her dilemma for somebody might have tried to come out after her and they would have got into difficulties, too. No, she would be safe, she would make it.

Dorothy never mentioned the danger she had felt herself in to any of the novices. When she reached shore she had simply walked up and down along the grass line above the stones, until she had gained some self-control and her breathing was quietened. Then she towelled herself back to warmth and joined the others for their picnic.

But that evening was the first time, at her regular place in the refectory, that Dorothy found herself being truly irritated by her neighbours. To her left sat Sister Mary Benvenuta, and opposite her was Sister Mary Margaret, who had been Maura Raftery. And it was Sister Mary Margaret who slurped her tea. Dorothy had never noticed that before and now it began to irritate her. She found herself watching the novice, surreptitiously, waiting for that ugly sound when she almost inhaled her tea with a slushing noise, then breathed out a loud *hhhaaaaa* sound. Dorothy shuddered. One of the nuns was reading from the *Martyrology* that evening and it was boring, a long list of the names of the saints, the virgins, the martyrs, whose memory was being recalled during this week, and all of this in Latin. Sister Mary Evangeline tried hard to focus on the names, though round about her some of the novices were beginning to giggle behind their hands as the poor nun found immense difficulty in pronouncing some of them. But Sister Mary Margaret continued to slurp. And Dorothy felt like rising from the table and running wildly down the long corridor to her little room.

Late summer turned into autumn and still Sister Mary Evangeline felt at peace, though troubled at times by her sisters' habits and foibles. She began to watch herself, to make sure that she, too, was not given to such irritating ways. At the singing of the hours in chapel she grew irked by Sister Mary Andrew who sang the Latin motets and the psalms with vigour and enthusiasm but sang off-key, her almost manly voice grating on the ear. But Sister Mary Evangeline relished still those prayers, those periods of grace and mystery when she was alone with her Christ, in that garden enclosed; *my lover is radiant and his skin is flush with health, he stands unique among ten thousand; his mouth is the source of sweetness, he is beautiful in himself; listen daughters of Jerusalem, for he is mine, lover and friend, and I am his, friend and lover.*

Sometimes the novices had to take a class for one of the nuns who had become indisposed. Sister Mary Evangeline did not enjoy the task, finding herself nervous among girls not much younger than herself, remembering how she had sat there, in those very desks, critical and negative, wishing to cause trouble and embarrassment to her own teachers. She took a class of girls one day, many of whom she had known in the earlier classes when she was in her final year. They wished to talk familiarly with her, and she with them, to ask them questions, about the town, about their games, about their families. But she knew she had to keep them at their studies, to hold them in quietness. So she assumed an authority and distance she did not really feel. She spoke crossly to them. She gave them work to do, an essay to write, while she moved about amongst them, her black habit swishing against the desks, the heavy beads of her rosary occasionally clunking against the wood. And she stood a while, gazing out the window at the trees and fields, how bare everything appeared out there, how dark and wet, and how the branches stood out cold and naked against the greying sky, how the fields beyond were black and fallow and empty. Several girls were whispering amongst themselves when she looked back, and giggling. For a moment Sister Mary Evangeline grew angry and was about to raise her voice and shout at them. But she held herself in check, smiled at the girls and quietly shook her head. They fell silent again and continued with her work. She was glad when the bell rang for the end of the class.

As she stood at the teacher's desk waiting for them to leave and the new pupils to come in for the next class, one of the girls approached her.

'Sister Mary Evangeline, may I speak with you a moment?'

'Of course you may. What is your name, please?'

'I'm Paula Meegan, I live in Crown Court. You know my family, Tom and Mary Meegan, they know your father well, he comes into their shop very often. And I know you, too, you're Dorothy, aren't you?'

'Paula, yes of course, I remember you. I think you were in second class when I was here, in final year. How are you? And yes, I was Dorothy, now I'm Sister Mary Evangeline.'

Paula smiled and reached her hand out to touch Sister Mary Evangeline on the arm. 'Yes, I know, you're Sister Mary Evangeline now. But I just wanted to say to you that you are still very pretty, Sister, you will make a very beautiful nun. The lads must be very annoyed.'

'Oh go along with you, Paula Meegan, what a thing to say!' said Dorothy, pretending annoyance. She smiled at the younger girl and began to leave the classroom. But she was pleased, she felt that her face must be flushed with pleasure, and she kept her head down and walked quickly along the corridor towards the convent. *How beautiful are your feet in sandals, my beloved, your legs are the work of a craftsman's hands; your breasts are rich like the clusters on the vine, and the fragrance of your breath is the fragrance of apples, sweet; your mouth is to me like the taste of good wine.*

The following spring, one day when Sister Mary Evangeline was walking in the convent garden, the small book of the Office in her hands, as she found herself distracted from the words by the wealth of buds on the rose bushes, by the vitality and strength of the songbirds in the flushed trees and hedgerows, she heard someone come walking down the gravel pathway towards her. She turned to see Sister Mary Clare approach her solemnly. At once, as she had often done before, Dorothy felt a vague guilt touch her, as if she had been caught in some activity unworthy of the high calling that she knew. She dropped her head again to read in her Office. Psalm 7:4: 'Why, oh God, does your anger rage against the sheep you have chosen? Remember your flock that you gathered together once before, remember how you redeemed and saved them … '

'Sister Mary Evangeline!' the mistress of postulants said, softly. She touched the novice gently on the shoulder, then stood back from her, folded her hands inside her sleeves and looked into the young woman's eyes.

'I have some sad news, I'm afraid,' the nun began. 'You will remember Nuala, I think she was a friend of yours? Nuala Coyne? You will remember her, how she had to leave us so soon, an illness that would not let her serve as one of us? You remember how she was?'

'Yes, Sister, I remember her well. I was fond of her.'

'Well, my child, she has been in hospital for a long time. And I am sorry to have to tell you that the Lord has taken her to Himself. God rest the poor child. God rest her!'

For a moment Dorothy did not fully comprehend. She stood looking at the nun for a while.

'Do you mean, you mean, has she died?'

'Yes, my child. She died last evening, peacefully, in the hospital. I think it was pneumonia, and that on top of her old illness, she simply was not able to survive it. She passed away into the embrace of her God. Now I want you and Sister Mary Margaret to go along tomorrow with me, we will be driven to Nuala's house where we will pay our respects to her family. We will pray quietly with them for a short while, and then we will come back here, you will say a final farewell to Nuala, and remember, dear child, she is where we all must go, she has merely left early, she is now finally in the care of the Lord where all we, after long travail, hope one day to be.'

All around her Dorothy could hear the singing of the birds in their mating, she could sense the earth itself swelling with life and new growth. She stood a long time, numbed. She could not find words of prayer. She closed her book of psalms. Three swans came flying in over the high sycamores beyond the convent grounds; she could hear the laboured breathing of their wings; she saw the clean white of their plumage, how their long necks were stretched out in front of them, how beautiful they were as they flew together, wheeling slowly down towards the river. She watched them until they had disappeared over the convent walls and had begun their descent towards the water. Then she turned slowly and made her way back towards the small oratory where she had prayed with the other postulants, and with Nuala. Perhaps she would find words to pray; perhaps she would find some consolation in the silence and loveliness of the presence there.

Mrs Coyne fussed about the Sisters when they arrived. A hush fell over the kitchen where people were gathered, trying to console the parents and Nuala's sisters, hoping by their presence to share a small portion of the burden, to ease the suffering. Sister Mary Evangeline felt strange in her heavy habit, her veil, the dark rosary at her side striking against the doorframe as she was led down to the parlour. She kept her eyes on the floor; she murmured vague consoling words to Nuala's mother. The Sisters were led into a cold parlour, scarcely ever used. The dark wood table had been shifted back against one wall. There was a large glass-fronted cupboard with the dishes that were used only on very special occasions. There were big uncomfortable chairs also pressed back against the walls and some of the neighbours were sitting there, not speaking, some of them saying rosaries quietly to themselves, some of them rising now and then to go up to the open coffin that stood in the centre of the room, raised on wooden trestles. A solitary high candle burned at the coffin's head. As the Sisters came in everybody stood for a moment and shuffled, awkwardly. Dorothy felt embarrassed, nodded to some of the people, then turned quickly towards the coffin.

Nuala lay, covered in a white-lace sheet, her hands joined together and a light-blue rosary twined through her fingers. There was a crucifix laid on her breast and Sister Mary Evangeline felt a strange horror as she recognised it; she wore her own crucifix over her pelerine and her fingers instinctively found it and held it. Nuala had been dressed in a light blue shroud; her head was lying back on a tiny white pillow. Her face, though it appeared a little yellow and drawn, seemed to Dorothy to show serenity. There was a small white ribbon tied under her jaw and around her head where the laced edge of the satin surround hid most of her golden hair. No words would come to Sister Mary Evangeline. She stood, the other Sisters stood on the other side. Mrs Coyne stood at the head of the coffin, her hand gently soothing Nuala's hair.

Dorothy reached her own hand in and laid it on Nuala's joined fingers. She was startled at the coldness of the flesh and hurt by the hardness of the skin. She closed her eyes, bowed her head as if in prayer. But no words came to her. Nothing, save for a strong resentment, and a terror for herself, a horror that she, too, would one day lie like this, cold, absent and other.

A small anger also grew within her. This girl had suffered so much in her short life, and others suffered little. Where, she wondered, was the love that could heal, without being asked, and heal from a distance; where was the voice that had offered comfort from the stern of a stricken craft, when all His friends were in terror of their lives? For the first time in such a short life, Nuala's body appeared to be fully at rest, there was no twitching, no limbs in torsion, no movement at all; the pain, the indignities, the involuntary jerkings of mouth and limb had vanished now into the white perfection of linen cloth and satin sheet. How is it possible, Dorothy thought, how can we live at all?

Sister Mary Clare muttered some prayers in a strong, though quiet voice. She held Mrs Coyne by the hand for a moment, gesturing towards the novices. Mrs Coyne glanced at Sister Mary Evangeline and smiled. The novice found, at last, that there were tears in her own eyes. She allowed them space a moment; there was nothing else she could say to the stricken woman. She saw the coffin lid standing like a sentinel against the wall; she saw the plaque already written and fastened to it, she saw the six brass screws shaped as small crucifixes that would soon fasten her down. Sister Mary Evangeline turned and walked as quickly as she could from the room.

For a long time, as that springtime lengthened, Sister Mary Evangeline could not find peace in herself. The words she loved had lost savour; *where has he gone, your lover, oh most beautiful among women, where has he gone? Which way has he taken, that we may hurry after him, to find him? I went down to the grove of hazel trees to see if he were there, and I could not find him. Return, O Shulamite, return to us, that we may gaze on you once more with pleasure …*

One of the older nuns, the Latin teacher, Sister Stanislas, was taken ill, and for several days Sister Mary Evangeline had to take her class and take her place at night in one of the dormitories. When she came into the class on the Monday morning she saw at once the young girl Paula Meegan, who had told her she was beautiful. Paula stood near the window at her desk, smiling at Sister Mary Evangeline. They said the prayers at the beginning of class. Sister Mary Evangeline had prepared the word 'this' for them; the 'demonstrative determiner', she told them and at once Paula's hand shot up.

'What does that mean, Sister, the demonstrative det …'

'Demonstrative determiner; it simply means the word "this", how it picks out one thing from a number of things. Here are some books for instance; I pick one up and say "this" book, or I pick a few and I say "these" books. You see? Demonstrative, showing. Determiner, picking out which one or ones.'

'Thank you, Sister. You explained it well,' and the young girl smiled up at Dorothy. For a moment the novice felt angry with the girl. Then she turned to the board, wondering where this anger came from. She wrote up the words on the blackboard: *hic, haec, hoc.* Then she turned back and explained masculine, feminine, neutral to them. And almost at once Paula's hand was up again.

'Why is table feminine in Latin, Sister, and why is book

masculine? How do you know when a thing is masculine or feminine?'

There was a small titter from the girls in the classroom and Sister Mary Evangeline again felt angry.

'You just have to learn them, that's all. You will know, sometimes, from the ending of the word. Such as, if it ends in a, like *mensa*, table, then it's feminine. So we say *haec mensa*, this table ...'

Several times during the course of the class the girls took down the forms of the word, copying them into their notebooks, with examples. While they wrote Sister Mary Evangeline glanced out the window. She felt uncomfortable, she felt annoyed at the persistent questioning by Paula Meegan. And then, suddenly, she felt as if she could understand that annoyance as she saw herself, several years ago, just like Paula, sitting in class, longing to understand, to know, to learn, and very much moved by her own Sister Bernadette at that time. Perhaps Paula was just like her, like another Dorothy, too much like her ... She was relieved when the class ended.

That night Sister Mary Evangeline had to take her place in number three dormitory. Most of the girls were from second year, including the class she had taken that morning. Each girl had her cubicle and it was Sister Mary Evangeline's task to go round during the preparation for sleeping to ensure quiet, to say the final prayers, to put out the lights. She had a large cubicle at the end of the dormitory and she was to sleep there. She felt tired after the day, very tired.

When silence had fully settled across the dormitory Dorothy stood at the end window and looked out over the darkening convent grounds. There was a quarter moon that sent a shivering silver light over the grounds, creating shadows that scarcely stirred. Over the trees she could glimpse some of the faint lights of the small town. She wondered about Nuala's family, how they were, she wondered about Nuala, lying out there in the silence of this night in the graveyard with its funerary sculptures, its stone angels gathering lichens and mosses, its bunches of flowers withering on the graves, and that same small and chill light throwing the gravestones into shadow.

She shivered and drew away quickly, turning into her own cubicle. She knelt a long while at the side of her bed, trying to pray. These days the words were still cold on her tongue and reluctant in her mind, the music lost and the images dead. She buried her head in her hands and leaned forward on the coverlet of her bed. Once again she found those inexplicable tears coming; she sobbed, quietly, once, knowing a shuddering of sadness through her entire body. Soon she changed into her nightdress and climbed quietly into bed, the heavy curtain drawn across the entrance. She folded her hands over her breast, closed her eyes and wished for sleep.

She came to with a start, she did not know how long she had slept, or dozed. Surely she had heard something, surely some noise had brought her awake. She sat up in bed and listened. For a while, there was nothing; a girl coughed vaguely in her sleep, a bed spring pinged, silence again. Sister Mary Evangeline laid her head back on the pillow and closed her eyes. And then she heard it, a girl's voice somewhere in the dormitory, calling '*Hic!*' That was all, but it was answered by a small giggling sound from someone else. Then it came again, '*Hic!*' followed somewhere else by '*Haec!*' and then a third voice chiming in with '*Hoc!*' Then there was quiet, but Sister Mary Evangeline could hear a smothered laughter somewhere. For a moment she smiled to herself; they had learned something, at least, from the hour in class.

It started up again, a voice here, a voice there, until many voices individually called out one of the sounds, and the demonstrative determiner was passed like a football around the dormitory: '*Hic*', '*Haec*', '*Hoc*', '*Hunc*', '*Hanc*', '*Hoc*', '*Huius*', '*Huius*', '*Huius*', '*Huic*', '*Huic*', '*Huic*', '*Hoc*', '*Hac*', '*Hoc*'. Dorothy had to grin to herself, it was funny, it was a gaggle of ducks individually quacking all over the dormitory. But she knew she had to do something, she could not simply lie there and let it happen. All the girls now appeared to be awake, there was a lot of laughter, and then she heard some girl call out 'Mary Evangeline is a determiner!' Again there was laughter. She rose, quietly, and put on her habit over the nightdress. She drew back her curtain and stepped out, in her bare feet, onto the wooden floor. She could see that the moon had lifted itself somewhat further into the night sky, but she had no idea what time it was. She began to move slowly about the dormitory.

But the girls knew her movements; they knew the creaking, however slight, of every board; they fell silent as she passed by the ends of the beds, all of them pretending to be asleep. And when she reached the far end of the dormitory someone up at the window end began it all over again, *hic, haec, hoc* ... For a long time Dorothy simply stood near the door of the dormitory, listening. She made up her mind to let them carry on; it was doing no harm, they would be tired next day, she would be tired herself, but somewhere deep down inside her a cold certainty had set in, like the first glaze of invisible ice over a pool of water. She felt the warmth of the heavy habit around her body and for the moment was glad of it. She buried her hands in the folds of her sleeves. She felt the crucifix lie against her bosom. She stood, and no prayers came, and she did not try to pray. When she got back to her cubicle, she closed over her curtain, took off the crucifix and laid it on the bedside chair, climbed into bed and promptly fell asleep.

Sister Mary Evangeline did not appear for Matins at six o'clock in the college chapel. At seven o'clock in the morning she was at hand to make sure that the girls were up and washing for the day ahead. When the seven fifteen bell rang she followed the last girl to the door of the dormitory, then went round all the cubicles to draw the curtains fully back. She went to her own cubicle, washed herself in the cold water from the delft jug, dressed in her habit and lay on the bed. She heard the bell for the seven thirty Mass ring out downstairs; she did not stir. After eight o'clock she heard the chatter of voices in the corridors below as the students were heading for breakfast. She lay on. After breakfast they would go out into the grounds, the day being fine, and enjoy a short period of free time. Then she heard the bell at five to nine; the girls would collect their books and bags and classes would begin at nine o'clock. She waited. Sunlight was flowing in to the dormitory and she could feel the warmth of a lovely day. There was a deep silence through the building.

She rose, gathered the few small things she had in the cubicle, her crucifix, her psalm book, her night clothes. She bundled them up in a towel. She gazed around the cubicle for a moment, then moved slowly down the dormitory towards the door. She could hear her own footsteps on the wooden floor. As she held the door open she glanced back into the dormitory; on one side the sun shone brightly through the windows; on the other the light was grey. There was a looming silence, a few dust motes floating on the air, a fine absence. She closed the door after her and walked along the corridor to the office of the Mother Superior. She knocked on the door and went in.

Several hours later Dorothy was being driven down the short, gravel path through the convent grounds and out onto the main road. The gardener, Johnny Traynor, had been given the task of bringing her the seven or eight miles back home. He was silent during the drive. Dorothy sat in the back, alone. She was dressed now in the old clothes she had worn on the day she entered as a postulant, almost two full years before. The clothes were ugly on her and ill-fitting. She leaned her shoulder against the car window and scarcely looked out, though the day was bright and the late spring was in full flower. There was heaviness in her soul that transferred itself to all her body. She had failed. She was a failure. Putting her hand to the plough, and looking back … In the boot of the car was her small suitcase, inside only a few of her poor belongings.

Johnny Traynor left her at the front gate of her house. He took her suitcase from the boot of the car and left it down at her feet. Then he straightened himself up and stretched his long, old body. He looked up at the clear sky, he looked at Dorothy's home. The engine of the old car was still running and the fumes from the exhaust rose white-grey into the air. He tipped his cap to Dorothy and got back into the car. He rolled down the window and called out as he revved the old engine: 'Good luck, Miss, may God be with you still!' Then he was gone.

Dorothy stood a long while at the gate. From far away she could just hear the tolling of the noon bell, the Angelus. Somewhere nearer at hand a dog barked, lazily. She could hear blackbird and thrush sing wildly in the escallonia hedge near the garden. The front door of her home was closed, all the windows were open at the top; she guessed her mother would be spring cleaning; it was a day for it, a day for an exact scrubbing and cleansing, for erasing the final memory of a wet and cold winter and airing the rooms with the finest airs of such a fine day. Dorothy wondered if her mother would be distraught. Dorothy had failed her. She had failed her God. She had failed herself.

The front door opened, suddenly, and Mrs Lohan stood there, her arms wide open, welcoming. Dorothy pushed the small iron gate open; it squealed its own welcome. Mrs Lohan began to walk down the short path to the gate, a smile of welcome on her face. Dorothy's heart lifted.

'Dorothy, darling, you're home!'

Dorothy lay into her mother's embrace, hearing the older woman hush her, hush, hush, hush, don't be afraid, we love you, we're happy you're home, Mother Superior telephoned, she said you had been wonderful, a good novice, but that you were unhappy, we don't want that, dear, no, we don't want that, hush, now, hush, and Dorothy wept, loudly and with great relief. After a few moments her mother took her by the shoulders and held her from her, gazing at her up and down.

'You look strained, darling, you have lost weight, and oh my God but that old brown suit makes you look forty years old. First thing, into town we'll go, down to Sweeney's and we'll get you all dressed up again. After a strong cup of tea, mind, come on in, come on in. You're home!'

THE RAVAGED EARTH

The first Sunday of September dawned bright and beautiful. Patrick sat on the men's side at First Mass that day, his mother sat on the women's side. She had a scarf on, a picture of the Blessed Virgin Mary in a blue veil marked the scarf; somebody had brought it back to her from Knock with a message that they had prayed for her and for Patrick's vocation, at the shrine. She was proud of that scarf, the face of the Virgin serene and pure and gazing out on the world with love. She knelt up straight and content in her pew and Patrick's heart shook for her; she would be lonely, of course, but it was a sacrifice she would offer gladly. Patrick's father was not there; he had muttered something at breakfast about having to go back on the mountain to care for sheep; there was a dog, harrying, he did not want to lose … but Patrick and his mother knew well that he was not able to face this day, to accept what it meant, what it would mean for himself and his own poor hopes.

Before the final blessing at Mass, Father Scott turned back to the congregation and asked them to sit up for a moment, he had a special word to say to them.

'My dear friends, my dear parishioners,' he began. 'Today is a special day in this parish. Today we will say goodbye, no rather, we will say farewell and God be with you, to a young man who has already brought some grace to our townland. Today Patrick Joseph Brennan is leaving to join the seminary where he will begin his studies for the priesthood. Now, when you look at me, I mean when you take a good look at me, your suffering curate for too many years, you will know how difficult and demanding a task it is; see how you have worn me out, and worn me down.' As he hoped, there was a small responsive snickering from his congregation. 'Seriously, it is a great grace when God calls someone to the religious life, it is a very special giving and a holy and sacred trust, and I want us all to kneel down today, at the end of this Mass, and pray for Patrick, and by our prayers to tell him that we will have him in our thoughts and prayers every Sunday from here out, until he comes back amongst us to say his first Mass for us. And if you, my dear parishioners, do not lay too heavy a burden on my poor shoulders, I shall hope to be here to celebrate that wonderful day with him, and with you all.'

Patrick held his head down during all of this; he felt a great burden being laid on his shoulders; he would have preferred to slip quietly away tomorrow, to leave behind no great expectations, no huge demands coming from his people on his young soul. But he knelt, too, and prayed for himself and for his mother. He glanced across at her and could see the glow of pride and happiness on her face, and in her bearing. For her he would make every effort, for her, and for himself.

Edward Brennan did not come home that day for his dinner. Nora laid his plate aside in the old Rayburn to keep it warm, but she knew it would shrivel and go dry. They did not speak of him, although his absence was heavy across the house all that day. Patrick was getting himself ready to leave for the novitiate, his black suit already bought, his white collarless shirts, the silver studs he would wear when he put on the priest's collar, his few books that he thought he might keep, his fob watch, still keeping exact time, his old missal.

The evening remained bright and still, the sea pool beyond the front yard scarcely stirred, save for the occasional ripple from a feeding mullet, or the sudden splash of a gull on the surface. His father had not come home and Patrick was anxious now.

'Mother,' he said at last. 'I expect he'll have taken a fair few bottles by now. He might be rough, because of what he is not able to face. About me, I mean. I hope you'll be all right when I ...'

She shushed him, though he could see the tension throughout her whole body.

'Ah God help him, sure he has his own dreams, the creature, and they haven't worked out for him. Though I'm probably the proudest mother in the country at this moment.' She ruffled his hair gently.

As the day darkened and the sky to the west was vivid in an orange and purple glow against a backdrop of small grey clouds, Patrick stood at the hedge at the end of the yard and gazed out on the world he was leaving. He had never felt it so small and hopeless, this holding at the brim of the ocean; behind him the shabby sheds where the turf and hay were kept, the wheel-barrow, the donkey and cart, and there, too, the old shabby dog with much of his hair matted and dirty, his old eyes shot with blood, his head hanging, his tail tucked between his legs. For the last time Patrick whistled him up and he came, pleased to feel safe in Patrick's presence, his tail wagging, though his eye was watchful for the older man with his quick and sudden cruelties. Patrick rubbed the old head for a while and whispered to the dumb creature, 'watch over Mother for me, Prince, be faithful to her, good dog, good dog …' Then he saw a fox, beautiful and cautious, appear from behind the hayshed and make its way slowly along the ditch, under the fuchsia. He saw at once that its late autumn russet colouring was almost the same as the beautiful glow across the evening sky and his heart surged for the wild creature, so few of her kind left along ditch and wood rim, bearing her own burdens silently. Patrick knew that her slipways were all wired now, to trap her, that her secrecies were almost all discovered, that she had been reduced to tarmacadam track ways and to the stench of man-sweat.

There was a price on her head, five shillings to any man or child that would bring a fox's tail in to the barracks. Edward Brennan was one of her most implacable enemies, out at night with powerful torchlight to inveigle her to her doom, to lure her out of safekeeping into slaughter. Patrick thought of the old dog, he thought, too, of his mother, anxious and nervous now sitting inside near the window, watchful, scared; it is a question of survival, he thought, and it has always been so. And how terrible for such a beautiful, wild and free creature of God's imagining, to be trapped in a cutting wire band that would hold her in torture through a long night, her howling reaching no sympathetic ears, how frightening and unbearable for her to be held weary in a cage, blank eyes fixed on her, she too, like Patrick himself, an anomaly, an ongoing exercise in meaning. He remembered, suddenly, the days he crept through the hedgerows up at Dorothy Lohan's house and how he relished the yield and softness of the dead leaves under his hands and knees, and he remembered the moment he had come across that battered panda bear and once again his heart lurched and pity for himself, for the dog, for his mother, for the beautiful endangered fox, flooded through him. 'I love you,' he whispered aloud to the evening, 'I love you, Jesus Fox, you Crucified, you beautiful, you slaughtered.'

Patrick watched the dog go slinking swiftly away, back towards the corner of the hayshed where it crouched, watchful. Then he heard the heavy boot falls of his father on the laneway, and the swishing of his hawthorn stick against the dandelions and rushes of the roadside. His father came staggering round the corner of the yard, pushing open the old half-rotten wooden gate and clattering it shut behind him. He was drunk, he reeled a little as he turned back towards the house. He saw Patrick and stopped.

'Not gone yet, then, your holiness?' and he laughed sourly.

Patrick did not answer. Out of the edge of his eye he saw his mother's face for a moment at the kitchen window. Edward stood a while, his heavy stick swishing lightly against his trouser legs. Patrick could see his face swollen with drink, his eyes rheumy, his lips lightly frothed with spittle. The older man simply said a loud, contemptuous '*Humph!*' and went unsteadily towards the door of the house. Patrick followed, slowly.

Nora called out, as the door opened, 'Edward, you're home. Your dinner will be on the table in a minute.' The old man stumbled in the doorway, took off his cap and tried to hang it on the hooks along the wall but it fell at his feet on the floor. He kicked at it and missed. Then he flung his stick onto the floor after it. He moved over to the table in the kitchen and sat, heavily, his misted eyes fixed on Patrick who came in after him, picked up the cap and hung it on its nail, and stood the stick up against the corner. Nora came over and put a plate of food down before the drunken man.

'What's this, Nora? What's all this? Is this what I'm gettin', this dried-out lump of meat and this mean old slop of cold spuds? Is this it? Is this what I'm worth? Or have you given all to our saint here? to keep him strong while he soaks up his books, while his father kills his self on the side of the mountain, keepin' sheep for our livin'? What's all this?' With a sudden rush of energy and anger Edward whooshed the plate off the table where it smashed onto the kitchen floor. He stood up, still unsteadily, and made to reach for his wife.

At once Patrick was at his throat. The son was now as tall as the father, and stronger in his sobriety. He held his father close, one hand against the older man's throat, and he pushed him back ferociously against the kitchen wall.

'You leave my mother in peace,' he shouted. 'You drunken old bastard, leave her in peace!'

His back against the wall, the old man's eyes were round as the plate that had been smashed against the stone floor, his two hands were weakly holding his son's hand, he was helpless, and frightened.

Nora came rushing up, calling softly 'No, Patrick, no, no, no, leave him be, he won't touch me, he won't, he's a good man, deep down he's a good man, don't harm him, leave him be, leave him be, please, leave him be.'

Patrick released him and stood back. Edward rubbed his throat carefully, eyeing his son. There was silence for a long while. Then the old man smiled, ruefully, and he moved slowly away out of Patrick's reach. 'Well, well, well,' he said. 'The baby's grown up, after all, the baby's not a baby no more. Not a mother's pet no more. He's maybe a man now, maybe, maybe.' He turned away and went stumbling out of the kitchen towards the bedroom. They heard the door closing quietly after him. Patrick drew himself up and sighed heavily. He was shaking. His mother came and took his arm and led him to the small fireside chair and sat him down. Then she sat in the chair on the other side of the hearth.

'Now Patrick, you are goin' for to be a priest and that's the most wondrous thing has ever happened in this sorry little corner of the earth and nothin', nothin' whatever must come between you and that great and holy calling. Listen to me now, listen to me. Your father is a good man. He has had it hard all his life, hard and tough and he grudges you goin', that's all, he grudges the loss of help, he grudges that you don't want to follow the life he had thought for you, and he sees that as an insult to himself, God help him. But he has never, ever laid a finger on me in violence, never, ever, and he won't, I know him, for sure if he does that's me gone for good out of this place, you being away now at the priesting, he knows it, I'm out of this house and away to my sister in Birmingham, has betimes tried to wheedle me away from him. But God help him, I'll be with him till the one of us dies, that's the truth, I'll be with him, and him with me, and we'll see each other into our graves in this place. You must not worry, my darlin' boy, you must not worry. An' there's your grandfather above in heaven and his one wish was to see this day come and you away to the seminary, his one great wish. So you'll go tomorrow, with our full blessing on you, and you'll write us when you can and maybe you'll get home for the odd day's holidays, and stay in your old room, and then, with God's mercy, you'll come home the priest and we'll be there, the two of us, dressed in our glory, to be given the Sacred Bread from your hands, and to be blessed by the sacred hands of our own, lovely son. You're to promise me now, you will not worry, things will be fine here, everything will be all right. I promise you. Now you're to promise me, you're not to worry about me.'

She sat strong and sure in her chair and Patrick's eyes were damp with tears. He leaned forward and took her hand in both of his and said, 'I promise, Mother, I promise.'

Father Scott drove Patrick from the small house at the edge of the estuary all the way to Kilruddery and the novitiate. For a while the boy stood before the high pillars of the front door and watched the car move away down the long and winding driveway, between fields with cattle and sheep, edged with high trees. He watched it stop at the big gates, then move forward and disappear away to the right on the main road. He felt bereft, that small and battered suitcase at his feet containing all his life and all his hopes. He turned and picked up the case.

The great wooden door of the mansion was of dark oak, with a huge brass knocker. Patrick knocked on it, gently, but the sound came back to him like a great thundering through a hollow space beyond. He waited, his heart thumping. He heard the flapping sound of slippers and the door opened, slowly, inwards. A woman stood there, surprising Patrick. She was elderly and plain, wore a large brown housecoat over indistinct jumper and skirt. She stood, gazing at the young man.

'Em, I'm Patrick Brennan, I'm expected?'

She nodded and beckoned him inside. 'Wait here!' she said, simply, as she closed the door behind him. It seemed to him that it closed with a deadening thud. He shuddered slightly. He was surprised to find himself in an enormous conservatory, not in a hallway or room. There was an unnatural heat in the place. It was high and there were green growths slightly darkening the glass ceiling. The high sides sloped gently down to the glass walls, to the rows of plants and flowers that grew on either side of the house, stretching away towards a small door at the furthest end. The woman slipped away between the rows of plants and he heard the strange sluppering sound of her shoes on the marble floors.

There were several high green trees down the centre of the conservatory, they reached and hung their heads against the high roof, their leaves thick and wide and dark green. Some of them were offering great, almost obscene, red and purple flowers, large as pineapples. Others trailed long thin thread-like seeds that hung down in utter stillness towards the floor. There were two rows of flower beds running parallel to this central bed, two more along the walls to the side. All the beds were filled with strange and wonderful flowers, in all colours, in all sizes. Patrick could name very few of them; some looked like lilies, save that they were scarlet coloured and had long yellow tongues reaching out from them; many of these tall plants offered bird-beak shapes, though they were in exotic and emphatic colours, yellows, oranges, blues. Flowers that took the shape of butterflies, or dragonflies, or birds. An almost overwhelming scent filled the conservatory but to Patrick it was pleasant and reassuring. There was a small plashing sound, constant and soothing, and he found, right in the centre of the conservatory, directly under the apex of the rounded ceiling high above, a pool where a small fountain dribbled water down over water-lilies and huge, green pods. He could see some golden fish move slowly through the stems, and here and there a larger fish, carp, he thought, though several of these had tails and fins of strange colours and intricate design.

Down at the end of the conservatory, over the door through which the housekeeper had vanished, was a large crucifix, the body yellowish white, the head fallen on the shoulder, the nails and the blood, the dribbling pus from the thorn-crowned head more realistic than Patrick had ever seen before. He realised that he had almost forgotten, in his surprise at the conservatory, where he had come and for what purpose and now, waiting, he gave himself up to contemplation of the crucified Lord. He felt that he could almost hear the hammering that fixed that too-sensitive body, with long nails, onto the wood, and how that sound, hammering still across the world, opened once and for always the abyss of our humanity. He knew that, in the fact of crucifixion, there would be no beauty in the body that hung there, that had writhed in its solitude, in its waiting, there in the bleak and uplifted perpetuity of time. For an instant his father and his contained violence slipped sideways into Patrick's mind but he dismissed the image, quickly. Humanity, he knew, was riddled through with the nerves of violence.

Near the floor, to the side of the small door, was a tree that Patrick took to be some kind of holly, though the large berries it bore were not red, like the blood-berries on the body hanging above, but a dark green. The leaves themselves, prickly and threatening, were green but with a core of rust, and beside the tree stood sunflowers, several of them tall as Patrick himself, but the flowers were stripped of their petals, the heads stood black and ugly and large, the stalks blackening and drooping, as a watcher might droop with sorrow before the crucified. For a while Patrick felt a strange and strong stirring within him, a determination that he would do his very best, as priest, to bring about the world of peace and love that this man had suffered and died for. He would offer the Christ his whole life.

As he kept gazing up at the sorry figure the door opened and a young man came in. He was dressed in a black soutane, he wore the full priest's collar and the very edge of a blue stock could be glimpsed; around his waist a double black chord, falling down in regular knots almost to the ground where it ended in two black tassels. He was handsome, with wavy black hair; his light blue eyes were bright and sparkling and his face glowed with inner contentment.

He shook hands with Patrick. 'Hello,' he began. 'My name is Mr O'Donnell. I presume you are one of the new postulants?'

Patrick nodded. 'Well,' Mr O'Donnell went on. 'You're welcome. I hope you'll be very happy here. The novitiate lasts a year, you know. Those of us who entered last year will be leaving next week for the seminary in Dublin, so we'll be a little crowded till then. I believe there's a big intake of postulants this year. And oh yes, by the way, we call each other by our surnames here. I'm Mr O'Donnell. And you are … ?'

Patrick hesitated. It felt strange to him to say Mr Brennan. 'I'm Patrick Brennan, I mean, Mr Brennan.'

'You're welcome, Mr Brennan. And oh by the way, we never come in here, to the conservatory, I mean. There's a main entrance round the side, through the archway. But of course you weren't to know that today. Come on, I'll show you to your room. I'm afraid you'll be sharing till next week, but I suppose it'll help to get you settled in. This way.'

Mr O'Donnell led Patrick out through the small door, along a short corridor with frosted glass windows on either side and into a larger hallway where the floor was of polished wood and there were rows of high cupboards in lightly varnished wood.

'This is the beginning of the sacristy,' Mr O'Donnell whispered. 'In here you'll keep your surplice and biretta.'

He led him through another door and Patrick was astonished that the house appeared so enormous, once you left the conservatory. They entered another long corridor, with the same wooden floor; this time there was frosted glass in the ceiling, allowing a cold light to shine through; on either side of the corridor were doors, all of them firmly closed.

'This is the priests' quarters, we never come in here, either, unless we have to speak with the novice master, or the bursar, or our spiritual director.' Mr O'Donnell was still whispering. Their shoes made a soft slither-sound along the floor. At the end of this corridor was another door that led into a small vestibule; to the right was an open door looking out onto a yard; to the left a staircase in light blue marble and beige stone rose steeply. They began to climb.

The first floor showed another corridor, rooms off on either side; it was very dark, save for a pale light coming from a larger room at the far end that looked like a washroom. Patrick shuddered a little; it was cold in here, even on this fine September day. They climbed another flight of stairs, reached a corridor similar to the last, and climbed again. Here there was another corridor exactly like the one below save that here, to the right, there was a door that Mr O'Donnell pointed to and whispered: 'That's the way down into the novitiate. And look, up there on the wall, that's the bell. That's what tells us the time of day, calls us to meals, prayer, study, work. And this corridor, this is for the novices, you'll be here somewhere. Names outside ...' He was still whispering. Slowly they moved down this dark corridor; outside each door was a small panel on which a name was written: Mr O'Reilly, another one had Mr Fagin, another Mr Doherty. They reached a door and outside it was a panel with three names: Mr Ryan, Mr Bergin, Mr Brennan. 'Ah!' whispered Mr O'Donnell with satisfaction. 'You're in here. Two others I'm afraid, but, as I say, it's just for a week. Then you'll have a room ... when the rest of us skip it, I mean. I'll leave you to it. Just put away your things. Then come on down, out that door I pointed to, come down to the yard, you saw the open door. I'll be there. So will Father Maloney, the novice master you know. He'll want to meet you.' Patrick opened the door and said 'Thanks very much' to the novice; he was already whispering; it was the thing to do;

it was perfectly natural. Mr O'Donnell touched him on the shoulder, nodded and smiled, then stuck his thumbs into the chord around his middle, turned and went slowly back down the corridor. Patrick had arrived.

There were three beds in the room, there were no cubicles; there was one small window; the beds were crushed close together; one wardrobe behind the door, no chairs, no other furniture whatever. Patrick could see he was the first to arrive in this room. He looked around at the sparse area in which he had to begin his new life. He chose the bed nearest the window and rested his old suitcase on top of it. He sat on the bed, knowing at once its hardness. There was a large crucifix over the door; there was one bulb in the centre of the room, under a dull white shade. Patrick sat a while, and a great heaviness and nervousness settled on him. He shook himself and opened the suitcase, drawing from it the old missal he had used in the scholasticate. He opened it at random, then shut it again quickly, laughing ruefully. The passage that struck his eye read: 'I dwell in darkness, like the dead, long forgotten, so my spirit faints inside me and my heart, heavy within me, is appalled.' But he knew he would get through this cold beginning, this distance. He gazed up again at the crucifix; the right hand of the figure had been broken at the wrist, giving the body an even more painful look. Patrick closed his eyes and tried to pray.

A bell rang at exactly six o'clock and all the new arrivals found their way to the study hall. There was a low buzz of conversation among them while they waited. The study was a low building, great windows down both sides, a podium at one end, desks in neat rows, like a large classroom. The novices, in their soutanes, flitted about among them, directing them to desks, urging calm. They sat and waited. Patrick felt very much alone; in spite of the years at the scholasticate he was the only one from St Canice's who had come to join the order. Most of the other arrivals looked sheepish and lost, too. Soon the door opened and a tall and angular-looking priest came in. His body was thin and ascetic, his face grave and stern. All the novices stood up, quietly; the new arrivals stood up, too, making something of a scraping sound with their desks.

The priest took his place at the podium. He gazed at the assembled young men. His eyes were piercing, his long thin fingers with immaculately groomed nails gripped the side of his high desk. He pursed his lips and blessed himself, aloud. They all answered Amen. He looked down at them again and said another prayer: 'Come oh Holy Ghost, fill the hearts of thy faithful and kindle in them the fire of thy Divine love.' Then he blessed himself again and sat down. The young men sat at their desks. Father Maloney made a small triangle of his joined hands, as if in prayer and gazed down at them for a while. Then he picked up a breviary and read aloud:

'Here is a song of David, who said, Blessed are you my God, my rock, who train my hands for war and my fingers for battle.'

He closed the book. 'I am happy to see so many of you. You are welcome to Kilruddery. I hope you will be happy here and that you will grow in the love and service of God. You are some thirty new men amongst us. We have eighteen who have taken their first vows and who are travelling on to the seminary in Dublin. Thirty of you. It is good to see that Holy Mother Church is still alive and strong. And growing ever stronger. We are here to serve God in His Holy Church. Now, at the beginning I quoted to you from David who said we are being prepared for war, and for battle. Because it is a war, it is a battle, the war for the salvation of the world, the battle to save our own souls. You will each find, in the desks before you, a copy of the *Rules and Constitution of the Holy Trinity Order*. Please now, quietly! open your desks and take that out. We will take a quick look at the contents of that book which shall be your battle orders for the coming year ...'

On the Friday of that first week, the young men were officially welcomed by all the ordained priests in the house. In the chapel of the novitiate, a small chapel with a beautiful rose window behind the altar, wooden pews in choir formation and a small organ gallery at the back, ice-frosted windows that allowed in a

pure light and high vases of flowers about the altar, they felt
warm and welcomed as Father Maloney called out each name:
Michael Aldington … James Peter Bourke … and each boy
responded, 'Here, Father, begging admission to the Order'.
Father Maloney then said 'You are given admission' and the boy
left the altar by a side aisle, into the corridor by the sacristy
where he collected his soutane, his chord, stock and collar and
came back in through the door in the sacristy. Father Maloney
welcomed each one back: 'Mr Aldington, you are now a novice
in the Order of the Holy Trinity … Mr Bourke …'

Patrick felt strange in his soutane; the collar and blue stock
felt tight under his chin, but he was deeply happy and at peace.
When they were all prepared Father Maloney began the
celebration of a Solemn High Mass, his singing voice high and
clear and finding delicate echoes among the timbers of the
chapel. The older novices chanted the responses in Latin and
everything was beautiful, slow, solemn and moving. Mr Patrick
Joseph Brennan was a novice.

'In the Holy Trinity Order we have three seasons,' the novice
master told them. 'This is the first season, between September
and Advent; then Advent to Easter, and Easter to September.
And in each season each novice will have a special function and
I will announce these functions now.' The new men were
seated in the study; the day was dark, there was rain and wind
outside. They knew, too, that tomorrow the professed novices
would be leaving by bus for Dublin and they, the new recruits
(for in the metaphor of war and battle this is how Patrick
thought of himself) would be on their own, with the priests and
their novice–master. The latter then read down through his list:
'Mr Aldington, regulator. Mr Bourke, grass verges. Mr Doyle,
sacristan … Mr Brennan, altar.'

Later that day each recruit was taken by the older novice who
had just relinquished that post and was shown how to do the
work. Patrick learned that he was to visit the conservatory every
morning and speak with the Brother in charge there, a gardener
who had spent many years on the missions in Lagos, who knew

the growth of the exotic plants, and the flowers that could be cut and delivered to decorate the altar. These flowers had to be changed every three days, the old ones brought out to the edge of the farmyard where they would go to make compost, the new ones to be arranged sensitively on the altar. On the other days Mr Brennan was to visit the priests' corridors on the east wing of the mansion and replace the flowers in the vases left on the corridor windows. The third day was given to gathering the normal flowers from the novitiate grounds where there were smaller gardens of roses and seasonal flowers, such as lilies, carnations, irises. Mr Brennan found himself happy in this task though it took him many efforts to get the balance on the altar right, flowers on the altar itself, flowers in the left part of the sanctuary to balance flowers to the right, the whole to be a tasteful and prayerful mix of the exotic and the homely.

Mr Brennan found that he could pray wonderfully while working with the flowers on the altar. He performed this task between ten and eleven o'clock when the chapel itself was deserted and he alone moved about the altar, close to the Presence. Above the altar was a statue of the Virgin Mary and at the base of this statue he began his work, usually with flowers that were small and gently grouped in a special vase; his task was to try and present a mixture of flowers that were blue and white. As he worked at the base of the statue his eye was always taken by the great Crucifix that was painted high on the wall, between the Virgin's statue and the rose window; it was an exquisite reproduction of a Crucifixion painting by one Duccio di Buoninsegna, the yellow-white body crumpled on a cross of plain brown wood; above the crossbeam were angels watching, all of them in tears and greatly distressed; the background of the painting was a vaguely gilt-coloured panel without landscape, all of the work looking a little like a Russian icon, the head of the Christ, haloed, drooped in the agony of death. Out from the burst side flowed a stream of blood and water and blood dripped from the burst hands and the feet. One great black nail pierced both feet and from it blood flowed down onto the bottom of the painting and Mr Brennan always felt that this blood dripped away onto a broken world imagined underneath, into the dark abyss of human suffering.

The Cross, he imagined, was dressed with a human flower, that flower having its roots in the dark abysm of human terror, the terror of that violence that has rent and seems destined to go on rending the lovely earth, and not even the angels in Heaven can support such horror. How is it possible for human beings to take another human being, and hammer rude nails through the wrists and the tender bones of the feet, cracking the bones, bursting the flesh, while the cries of the most gentle of human beings echoed through the air, the cries of agony whimpering out over the hours?

The Crucified Christ, Mr Brennan thought, hangs forever in a desperate present. Beginning every day with this image before him, he found his thoughts so often focusing on human hurt that he always hurried to his reading of the psalms, at Lauds and at the other Hours, to give him some joy in his living. For the novitiate was difficult. They rose each morning, with the harsh ringing of the electric bells along the walls, at ten minutes to six. They retired each evening with the final ringing of the bells, at ten o'clock. Between those times they sang, in Latin, the Hours, Matins, Lauds, Vespers and Compline, and recited to themselves, in quietness, the minor hours, Prime, Terce, Sext and None. They had classes morning and afternoon with the novice master; they had their morning periods of manual labour when they performed their allocated functions and sometimes, in the afternoons, they were allowed to play games – football, basketball, tennis – if they were not needed for work on the farm or gardens, picking potatoes, snagging turnips, weeding the onion patch. They had time for study and for private prayer. Their meals were all taken in silence while one of the novices read from the martyrology, in Latin, and then from a spiritual book or life of the saints.

For Patrick it was all delightful, he felt his soul expanding to the glorious but demanding God that he was coming to know. He relished those Hours in the chapel, the Latin chants, the kneeling and praying, the solemn liturgies. He felt, with the long hours of meditation, reading and silence in which he moved, that he was back in the Middle Ages when God was moving amongst the people and the people responded to Him, with service and with love.

'Now,' the novice master began one day, 'we must talk about the vows of poverty, chastity and obedience. These are the vows you will take at the end of the year, when your novitiate is completed and before you go to Dublin for the next stage of your studies. We will take them, one by one. And the first of these is poverty, holy poverty …'

Patrick knew that this would cause him little trouble; he had ever been but poorly off, there was nothing in the world he considered his own and among the priests there was little that they would acquire through a long life of service. Father Maloney asked them to consider, all that afternoon, that if there was any object whatsoever among their possessions, in their rooms, anything to which they attached any particular personal importance, then they had not yet moved towards holy poverty. They were to go and examine their rooms, even their places at chapel, their work places, and if they found anything they were to bring that, at once, and with love, to present it to Christ in the presence of the novice master. They were to give up the world, all the goods of this ephemeral planet, and live in the poverty of Christ and they would have treasure in heaven.

That afternoon, in the quietness of his room, Mr Brennan found, in a small drawer in the cupboard at the side of his bed, the fob watch and chain that he had received these many years ago. Instinctively he wound that watch every night. It kept perfect time. It had never failed him over the years. He loved it and had assumed that it was an essential part of his living. He had no wristwatch; he had lived and circled his living around this fob watch. On the end of it still was the chain that John William Mills had given him, so long ago now, it appeared, with the sodality medal on which was inscribed that boy's initials. With a great pang of grief he realised he was wholly attached to that watch. He remembered, too, the day with Dolly … and the watch seemed to hold a great deal of the urgencies of his life in its perfect shape. At once he knew he had to give it up. He kissed it. He put it into the deep pocket of his soutane. He made his way to Father Maloney's office.

On a fine mid-October afternoon, Mr Brennan was out in the novitiate grounds, in soutane and collar and stock, where he wished to pray the minor hours in the good God's air. The grounds were laid out between trees with neat walkways, the grass edges perfectly trimmed, flower-beds beginning now to fall into autumnal dismay, yet there were roses clinging to their bushes and many of the trees were still full-leaved and beautiful. Mr Brennan walked slowly across the nearer grounds, the ordered walkways, on the soft and softly sounding gravel. Then he passed through a gap in the cypress trees and moved out by the playing fields towards the far ends of the grounds. The day was so lovely, with only the faintest sense of a chill in the air, that he relished every moment of the silence and the freedom about him. At the far end of the novitiate grounds, well out of sight of the building itself, a high hedgerow closed off the acres from the world beyond. And down there, at the very furthest edge, was a fine Calvary, the figures of the Crucified Christ, with his Mother Mary and Mary Magdalene standing gazing up in sorrow at Him, all sheltered in a high concrete niche. Many of the novices liked to stand here, gaze up at the statues, and pray.

He stood for a long time; he recited to himself, from the Office, the psalms and prayers of Sext and None. Sometimes he whispered some of the psalms out loud, to the air, to the trees, to the Crucified Christ. 'God,' he whispered, 'the artist, crazed by eternity, crazed by loneliness and isolation, shaped a cross against a sky in chaos; He took his Son for model, the Christ impressed upon the wood, to see how mankind might suffer, to know the inner focus and point and stress of human pain, and there were soon, on the sacred body, blood-dribbles standing bright against the drained-clay flesh; and afterwards, to the consternation of the God, other humans came, they buried the bones, the Jesus Bones, and left them in the earth, and went away.'

Somewhere in the bushes a bird flitted, distracting his eye. He moved to the edge of the path, to where a thicket of fuchsia bushes hung their still flourishing florets of Christ-blood red over the path. He thought a moment of the fuchsia bushes that grew scraggy and twisted down by the shore where his own poor home shrugged itself in against the sea-winds and his heart gave a huge lurch of loss; his mother, God help her, how was she? The letters he could write home only once a month were read by the novice master and any letters he received came to him, the envelopes slit, and he knew the master read these, too. In this way, he could not be certain of her actual wellbeing, her letters short and generalised and confined to offering prayers for her son and begging his prayers for her and for his father. Already he longed to see them both, to walk again the wild-grass and salted lanes to the pier, to watch the sea pool fill slowly, to hear the gentle plopping sounds of the fish, to see the heron come planing in from the boglands to stand, erect and watchful, on the encrusted stones by the pool.

A sudden hissing sound startled him. '*Sssstt!*' it sounded, like a snake. He wondered if it was some small bird, a wren, perhaps, and he went nearer to the fuchsia hedge. Then he heard a voice, a male voice:

'Father, Father, over here!'

He glimpsed a face peering at him through a small gap in the hedge, the face of a young man, about twenty-five years of age, a face brown and somewhat ugly, the brow ridged under black hair scarcely brushed, a large nose and a badly shaven jaw. The novice was startled. Between him and the man was the fuchsia hedge, then a fence of barbed wire. The man now glanced about him, beckoned to the novice to move a little further to his right, along the hedge. Mr Brennan did so, with some trepidation. There was a gap in the hedge where the wire had been cut or broken, the novice could see through onto a muddy lane beyond. The man beckoned to him.

'Here, Father, come and see, come and see!'

The man skulked somewhat. Mr Brennan passed through the gap and found himself held by the elbow and drawn, gently but forcefully, by the man outside. 'Come on, Father, come and see!'

Mr Brennan saw a donkey, lean and hungry-looking, tied by a rough rope to a fence-post; beyond the donkey, its shafts drawn up and pointing skywards so that underneath it was a space of shelter, was a painted cart, the big wheels missing some of the wooden spokes. And in the sheltered space was a roughly put-together canvas tent, small and mean-looking, with a forked stick holding it up and offering an opening within. The novice could at once see a woman inside, sitting on a sack of some kind, and holding an infant on her lap. The scene was one of abject misery and poverty and Mr Brennan was shaken by the sight.

'You see, Father, that's Janey, she's my wife, Father, an' that's my daughter, Maura Jane, she's barely two month, Father, an' we're findin' it tough to live, you know like, an' you'd be doin' God's good work now if you could get us some food, mebbe a drop a' milk, too, such like, Father, and God will be good to you so He will.'

The man's wheedling voice irritated the novice. 'Have you no work you can be doing?' he asked.

'Ah sure Father, where's the man nowadays'll give work to a poor traveller like me, an' sure haven't I to give all my time to me wife an' chil', an' to the oul' ass there, you know. Sure, you might be able to get us a wee drop a' milk now, mebbe a slice a' bread or some such?'

'Why don't you go up to the farm there, at the novitiate, just around the back of these fields? Or even up to the novitiate itself, only don't go in through the conservatory, just through the arch over at the side ...'

'Ah sure, Father, haven't I bin up an' down the road time an' again, an' there's a priest there ran me, Father, ran me, an' me simply askin' for a drop a' milk for the chil'.'

'A priest, are you sure? Maybe it was Brother Luke, he's in charge of the kitchens.'

'Priest or Brother, Father, sure I wouldn't know, but he ran me like, you know, he ran me, so he did. The twice I was up at him, he ran me. An' look at the poor chil', she's sleepin' now, thanks to God, but she does wail and weep a deal, Father, a great deal, with the hunger you know, an' the thirst.'

'I'm not a priest, by the way, you can call me Patrick, if you like, or Mr Brennan, I'm not a priest, I'm only a novice.'

'Sure Father, I don't know nothin' about them things, nothin' at all, only I know you'd be doin' God's good work now, if you could ...'

When he got back to the novitiate, Mr Brennan made his way through the refectory which was empty though all set out for lunch, the tables covered in perfectly white linen, the cutlery arranged, the water-glasses upside down at each place. He knocked on the door that led into the kitchens but there was no reply. Cautiously he pushed the door open. The kitchens were empty, a boiler bubbling softly in one corner, great pots on a large range, all gleaming, dishes and pans stowed away and stacked in their places. Even the flags of the floor were shining clean. Mr Brennan hesitated, then moved quickly towards a cupboard. He found several loaves of bread wrapped in greaseproof paper, one of them already opened but leaving most of the bread untouched. He took the loaf and moved over to the scullery where he found a large can of milk and, under a wrapping of silver foil, several slices of cooked beef. Carefully he took some slices, shoved them into the loaf of bread, then dipped a tin porringer into the can of milk and filled it. There was complete silence in the kitchen, save for the murmuring of the boiling water. Mr Brennan opened the door that led out into the farmyard of the novitiate; the yard was empty, too, and slowly and carefully he carried the treasure across the yard and out into the novitiate grounds.

As he arranged the exotic flowers about the altar next morning, the lilies, the orchids, the strange palm leaves that were shot through with scarlet and purple lines, Mr Brennan gazed up a while at the Crucified in Buoninsegna's picture. It occurred to him that the closed eyes of the Christ were not really closed at all, that they were watching the young novice in his efforts, that the arranging of the flowers, these hothouse and sheltered beauties, was in itself a prayer but that there was a greater prayer from yesterday, that of bringing simple gifts to the travellers beyond the fuchsia hedge. And either side of the tabernacle, in two small glass vases, Mr Brennan had set two beautiful sprigs of fuchsia from that hedge, the blood-flowers perfect in their humble hanging, the simplicity of the leaves and the long slender sepals wholly beautiful and for the first time, as he arranged the sprigs as close to the housed Sacred Host as possible, the novice noticed the thin branches and how red they were, like veins that lead to the bleeding fingers of the flowers.

'The suffering of Jesus,' he thought to himself, 'and the suffering of the poor. All linked here, on this altar. And let it be a prayer for peace, for the ending of violence, for the bringing into human love of all suffering peoples.'

The novice knelt on the bottom altar step a long time, his heart full, the silence of the empty chapel about him resounding with praise of the world and of God.

As the novices came filing out of the chapel some days later, having sung Lauds together, the novice master beckoned to Mr Brennan. At once a chill passed over the young novice's body. He followed Father Maloney along the corridor, the priest's tall figure erect and challenging, the stride determined and sure. They climbed a stairs to the priests' corridor, Mr Brennan trailing behind. Father Maloney opened the door of his office and beckoned him to come in. The room was large and bright, two high windows looking out over the ordered novitiate garden. There was a large desk in the centre of the room, two horsehair chairs facing it and a high wooden chair where Father Maloney sat. There were filing cabinets against the wall to the right, a fireplace with a plain wooden fireguard in front of it, and over the fireplace a wooden cross, without figure.

Father Maloney sat at the desk and motioned the novice to sit at the other side. The novice sat, nervous, wondering. Father Maloney then laid his elbows on the desk before him, joined his hands in prayer, closed his eyes. His lips moved soundlessly a moment. Then, suddenly, his eyes were fixed on Mr Brennan's and the novice knew the piercing power and directness of that gaze.

'Brother Luke has been telling me a strange tale, Mr Brennan, and I wonder how you will respond.'

'I'll try, Father.'

'Yes, yes, yes, but it's quite serious you see. Here we are

touching on one of the vows you will be expected to take if you stay with us. The vow I speak of is obedience. Obedience. Now that does not simply mean that you do everything you are told by your superiors, it means far more than that. And in this case I am shaken and astonished at the news I hear.'

He paused and the novice sighed softly to himself.

'It appears that a tinker, a young man of scruffy appearance, came to the kitchen door some days ago. Brother Luke gave him food, he tells me, some cooked chicken, I believe, some bread, some milk. Good, nothing strange in that. But the man returned the next day, begging again, and this time Brother Luke turned him away. We are not in a position here in the novitiate, Mr Brennan, to feed the beggars of the countryside. Now, it appears that someone by the name of Father Brennan, again according to Brother Luke, entered the kitchen, took away some food, beef this time, I am told, some bread, and a metal bowl in which there was probably some milk, and gave this to the tinker. Because the tinker returned, a Timothy Stokes, I believe and when Brother Luke told him he was not to beg here again, he retorted with the story of Father Brennan. Now there is no Father Brennan in this building, but there is you, Mr Patrick Brennan, there is you.'

'Yes, Father, I found the family down at ...'

He was interrupted. 'I have no wish to know the details. None at all. What I need to know is this, Mr Brennan, do you really consider it your place to take food and other stuff from our kitchen, without leave of anybody, and distribute it where you see fit?'

'No Father, but there was a baby ...'

Father Maloney raised his hand, a long El Greco-figure hand, the fingers delicately long, the shirt sleeve with its stud showing. Then he lowered his hand and began to handle papers on his desk.

'Now, I speak of obedience. This is a sin against obedience. In the order you must subject your will wholly to the will of Jesus, and anyone in a position over you stands in the body of Jesus, and him you must obey. Implicitly. You would now have seriously, quite seriously, broken your vow, if you had taken such a vow. But you will take such a vow, if you remain amongst us. I see here that you were in some faint trouble in the scholasticate, it appears you did not accept the authority of the priests set over you there.'

'But that was …'

'No, no, and again no! I do not want to know details. What I see is a propensity here to take the law into your own hands and to behave as if you were not responsible to anyone. It will not do, Mr Brennan, it simply will not do. Now, I have seriously considered dismissing you from the novitiate.'

Father Maloney again put his long fingers together as if in prayer, brought the tips of his fingers to his lips and gazed at Mr Brennan. The novice knew a strong pain deep in his stomach; he saw his mother, standing at the door of their old house, watching him return in disgrace; he saw his father standing in the door behind her, a smirk of satisfaction on his face.

'I am sorry, Father … truly sorry, I was simply trying to help in what appeared a desperate situation. The baby …'

Once again that hand was raised to terminate the conversation.

'You will need to be more true to your Christ, Mr Brennan, you will need to obey, in all its details, and in all its facets, your superiors. You will not act without permission, of me, or of Brother Luke, or of the head novice, you will even obey, as is your duty, the oldest novice on the walk when you go out in threes each week. This is obedience, Mr Brennan, and I shall be expecting it wholeheartedly from you. This is a serious black mark against you and it saddens me, it saddens me greatly. Go now, go back to the chapel, kneel before the altar and pray, pray for forgiveness, pray for a heart that is truly open to obey, pray for a heart that has stripped itself of any pride, pray, Mr Brennan, pray for a true vocation to our order. That is all.'

The novice master bowed his head again over the papers. Mr Brennan stood up, conscious of a small scrape of the chair leg across the wooden floor. He moved, backing slowly, to the door, opened it and slipped out. For a moment he leant back against the door when he had closed it, shut his eyes and sighed deeply. His whole body was trembling. He felt cold. He was hurt.

He had no idea what time it was when he woke suddenly. He felt very, very cold. For a long time he had no notion either of where he was or what he was doing there. Somebody was shaking him gently by the shoulder. And then a torch was shone, obliquely, on his face. When Mr Brennan sat up with a cry of fright, the man stood back from him, shone the torch on his own face and said, 'It's OK, it's OK, Mr Brennan, it's just me, Brother James, you're in the conservatory, you must have walked in your sleep. It's OK, it's OK.'

The novice stood up quickly; he found he was wearing his soutane over his pyjamas, though he had not tied up the buttons of the long black garment. He shook his head and rubbed his eyes. The terror of what he had done struck him and he dropped down on his knees on the cold floor of the conservatory. He bowed his head and sobbed.

'It's OK, young lad, it's OK. It's normal enough, maybe you got a fright or something. Don't worry about it. It's OK.'

The novice stood up again, slowly. He had tears in his eyes. He had not experienced this for many years. At once he remembered the tinker, the novice master, the threat ...

'Yes, Brother James, I am feeling anxious these days. I'm sorry, I hope I didn't wake you up, or anybody else. What time is it?'

'It's about half past three, and no, you didn't wake me. I don't sleep too well. But you left the door of the conservatory open and I heard it banging slightly so I came to look, and glad I am that I did. You see,' and he shone the torch over some of the palm trees in the conservatory, then up to the windows in the ceiling, 'I have brought in a few exotic butterflies, to help with the pollination, as an experiment you might say. The best of good butterflies they are, I'll show you them in the morning if you come in, say before you collect the flowers for the altar. And I was worried about the open door, it wouldn't do to have these ladies and gentlemen fly about amongst your simple novices, now, you might think you were seeing angels, the best of good angels, and I have nets over the windows above, see! so they don't get out when the airing has to be done. Come on now, I'll help you back to your room, and I wouldn't worry about it, if I was you. There's a lad, the best of good novices, the very best.'

He took Mr Brennan by the arm and led him back along the corridor and up the stairs to his room, shining the torch on the walls and floors before them. At the door of his room the novice turned and hugged the Brother who drew back, embarrassed, whispering, 'it's OK now, it's OK, everything's OK, sleep good, good lad, sleep good …'

Patrick slept fitfully for the rest of the night and was glad when the bell rang at ten to six and he rose to announce the praises of God, to dip his face in cold water and to go down for prayers. Brother James was waiting for him at the door of the conservatory when he went later that morning to collect flowers for the altar. Brother James was small and compact in his body, he was over middle age and had a shock of straw-coloured hair that was always immaculately curled. His face seemed ever wreathed in smiles, his deep brown eyes twinkling. The world called him foolish; he had had some kind of breakdown but now appeared to be the happiest of men. He was a miracle-worker with the strange plants and flowers of the conservatory. Now he wore a brown apron over his soutane, the half-collar slightly soiled over the blue stock.

'Good lad, good lad, come in, I have some glorious heliconia for you today, for Jesus I mean, for the altar. Set them up, I'd suggest, in the midst of a bunch of white geraniums and they'll sing hosanna for days on end. Come in now and we'll see if we can't find the best of good butterflies. Shut the door after you there, now, good lad.'

There was a weak sun forcing its way down through the canopy of palms and the branches of other dark green trees in the conservatory. Brother James moved in to the centre and stood near the fountain; he gazed up at the huge and ungainly flowers of a banana tree and suddenly clapped his hands loudly. Almost at once some half dozen butterflies rose from various parts of the high shrubs and the rabid flowering trees. Mr Brennan stood astonished; he watched a large butterfly soar high towards the ceiling and flutter downwards again. 'Kingfisher!' he breathed. Brother James laughed and pointed.

'That wee fella is called Ulysses, he's from New Guinea. What a beautiful blue, like a tropical sky, isn't it, and black all around the outside. Iridescent, isn't that the word? Oh yes, a beauty, truly an angel. A tiny glorious kingfisher, indeed, you're right. Good lad. And look, there!'

He pointed to the huge blossom on the banana tree; there was a smaller butterfly, sylphlike, trembling on the flower; the front part of its wings was white, with black spots setting it off, the hind wings were black and white with crimson spots so that when the butterfly shuddered, there came a rainbow colouring of great beauty.

'That little lady is Cressida, isn't she gorgeous? She's from Indonesia, you know. Far from home, but I think she'll like it here. And that one over there, on the window, see him? that's Sardanapalus, now there's a name for you, I think the full name is more than that, *Agrias Sardanapalus*, oh the best of good names, the name is bigger than the fella himself. Isn't he a dote, though? Oh my God what a beauty.' The butterfly was clinging to the window glass that was stained with a light green scum; against it the butterfly was dazzling in its beauty, the front wings crimson and black, the hind wings black but shaded by a cobalt blue and a string of creamy white; its dark body also sported small yellow feathers that shuddered too, as if in ecstasy. 'That beauty has come all the way from Peru, you know, well, maybe not the whole way, he was reared in London, in fact, I get all these beauties from London, you know. A great place, London. You can get anything …'

'And do you think they'll live here, Brother James? Will they survive in our climate?'

'I hope so, oh yes, I hope so. I even hope they'll breed here, make a wonderful show among the flowers now, won't they? So I have to keep the place at an even temperature you know, hot, and moist, so I have to have the doors shut, the windows netted. These beauties wouldn't last long out in the real world, you know. Not these lovelies.'

Mr Brennan stayed a while longer and noticed two smaller butterflies, shivering together on a long, wicked-looking spine of some other plant; their wings were a soft yellow colour, with a strange though regular pattern of black and orange spots and lozenge-shapes. For some reason the French name for butterfly came to his mind and he said the name aloud, pointing, '*Papillon!*' Brother James looked and laughed. 'Good lad, good lad! Sure you might take over from me here when I pass on. It's a great place to spend your life, believe me. *Papillon*, yes, that's French, isn't it? Those little creatures come from Spain, one male, one female, don't ask me though, don't ask me. I believe they're actually called *Papilionidae*, something like that. So you were close, good lad, you were close.'

As Mr Brennan was leaving the conservatory, a bunch of white geraniums in his arms, and several stems of what Brother James called heliconia, the Brother came close to him and whispered, conspiratorially. 'Mum's the word about last night, OK? No need to worry Father Maloney, I won't say a word. Just rest easy, there's a good lad, take your sleep in the kind lap of the loving God. Just think, He created all these wonderful flowers and butterflies and trees, imagine what it must be like in Paradise itself, if Jesus said, or was it Jesus? I don't know, somebody anyway, who ought to know, he said no eye has ever seen and no mind has ever imagined what wonderful things God has prepared for those that love Him? Eh, eh? Must be a good God, most loving, most wonderful. The best of good Gods, what?' and he laughed quietly to himself as he turned back to his care.

It was on the feast of the Immaculate Conception, the eighth of December, when Mr Brennan was again summoned from his work at the altar. It was Brother Luke this time, who came noisily up the centre aisle of the chapel to where Mr Brennan was working. Luke was a bald, thin man with a hard face and jerky manner. The novice had never liked him, fearing his sarcastic comments, his sudden angers, remembering, too, his speaking of the tinker to Father Maloney. This time, however, he spoke quietly and gently. He took the novice kindly by the elbow, glanced around the empty chapel, then spoke conspiratorially into his ear.

'Mr Brennan, Father Maloney has asked me to fetch you. You're to go to his office. Now, please. And God be with you, God be with you.' The blessing was said softly, without mischief intended. The Brother pushed the young man gently towards the door. 'I'll take over from you here. You needn't come back today.'

Mr Brennan hesitated outside Father Maloney's door. If this was about his sleepwalking he would surely be worried; health was important in a novice, he knew that. And there was nothing else on his conscience, although he probed his memory quickly. He knocked, softly, and heard that sharp and certain voice call 'Come!'

Father Maloney was seated at his great desk but as soon as Mr Brennan closed the door and came forward into the office, the priest rose from his place and came round the desk, stretching out his hand.

'Ah, Mr Brennan, I'm afraid I have some bad news for you.'

The boy shuddered; was he being sent home? Had Brother James said something? But Father Maloney was taking the novice by the shoulder and leading him gently towards one of the chairs.

'Please sit down, please.'

Mr Brennan sat on the very edge of the chair while the priest returned to sit on the other side. Now the novice could scarcely see him, only a blurred outline of the figure against the grey light of that winter's day. But he knew Father Maloney had again joined his long fingers in a praying shape.

'It's your father, I'm afraid,' he said, very quietly. 'He was taken to the hospital yesterday evening, I believe. Your Father Scott has been on the phone to me. I didn't know your father was a fisherman?'

'A fisherman? No, Father, he's a small farmer. But he goes out with the men sometimes. Is he in hospital? Is he all right? You said … "was"?'

'He was fishing, it appears, helping others perhaps, a boat called *Sunrise*, I believe. Father Scott was not clear. Something about the age of the boat, a half-decker, I'm led to believe. And a wave, a freak wave, and two of them, including your father, were swept overboard. The weather was fairly rough, and of course the water this time of the year …'

Patrick sat quietly. 'Did he drown?'

'I'm sorry, Mr Brennan, yes, it took them some time to recover the body. I am sending you home. I have your train ticket here. Brother Luke will drive you to the station. Father Scott said he would meet you in Westport. Take a few days but I will expect you back here at the beginning of next week. These things happen, as you know, and I am dreadfully sorry that it should happen to your father. I know your mother will be devastated. I shall go now, with Father O'Brien and Father Mellett, and we will offer a special Mass for your father, and for you, Mr Brennan, and your mother. Brother Luke is waiting for you. You may travel in your suit, of course, wear the stock and collar and remember, you are a novice in our order, you are to maintain your dignity, the dignity of your faith, and the dignity of your calling. Go now, and God be with you.'

The priest rose and came round the desk. Patrick sat on, utterly stunned. Father Maloney touched him lightly on the shoulder. Patrick stood up.

'Thank you, Father,' he said, and turned to the door.

Those days were a fug of confusion and sorrow. Patrick was grateful for the words and actions of people all around him. In his presence they were unsure, this young man in priest's clothing, who was not a priest, but who held himself strong and moved with some confidence. His mother, Nora, hugged him close when he arrived, hugged and held him, wept and could not speak. Patrick went down to the lower room where the people sat on hard chairs around the walls, murmuring, watching. Edward Brennan lay in the open coffin and Patrick was shocked at the strange dark-blue bruising on his face. The hands were almost yellow and the fingers were bound with a new rosary beads. Patrick touched those hands and was hurt by the coldness.

Later he stood down by the pier and watched out over the sea. The evening was very cold, a bitter wind blowing in off the ocean but Patrick stood in his greatcoat, his hands in his pockets, and tried to imagine his father's dying. Beneath the surface of the ocean you can hear your own breathing; he remembered that, he remembered the few times he had dared to take his own body underwater, to open his eyes; he remembered those unnamed things that went drifting by on invisible pathways, sea-seeds and plankton and pieces of fish-flesh, the whole detritus of underwater history: and he imagined the wreck of the old trawler that now lay almost wholly washed by tides into nothingness, there in the thick oozing mud of the estuary, only the black ribs showing, its angular repose and gashed perfection, and how the name of that small half-decker from which his father drowned was so full now of hurt; *Sunrise*. He imagined his father's body afloat half over, half under the sea's surface, the lifting away of awkward articulated creatures from the drifting corpse, and how the crew must have felt, watching, waiting, as if they had come to a festive gathering only to discover nobody home, lights out, and all doors locked; and for a moment he felt a deep anger against his God, for the son's own sake, for the mother's sake, and how suffering seems prevalent over the earth, and now here, in this parish, on this shore, in this heart and once more the unavailing cries of loss swept over him.

When all the rites were accomplished and the people had left mother and son to go back to their own living, Patrick and Nora returned together to the empty chapel, to pray. The once familiar building seemed wholly other now to the novice as he stood, a man called to the service of this somehow-alien God. His mother knelt below the statue of the Virgin, with its right hand broken and the wire bones protruding. She lit a candle and placed it among the dead candles on the stand. Patrick moved slowly back down the chapel, looking in along the once-familiar pews. He heard the sorry scratching of the match. He saw here and there among the pews some dropped memoriam cards, a small red glove lying on the floor, and all the tiny scratches made on the polished wood by idle hands. He stood then, watching his mother where she knelt, gazing up at the bland statue above her. The Virgin stood, twelve stars set in a ring of iron about her head; five of the small white bulbs fastened on the ring were smashed, the rusted rod protruded where the right wrist had been. Theotokos. God-bearer. Woman. And how obedient she was, Patrick thought, to the love-demands of God, and to the sacrifice she was to make to violence.

There was still a scent of incense on the air in the chapel. Patrick saw how his mother seemed old, all at once, as if being suddenly a widow had also taken years of her own life from her. Quietly he came up behind her; her body was drooping in its black coat and skirt, there as she knelt before the Virgin. He could see the pale hocks between the holed black-wool stockings, and the fall of the old black coat. He could hear the sibilance of her whispered prayers, that sad lisping sound, and he saw that she had her eyes shut though her face was raised to the Mother. And then she spoke, frightening him, and she knew he had been there, close to her.

'Patrick, you know he loved you very much. And he was proud of you, too, though that same pride wouldn't let him show it. He was proud that a son of his would one day be a priest of God. And that morning you left he stood in the window of the room and watched when Father Scott came to gather you away from him. He was weeping, Patrick, he really was, and he waved to you, but I know you didn't notice him, how could you? But I saw him and felt such pity ...'

She bowed her head a moment. Then she blessed herself, the rosary beads dangling from her fingers. She stood up and turned to him and smiled.

'I'll be all right, you know. I loved him, I really loved that old fool of a man. And I suspect he'll be watchin' out for me from above. The poor devil. The poor gom. He was a good man, Patrick, never forget that, a good man, made to work a hard holding, a mean and scutchy knot of fields, and he tried his best. And never, ever did he lay a finger on me, never, Patrick, though he might have raised his fist betimes, an' that in his drunken state only, other than that he was good to me, an' he loved you, an' I'll be all right, I'll have a widow's pension, I'll set the fields, some neighbour'll pay me to graze his sheep an' cattle, an' you go back now, go and be a priest, an' he'll be prayin' for you, as I will, as I will, an' you me own son a priest, sure how could I possibly go wrong?'

Patrick moved swiftly and took her in his arms and held her closer to him than he had ever done before.

In the early days of Advent the novices changed their functions. Patrick was replaced on the altar by another, and he replaced the 'regulator'. It was the regulator's job to be at hand to ring all the bells for the hours, for waking, meals, prayers, it was his job to ensure that everything began on time and ended on time. Patrick went to Father Maloney's office and, when admitted, stood before that desk and mentioned his old fob watch; he needed a reliable timepiece to help him with his function and Father Maloney, smiling, produced the watch from a cabinet in a corner of his office.

'You will bring it back when functions change again, Mr Brennan,' the priest said. 'You realise that it is now being given to you on loan; it is no longer your watch. Holy poverty does not allow individual possessions.'

'I know that, Father. It will help me fulfil my function. Thank you, Father.'

Patrick kept the watch in the breast pocket of his shirt, the chain closed in to one of the buttonholes of the shirt. He felt good with the watch close to his body. And for the next four months he was up before everybody else, standing in the small cupboard space where the bell system was housed, his watch in his left hand, his right hand poised over the button that would start the bell. He was in bed last every evening, too, waiting for the ten o'clock moment to ring the bell for the beginning of the Great Silence that took the novices through the night. And he had to present himself at the great bell of the chapel, to ring the Angelus at noon and again at six o'clock. He was happy doing this, the watch close to his breast keeping him alert to the duties, also keeping him mindful of his mother and father, and how each moment was bringing him closer to his first vows, and closer to his Christ. And life moved on gently, regularly, with the quietness and assurance that following a strict routine will bring, and a knowledge that every moment, known, counted and rehearsed, was garnering for him treasure in Heaven.

The monthly letter from his mother reassured him; she was well, she was content; the fields were set, she was praying for him, she hoped he was praying for her. And his regular monthly answer was in the same vein, he was happy, settled, he was learning the story of God and the story of his own soul, and of course he was praying for her and begged her prayers for him.

When the last four months of the novitiate began, Patrick gave up his watch again with a certain pang of regret that he found unholy in himself. Easter had passed; the long run into Pentecost and the long retreat of the summer would follow. Then would come a week of intense preparation for the taking of first vows. There would be three days of holiday when the novices could go for walks each day, rise an hour later each morning, play games in the afternoon. And then the new men would arrive and preparations would be made for the next stage, the seminary in Dublin and the study of philosophy. Patrick's new function was that of librarian. He was taken aback; he knew nothing about such work but the novice who was there before him helped him through the first week.

Every morning, for an hour and a half, Patrick would unlock the library that stood at the end of the novitiate building, where a door opened into the precincts of the Fathers. The novices were allowed to come to the library for the first half an hour, to borrow books and to leave back those they were finished with; lives of the saints, the life of the founder, books on the spiritual life … rare and rarefied works. For the next hour the priests could come and do the same, save that they had a special section of the library where the novices could not browse. This section contained the works of some of the great novelists, Jane Austen, Charles Dickens, Graham Greene … There were sections on world geography and world history. There were back issues of the *National Geographic Magazine*, and of religious magazines and journals from around the English-speaking world. And there were histories of the great Missionaries and the Foreign Missions, as well as works in dispute, and works that were banned in Ireland or banned by Holy Mother Church. The banned books were all kept in a large glass case that was locked and only Father Maloney himself kept that key. The books were used only by priests engaged in research and in the preparation of refutations and theological studies.

Patrick stood, one of the first days he worked in the library, and gazed at the range of books behind that glass; most of them looked old and fusty, they had heavy bindings, though some of them were on flimsy looking paper. Many of the authors had French names, though the books appeared to be in English: Rabelais, Voltaire, Sade, Balzac, Sartre. He saw novels by Lawrence Sterne and Jonathan Swift, books by John Milton and John Calvin. There was one book by Samuel Richardson, titled *Pamela*; the novice wondered what that book was doing in there, whoever read it, and why it was banned. As for Jonathan Swift, all he had ever known of his work was *Gulliver's Travels* and his mother had read most of it to him when he was a child.

Each book in the library available to novices had a little ticket, with a number, held on the inside of the front cover. Patrick had to take out the ticket, write the borrower's name, the date, and file the ticket away in a box. When a book was returned, he found the ticket and reinserted it in the cover of the book. Almost every day there was a period when he could read for himself, when nobody disturbed either him or the books. He rifled the geography and history sections. He hopped and skipped through the *National Geographic Magazines*, breathing in the breadth and depth and width of the wonders of God's creation. And almost every day he read a piece from a book called *The Ravaged Earth*, by Gabriel F. Richards. Reading this alongside the *National Geographic Magazines* made him ever more aware of mankind's destruction of the planet. As he read he grew more angry and impatient to be out in the world to conquer the inherent violence and destructive urges in mankind. As a priest, he felt, perhaps he could do something to right the balance. Perhaps he could do something. Perhaps.

The book began with the Trojans and the fight against the Achaians, as recounted in *The Iliad*. In the scholasticate he had studied small bits of that great epic but had never touched its details. Now he read about Hector, how he had taken the lead and followed the Achaians when they fled the walls back towards their own camps, how he struck down the stragglers without pity, how he leapt, like a hound headlong as if biting on the flanks of a lion or a wild boar, how he swerved with the swerves of his quarry, twisting and turning with its twists and turns. Until at last he had driven those who remained over the moat and stakes of their own encampment, how many of them were bloodied and ripped to pieces, and how they prayed aloud to their gods in the heavens, their hands held aloft in supplication. But Hector and his companions wheeled their horses about and again about, bloodthirsty, and scoffed, like the gods of war, at all human suffering.

He read an account and a translation of the great medieval poem, *The Dream of the Rood*, how Christ, to redeem such suffering, made himself climb onto the Cross and die for humankind. And the novice shuddered to know how men have continued, and will ever continue, to inflict the most dreadful suffering upon one another, in spite of all that history has taught.

He read of Vlad Tepes who, in the fifteenth century, became known through the world for his cruelty, how he impaled his enemies to drive terror into the countries he invaded. He had a horse attached to each of the victim's legs and a sharpened stake was gradually forced into the body. The end of the stake was oiled and care was taken that the stake not be too sharp, else the victim might die too rapidly from shock. Normally the stake was inserted into the body through the buttocks and was forced through the body until it emerged from the mouth. However, there were many instances where victims were impaled through other body orifices or through the abdomen or chest. Infants were sometimes impaled on the stake forced through their mother's chests. The records indicated, the young man read, that victims were sometimes impaled so that they hung upside down on the stake. Vlad Tepes feasted on the flesh of animals at his table on a clearing in a forest of the impaled; he was credited with killing between forty thousand to one hundred thousand people in this fashion.

For days after reading these passages, Patrick found himself shuddering inwardly and in great doubt about what he was doing himself. Memories of what he had heard and read about his own country, Ireland, and the dreadful sufferings its people had gone through at the hands of the English for over eight hundred years, disturbed him. Where was the love and friendship, the self-sacrifice and kindness that the Christ had come on earth to offer and to display? He read of the great battle of Maldon, in Essex, when the Vikings invaded the country of the Britons. He read of Genghis Khan, he read of World War One and World War Two. He believed, more firmly than ever, in the existence of Hell. And slowly, ineluctably, his heart misgave him.

It was on a day when such thoughts were touching him deeply once again that he walked out on the far avenue of the novitiate to gather himself into prayer. The summer was about to begin; the trees were rich in foliage and the bushes were beautiful with their flowers. Along the avenue the whitethorn was in blossom and bees and insects made a delightful music through the hedgerows. And once again, as he paused before the great Crucifix in its niche at the end of the avenue, he heard a voice go '*Hissssssst!*' through the leaves, and saw the face of the tinker grinning at him, saw his finger beckoning.

The novice was shocked, and for a long time he hesitated. What of the vow of obedience? What of the warnings, long ago now, of Father Maloney? And yet, he thought, what of the suffering of this small family? How could he simply turn away? He stepped through the hedge once more and out onto the small laneway beyond.

'This way, Father, just along here.'

The tinker led him up along the grassy margin on the other side of the laneway and into a small cluster of trees. Hazels and alders formed a copse and in the clearing in the centre of the copse, shaded from the sun and somewhat sheltered from rain, the small family had set up their painted cart. The mule was tethered to one of the trees nearby and this time there was a small tent, of dark canvas, and a fire burning on a nest of stones to one side.

'This is Janey, this is my wife. Janey, here's Father Brennan that I said, gave us the porringer and the meat an' all, that time. And here, Father, is little Maura Jane, our little Maura Jane Stokes.'

A young woman, pretty, dark-haired, the hair streeling down over her shoulders, was tending to a child, a girl just about one year old, who was smiling broadly and chewing something in her dirty mouth. The woman held the child and was rocking it gently, but proudly. She beamed up at the young novice.

'Ye're heartily welcome, Father,' she said, 'heartily welcome.'

The tinker stood back proudly and watched for a moment. Then he took the novice by the sleeve. 'You might give the chil' a blessing, Father, 'twould be a great blessing to us all. Would you do that, Father? Please?'

'I'm not a priest, you know, I'm only a novice. I wouldn't be able ...'

'Priest, novice, I don't know, Father, but I do know you helped us out at a time when we was in bad trouble, with our own family, too, so we had to go the roads on our own. You were more than good an' I know it might have got you into bother. So a blessing would be certain good. There now!'

Patrick smiled and moved towards the child. The little girl at once dropped the piece of wood she was chewing on and reached her hands up towards the novice in his black soutane. Patrick was a little taken aback.

'You'll hold her, Mrs, ah, please, and I'll just say a word or two. Will that be all right?'

'That'll be sure and certain welcome, Father, an' God will be good to you.'

The young man closed his eyes, joined his hands; 'May the God of wandering people and the God of pilgrimage bless this child, em, Maura Jane, and bless her parents and keep them all safe on the roads of life until they meet Christ Himself in glory in the last times. Amen!'

'Amen, Father, and thanks!' the tinker said. Then he

disappeared down into the small tent. The young novice smiled down at the woman and child who were both beaming up at him. Almost at once the tinker was out again, holding the tin porringer in his hand.

'Look, Father, I done mended it. The handle come off, like, but us folks, we know how to meld it all back on again. You'll scarcely notice the healin', just a little drop of solder, there, on the base of the holder. An' thank you for it, we've blessed you every time we made use of it.'

'Oh but you're welcome to keep it …'

'No, no, Father, no, you have it back now, but if you could see your way to bringing another bite of meat or something …'

The novice hesitated a moment. A blackbird was singing loudly somewhere beyond the copse and the sound filled the afternoon with its strength and beauty. He made his decision.

'Look,' he said, taking the tinker by the arm. 'You come with me now and we'll both go up to the kitchen above. You'll come in with me and we'll see what we can find.'

A few minutes later the novice and the tinker, who was by now shyly following behind, came in through the yard and entered the kitchen door of the novitiate. There was nobody there. At once Patrick went to the top of the long sideboard and took a tea towel off a tray; there were four loaves of brown bread. Patrick took one of them and shoved it into the arms of the tinker. Then he opened the door of the great cooler and found half a ham carefully wrapped in tinfoil. This, too, he shoved into the arms of the tinker. At that moment the door opened. It was Brother Luke.

All three stopped, and looked at one another. There was a long silence. The door closed slowly behind the Brother. Once again Patrick made a decision.

'I am giving of our surplus to a needy family, Brother Luke. Of our surplus, mind. There is a child down there, in the open air, and she needs food, more than we do. Off you go now, Mr Stokes, and give my best regards to Maura Jane and to your wife. Off you go.'

At once the tinker made for the door, avoiding the eyes of the Brother, who stood aside quietly, and let him pass. When the door had closed behind him, Brother Luke gazed back at Patrick who stood, peaceful and tall, the tin porringer tied by its gleaming handle to the cincture around his waist.

'Believe me, Mr Brennan,' the Brother said. 'I know what Christ has said, I know as well as you do. But he will be back, mark my words, and with him will be his clan. And his extended clan. You can all starve yourselves like hermits and ascetic saints for all I care. I'm in charge of the kitchens, however, and it is me has to answer to Father Superior. I'll thank you to remember that.' The Brother moved swiftly across the kitchen and out into the refectory. Patrick stood a while, then he sighed deeply and moved, head bent, towards the chapel.

He sat a long time before the altar, in unechoing quietness. Flowers in their places sent a rich scent out over the pews; the gilt-closeted doors of the tabernacle gleamed in the summer light through the high stained windows. The tiny red light withering in the lamp gave little comfort. Words would not come to him. He tried the well-rehearsed prayers but found his mind instead wandering out over the fields towards the tinkers in their copse, and towards the tidal pool beyond the door of his mother's house, the waters now at their warmest meeting the chill fresh waters from the hills. As he sat, the black sleeve of his soutane, its edge frayed against his wrist, the tiny particles of dust still visible, began to irritate his skin. He knelt a while, buried his head in his hands and still no words would come. Soon, he knew, the other novices would be coming in for Vespers and he would take his place again amongst them, singing in that distant tongue a distant music that pleased him deeply but left him quivering with a small emptiness.

He sat again, allowing all his mind to wander the sand and gravel road of the village at home. He could hear the hissing of disturbed geese in a neighbour's yard, the glory-braying of a donkey from high along among the houses, the barking of a bored dog against the shifting shapes of summer clouds and then, down so deep in the soundless well of his being he could hear his own voice calling, hopelessly, hopelessly, her name;

Dorothy, the call rose, Dorothy, Dorothy, Dorothy. Abruptly he stood up, genuflected before the altar and its gold indifference, and left the chapel. He would not attend Vespers, he could not. He walked out again into the novitiate grounds and moved, vaguely peaceful in himself, along the gently landscaped gardens.

Patrick did not rise with the bell the next morning. Instead, he stretched himself luxuriously in the bed and tried to go back to sleep. But he could not. Nor did he appear for breakfast in the refectory. He rose, washed himself carefully, gathered together what he wished to keep out of his room, the black-leather covered book of prayers and psalms, the light-blue scapular of the Virgin the novices wore against their hearts, and the sheened tin porringer he had taken back from the tinker. These he left on the small cupboard by the bed. He sat and waited.

When he heard the bell ring for the end of breakfast he knew the novices would be making their way, in silence, towards the study where there would be half an hour of spiritual reading before the hour of manual labour. He waited another five minutes then made his way, quickly, to Father Maloney's door. He knocked and was admitted.

Father Maloney looked at him for a moment. Patrick stood wordless before him. The priest smiled, wryly, then stood and, still without speaking, took out a key from his desk and moved over to the filing cabinet at the side of the office. He opened a drawer, drew out a small packet. He locked the cabinet again and laid the packet down on the desk before the novice.

'You will find in there everything you came in with, your watch is there, some coins, I think, and I have added some money with which you may buy your train ticket. You will go down now to the basement and there you will find the clothes you came in, as well as your suitcase. Take with you what you need. What you leave will be distributed wherever it is required.'

Patrick took up the packet. Father Maloney came closer to him and stretched out his hand. Patrick took it. The hand was firm, the handshake was short.

'I am sorry to lose you, Patrick, very sorry indeed. But from almost the very start I could see there was something in you of too much independence for our life, too much self-will. I wish you every joy and happiness and success in your life. When you have your suitcase ready Brother Luke will collect you from the front door. Say in about twenty minutes. I will telephone Father Scott and tell him to expect you on the train at Westport. He will, I have no doubt, inform your mother. I dare say she will be saddened. But that is God's way. God's will be done. And God go with you.'

'Thank you Father. I'm sorry. I am truly sorry. I have been very happy here, but …'

Patrick turned quickly and left the office. He collected his old suitcase, his old clothes, finding some difficulty in putting on his tie again. He left the black suit carefully folded on his bed. He hung his soutane, cincture and stock behind the door of his room. He glanced once around the room. Then he left.

The morning was bright and cheerful when Patrick moved for the last time through the great conservatory towards the front door. He moved cautiously, closing the cloister door quickly behind him. There was that same rich silence in the hothouse, a silence almost tangible while the exotic plants inhaled and exhaled, and the soft plashing of the fountain cast a gentle goodness over all. Patrick watched for butterflies. But nothing stirred. As he gazed upwards he was astonished to find that the high cooling windows were opened and there was no netting that might prevent the butterflies escaping. Cautiously again he clapped his hands, softly. Nothing stirred. He moved quietly under the great palms, the huge banana-tree boles, the foliage of fern and thickening undergrowth. Until suddenly there was a violent sneeze that startled him and that was followed almost at once by a loud, unholy screech that made him jump back against the glass wall behind him.

Brother James emerged from a corner of the conservatory, thick gloves on his hands, a secateurs in his right.

'Ha, it's my old friend Mr Brennan,' he said, smiling broadly at Patrick. 'Come to pay me a visit, eh? But there you are now, all dressed up in worldly clothes, like an ordinary layman. Are you on your holidays or something?'

A little sheepishly Patrick explained that he was leaving the novitiate and going home. Brother James looked at him for a while, somewhat sadly. 'Ah well, it's God's way, that's what it is. You must follow your heart, surely, follow your heart. Ah but sure you were very good with me here in the conservatory in your time. I'll miss you, there's a good lad. But I wish you well. Wish you well.'

'Where are the butterflies, Brother James?'

'Ah, my darling butterflies. I think they must have been homesick, you know, the poor creatures. They just died on me, one after the other, just upped and died. I don't know. Too cold here for them, maybe, or not enough space for them to fly around in. Almost broke my heart, they did, till I got my good friend Wally to take their place.'

'Wally?'

Brother James grinned. Then called out, loudly, into the heart of the greenery.

'Wally, come on out! Come out!'

There was another unholy screech and both of them winced. Patrick heard a slight rattling of chains and then, almost before his face, appeared a most magnificent bird, its right leg trailing a long, thin chain back into the midst of the greenery. The bird had beautiful blue wings shading to even deeper blue; its breast and body were a bright golden colour and it had a small cap of green on its head. Its black beak curved ferociously, emerging aggressively from white cheeks.

'A parrot!'

'No, no, no, not a parrot, Mr Brennan. This here's Wally. Wally, say hello to Mr Brennan. Say HELLO!'

The bird hopped a little on its branch, raised the claw with the chain attached and scratched at its neck. 'Thon's a macaw, Mr Brennan, the best of good macaws, brought back all the way from Brazil by Father Goldenby, who's retiring now. He screeches good, Wally, I mean, not poor old Goldenby, and I've been trying to get him to speak. Trying to get him to say

Benedicamus Domino, but he won't even try. So I am working on
a simpler thing, Hello, but he's refusing even that. But isn't he
a beauty? His wings are scutched a little bit, but to be safer still
he has a long chain. Keeps him in check. And he eats the seeds,
you know, and nuts and fruit and even sometimes bits of my
own white bread. Only problem is, if you'll forgive the
expression,' and Brother James raised his eyes piously to the glass
ceiling, 'he shits all over the place. God bless him!'

The bird was edging itself along the branch towards Patrick,
its big eye focused on him. 'You'd better not get too near that
beak now, Mr Brennan, for it can take a queer swipe out of the
bark of a tree if he has a mind to.'

At that moment a car honked impatiently outside. Patrick
shook hands warmly with Brother James, then turned quickly
and went out through the conservatory door. For the first time
since he had arrived at Kilruddery, Patrick stood in the marble-
tiled great hallway of the novitiate. Before him was the heavy
door that had been opened to him, oh a lifetime ago. He paused
a moment, then gathered himself together, opened that great
door, closed it as softly as he could behind him, then turned to
face Brother Luke.

For Patrick the slow meandering of the train towards the west
brought many anxieties to his mind. It was his mother most of all
that worried him; how would she take it? Would she be greatly
upset, greatly disappointed? He remembered his grandfather and
his prayers for him. And of course the people held in some
contempt those whom they called 'spoiled priests', and Patrick
himself remembered the words, 'No man putting his hand to the
plough and turning back is fit for the kingdom of God'.

He tried to settle himself more comfortably in the
compartment but the train rattled and shook though the day
outside was bright and the fields were rich in summer growth.
He was restless. After all these years what had he to show for the
care and support that Father Scott had found for him? And how
would the priest treat him now? He had let his family down; he
had let his priest down; he had let the parish down.

When, at last, the train began to draw in to the station at Westport, clanking over the bridge across the road, then puffing loudly as it slowed, letting out a scream that reminded Patrick of the macaw, he lowered the window by its old leather strap and put his head out. He was watching for Father Scott. The platform was crowded with people eagerly watching towards the carriages. When the train had finally jolted to a halt, Patrick could not see the priest. As he opened the carriage door and stepped down onto the platform he was anxious; what if Father Maloney had not telephoned? What if nobody knew he was coming; he had still over thirty miles to travel. He moved slowly towards the station exit, people crowding around, calling, hefting luggage, and greeting one another. And then he heard his name called out; he turned. His mother stood near the exit, a broad smile on her face. Patrick rushed to greet her. She held her arms out and he hugged her.

'Welcome home, boy, welcome home!' she said and there were tears in her eyes but Patrick could see at once that they were tears of pleasure. He stood back from her. 'I'm sorry, Mother, I just am not good enough ...'

'Of course you're good enough! But there's nothing to be sorry for, nothing at all. Sure I'm very glad to have you home with me. I didn't want to be selfish, to steal you back from the Lord, but I have been so lonely, Patrick, so lost ... Oh God, it's good to have you home.' And she hugged him tightly again. 'Come on, Father Scott is waiting outside, with the car.'

Outside the station Patrick could see Father Scott leaning up against the side of the old red Ford; he looked exactly the same as ever; he was smoking, watching out over the fields, watching the clouds that slid lazily across the sky. Then he turned, saw Patrick and his mother, and flicked the cigarette away across the road. He came sloping round the car, that long arm stretched out to greet the boy.

'Well, well, well, St Patrick back to live among the natives! Good to see you back, boy, good to see you back!'

Patrick was overwhelmed at the welcome and sat into the back seat of the car gratefully.

'I'm sorry, Father,' he said, 'I simply am not good enough …
I tried. God just didn't want me.'

'Well, do you blame him? Who'd want a twerp like you? A
slug in the cabbage of bliss, what? But seriously, I know you
tried, lad, and Father Maloney was full of your praises. And
remember, there are other ways of living out your life, your
mother needs you now, you know, and the parish needs you,
too, so just be glad you got a good education into you, sure that
must have been what was in God's mind all along. He uses
strange ways to bring us to where we should be, that's the truth,
that's the whole and holy truth of it now.'

When they were alone in the kitchen at home, Patrick spoke
eagerly to his mother about his hopes. There was no bookshop
in town, just a small grocery that sold newspapers and Catholic
Truth Society pamphlets. He wanted to set up a real bookshop,
with all the great books, and he wanted to create a place and
space of beauty, with beautiful things, things like wind chimes,
like special books for children, and an area in the shop where
they could play with toys and read great picture books, a wall
perhaps to exhibit new good paintings by local people, even a
coffee shop where people could sit and chat and where he
would display cards and books and things to do with peace, with
the history of the world, with picture books about all the
wondrous things in the world, he wanted to create a space
where the wonderful things of God's creation could be put into
the balance against all the horrors of the world, the wars, the
human disgrace, the suffering …

The night closed in on them slowly, the long warm dusk of
summer stealing in on their contentment, the sounds of gulls
and the occasional squawk of a heron coming like dreams into
the kitchen. Later, before he went to bed, Patrick stood out on
the edge of the pool, hearing that familiar gurgling in the
darkness, watching the stars as they stood in their perfection in
a perfect sky, and his heart was filled with hope, and gladness,
and a new and catching loneliness.

EPILOGUE

A SHARE IN THE HARVEST

The day was warm. Dorothy stood, arms akimbo, leaning back against the wall at the side of the open front door. On days like this there was no reason to close the door; the warmth of the sun and the freshness of the air would be free to enter, like the most welcome of guests, and ramble through the big house. Between the front door with its frosted glass windows on either side and its golden stained fan-window above the door, between that front porch and the gate leading out onto the roadway, was a large garden, the lawn immaculately cut, the hydrangea bushes in glorious bloom, the standard roses down along each side of the footpath to the gate perfectly pruned and in blossom. Her grandchildren played on the lawn, Paddy and Doodles, six years old and four years old. They were absorbed in something in the grass, some tiny flower, or insect, or other wonder. Dorothy's youngest, Nuala, 'Mumsy', dozed in a gold and red-striped deckchair. There was a quiet that was filled with the scarcely audible rumours of summer living and Dorothy sighed with the ease of it.

She felt as if somebody touched her, then, ever so gently, on the tip of her right shoulder and at the same time she was certain she heard somebody's voice call her, from a very great distance. She turned her head and moved away slightly from the wall to see who had touched her but there was nobody. She was astonished, too, that the voice she heard called her by that old name: Dolly, three times calling, Dolly, Dolly, Doll ... She had not heard that name oh for so many years. She looked down towards the small front gate and out over the road, but there was

nobody in sight. The children had not stirred, nor had her
daughter shifted from her dozing. She must have been mistaken.

She knew a small pain in her shoulder, where she had felt the
touch. She shifted her shoulder to ease it but the pain seemed to
move, down along her right arm until her fingers tingled, not
unpleasantly. She felt a little tired. She was going to call over to
Nuala that she was just going upstairs for a little rest but she
found a stiffness in her jaws that threatened pain. She turned,
quietly, and went indoors. No need to bother her daughter, nor
her grandchildren. It was cool in the hallway, the soft plum-
coloured carpet welcome to her tired feet. On the right was the
small bookcase with those books Patrick, 'Packie' – she
whispered the name aloud and then laughed, she hadn't used
that name for years, oh for so many years – those books that
were bound in the same richly-gilded binding that he had
collected from his own bookshop over the years. They were a
series of the great English classics, from Defoe to Masefield, a
whole row given over to Charles Dickens, books he would read
to the children at bedtime, books he would carefully put back
in place, dusting them cautiously every so often. Packie. She
giggled again, then brushed her hand lightly against the tiny
marking silk tassels that dandled from each book. As if she
tickled them. As if she could touch him again.

And suddenly he was vividly before her mind once more, that
great question he always asked he was asking her again. Did his
bookshop help? Did the fictions, the geographies, the histories,
did the beautiful objects he filled the shop with, did the
meetings, the coffees, the talks he got together, did any of that
make any difference? Sometime in the deep of the night before,
she had seen thousands of young men and women wade slowly
out into the waters of the old lake that was now almost wholly
coated in green scum of some kind. Men, women and children
wading out in utter silence while the oozing bottom-mud
sucked them further and further in, their arms moving slowly in
the air as they advanced, and then, oh so slowly they disappeared
with that soundless howl that is possible only in dreams though,
as Patrick used to say, the howl is audible day by day,
everywhere, in this country, in this world, and now, at this time.

The old woman paused, her hand on the banister, her foot almost prepared to take the first step. Why the force of these thoughts right now? And why the weariness? Life was so quiet these days, indeed it had been quiet and filled with an undemanding grace ever since the day he had called her from the till at the back of the bookshop, smiled at her and said: 'Dor, I think it's time we handed on The Golden Page. I think that Eamonn is ready for it. I think that you and I are ready to let a younger generation expand and develop the place. I have lost zest, with all these books flooding in, bestsellers, florid covers, great thick paperbacks I hate to sell, even though they bring in the profit, useless things, empty-minded, good only to balance an old chest of drawers ...'

'Now, now Patrick, they have been good to you, you know that. You've sold more books in the last five years than in the first twenty-five or thirty. Maybe they're rubbish, they sure as blazes aren't Dickens, but we're in a fast age now, people move fast, they eat fast, they live fast and they sure as blazes read fast. But I agree with you; it's time Eamonn took over, and it's time Nuala took over from me. We have lives to live yet, you and I, a great world out there to visit.'

That was what? Nineteen years before? Twenty? And it seemed like three. It seemed like a week. And now it's been eight since poor old Patrick ...

Can a poem touch on the heart of politics? he would ask, in some frustration as he glanced through a morning's newspapers. Can a poem tell the world about the beauty of the blood-red bill of the chough, its blood-red claws and the wonder that there is when it does its acrobatic stunts under the cliffs, its cry echoing with intense music off the wet rocks? Do our politicians know, and does it matter to them, how beautiful it is to sleep by an uncurtained window while the dark side of the mountain rises as a guardian over you and a high star moves slowly across the glass, its colours shading from gold to turquoise-white? I could sell so little poetry, Dor, he used to lament, and yet there was no other way to make those politicians grow aware how the skylark fills the sky, the sky that is its world, its ocean, full of water-fire music as it lifts away up over the sand-dunes, and when I wanted to tell them about the scent of the wild cotton, he would say, the glorious smell of the heathers when the summer bog is warm, how stupid all that was to them while they stood in their chambers hurling lies and accusations across the hurting spaces of the world. Nobody now, Dor, he used to say, nobody bothers now with Christ, they have no time, there is no silence to hear Him, and yet there He is, waltzing across lake waters, alive in the light, in the stones, in our bones.

Ah yes, Dorothy thought, that is where my dream came from, the lake waters, the day he and I bumped into each other, Packie, Dolly, both of us about to give our lives to that same Christ. And once I remember, after the visit of some politician to the shop, poor Patrick called out after him as he headed in his rich shirt and his indifference to the suffering, Patrick called out: 'Do you hear the Christ calling to you? you the anointed of the people, you the disappointed, the disappointing.'

Dorothy shook her head, to loosen the thoughts and memories that came flooding in. She looked up the stairs towards the landing, not that far above, and decided she just might not have the energy right now to climb up that far. What about a nice cup of tea first of all? With a sense of relief she moved instead down the hallway towards the kitchen.

She took water from the filter jug and poured it through the spout of the kettle until the little red ball within showed her the water was far enough up in the electric kettle. She pressed the button; the yellow light came on. She sat down at the kitchen table to wait. She noticed once again that the old clock her grandfather had given her so many years ago, was standing in the glass cupboard where they had kept the millennium souvenir milk bottle, the beer mug – the 'stein' – Patrick had brought back from their holiday in Munich, such things. She remembered her grandfather saying 'Time is something we don't have enough of', and she sighed in acknowledgment. It was the small gilt carriage clock he had been presented with when he left the RIC and the double-ended key for winding it and shifting the hands still hung on the back. But the clock had stopped long, long ago and she never wanted a watchmaker to look at it in case he broke it. The hands stood, for at least forty-five years now, at twenty minutes after two. Idly she wondered what had happened right then, at that precise moment, that the clock had given in. She stood up, cautiously, feeling her bones too fragile now within her, and opened the glass door of the press; she took out the clock and put it on the kitchen table. The kettle was spewing out steam; the light went out with a small click.

She sat, gazing at the clock, sipping her mug of tea. That mug she had bought herself, in Tintagel, on that honeymoon trip they took to the shires, motoring slowly and with intense joy, through Devon and Cornwall, and now she gazed at the pictures printed on the side of the mug, the ruined castle, the face of a knight, a cormorant wheeling in the sky of history. And then she thought of that last holiday they took together, to Munich, to celebrate the fact of a direct flight between Dublin and that city. How they had sat together in the vast foyer of the Hilton, she and he, drinking tea (and such a bad cup of tea, sure they can't make proper tea in Germany) and giggling as they watched, like naughty children all over again, as big business happened in nooks and corners everywhere around them. Men in suits and ties, some in immaculate shirts, sitting there at small tables, many of them with coffee cooling on the surface and a laptop open on their knees, and the metre ticking in a taxi outside, palm trees in discreet corners by marble pillars that rose, as in some great temple or conservatory, chocolate-veined, towards a glass ceiling. There was a small and deathly silent aquarium with angel-fish swimming in deadly boredom against some picture that gave the illusion of distant yachts moored in a distant harbour; the lovers, old now and utterly familiar to one another, played the childish game once more, guessing who was who and what was what amongst these hassled and harrying men, and had they wives, and did they know the names of their children, and did they eat sausage and go to spas, and did they have any sense at all of what the World Wars had done to the hearts and souls of people.

Dorothy sighed again. There was no great sadness left in her any more. There was no longer a sense of loneliness. There were no questions left, and there were no answers either. Their life together had been too good for that. There was a sense of gratitude. There was even, she would admit, a sense of impatience with her own living now, as if it made no sense any longer that she should still be lingering in this world. She took up the small carriage clock, shook it gently close to her ear, heard the mechanism within complain slightly. She finished her cup of tea, took the clock with her and passed into the library.

The patio window was wide open and a gentle breeze came in from the back garden. She was a little worried now; there was nobody to take care of the garden, the raspberries were growing wild and creeping plants were beginning to choke the gooseberries. But the plum tree was already showing a lot of small, hard green fruits and with the early autumn she knew there would be a good crop. Last year the wasps had taken many of the fallen fruits, and she had to keep the children out of the garden. Patrick had been such an important part of her life it felt that with his death most of her, too, had fallen away.

She moved past the shelves of books and stopped at the old bureau that she had brought from her parents' house. Her own father had spent years working at its surface; the little drawers and the almost hidden spaces were scratched now, and there were old ink stains everywhere, but she had often sat at that desk herself, writing letters, dreaming, remembering. She sighed and pushed at the sliding door that led into the sitting room. She had forgotten her shoulder and a pain shot through her right arm, reminding her forcefully that she must have twisted it just now. Old age, she thought, is not a pleasant thing, especially when you are conscious of the fragility of almost every part of the body, every part, that is, still working. She giggled aloud. Age has its compensations, too, she thought. But right now she could not quite remember what they were. Gingerly she closed the door behind her and moved into the sitting room.

The television built into the wall seemed to dominate the room, in spite of all Dorothy's efforts to the contrary; she had put flower vases on the small side tables; she had placed decorative candles along the mantelpiece and even on the shelves above and below the television. She had enjoyed some of the movies they showed, some of the old movies, but the newer ones seemed intent on portraying every possible kind of violence and how she hated that! His special chair, where he read his novels, his studies of religion, his poetry, was faced away from the television and she felt, even after these years, she was an intruder when she sat in it herself for a while. The back of the armchair held his own back still in vague outline, where his body had rubbed so often that a trace was there, in the darker colouring of the already dark green of the stuff. And once she had taken apart the armchair, when he was away on some bookshop junket, and had found coins fallen down at the sides, she had found one of his favourite pens that he had thought somebody had filched from him, she had even found some of his fingernails and she had reproached him, jokingly, that he sat there, absorbed in some book and absent-mindedly bit his nails and hid them down the side of the chair. He had blushed when she said that and she had rushed to reassure him, it's only a joke, I'm teasing you.

She glanced at the face of the television, its grey blankness that would soon light up when the children came running in for cartoons or some other harmless tales. And suddenly, and for what reason?, she remembered Locke's Field, and that evening when she saw her first movie, and she scolded herself because surely there was a violence there, too, a violence in the heart of humankind that was portrayed in those black and white horror movies she and Patrick had loved so much. Stories about werewolves, about vampires, that great story of Jekyll and Hyde, and then, of course, there was Locke's Field itself, that expanse only recently sold, those wet and useless few acres that had been bought up for some astronomical sum just a few years ago, proving to Dorothy that now she knew she had lost it, she had lost touch with whatever reasoning there might still exist in the minds of contemporary human beings. Millions, for that old scutch-wild field of grasses and rushes and nettles! Ludicrous! Madness! Fools!

And there, standing where it had stood for years, was that old special porringer of Patrick's, that battered and dulled old porringer that he always insisted be used for his coffee when he came home after work because, he said, everything tasted better from that porringer, better than any other drink he had ever had. Even when their own son was going through his crisis, their own Eamonn, God be good to him, and the pressure on their lives was so awfully great that he often took a good sup of whiskey in that old porringer along with his coffee, even then he seemed to find some consolation in that old battered thing. She reached for it now and took it down, tucking it into the deep pocket of her old apron. Even the touch of it on her fingers seemed to warm her, as if he was sitting there, in that old armchair, waiting for her to bring him his coffee and then he would say to her how good she was, how he loved his own old goose of a woman, and she would chide him and murmur proudly deep inside herself how she loved him. The old codger!

Carrying the carriage clock with her, she went out the sitting room door into the hallway. She would head upstairs now. This reminiscing was beginning to wear her down. She began to climb, her left hand holding to the banisters, her right grasping the carriage clock. After the fifth step she felt so tired she had to turn and sit down on the step. Her breathing was difficult. She must be tired, more tired than she had thought. Lovely strips of scarlet and cobalt light lay along the carpet on the hallway, passing through the fanlight above the open door, and through the frosted glass on either side. She could just see out, from where she sat, as far as the edge of the lawn. She breathed more easily. She felt at peace.

Aunt Lily Graham came floating into her mind. That day she and Patrick decided to visit her in Westport, because Dorothy hadn't seen her since the day she had become a novice, in another world, another life. She was sorry for her, that memory of a lonely woman, big in the world, yet seemingly scared of that world. They found her place at the top of the town, where three streets came together; she had a small flat above a sports shop and they had to pass in along a dark hallway to the door that led to her rooms. They walked quietly through that door and found a staircase, uncarpeted, dirty, and dirt-marks on the badly-painted walls. The stairs were steep and Dorothy remembered wondering if poor old Lily had to go up and down these steps very often. There was a door opening directly from the top of the steps and when Dorothy knocked, gently, she heard a feeble response from within.

Aunt Lily was sitting in a fireside chair, her back to a small window, her feet up on a footstool and a cup and saucer balanced on the arm of her chair. Dorothy was stunned by how small and shrivelled she looked, wrapped up in several layers of jumpers, black woollen stockings visible from under a heavy red skirt. Her face was pinched and sallow, she wore rimless spectacles down on her nose and she had a scarf about her head, hiding what hair she might have left. There was a one-bar small electric fire glowing to her left, in an otherwise black and dead fireplace. She did not stir when Dorothy and Patrick came in.

Patrick stood back against the door and allowed all the space to Dorothy. She moved quickly over to Lily and took her hand.

'Well, well, well,' the old lady said in a whining, high-pitched voice. 'So the little fairy has at last consented to visit her old aunt. You're welcome, my dear, but you know you cannot stay for very long now as I have to watch a programme soon, it's dear old Oprah, you know, always good for a laugh.'

Lily had a television strategically placed in front of her, a big colour TV and she was keeping one eye fixed on a cartoon. Dorothy felt like an intruder.

'Sit, sit, sit,' Lily motioned to a chair beside the table, then she glanced over her glasses at Patrick who stood by the door. 'So, this is the lucky boy, is it?' She turned immediately back to Lily and asked: 'And are there any young fairies flying about your house yet?'

'No, Aunt Lily. We're not long married. But how are you? We brought you a box of chocolates, didn't really know …'

'Chocolates! Lovely, lovely! You always were quite a fairy, you know.'

'How do you manage these days, Aunt Lily? I mean, for shopping and all that.'

'Shopping? Old Tommy Hugget from downstairs, in the sports shop you know, goes and gets my groceries and my necessities. Not there are many of those nowadays, just the food, a bottle of gin now and then, and the television guide.'

Dorothy moved gently towards the window; the room was very stuffy and she thought she might open the top of the window, ever so slightly. Lily reacted at once.

'Don't you dare open that window, young lady! Don't you dare! Do you want to kill me off or something?'

Dorothy sat down again, a little shamefaced. She moved restlessly on her seat.

There was a moment's silence. Lily laughed then at something on the television. She picked up the remote control from her lap and flicked to another channel. 'Telly bingo will be on in a minute, you know. Do you play it? It's great fun, and Tommy below helps me with it.' She strained forward for a moment, as if to dismiss her visitors.

'Aunt Lily,' Dorothy tried. 'I wanted to tell you about Father Scott …'

The old woman stiffened a little but kept her eyes on the television. She waited. Then she looked at Dorothy. 'What about that old bastard? Is he still alive?'

'Well, that's just it, he died about a month ago. A heart attack, I think. We'll miss him. He was …'

'He was a slug in the cabbage of bliss, the old bastard!' Lily said, but gently and affectionately. She lowered her head a moment and sighed deeply. Then, almost whispering, she said, 'The slug, oh the lovely, lovely slug he was, to be sure!'

She seemed to be absent for a while, nodding her head gently up and down, her eyes closed. Then she spoke again, though she seemed to be addressing her words to the electric fire beside her. 'Some of us, you know, dear, some of us never had a share in the harvest. No sir, not us. Mother Church didn't want some of us about, sullying up the parlours of Paradise with our longings and our needs. No sir. No share in the harvest, some of us, no share at all.'

She was silent for another while. Dorothy shifted uneasily. She did not know what to say next. She glanced at Patrick who tried to beckon her, with a movement of his head, to leave. But Lily had turned back to Dorothy. 'I was in love with the bugger, you know, I loved him. And I think he loved me, too, I think he did. But he was too good a man for me, far too good. He was married before ever I got to know him, married to Mother Church, and I never got a look in. Never. Not a chance. So, so, poor old Jim, poor Jim, so he's dead and gone then, eh? Dead and gone. God has him finally where he wants us all and sure maybe up there the rules and regulations might be different, we might have a little share in the happiness then, us poor fools. God help us all. Soon enough, too, soon enough.'

She lay back then on her chair and closed her eyes, though her right hand held the remote control and her left hand lifted slowly to brush back an imaginary hair from her wrinkled brow. Without moving she said, 'Go now dear, and thank you for coming to see me. But I'm very tired now. I might doze a while, before Oprah, you know. And then there's *Neighbours*, before the evening news. More deaths and murders and drugs and shooting, no doubt, no doubt.' She waved her left hand vaguely in the air.

Dorothy moved softly to her side and took her hand gently. She raised the frail hand to her lips and kissed it. The old lady opened her eyes and looked up at her. She smiled and whispered, 'What a little fairy you are, to be sure, to be sure.'

There were tears on Dorothy's cheeks now, where she sat on the stairs. She wiped them away, then rose carefully and climbed the rest of the stairs. When she reached the top she spoke out loud, as if her aunt were listening to her. 'Ah yes, the panda bear, the black and white panda bear. You little fairy you, and God be good to you, my own sad Aunt Lily.' She turned left at the top of the stairs, and opened the door into what had been Declan's room and was now used by the children when they came visiting. The room was in a mess, but Dorothy always kept a small part of it out of the childrens' reach, a small locked drawer at the base of the wardrobe. She reached for the little key over the mirror door of the wardrobe and her shoulder hurt her as she reached. She let out a small, hurt animal cry. But she got the key. She went down on her knees to open the drawer and found herself crying.

'Silly me!' she said out loud. 'Crying over a pain in my shoulder!'

But she knew she was not crying for that reason. She was crying for Declan. It had been a terrible shock when they were told that he had contracted acute leukaemia and the doctor had talked to them a lot of stuff about bone marrow and the lymph system. All they knew was that Declan, their eldest, was only eight years of age and was often in severe pain. He had been a strong and outgoing young boy and suddenly all that had changed, as if overnight. It began, they thought, with the tonsils and they had not worried about that. There was a small operation, but he did not appear to be recovering. He lay in the hospital bed, the curtains half drawn about him, and he smiled up at them weakly. He did not complain, he never complained but he had told his doctor that he had felt very tired for a very long time. He had grown thin, too, and that in spite of the best food that they could coax him to take. His arms were what caused Dorothy most sorrow, how thin and feeble they became, how she could notice bruising from the smallest thing and how, once when she had hugged him, he had cried out with the pain of it and then apologized to her for calling out. That was when her heart began to break, that was when she first heard of acute lymphoid leukaemia, and when she could sense real anxiety in the doctor and terror in Patrick's face.

'Will he be all right, Patrick? For God's sake, tell me, is he going to be OK?'

Poor Patrick. He had tried to smile at her and say of course he's going to be all right. He's a young boy, he's got his whole life before him, God is good, Dorothy, God is good, and you and I know that very well.

Dorothy noticed how often Declan had nose bleeds then and she wept openly when she saw how his hair had fallen out, how he lay, small and reduced and pale, in the bed, his small skull barely pressing a shape into the pillow. And yet he never complained, he did not whine nor beg nor ask for anything. He smiled at them, and whispered to them. About the lake. About school. About his pals. He never seemed to ask about his illness, when he would be well, when he'd be going home, nothing,

nothing, and it appeared to Dorothy as if he had already made up his mind, as if he knew, as if he had not the will nor the strength to fight.

Only once had she heard him scream, and that was when she accompanied him as a nurse pushed him in a wheelchair down to surgery where he was to have a spinal tap done, and she heard him scream with pain and she had clenched her teeth and her fists together and wished that it was she and not little Declan who was there. It was then that she had really begun to pray; she had taken out the crucifix that she had brought with her from her days in the convent and had spent hours kneeling in their room before it, and hours in the chapel, too, before the great crucifix over the altar, pleading, reasoning, promising. And when the boy had died she had put the crucifix away, both she and Patrick had stopped going to Mass, they had ceased praying together, they had slipped down some terrible black slide into despair.

It was years before either of them began to live with brighter eyes and renewed hope, and they could trace that to the day when their daughter, Nuala, qualified as a solicitor and they both stood, watching her as she stood with others, smiling proudly, accepting her parchment. She was very pretty, they both knew, and she was healthy and it was for her they decided, without even speaking to each other about it, that they would work to find a way back towards hope.

In the wardrobe Dorothy quickly found the panda that Aunt Lily had given her so many years before. Its two eyes, those lovely brown button-eyes, had long since disappeared; the right arm and the right leg had also vanished and the ends been crudely sewn together. The colour that had been white was now a dirty grey; what had been black was almost the same dirty grey. It had fallen somewhat out of shape ... but now, when she sat it up against the back of the door, you could tell what it was meant to be, you could tell, and you could tell how a life falls slowly into its own ruin and yet remains that one life, unique, beautiful, and sad.

She reached deeper into the wardrobe, under letters, an old notebook, some clothes that she had secretly kept of Declan when he was a baby, and found that crucifix … It was exactly as she had remembered it … She took it out now, kissed it gently, held it for a moment against her bosom, closed her eyes and smiled, upwards, towards the ceiling. Then she pushed the drawer shut, leaving the key where it was, and carefully stood up again. She gathered up her treasures, that small harvest of so many years, the panda, the porringer, the carriage clock, she felt for a moment the watch in her apron pocket. She held them carefully against her apron as she left Declan's room and headed across the landing towards her own bedroom.

She paused to gaze through the landing window where it looked out over the fields and meadows, the far village and the harbour, to the sea. And there was Locke's Field, transformed beyond all knowing. There were giant yellow cranes, lank and stilted, like exotic migratory birds feeding in what had been marshlands. They stood tall and defiant amongst a disarray of bricks and piles of timber beams and Dorothy knew that within a few months a new estate, a rich away-place for absentee owners, would rise, lovely and mostly abandoned, among instant gardens, instant trees, instant summers. She watched a grey heron flap its confused way between two of the cranes and veer suddenly, as if it had thumped into an invisible wall of air, off towards the sea. And Dorothy, watching, knew that all of this, the cranes, the heron, the panda bear, the crucifix, all of them are listed in the one, ongoing annals of an incomprehensible world. The field was now just one great mess, the few rhododendron and furze bushes were dumped over, their branches, twisted and contorted, reaching out of mud like lopped limbs in a war zone. Men in daffodil-yellow hats moved about like robots, carrying wooden planks, they were the earth shakers, the world movers. Dorothy shook her head slowly; she was not sure if this was stitching or unstitching of the world.

She opened the door of her own room. She closed it behind her, then arranged her small harvest of goods along the dressing table, the crucifix in the middle, the porringer on the right, along with Patrick's old fob watch, the panda on the left where it slouched back against the dressing-table mirror, the carriage clock at the end. So, she thought, everything enclosed in time.

The clock, the watch; how quickly it sped after all. It seemed to her that it was barely a few days ago when she stood in the new bookshop in Crackley, delighted and amazed at the wealth and beauty of the place, the great shelves of wonderful books, how she stood, absorbed and enthralled in a book – it was a book of stories, how could she ever forget? – by D.H. Lawrence, an author she had never heard of, but it intrigued her, and the binding was rich and lovely, a dark green, with gilt edges, and the letters in embossed gold. She held the book in her hands and closed her eyes and relished the scent of it, as well as its weight and the pleasure of its feel between her hands. And how she had jumped, suddenly, when somebody had tapped her on the right shoulder, tap, tap, tap, gently, yet urgently, and she had turned, and there he was, there was Patrick! And oh, she had thought he was still in Dublin, still studying for the priesthood, and there he was now, smiling at her, speaking to her, about something, she did not know what, she was so thrilled, so delighted ... How ridiculous it is to say we have time. Time is something we don't have enough of; somebody had said that to her, a long, long time ago.

She was tired, now, so very tired. She shook off her shoes and lay back on the bed she had shared with him for so many years. He was still with her, she knew that, yet all those years when they had snuggled in together and they had relished the physicality of each other's presence, the warmth and assurance of a loving body against her own, there had scarcely passed a moment when she was not aware that some night, some night it would happen, some night would be the first night she would have to sleep alone, knowing he would not return, he would not be there, not physically anyway, ever again. Now she folded her hands over her breasts and closed her eyes and sighed, deeply.

Since Patrick's death she had slept every night in the big bedroom without ever drawing across the curtains. She was happy to watch the stars as they appeared, or the moon, or simply know the easy and unremarkable shifts between light and darkness, between darkness and light, that made the movement of the earth. Now it was bright afternoon and the light was warm and comforting coming in through that window. She closed her eyes, tightly, then opened them again, to know the comfort of the room. She felt so good, so comfortable in her body, so much at peace, yet oh so very, very tired. She was surprised to see that darkness was already growing in the room, as if a curtain was being very slowly drawn across against the light.

THE HEATHER FIELDS AND OTHER STORIES

John F. Deane

Set in island communities in small-town rural Ireland, peopled with the marginalised and forgotten, the nine stories in John F. Deane's stunning collection address life's most profound questions – the nature of existence and the purpose of being.

Haunting, occasionally comic and always beautifully written, *The Heather Fields and Other Stories* showcases the mastery of form for which Deane is universally renowned.

PRAISE FOR JOHN F. DEANE

'Few Irish writers have mastered the art of eloquent, impassioned expression as artistic statement as beautifully as John F. Deane … In gravitas, sophistication and magisterial urgency of intent, Deane looks to Kinsella and beyond him to Yeats.'

Irish Times

'When John Deane fuses the music of thought and feeling with the music of language itself, there rises in me that eternal Yes! that we unconsciously hunger to experience as we approach a poem or any work of art.'

DENISE LEVERTROV

978-0-85640-800-7

£7.99

THE PEN FRIEND

Ciaran Carson

'I write to try to see you as you were, or what you have become. You left no forwarding address: that was part of your intention. For when we wrote those letters to each other all those years ago, we wrote as much for ourselves as for each other.'

More than twenty years after the end of their love affair, Gabriel receives a cryptic postcard from an old flame. It is the first of thirteen cards from her, each one provoking a series of reveries about their life and love in 1980s Belfast.

The Pen Friend is, however, much more than a love story. As Gabriel teases out the significance of the cards, his reveries develop into richly textured meditations on writing, memory, spiritualism and surveillance.

The result is an intricate web of fact and fiction, a narrative that marries sharp historical insights with imaginative exuberance, a strange and wonderful novel that confirms Ciaran Carson as one of Ireland's most engaging and ingenious writers.

PRAISE FOR *THE PEN FRIEND*

'a slyly elegant "mystery" fiction which is fascinating and absorbing from beginning to end.'
Times Literary Supplement

978-0-85640-815-1

£14.99

THE DANCERS DANCING

Éilís Ní Dhuibhne

It is 1972. A group of teenage girls are sent to the Donegal Gaeltacht to improve their Irish and experience the local culture. Liberated for the first time from the reins of parental control, they respond to the untamed landscape of river, hill and sea, finding in it unnerving echoes of their own submerged – and now emerging – wildnesses.

PRAISE FOR *THE DANCERS DANCING*

'Éilís Ní Dhuibhne in *The Dancers Dancing* has produced one of the most compelling and understated exercises in the female Bildungsroman.'

DECLAN KIBERD

'With a delicate touch not unlike Arundhati Roy's in *The God of Small Things*, Ní Dhuibhne sneaks under the ill-fitting skin of her metamorphosing Derry and Dublin cast. Their stories unravel in shifting voices with all the wisdom and perspective of an omniscient narrator.'

Sunday Business Post

'Ní Dhuibhne's writing is marvellous, building layers of impression until a complex, vital and true-false picture of liberation is revealed.'

Irish Times

'Her observations are lemon-fresh, her writing beautiful, witty and wry.'

Sunday Express

978-0-85640-860-1

£7.99

FOX, SWALLOW, SCARECROW

Éilís Ní Dhuibhne

Anna Kelly Sweeney is a writer of popular fiction intent on worldly success. Leo is an idealist who lives in rural County Kerry and devotes himself to poetry, culture and innumerable worthy causes. When Anna falls in love with the handsome and enigmatic Vincy, and Leo with troubled publicist Kate, the consequences of their glimpsed happiness reverberate beyond their own insulated worlds. Inspired by Tolstoy's *Anna Karenina*, this panoramic and compulsively readable new novel is an intelligent, witty and fiercely humane insight into modern Ireland.

PRAISE FOR *FOX, SWALLOW, SCARECROW*

'Thank goodness for Éilís Ní Dhuibhne and her novel – a warm, sardonic, unflinchingly and horribly accurate examination of the world of Irish letters.'

CARLO GÉBLER

'... possibly the finest novel to emerge from Ireland in the early twenty-first century. It is a formidable critique of a culture, so intelligently and artfully conveyed that the book fairly crackles. Magnificent.'

MARY O'DONNELL

'*Fox, Swallow, Scarecrow* is that rare thing – a clever, intelligent book that is also highly readable ... a must read for anyone interested in the state of the modern Irish novel.'

SARAH WEBB

'This is the Celtic Tiger novel we've all been waiting for ... Brilliant.'

KATE HOLMQUIST

978-0-85640-807-6

£8.99